LAST GIRL STANDING

Center Point
Large Print

Also by Lisa Jackson and available from Center Point Large Print:

One Last Breath
Liar, Liar
Willing to Die
Paranoid

Also by Nancy Bush and available from Center Point Large Print:

The Killing Game

LISA JACKSON

AND
NANCY BUSH

LAST GIRL STANDING

CENTER POINT LARGE PRINT
THORNDIKE, MAINE

This Center Point Large Print edition
is published in the year 2020 by arrangement with
Kensington Publishing Corp.

The text of this Large Print edition is unabridged.
In other aspects, this book may vary
from the original edition.
Printed in the United States of America
on permanent paper.
Set in 16-point Times New Roman type.

ISBN: 978-1-64358-654-0

The Library of Congress has cataloged this record under
Library of Congress Control Number: 2020934784

Prologue

*B*eep . . . beep . . . beep . . .
The rhythmic sound of the monitor was soft and reassuring as nurse Alice Song stepped into the private hospital room and zeroed her gaze on the patient. The respirator was breathing for him, and there'd been no change in his condition. She'd allowed the three women in their early thirties into his room against everything she believed in. She didn't trust them. Someone had stabbed Dr. Stahd repeatedly, and it could have been one of them. But the police officer assigned to watch over the patient, and the hospital as a whole, had made an exception to their no-visitation rule, mostly at the behest of Dr. Stahd's father, also a medical doctor and a high-handed egotist if there ever was one.

The three women were pretty, to a one, apparently friends of the victim since junior high school.

Alice checked Dr. Stahd's vitals.

"He's doing okay, right?" one of the women asked anxiously.

5

"He's stable," Alice answered shortly.

"But he's going to be all right?"

Alice regarded her suspiciously. The real thing, or an act? She was petite with light brown hair streaked with blond and enhanced breasts that made her look as if she might fall forward with a good clap on the back. The diamond ring on her left hand was worth a small fortune, and her Louis Vuitton handbag and Christian Louboutin heels shouted money as well; Alice had seen the Louboutin's distinctive red soles as the woman had tip-tapped down the hallway. Nothing understated about that one.

"His condition is stable. Far better than critical," the tall blond one told the shorter anxious one. She was the epitome of the icy bitch. The lawyer, Alice had heard.

"Who did this?" asked Anxious Moneybags.

The third one, who seemed a bit removed from the other two, said determinedly, "The police'll find out." She was a redhead, complete with freckles and pale blue eyes. There was something familiar about her Alice couldn't quite place, but the steeliness beneath her words was unmistakable.

"Yes . . . yes . . ." Anxious Moneybags nodded, though it sounded like she didn't believe it.

Alice glanced at the officer standing guard, who nodded at her, as if assuring her he was on the job.

She nodded back and headed out. She was almost out of ICU when suddenly an urgent *BEEP! BEEP! BEEP!* from the patient's monitor brought all the staff to attention.

She yelled for the crash cart and saw another nurse already busting for it.

"Shit . . . ," the tall blond muttered as Alice raced back.

Moneybags burbled, "What? What?"—then clapped her palm to her mouth as Alice leaned over the man in the bed.

"Get back!" Alice snapped as they hovered together. "Get out of here!"

They shuffled as one toward the door but hung there in a frozen clutch as Dr. Evanston and the crash cart clattered in.

Dr. Stahd suddenly woke on a gasp, lids flying open, mouth a wide O. He croaked out, "Dee!" before his eyes rolled back in his head and he collapsed into unconsciousness.

"Oh, my God!" one of the women whispered. The redhead, maybe. Alice was too busy to look.

"He's going to be okay, right?" Moneybags again.

BBEEEEEEEEEEEPPPPPP.

Flatline.

Alice inhaled sharply as Dr. Evanston, sixty-five and hard as granite from his rigorous daily workouts, readied the paddles and bellowed, "Get those women out of here!" Alice whipped around

7

and glared at the three of them, but they were already backing out through the door, practically stumbling over each other, herded by the police officer.

Immediately she turned her attention back to the man in the bed. His pallor was white, his skin icy.

Not long for this world, Alice thought. Sometimes she could almost see a silvery, gossamer death shroud descend upon a patient. It was a psychic gift she didn't talk about to others.

But right now, Dr. Stahd's handsome face was growing shimmery. A preliminary sign.

"Clear!" Dr. Evanston yelled again, swooping down to shock the patient with the paddles.

Ellie O'Brien stood just outside Tanner's door. She wasn't leaving till they physically pushed her out. Her ears still rang from his cry of: *"Dee!"* Clear as a bell. A confession, she'd wager.

But, of course, *Dee* wasn't here. How could she be? *Dee* was in police custody, or being questioned by them, or just not interested in Tanner's fate. *Dee* had never given a damn about him. Not really. She'd only cared about how he'd made her look good. As far as Ellie was concerned, it was only a matter of time before the evidence proved she'd stabbed him, over and over again. He was damn lucky to still be alive.

Her heart galumphed painfully. He couldn't

die. Not Tanner. The coolest guy in high school.

She regarded the scene beyond the open door in subdued shock: the team of nurses bustling about; the white-haired doctor trying his best to bring him back; the tubes and screens and wires filling the room . . .

Was this how it was going to end? *Was this it?*

A cold knot of certainty tightened inside her. Dee was for Delta, Tanner's wife, known as "D" to her group of friends. Amanda, "A," and Zora, "Z," were standing a few feet away from her, waiting for Ellie to join them even though she was more a frenemy than a friend. Not invited to be the "E" of the Five Firsts.

Now Ellie pulled her gaze from the frenzied tableau inside Tanner's room to regard Amanda and Zora. "She tried to kill him," Ellie said with certainty.

Zora shook her head, her eyes huge. "We don't know that."

Amanda didn't utter a word. The strong, silent type. She was a sphinx. Just like always.

Briefly Ellie thought of Carmen and Bailey . . . the "B" and "C" of the group since grade school. Those five girls had practically run West Knoll High School when they were students. They were the popular clique that had moved like a tsunami through the school, swallowing up anyone who dared defy them, leaving them bared and broken in their wake, like Ellie herself. She'd long ago recovered from the mean snub, had made her way in the world to a place of respect, but she would never forget.

"Are you going to be reporting on this?" Zora asked her.

"No," Ellie said curtly. No, she would not be reporting. That was a sore point. But she would be investigating on her own . . . and she was going to start with *Dee.*

"I just thought—"

"Let's wait till we find out what happens," Amanda cut in.

The three of them then stood in silence, each wrapped in her own thoughts.

But all they could hear above the frantic efforts to save Dr. Tanner Stahd's life was the ominous monotone of the flatline.

PART ONE

The Five Firsts

Chapter 1

West Knoll School
Fifteen Years Earlier

Delta Smith slammed her locker shut with such force that the sound reverberated down the empty school hallway like a gunshot. She slammed it shut even though her books and belongings were still inside. If she didn't have to run the combination again, she would yank it open and smash it closed again. She was so angry she could spit. Or let loose a primal scream. Damn that bitch, Amanda! Damn that smug, cheating *bitch*. Her *friend*. One of her *best friends!* Well, no more. You didn't steal somebody's boyfriend and get to stay friends. *Ever!*

Delta swore a blue streak under her breath as she furiously tried to reopen the locker, messing up the combination enough times that she slammed her palm against the metal door and shrieked in total frustration.

How? How had this happened? Amanda knew Tanner was hers. She *knew*. They all knew. There were rules. And you didn't mess with the rules!

Taking in and releasing several deep breaths, Delta was finally able to reopen her locker, her heart racing with fury, her breath coming fast, her face hot. She couldn't stand it. The idea of going outside the school and running into *anybody*—because the whole school knew! *They all knew!*—didn't bear thinking about.

She grabbed her books and purse and cell phone—her mom's, because her parents didn't trust her to not lose one of her own. "Be careful with it," Mom had warned. Delta turned the phone on now and called home. "I need a ride," she choked out to her mother. Outside the window at the end of the hall, the one that looked toward the parking lot, Delta could see groups of kids heading to their cars or their rides or starting the walk to their nearby homes.

"Thought Tanner was bringing you home."

Tanner.

"No," Delta said, steeling her mind against the quaver that wanted to infect her voice.

"Well, I've got a couple of things to do, so I can't be there for half an hour at the earliest. Maybe you should see if someone else can drive you?"

The hopeful note in her mother's voice was the last straw. "I'll wait," Delta answered, clicking off, then broke into silent, angry tears.

She moved blindly toward the girls' restroom, where she locked herself in a cubicle to wait the half hour Mom had said it would take before she could pick her up. Hopefully all the other kids would be gone by the time she headed outside.

She cried silently for another few minutes, wiping the tears away with her right index finger as soon as they reached her eyes, infuriated by the sculptured nail of her pointer finger with the tiny red and gold flower painted on it. Just like Amanda's. *And* Carmen's. *And* Bailey's. *And* Zora's. All of the members of their group, the Five Firsts, the most popular clique in school. They'd all gotten the little red and gold flower on their right index fingers, their colors—the colors of West Knoll Grade School, where they'd all met and realized their initials were A, B, C, and D. They'd been friends with Ellie, too, then, but she was such a judgmental whiner that it had been Amanda's idea to have Zora take her place, tacking on a Z for the First Five's last member. Bailey, the peacemaker, had suggested maybe they could invite Ellie and be six, but the First Six? The alliteration hadn't really worked, and Amanda had said no, and when Amanda said no everyone listened, because Amanda's family was rich. Richer than Zora's, even. The Forsythes had that swank house above the West Knoll River and all that property for acres, damn near miles, around it. Their class was supposed to go there next month for a big senior day trip and barbeque, and maybe overnight, if the would-be classmates' parents allowed them to, with some of the faculty as event supervisors.

Delta choked out another sob. But how could she go now, with what she knew about Tanner and Amanda? Zora had caught them *making out* at her house last weekend after Delta had left the impromptu party early because she had to get up early and work at the store for her mom before school.

She hated the grocery store. Smith & Jones, the mom-and-pop place at the corner that her parents owned, formed from her dad and mom's last names, Smith and Jones. It was almost embarrassing, even though all her friends loved to stop by and talk to her dad, who always gave them free stuff, even though Mom constantly chided him for "giving away your daughter's education." Delta didn't much care. She planned to marry Tanner as soon as she could. They'd met in junior high, and all the girls had fallen head over heels for him, but he'd shined his smile on *her*. Delta Smith! Oh, man. She'd glowed under the attention. And she could *feel* the way the other girls glared at her when they thought she couldn't see. It was just so perfect. Tanner was so perfect. And he was captain of the football team. Quarterback and team captain with an academic scholarship to the University of Oregon. Delta was trying hard to keep her grades up and save her money so she could go to Oregon, too.

But now . . . all her dreams were dust.

Had it been thirty minutes yet? Probably not.

She was loath to leave the bathroom. She looked at her blotchy face in the mirror and could have cried again. After turning on the tap, she cupped water in one hand and dabbed it on her hot cheeks with the other.

She was just getting ready to brave the halls when the door swung inward and there was Zora . . . with Bailey and Carmen, two peas in a pod. They were always together. The kind of best friends that make it hard to be with them. Even though they were members of the First Five, Bailey and Carmen could be the Only Two, the way they acted sometimes.

"There you are!" Zora declared. "God, we've been looking all over for you. We thought maybe you went home with somebody else."

"Tanner was looking for you, too," said Bailey.

Delta couldn't contain the squeak of despair that squeezed past her lips. "I'll bet," she said bitterly.

"He was," Bailey insisted. "I don't know what happened between you guys, but he was really trying to find you."

"Oh, you know what happened." Delta could hardly get the words out. "What are you guys still doing at school?"

"Looking for you," Carmen said. "And Amanda. We saw her leave with her brother."

Delta held up her hands. "I don't want to hear about her!"

Zora, Bailey, and Carmen all looked at each other, as if silently asking each other how to proceed. Delta turned away from them, filled with anguish. She heard Zora say, "Guess I shouldn't have told you about them. It wasn't that big of a deal."

"Not that big of a deal?" Delta's head shot up. "You would keep it from me?"

"Of course not. I mean, it was just . . . it wasn't a big deal. Just a little making out."

"On your parents' pool table!"

"Well, they were . . . playing pool," Zora muttered.

"That's not what you said the first time. You said they were *on* the pool table!"

"Playing pool on the pool table! Jesus. I don't know, Delta. It wasn't like that!"

"What was it like?"

"Not like that."

Delta wanted to believe her. She really, really wanted to. And Zora was trying to take it back now, but she'd been pretty clear before. She just didn't like conflict. Delta could tell she was sorry for spilling the truth.

Bailey said, "All I know is, Tanner was looking for you."

Carmen added, "I bet Amanda's sorry for what she did."

All three girls turned to look at Carmen. They all knew that was undoubtedly a lie. Amanda

Forsythe was rarely, if ever, sorry about any-thing. She was their uncrowned leader. What she said, went. If she didn't like something, the rest of them didn't like it, either. There was no feeling sorry . . . no ruing the day. Blond, regal Amanda was tough, smart, and uncompromising.

Delta wanted to hate her, but Amanda was also fiercely pro the Five Firsts. It was mostly owing to her efforts that they were *the* most popular group of girls. Everyone wanted to be them. If Delta challenged Amanda, who knew what would happen next? Delta could be left out in the cold. Amanda had that much power.

Didn't mean she wasn't a bitch.

"It was nothing," Zora said again. "Stupid drunk stuff. She just gave him a good-bye kiss, or something."

"That's not what you said," Delta reminded again.

"I was a little drunk, okay? I'm sober now, though."

"Maybe you should talk to Amanda," Carmen suggested to Delta.

"Maybe you should talk to Tanner," countered Bailey.

"Oh, I'm mad at him, too, believe me," Delta said darkly, though she wasn't nearly as mad at him as she was at Amanda. She *loved* him. With-out Tanner, she didn't have a dream. A future. It was . . . frightening to think of what she would have to do if she lost him. "My mom's picking me up. I gotta get outta here." Delta squeezed past them to the door, and they followed after her.

As she pushed through to the back parking lot, Delta saw Ellie O'Brien's dark red hair . . . and Tanner's blond streaked, longish surfer locks practically touching Ellie's; their heads were close together, and they were laughing and talking and totally unaware or uncaring that his girlfriend was approaching. Delta's heart lurched painfully. They were leaning up against Tanner's dark blue Trailblazer, into each other.

Delta's fury instantly switched from Amanda to Ellie.

"What the hell?" Zora asked, echoing Delta's reaction.

Ellie had turned on her personality for Tanner; Delta could tell. For someone usually so restrained and controlled, she was grinning like a goon at something Tanner had said. She didn't even glance up and look at them—couldn't tear her eyes from Tanner's—even though Delta had stopped short at the top step and Carmen, Bailey, and Zora had nearly barreled into her.

Mom's Volvo wagon was idling a few cars from Tanner's. Upon spying her daughter, Karen Smith put her arm out the window and waved Delta toward their car.

"Hey . . . ," Tanner suddenly called, his gaze finally ripped from Ellie's to take in the four girls gathered, frozen, on the top landing of West Knoll High's back steps. He straightened and moved past Ellie, who was half-blocking his way to them.

Delta wanted to scream at him . . . shriek like a harridan that he was hers and he couldn't flirt with other girls! She wanted to have an out-and-out fit, but she knew that would get her nowhere. She needed to be cool. Calm. Collected. The fun girl, not the snarling horror who made everyone raise their brows and silently ask, *What's he doing with her?*

And, above all that, she just wanted him to take her in his arms and tell her he loved her in that way that made her feel so safe. She swallowed, unsure quite how to handle this, wondering if her face looked okay. No time for new makeup. She hadn't really believed he was waiting for her, so she hadn't put herself together in the way she should have.

Forcing a grim smile, she said, "My mom's here," as he headed her way.

Tanner glanced around and hitched his chin in recognition at Mom, who gave him a short nod in return. Her mother didn't share Delta's love for Tanner. She wanted her daughter, her only child, to go to college and succeed. Both of her parents constantly talked about the importance of success. Smith & Jones was a success! They were successful people, and they wanted that for their daughter as well. Delta felt kind of small for thinking it, but she questioned just how much of a success they truly were. Her father had risen from near poverty to own his own business, and that was an accomplishment, for sure. But in the world Delta craved, there were a lot more steps to be taken beyond a business that barely supported three people. Smith & Jones was fine, but Delta dreamed of much bigger things.

"Can I come over?" Tanner asked Delta now, the guilty look on his face telling her more than she wanted to know about how he felt about his behavior. Her heart sank further.

But she really, really, really wanted to see him. Zora, Bailey, and Carmen were waiting with bated breath to see what she would do. Ellie's animated expression had shut down as if a blind had been drawn over her face, and she was standing by, waiting to see how Delta played it, maybe.

"Sure," she said. Her smile felt like it was cracking.

"I'll be there in an hour, okay?"

What do you have to do for an hour? It could be anything, she reminded herself. Sports training, most likely. He was religious about working out. "See you then."

"So, where's Tanner going?" her mom asked once she'd slammed into the passenger side of the car after sauntering across the parking lot as if she didn't have a care in the world. Her other friends were all climbing into Zora's white Mazda. It made Delta feel a little bit foolish going home with her mother.

"I don't know."

"Something going on?"

"No," Delta said shortly. Mom was keeping her voice neutral, but Delta suspected her mother was hopeful there was trouble in paradise. She felt Delta's obsession with Tanner wasn't the best thing for her daughter.

"What happened to your ride with him?" Mom asked now.

"He has somewhere he has to be."

"Ah."

Delta didn't appreciate the all-knowing "Ah," but she managed to keep herself from sniping at her mother as that never paid off.

They didn't speak the rest of the way home, and as they pulled into the driveway, Delta despaired of the small, two-bedroom white clapboard house, built by her great-grandfather, that was nothing compared to Amanda's and Zora's parents' palatial homes. It was amazing that Tanner, whose family might not be as affluent as Amanda's and Zora's but was way further up the economic scale from Delta's, could even look at her. The Smiths were arguably the least wealthy of the Five Firsts' families. Not that it should matter, but it did. Some. Delta had learned to purposely use her charm and personality to make up for what she lacked financially, and for the most part, it worked. She was well-liked, and she liked people right back. Maybe that's what had won her Tanner. Where some of her friends could be anxious, bitchy, or downright cold, Delta always made a point to be friendly and nice, as if she were on top of the world.

Well, at least that was the goal. Sometimes she felt as mean and infuriated as Amanda. She just hid it better.

Ellie O'Brien could take a lesson, too, Delta thought with a sniff. There was a dark cloud over her head most of the time, and when she spoke, it was about all the things they needed to do to graduate and be good people and, oh, just everything. She was a born lecturer. Too judgmental by half . . . but . . . though she'd been flirting with Tanner, it was really *Amanda* who'd betrayed Delta.

Before her mother could make her help with dinner, or pick up the living room, or come up with some other chore, Delta ran into her bedroom and slammed the door. She needed a few moments to pull herself together before Tanner showed up.

Would they talk about Amanda? Delta wondered anxiously as she applied new lipstick and corrected the smudge of her eyeliner. How long had that black smear been at the edge of her eye? All day? She shuddered at the thought, how Amanda and the others might have been tittering behind their hands all day, no one bothering to warn her.

Some friends.

Tanner drove up about forty-five minutes later. She heard the roar of his Trailblazer as he approached; he'd done something to the engine to purposefully increase the loudness. She smoothed down her blouse. It was pink, which looked good on her, with her hazel eyes and dark hair, and she'd brushed a little bit of blush on her cheekbones.

She came out smiling, greeting him at the door as he sauntered up the walkway. His face brightened upon seeing hers. She realized that, for all her forced cheeriness, she'd been as dark and dreary as Ellie all day, up till now. Okay, then. Showtime.

"Hello there," she greeted him.

"Hi." One word. Full of relief.

"C'mon in." She held the door, and he followed her inside. She would have loved to take him to her bedroom, where they could be alone, but Mom would never allow it. Dad was even worse, though he was still at the store.

"Wanna go out to the back deck?" she invited. It was late April. Pretty iffy weather-wise this time of year, but Oregon was known to have a week or two of fabulous weather most springs, and each day this week had gotten better than the last. There was still a chill in the air, but the sun was out at least.

They walked out together. The grayed teak furniture was mostly dry, but some slats held moisture from last night's rain. Delta perched on the edge of her chair. She'd debated about whether to put on her good white pants but had settled for blue jeans—a better choice, as it turned out.

Tanner was in jeans and the gray hoodie Delta had bought for him, a name brand that she'd saved for, putting away any extra money she made working at the store. It had been expensive, but it looked great on him, making his eyes even bluer.

"Gotta go work out with the guys soon," he said apologetically.

"It's Friday night. Supposed to be . . . our time."

She spoke lightly and pretended the words didn't have as much import as they did for her. "Their time" seemed like a joke from an era that was out of step with current reality.

Tanner launched into all the reasons he had to stay in shape to keep up with his football career. Though he didn't say it, she knew he fretted he wasn't quite tall enough to be a really great quarterback. He cited other shorter NFL quarterbacks who were doing well, but at barely six feet he was overshadowed by others who were six-five or even more. Still, he'd been offered a scholarship, so Delta wished he would cool it a little on the football obsession, at least for today.

After a while, she brought them each a Sprite, but she barely touched hers while Tanner poured his down his throat. She was watching her weight and had made herself a rule that she wouldn't drink calories if she could help it. All calories had to come from food she chewed.

When he was finished, he wiped his mouth with the back of his hand and said, "Wellll . . . I'd better get going. We'll catch up later?"

Delta's heart was beating hard, and her hands were trembling a bit as she thought about whether she should bring up Amanda. Was she going to? What if her questions made him mad? But she needed to know!

They walked back through the house and then out the front door. At his car, she took a deep breath and asked quickly, "Did you kiss Amanda?"

He was opening his driver's door and jerked as if she'd goosed him. "Uh . . . no . . ."

"No?"

"No." Then he mumbled, "Not really," as it probably occurred to him there was no escaping the truth of the hot gossip surrounding him and Amanda.

"What does that mean?" she asked sharply.

"It means nothing happened."

"C'mon, Tanner."

"Amanda was just fooling around, and we were kind of wrestling."

"Wrestling?"

"Just horsing around. You know." He sounded almost angry.

"Did you kiss her?"

"I just told you. It wasn't like that."

"Did you kiss her?" Delta stressed.

"Did somebody say that?" he demanded, eager to spread the blame to the messenger.

"I heard you were on the pool table together . . . making out."

"What? No. We were just . . . that's not . . . who said that? Did Zora say that? She wasn't even in the room!"

Zora had said both. First, the story had been that they were making out on the pool table, and second, they'd shared a quick kiss good-bye on the way out. The second part sounded like Amanda had gotten to Zora, asking for the change of story. What mattered was that Amanda and Tanner had kissed . . . and it looked like it happened on Zora's pool table.

Delta wanted to believe they'd shared a quick peck good-bye, and nothing else had happened. She really wanted to. But "making out on the pool table" had a ring of authenticity about it, the kind of thing Zora just didn't make up out of whole cloth. And anyway, her best friend and her boyfriend shouldn't have been kissing at all!

But it was Amanda's fault. She was the one, not Tanner.

"Did Zora say that?" he repeated, indignant now.

"Do you know how it makes me feel to have the whole school know something happened between you two?"

"*Nothing* happened between us. That's what I'm telling you!"

"It was something."

"Jesus Christ, Delta." He jumped into the Trailblazer, slammed the door shut, and glared at her through the window.

She wanted to take it all back. Pretend it hadn't happed. Prostrate herself on the ground. Climb in the car with him and make love with him right in front of her parents' house.

She did none of those things. Just stood by forlornly as he burned away in a chirp of tires and the roar of his engine.

Chapter 2

Zora DeMarco drove Bailey and Carmen to their respective homes. The girls, each in turn, ran into their houses to dump their books, promised to do their homework as soon as they got back, then raced back to Zora's Mazda. Carmen took the front seat. She always forced the smaller Bailey into the back, but Bailey didn't seem to mind. She and Carmen were too tight to quibble over such small issues. Zora had accused them of being gay, and they'd just laughed. The truth was, Carmen kind of had a thing for Tanner Stahd—didn't they all?—and she got all moony-eyed around him, which drove the rest of the Fives crazy, although Delta kind of smiled with indulgence, like she knew she had Tanner and the others could all go screw themselves.

Zora said, "My parents are onto me, so we can't break into their booze anymore. They took away my phone, too."

"That's okay. I can't drink. My dad can smell it on me," Carmen said.

"He can't smell vodka," Zora said.

"He can smell anything," Carmen insisted.

Zora would have liked to argue further, but

Carmen's dad was Reverend Proffitt—*the* Reverend Esau Proffitt—as her father would boom out almost whenever he heard the man's name. And it wasn't a term of respect. Zora's dad thought *the* Reverend Esau Proffitt was a hypocritical fake. Something about the reverend and a parishioner that none of the adults would talk about. Zora had even gone so far as to ask Carmen what the big secret was, but Carmen wouldn't talk about her family. She had a brother and a sister, and was apparently the bad seed in between an older angelic sister and a younger, totally sports-minded brother, both of whom had great grades. Carmen was smart enough but didn't apply herself, so the counselor had said, and she was athletic enough to maybe play volleyball in college, if she had the mind-set, which she didn't, if anyone had asked Zora. Carmen hadn't been offered a scholarship like Tanner. She was "exploring her options," as she was wont to say, which meant she had no plans set for college, like all the rest of them.

Bailey said, "I thought you broke your phone."

Zora and Amanda were the only ones of their group whose parents had added their daughters' cell phones onto their family plans.

"I did. That's why they took it away. It's just not fair."

"So, none of us has a phone," Bailey sighed.

There was a moment of silence on that,

then Carmen said, "I have Tanner's number memorized."

"Hell of a lot of good that's going to do us without a phone to call him," Zora pointed out.

"Why would we call him? He's Delta's boyfriend," said Bailey.

Zora snorted. *Well, kinda.* She felt a moment of guilt, then said aloud, "So, what are we doing tonight?" Friday evening was looking like an epic fail before it even began.

"Let's go to Amanda's," Carmen suggested. "That's where they're going to have the graduation party. I want to see where to stake my tent."

The parents and teachers had planned a supervised party for the upcoming grads; it was scheduled for a couple of weeks before graduation on the Forsythe grounds, where the kids could all camp overnight. Though Amanda's parents had agreed to the use of their property, Amanda herself wasn't all that keen on having the whole class at her place.

"If there are tents, I'm in a tent with you," Bailey chirped to Carmen.

Bailey's father was a police officer, Bob Quintar, whom everyone called "Quin." Some of the kids in their class had tried to call Bailey by the same nickname as well, but she'd shut them down. Quin was her father. "If you call me that, I'll look around for my dad," she'd told them.

Her father wasn't all that keen on having

Bailey at the overnight event. The Reverend Proffitt hadn't even been going to allow Carmen to go at all until he learned that several members of the school staff would be there, along with the class do-gooders, Rhonda Clanton and Trent Collingsworth. Grudgingly, the reverend had okayed his daughter to attend for the day only.

Zora said, "I'm supposed to be bunking with Amanda and Delta, but I don't know now."

"They'll kill each other if they're together," said Bailey.

"We're definitely going to need at least two tents," added Carmen.

"No way Amanda sleeps in a tent," Zora pointed out.

"Not even if Tanner sneaks in?" Bailey suggested.

"No one's sneaking in." Carmen shut that down immediately.

"How are you planning to spend the night?" Zora asked Carmen. "Thought your dad nixed that."

"I'll find a way," she said determinedly.

Zora shrugged. Carmen's interest in Tanner was starting to get in the way of her every thought.

"Let's go ask Amanda about it," Bailey said. "I gotta admit, I'm kind of pissed off that she kissed Tanner, or whatever happened."

"Delta doesn't own Tanner," Carmen said, staring forward through the windshield.

"She's his girlfriend, and he cheated on her with her friend, one of the Five Firsts. That's not okay," Bailey came right back.

In the rearview, Zora could see how lost Bailey was after Carmen's comment. It was doubtful Bailey could see the pinkening of Carmen's cheeks, but Zora could. Bailey was over Carmen's obsession with Tanner, as they all were, but she mostly kept her thoughts to herself. This was the most dissension between the two friends that Zora had heard in a long while.

"I just meant that she acts so . . . proprietary," Carmen mumbled.

Bailey had no comment for that. Or maybe she knew better than to push too hard because who knew how Carmen would react. Like Carmen, Bailey wasn't clear on what her plans were post-graduation. Zora figured that whatever Carmen decided to do, Bailey would likely do the same.

Into the awkward silence, Zora said, "We just told Delta how we were on her side about Tanner and Amanda. Now, what do you want to say to Amanda?"

"I don't know." Carmen leaned down in the seat. She was on the tall side and had been playing volleyball competitively all her life, as far as Zora could tell. If she didn't get a scholarship, that would be it. Her parents couldn't afford college. She would probably go to the local community college. Her older sister was on academic scholarship.

Zora, on the other hand, had the means to go wherever she wanted. She just didn't have the grades. She could maybe get into U of O or Oregon State, if she was really, really lucky, but she really wanted to go to the University of Arizona in Tucson. Hot, dry desert . . . oh, to be out of this *rain*. But . . . she'd blown her SATs, and she just couldn't bear facing them again. And her grades this year had been in the toilet. She'd been to a few raves with her cousin and used ecstasy, though mostly she'd just been a boozehound. But being out all night . . . it was a kick . . . And it had played hell with her GPA.

She might end up in community college as well, she thought glumly.

And there were those troubling fights between her parents . . .

Zora gnawed on the side of her thumb. She'd heard her dad mention something about "the eastside deal," a real estate venture that was supposed to be a serious moneymaker, but maybe not . . . ? Black clouds on the horizon? She wouldn't think about it. Everything was fine, just fine.

"What did you think of Ellie talking to Tanner?" Zora asked them, pushing her troubling thoughts aside.

"She's just helping him study," Carmen dismissed with a shake of her head.

"Ellie? Isn't Delta helping him?" asked Bailey, frowning a bit at her friend, who was suddenly so knowledgeable, apparently.

"Ellie's like a math wizard," said Carmen.

"Is she?" Zora asked, sliding Carmen a sideways look.

"If it wasn't for Ellie, I woulda flunked Algebra II. That stuff was hard."

Zora let that nugget of information settle into her brain. She could've used some help in math herself. If she'd known Ellie was tutoring, maybe she could have asked her? But then maybe not, because Ellie didn't seem to like Zora very much. Maybe—probably—because Zora had taken Ellie's spot with the Five Firsts, which was totally unfair because it hadn't been Zora's idea. Amanda had come to her and said she and Delta had talked it over and wouldn't Zora be a better fit than Ellie O'Brien? Zora had been flattered and agreed. It wasn't her fault that Ellie had been discarded.

She put herself in Ellie's shoes for a moment, thinking about how hurtful that must have been. A total betrayal of friendship.

Immediately she shoved the thought aside. It wasn't Zora's fault Ellie had been pushed out in favor of her. It just wasn't.

They pulled into Amanda's driveway, a long,

straight cement road that led to the two-story Georgian house on the hill with a matching two-story, double-bay garage set apart from the house, so as not to get in the way of the view. Behind the house were acres and acres of Forsythe land, the West Knoll River cutting a jagged chasm of both slow-moving and whitewater rapids through the Forsythe property. The graduation committee was staking out a part of their land for the over-night party, and there had been raging discussions about whether it was safe or not to have them so close to the cliff side and river. The Forsythes had nearly pulled back their invitation, but Mr. Timmons, the senior math teacher, and Miss Billings, one of the school counselors, had talked them back into it, though the school district had made it clear they were not sanctioning or hosting the event in any way.

So many rules. Zora was going to be glad when school was all over . . . sort of. The great uncertain beyond gave her a chill, whenever she thought about it.

So just don't think about it.

"What?" Bailey asked, and Zora realized Carmen was looking at her askance, as well.

"Never mind." She must've spoken out loud. Too much on her mind.

They pulled up to one side of the Forsythe home, where there was space to fan out a dozen cars in the stone parking area between the house and the two-story garage. Amanda's father was a lawyer who made a buttload of money—more than Zora's father, it sounded like, though Zora's parents were very tight-lipped about it, whereas Amanda's dad was one of those guys who was proud of his accomplishments and liked to kind of brag. He'd even once brandished a big bottle of some fancy champagne and invited Amanda and the rest of the Firsts to join him in celebrating a big deal of some kind, but Amanda's mom had intervened and shooed them all out of the big den with its black-leather bar. Amanda took it all in stride. She had a tendency to hang back and just absorb everything, a character asset Zora's mother told Zora she should learn from.

"Amanda Forsythe knows when to talk and when to keep her mouth shut," Mom said more than once. "You could take a lesson."

Zora had been pissed, though she knew her mother was just trying to help, but Zora was Zora. She knew how to have a good time. And Zora had seen Amanda shed that icy, blond-bitch persona, which was more of a cover-up than a thing anyway, when it suited her. She could flirt like a randy whore. Hadn't she done that with Tanner?

Tanner Stahd . . .

Zora bit her lip, thinking about him.

As if reading her mind, Bailey piped up, "Tanner isn't the only hot guy in the class," as the three of them walked up to the Forsythe front door. "There's McCrae and Justin Penske and Brad Sumpter . . ."

"Brad Sumpter?" Zora sniffed.

"None as hot as Tanner," Carmen defended loyally.

"Tanner Stahd, the teenage god," Zora murmured, repeating her mother's ironic words as she rang the bell.

"Well, he certainly thinks so," said Bailey on a short laugh.

"He's not as much of an egotist as McCrae," Carmen defended.

"Okay, Chris McCrae and Tanner Stahd both have inflated opinions of themselves," Zora said. "Doesn't mean they're not hot."

The door was opened by Amanda's mother. Marilyn Forsythe was rail thin, and the skin around her face had been stretched to remove lines. Tastefully so. Zora's own mother had tried a similar procedure, but it hadn't worked quite the same way. She was still a little dumpy, with a cloud of curly brown hair—dyed—whereas Marilyn was slim elegance, with blond hair swept into a ponytail at her nape. She wore cream-colored pants and a matching blouse. She was beautifully put together, creased and combed and her makeup flawless, with just a hint of blush on her defined cheekbones. She smiled at them all a bit tightly and told them Amanda was in her bedroom, a room that had once been a private den, accessed only by a wrought-iron stairway and now Amanda's very private, very *chichi* bedroom.

The three girls clambered up the stairway, their footsteps clanging through the cavernous house, and they were greeted at the bedroom door by Amanda, who seemed to let them into her room a bit grudgingly. Zora walked to the floor-to-ceiling windows that curved around the turret that made up this end of the house. Below Amanda's room was a dining room with the same nearly 360-degree view as this bedroom.

"I can see the river from here," said Zora.

"No, you can't. It's down in the ravine," said Amanda.

"Well, I mean, I see where it is. I can see the jogging path that runs along the edge and the rail." Zora flushed. Amanda could be so mean sometimes, without even trying to be.

"Can you?" Bailey asked.

"You must have great eyes," said Carmen, squinting.

Zora didn't answer. In truth, she'd just been making conversation.

Amanda's gaze was trained out the window as well, but her blue eyes held a faraway glint, as if her mind were anywhere but with her friends. It was just as well, as Zora didn't want her every comment analyzed and thrown back at her.

"What are you thinking about?" Zora asked.

"Nothing."

Amanda could be very hard to know. Truth be told, the rest of them were all vying for her attention, whenever they were together. Well, everyone but Delta, who, even before Amanda kissed Tanner, or vice versa, had been on her own path, a little distant from the rest of them. Zora had secretly admired and wondered about Delta, whose family had far less money than all the other Firsts, even Bailey or Carmen, or at least that's what Amanda had said.

It's not about money, Zora reminded herself. Sometimes she was a little bit embarrassed by her own thoughts. She looked around quickly, worried someone could see through her, but Bailey and Carmen were animatedly telling Amanda about the arrangements for the Five Firsts' tents, while Amanda listened as if she were just indulging them, which she probably was.

It was Bailey who finally got around to asking Amanda about kissing Tanner with a kind of bumbling, ass-backward question about whether Delta and Tanner were still a couple.

"Why wouldn't they be?" Amanda asked provocatively.

"Because you were making out on Zora's pool table," Bailey blurted out after a charged moment.

Zora held her breath, and Carmen looked worried. It wasn't smart to piss Amanda off.

Amanda didn't immediately meet Bailey's gaze. She still seemed locked in her own reverie. But then her gaze dropped to the floor for a moment before she looked at the shorter, wiry girl. "Jesus, Bailey, people make such a big deal over things. Tanner is with Delta. We just got caught up, messing around, you know."

"Yeah." Carmen looked relieved, clearly wanting the conversation to end.

"Does Delta know that?" asked Zora.

"I haven't talked to Delta. Obviously." Amanda sighed with exasperation. "She's really pissed off. I get it. I would be, too. But it was nothing. Tanner knows it was nothing. And now you all know it was nothing. Right?"

"Right," the three of them chorused with much relief.

Zora wanted to believe her. Really, really wanted to believe her. Amanda was their leader . . . and Delta too, sort of. And she didn't want all kinds of confessions and soul-baring to get in the way. She had her own needs for privacy.

"Amanda!"

The call came from outside the bedroom door, and they all turned to heed Amanda's mother's call. "What?" Amanda yelled back snappishly.

"We have that appointment. We gotta go before

43

your brother gets home from practice. Chop-chop."

"Oh, shit," Amanda muttered. "I forgot. I have an audition for a commercial."

"On Friday?" Bailey asked.

"I know." Amanda made a disgruntled sound.

"What's it for?" Zora asked. She knew Amanda tried out for acting jobs here and there, and she hoped to somehow work her way into it, too.

"I won't get it. It's a local commercial for a real estate company, and they always want young kids and parents. I'm sick of doing things that don't pan out."

"On Friday?" Bailey repeated.

Amanda didn't bother to answer as she stomped out of the room. After a moment, Zora, Carmen, and Bailey followed her down the winding staircase. They hovered by the front door a moment, listening to Amanda argue with her mother about the audition, but in the end, Mrs. Forsythe shooed the girls out and took Amanda in her car. Without Amanda, Zora sort of lost interest in hanging out, and since the debacle of her father finding out that their liquor supply had been diminished, he wasn't keen on having Zora host her friends at their house any longer. It was the boys, of course, who'd really done damage to the fifths of bourbon, rum, and vodka, but since Dad didn't really know the guys in her class, he took out this displeasure on the Five Firsts.

"I'd better take you guys back," Zora said to them.

"Take me to Carmen's," Bailey said, not bothering to hide her disappointment. "My mom's probably there."

Joyce Quintar and Elena Proffitt had met in Lamaze class and become good friends. Their daughters had followed suit, and their friendship had lasted even through Bailey's parents' ongoing trials, though the Reverend wasn't all that keen on his wife hanging out with a divorcée. . . . He truly was old school.

After Zora dropped off Carmen and Bailey at Carmen's house, she returned to her own home, a Tudor with leaded-glass windows and a grand entry hall. She was disappointed, too. It was really Amanda's fault their Friday night had gotten blown up. If she hadn't been fooling around with Tanner . . .

Momentarily, Zora allowed herself to think about Tanner Stahd in the way she only did in her most private moments. The guy had a lean, easy, open way of being. Zora had caught his eye lingering on her once or twice, and each time her heart had beaten a little faster. He was a cool guy, and it felt good to be noticed. Though she thought it was pretty rotten the way Amanda had ignored the fact that Tanner was Delta's boyfriend, and kissed him and climbed up on the pool table, laughing and joking around and generally being more frenemy than friend, there was no denying Tanner was hot. The hottest guy in high school. And really . . . who was to say that Delta had dibs on him? Sure, Delta and Tanner were assumed to be a couple; they'd been one for years. But it wasn't like they were married or anything. Sure, it wasn't right to treat your friends like Amanda had treated Delta, but maybe it was time for some kind of shake-up. If Tanner were suddenly free of Delta he'd be . . . well . . . *free.*

Zora parked her car in the third bay of the garage, then pushed through the back door into the mudroom off the kitchen. Immediately she heard her parents screaming at each other, calling each other names that blistered her ears. Her blood ran cold. This was the new reality. Mom and Dad couldn't get along. Was divorce the next step?

Zora sneaked up the back stairway to her bedroom over the entryway. She grabbed her iPod and plugged the earbuds into her ears, anything to stop the noise. But above the music she could still hear her parents going at it . . . and in the back of her mind she heard Bailey's voice: "My parents yelled and screamed at each other for years before they decided to get a divorce. Broke my dad's heart, but Mom didn't want to be a cop's wife anymore. She's found someone new, and it's like Mom's the one in high school now. My sister's with her, but I stayed with Dad."

Is that what I'm going to have to do? Zora despaired. Pick a parent to live with? Sure, she was going to be eighteen in a few months, but she still depended on her mom and dad.

Bailey's father was the West Knoll River chief of police, and Bailey had stayed with him when their mother went to find her new life. The only time Bailey even saw her mom was when she was visiting Carmen's mom, which used to be every Friday but had become spottier and spottier as Joyce Quintar pulled away from her ex-husband and therefore her daughters. Or so Bailey had said when Zora questioned her.

Zora didn't want any of that. *Please, please, please. Please don't let them divorce and sell the house and move away. Please . . .*

Chapter 3

Ellie sat at the dinner table with her mother, stepfather, and two half brothers, the twins, Michael and Joey, and listened to Oliver Delaney go on about his latest case, a drunk-driving fatality in which the driver had killed himself and his date, and now the deceased date's family was suing for millions, as said drunk driver had been wealthy. Said drunk driver also had nine children, and Oliver was representing them.

"Stop it," Ellie's mother said to the twins, slapping the air in their direction as the six-year-olds were squirreling around, laughing and knocking their chairs together. A glass of milk shivered and sloshed white liquid onto the table.

Ellie grabbed Joey's hand to stop him. He tried to wrench himself free, and she hissed at him, "You want to go to your room?"

"Ellie, I'll handle the boys," Mom said as Oliver grabbed Michael's hand and squeezed hard enough for the boy to yelp.

"Stop it." This time, it was Ellie who snapped. And she snapped at Oliver, who never took having his behavior questioned well.

"I wasn't hurting him," Oliver said coldly.

Michael, suddenly realizing he had some

49

power, held his wrist limply and whimpered, as if he were gravely wounded. Joey pushed him, not buying it at all. Michael immediately pushed Joey back, and the wrestling match was on again. Mom had to get up from her seat and take the two boys away, scolding them as they each howled that it was the other one's fault. The bedroom door slammed, and in the relative quiet that followed, Ellie sat with her stepfather, whom she couldn't stand.

"How was school today?" he asked her when the silence had stretched to uncomfortable limits. This particular question was about the extent of their entire interaction with one another.

"Fine."

"About six weeks till graduation now."

"Uh huh."

"Your mother and I talked about the Forsythes' overnight party. We both think it would be better if you didn't attend."

"Oh, I'm going," Ellie said. Her father might be gone, taken by a heart attack when she was only eleven, but everyone said she'd inherited his stubborn spirit, and she wasn't going to let Oliver Delaney dictate to her . . . ever.

His face flushed, and his dark eyes glittered. He hated her, she knew. What he didn't know was that she hated him right back. Just like she hated pretty much all the boys in her class, except Tanner . . . and maybe Chris McCrae.

Those two she lusted after. She was going to get one of them in bed before the end of the school year, hopefully Tanner. She couldn't believe Amanda had jumped in ahead of her, kissing him, wrestling around on Zora's pool table.

She thought of Delta, her dark good looks and vibrant smile. Ellie had wondered about the spell she'd cast on Tanner for the best part of high school, but now, at least, it looked as if that spell had been broken. If Tanner was with Amanda . . . no matter how minorly . . . then he was ripe for the picking.

Delta could just eat shit, as far as Ellie was concerned.

"You're not going to that overnight party, and that's final," Oliver said, stabbing up a bloody bite of steak with his fork.

Ellie simply got up from the table, put her half-eaten plate in the sink, and followed after her mother and brothers. She'd been working as a server at the Commons, an independent-living adult-care center, for the better part of the last two years and had been saving up for college. All senior year, she'd been taking courses at the local community college, and she planned to go to the University of Oregon, where Tanner had a scholarship for football.

"Where are you going?" Oliver boomed after her.

To my room, asshole. Normally she was at her

job during these hours, but she had Fridays off, and without anything to do, she'd come home and gotten a jump on her homework, though unfortunately that meant she was around for dinner and therefore Oliver's tyranny.

She closed the door to her room, which would also piss Oliver off. "No closed doors" was his policy. He lived in terror that she would do drugs. Not that he cared a whit about her welfare, but it wouldn't look good.

Also, though she knew he would never admit it and her mother would never believe it, she had felt Oliver's lustful eyes on her a time or two and not in a fatherly way. If she was bolder, and he wasn't such a toad, she might take him up on it. Maybe that would wake Mom up. Except there were the twins, and as much as they drove Ellie insane, they were her brothers, and she loved them, sort of, and she couldn't be the reason her mom and Oliver broke up. Why Mom stuck with him and supported him, maybe even loved him, was an enigma Ellie had tried to understand the last eight years since their marriage, but it was as unsolvable now as it had been in the beginning. No, the best thing she could do was make it through the summer and then hightail it down to Eugene, find a roommate, and go to college. She didn't think Delta would be following Tanner. First, because Delta didn't have the money, and second, because this Amanda thing had really put the kibosh on their romance . . . hopefully.

But Amanda? With Tanner?

The thought of that icy blond robot with Tanner irked Ellie deep down. And wasn't Amanda supposed to be Delta's best friend or something? Not that Ellie could stand either one of them.

She flung herself on her bed, then rolled over and stared up at the ceiling.

Once upon a time, she'd been the third of their group of three: Amanda, Delta, and Ellie. Third grade and into fourth. She still had the pictures of that time, when the three of them were inseparable. They'd all styled their hair in chin-length bobs. They got the same black ankle boots. They each had a bracelet with their name engraved in scrolled letters, and they swapped them around. Sometimes Ellie would have Delta's, sometimes she would have Amanda's. At some point in that year, she ended up with her own back, and Bailey and Carmen moved into the school—not at the same time, but it felt like it somehow—and they joined their group. Ellie had protested, had given both Bailey and Carmen the cold shoulder for the last half of sixth grade and that summer and into seventh, and suddenly Ellie was out, and Zora DeMarco, whose businessman father broke into the cell phone business when it was really starting up and suddenly had money coming out his ears, was brought in. And then Ellie's dad died, and she didn't give a rat's ass about her fair-weather friends, and then . . . she was no longer one of the Five Firsts, she was an ex-First.

Ellie climbed off her bed and went to her closet, searching on the shelf above her clothes for the jewelry box with the Scottie dog shaped out of "gems" on its cover. She opened it up, and the song "You're the One That I Want" from *Grease* started playing. She dug through several tangled necklaces to find the bracelet with the letters of her name scrolled in silver. She'd saved it. What a laugh.

She put it on and twisted her arm, letting the overhead light bounce off it.

Maybe she would wear it when she had sex with Tanner.

Maybe on the night of the overnight.

Bailey sat at the kitchen island beside Carmen, eating an oatmeal cookie, while Carmen's mother and her own mother shared cups of coffee and conversation. Bailey had been surprised to find her mom at the Proffitts', as the once-sacred Friday afternoon confab between the two women had sort of dissolved since Joyce split from Bailey's dad and apparently took up with an old boyfriend from high school. When Joyce had rushed over to hug her, Bailey had tried to reciprocate, but truthfully, she was still pissed off at her.

Carmen's mom, Elena, didn't have any reservations, and she was sharing tea cookies and even a shot of bourbon in the tea with Joyce and generally having a grand old time when Carmen and Bailey showed up.

"You're back," Elena had said in surprise.

Joyce had momentarily frozen as well, then rushed over to Bailey as if to make up for the half second of shock at seeing her daughter. Though Elena and Joyce's friendship had lasted through thick and thin, the Reverend Esau Proffitt still had problems with the fact that Joyce had left her husband. A wife cleaves to her husband and all that. Though Bailey wasn't as old-fashioned and hard as the reverend, she, too, had struggled with her mother's defection, seeing her less and less this last year and a half, even though she'd only moved about forty-five minutes away to Vancouver, Washington, across the Columbia River from Portland.

"My, your hair's grown," Joyce said, fluffing at Bailey's ponytail.

"It does that," said Bailey, swallowing a bite of cookie on a dry throat.

"Oh, you're mean. Don't be mean." Her mother smiled at her indulgently but was already turning back to Elena. "How did my girl get so mean?"

Elena wasn't as blithe as Joyce and offered a tentative smile in return.

"Bailey's not mean," Carmen defended. "Give

us a break. We're just heading toward graduation and a whole new world. It's crazy scary."

"Oh, I'm just kidding," Joyce said.

Oh, sure, Bailey thought.

"Weren't you going to Zora's?" Elena asked as Joyce waggled her cup in the direction of the bourbon bottle.

"Amanda's," Carmen corrected. "Zora took us there, but Amanda had some kind of audition, and then we just didn't have plans, so we came back here. We can leave, if you'd rather be alone."

"Don't be silly," Elena said, picking up the bourbon and bringing it to where Joyce was sitting, pouring a generous dollop into her mug.

"I've got to get home anyway," Bailey lied.

"Pooh," said Joyce. "You're an adult."

"Not eighteen till August," Bailey pointed out.

"And you're with your mother," she singsonged.

Who's drinking and laughing with her friend and doesn't give a damn about me.

The words were on her tongue, but she reined them in. Nothing good ever came of arguing with either of her parents, though her dad was really easier to talk to, quicker to realize he'd maybe stepped in it with his youngest daughter. Joyce never seemed to get any wiser, which was completely fine in Bailey's estimation. She'd left them with hardly a backward glance. Running into her at the Proffitts' on the occasional Friday was more heartache than joy. Bailey had worked very hard on becoming inured to her, and for the most part, she'd succeeded. Her mom couldn't get to her like she could to her older sister. Bailey warned Lill to toughen up, but Lill didn't pay attention to Bailey and spent a lot of time still trying to be with their mother, setting herself up for disappointment time and time again.

"What kind of audition?" Joyce asked now.

"Mom," Bailey said, pained.

"What?" She threw up her hands. "Can't I ask *anything?*"

"I just . . ." For one terrible moment, Bailey thought she might actually tear up. She'd prided herself on being able to handle her emotions.

"Hey, c'mon," Carmen said, sliding off her stool. "Let's go to my room."

"Don't get on the Internet," Elena warned.

Carmen snorted in exasperation as she led the way up the stairs to her bedroom. The Proffitts watched over their children's online time like hawks. It drove Carmen half-crazy, but Reverend Proffitt was fiercely concerned with the behavior of teens and making certain they didn't head down the wrong path.

Bailey appreciated her friend looking out for her. Joyce tried to stop her from leaving with a "I never get to see you anymore" plea that sounded like a whine, but Bailey covered her ears, physically putting her hands over them, to block her mother out.

"I can't stand it," she said, once the bedroom door was closed behind them.

"I don't want to think about anything but the overnight," Carmen said, stretching out on her twin bed. Bailey took the beanbag chair, the only other place to sit in the tiny room. Carmen's bedspread was pink checks with ruffles, a remnant from girlhood that no one in her family seemed the least inclined to change, and when Carmen had complained about it, she'd been ignored completely. The reverend and Elena had no clue what went on inside Carmen's head. Bailey could have told them she was obsessed with Tanner Stahd, and they would have fallen over themselves trying to deny it. It wasn't a subject Bailey and Carmen talked about much, as Bailey thought Tanner was cute and all, but maybe overrated for all the fuss about him. But Carmen's every other thought revolved around him. Though Carmen hadn't said it, Bailey knew she was kind of counting on the overnight above the river as a way to be near him.

As if divining Bailey's thoughts, she asked, "Do you think Tanner and Delta will break up?"

"Do you . . . want them to?"

"I don't know. They've been together forever. I just wondered . . . you don't think he and Amanda are really hooking up, do you?"

There was an edge of desperation in her voice, as if she could live with Tanner being with Delta, but the thought of him with Amanda was anathema.

"Nah. Amanda's never serious about guys." Bailey actually had no idea what Amanda's thoughts were. The girl was a cipher, only showing what she wanted to be shown. But Bailey wanted the subject to change to steer Carmen away from her obsession, no easy feat.

"Amanda won't go to Oregon," Carmen predicted. "She'll go to some other school. Maybe back east. Something prestigious and cool."

Bailey didn't respond to this. She wanted to give her friend some hope, sort of, but she also wanted her to face reality. Carmen didn't have a chance with Tanner. He was too popular, and Carmen, even though she was one of the Five Firsts, was a little too nerdy, a little too needy, and her dad being the reverend only made it worse. None of the guys wanted to be with her. They all wanted Amanda, or Delta, or maybe Zora . . . and even Ellie. Bailey knew Carmen yearned to be in that grouping—the one the guys lusted over—and felt a little bad that she was glad she wasn't. Bailey had no interest in giving her heart to any of the high school boys. It wasn't that she didn't find them hot, despite some of them saying she and Carmen had to be lesbians because they were always together and had never had boyfriends.

She just knew that, as the daughter of one of the town's policemen, if she was going to sow her wild oats, it was going to be outside of high school, somewhere far away from West Knoll.

Carmen broke into Bailey's thoughts with, "Don't you just want something to happen? Something good?"

The words sounded wrenched from her soul. "Well . . . yeah, I—"

"I just feel like we're waiting, you know? It's just . . . waiting and waiting. I want it all now. Don't you?"

"Depends on what *it* is, I guess," Bailey said cautiously.

"It's Friday night. We're not going to get drunk. We're not going to be with our friends. We're not going to see the guys."

For guys, read "Tanner."

"We're just *waiting* for the rest of our lives to start. My dad's freaking that Amanda's party's an overnight."

"It isn't really Amanda's party. It's the whole class, and—"

"I know, I know. Coach Sutton, Mr. Timmons, and Ms. Reade . . . They'll all be watching us. And some others, too, I think. I've told my dad that, but I don't know. At least your dad gives you some freedom, but not mine. Mom'd probably let me. But she can't go against him."

"Some of the kids are just going for the day—"

60

"I don't want to be one of them!" She leapt off the bed and paced the room, stopping in front of the window and throwing back the curtains. It was just getting dark, and the sky was purplish, with a crescent moon rising on the horizon. "I want to spend the night with the guys. It doesn't have to be a sex orgy, like my dad thinks it's going to be. I just want to camp out. Roast hot dogs and marshmallows and swim in the river by moonlight. I know. Never mind," she said quickly as Bailey started to protest. "The river's too high in the spring. It wouldn't be safe."

"I was going to say, it would be hell getting down the cliff to the water. I know there are steps, kind of, and we're going to do it, but in the dark . . ."

"I just want to get out of here," she moaned. "I just want to be with . . . a guy."

This was as close as Carmen ever got about admitting her deep, deep crush on Tanner Stahd.

"I can't believe Amanda was with Tanner," Carmen muttered.

"I can't believe she had an audition tonight. She seemed really irked at her mom about it all."

"And then Zora just went home. I guess we're not cool enough to be with her."

"Maybe we should call some of the guys?" Bailey suggested, though it was about the last thing she wanted right now. But it was what Carmen wanted, and whether Carmen knew it or not, Bailey was a better friend to her than she was to Bailey.

"You don't think Tanner's with Delta?"

"I was thinking more of McCrae or Justin Penske or . . ." She trailed off at Carmen's snort. Her friend was back lying on the bed again, glaring at the ceiling.

"What do you think's going to happen with Amanda and Delta?" Carmen asked.

"Nothing good," Bailey said with feeling.

"Maybe Tanner'll decide to quit them both."

"Maybe."

"I applied to U of O," Carmen said now, surprising Bailey. They'd both planned to take courses at Portland Community College and get part-time jobs.

"You did? Oh." How could she forget that Tanner had won an academic scholarship there and hoped to make the football team?

"He's really smart, too, y'know," Carmen said defensively.

"Did I say he wasn't?"

"His dad's a doctor, and his mom was pre-law."

Bailey nodded slowly. Tanner's dad had been a medical doctor before he got involved with drugs himself—or so the story went—and had his license suspended. His parents had divorced, and his mom had gone to work for a law firm, while ex-Dr. Stahd had turned his life around and now prescribed over-the-counter herbal supplements with his new, younger-model wife.

"Tanner's going to be a doctor, too," she said.

"I know."

"Bailey? Honey? I'm getting ready to leave, and I want to say good-bye." Her mother's voice called up the stairway.

"Gotta go." For once Bailey was ready to leave. She'd hoped Carmen's obsession with Tanner would dissipate as the school year came to a close, but for some reason, their imminent graduation seemed to have only heightened it.

"I'm going to spend the night at Amanda's, no matter what," Carmen told Bailey with conviction. "My dad can ground me or whatever. I'm already eighteen. He can kick me out. I don't care. I'm going."

Chapter 4

The party at Amanda's took place three weeks before graduation. Delta stood to one side of the barbeque pit Coach Dean Sutton and one of the school counselors, Clarice Billings, had created with the help of the senior boys. Tanner had been involved in the dig as well, taking off his shirt on this unseasonably warm May day, creating a minor stir among the girls, who hooted and hollered as if he were a Chippendales dancer.

Delta had grinned until her cheeks hurt, pretending to think it was all so much fun, when in reality she wanted to sink down onto the blanket on the grass and sob her heart out.

Things had not gotten better with Tanner. Maybe she'd let him off the hook too easily. He'd stopped talking to her about Amanda, but worse yet, he now acted like she'd given him carte blanche to hang around with her ex-friend and generally behave as if his kiss with Amanda was no big deal. In fact, it almost felt like he was flaunting his independence from Delta.

The last few weeks had been horrifyingly awful. How had this become her problem and not his? And Amanda? Like Tanner, she acted as if nothing had happened. She treated Delta like they were still friends, with just a shade more distance between them. The rest of the Firsts had taken their cues from both Delta and Amanda and pretended as if the make-out session on the pool table was a myth. But one little kiss, it wasn't. Delta was pretty sure about that. There were vibes, undercurrents, tacit agreements, sideways looks that were meant to be bland but held secrets.

It was torture. Her heart clutched, like it had so many times these long, miserable days. She'd already lost him. It was over. Her dreams, her love, everything.

And it was Amanda's fault.

Delta realized she'd been lost in a fog for most of the day and made an effort to resurface. There were a couple of pitched tents, but the parents had all gotten together and sent e-mails swirling and put the kibosh on a big, overnight campout. The tents that stood in the field belonged to Amanda's family, who'd turned them into board-game centers where the seniors could get out of the sun and hang together. There was also a badminton net strung between two poles and a croquet field. Coach Sutton had decided to have a pig roast, and he'd been at the site for hours and hours, and apparently there were still hours to go.

So . . . no overnight, which was fine with Delta. The thought that she might fall asleep while Tanner and Amanda were still awake and somehow escaping the adults' watchful eyes, maybe heading into the deep woods on the north side of the property above the river canyon for some extracurricular activity, was more than she could bear.

She inhaled and exhaled. Carmen and Bailey were playing badminton with McCrae and Justin Penske and having a good time, if Delta could correctly read the squeals of laughter and ribald jokes zinging back and forth. Ellie was being her usual brownnoser self, hanging around the barbeque pit and talking to Miss Billings and the coach. There was another teaching assistant with them as well, but Delta didn't know his name. He seemed more interested in Miss Billings than anything else.

Amanda was riding a golf cart back and forth between the house and the picnic/party/barbecue near the river, fetching items from the kitchen—sodas, water, paper plates, and other supplies. Sometimes Tanner would jump into the front seat with her, and Delta had seen them turn to each other and share a grin.

Should she leave? Just turn around and go? She shaded her eyes from the bright spring sun and stared into a deep blue sky. She could barely recognize what a beautiful day it was. Just made for a picnic.

She closed her eyes, and when she opened them again, it was to see Coach Sutton's tanned, knobby knees as he prowled around the pit, checking the temperature. Miss Billings was seated on a lawn chair, smiling up at him. Delta felt ill. It seemed like love was in the air for everyone but her.

She realized there was someone just behind her left shoulder, and she turned around swiftly to find Woody Deavers sliding her a sly smile. She turned back around just as swiftly. Woody was always trying to get a laugh, most times at someone else's expense. His hair was too long—much longer than Tanner's—and he wore jeans so faded and worn they were almost white and looked like they could shred into cotton puffs and float away. He'd taken off his T-shirt and laid it over his shoulders, exposing a hard, deeply tanned, muscular torso for all to see. A tattoo of a landing eagle, talons extended, ran along his shoulder and collarbone.

Delta hated tattoos.

"Hey, Ms. Smith," he said lazily. "What happened with your man there in the golf cart?"

She didn't respond.

"He and that ice bitch together now?"

"They're just bringing stuff up from the house," she stated shortly as he strolled into her range of vision.

He thrust his fists in his pockets and gave her a long look. There was something aggressively male about him. She'd seen him in a short, comedic play, and he hadn't been half-bad, but he was not one of the cool kids, and she'd spent a lot of time working on her own popularity, which could be undermined by even talking to him.

"Where's Crystal?" Delta asked, referring to his girlfriend. If Woody had one tattoo, Crystal had a dozen.

"Crystal wouldn't be caught dead at a class party." He smiled, a brilliant shot of white. "Don't know what I'm doing here. Actually, I do. I came for the pig. Crystal's a vegetarian, so that didn't interest her, either."

Delta smiled tightly.

"Seriously, what's going on with Tanner and Amanda?" he asked.

"What do you care?"

"I don't. Much. But you do."

"They're just friends. We've all been friends for years." She shifted away from him a few feet, wondering if she could just run for it.

"Sure. That's why you're so miserable."

"I'm not miserable. I'm just tired."

"You gonna stay overnight here?"

"We're not doing that anymore. Did you miss the memo?"

"Maybe the adults in the room are leaving," he said, shooting a glance toward the coach, Miss Billings, and the assistant guy, "but that doesn't mean we have to, does it?"

"The Forsythes aren't letting us stay here," she informed him tightly.

"Ice bitch's parents don't have to know."

Just the idea made her heart clutch. She was a hard sleeper, and what if she fell asleep and then Tanner and Amanda got together and everyone knew and they had sex and it was all over for her and Tanner? Maybe she should have put out. They'd certainly had their make-out sessions, and some had come pretty close to them doing it; Tanner had certainly pressed her. But Delta had held off, not because she didn't want to, but because of some nebulous impulse for self-preservation that she'd gleaned from her friends, who seemed to have sex with one boyfriend, then get dumped, then have sex with another, just to have the whole thing start all over again. That's what had happened with Zora and two guys from their school, both of whom had been older and had already graduated. She acted like it was no big deal, but Delta wondered. She now had a reputation for being easy, which didn't seem to bother her, but it would bother Delta.

Still . . . was that the reason Tanner had jumped to Amanda? As far as Delta knew, Amanda hadn't even had a serious boyfriend, so far. She was, as Woody put it, an ice bitch, and kept guys at arm's length . . . or at least she had.

You should've made love to Tanner. You should do it tonight.

70

"Excuse me," she said shortly, walking away from Woody. It was a long trek back to the house, and by the time she got there, Tanner and Amanda would probably have loaded up the cart and be on their way back to the party.

She hesitated, wondering if she should wait. She had to get Tanner away from the party entirely. They needed their own special time together. Somewhere else.

"Have you seen Amanda?" Ellie asked Delta. She'd been talking to McCrae, flirting, Delta had noted, but now she was looking at Delta in that intense way of hers.

"She and Tanner went up to the house to pick stuff up," Delta said, purposely making it sound like no big deal.

"Ah, yeah, the golf cart . . ." She glanced in the direction of the house.

"It's getting hot out here," McCrae said, squinting toward the sun. "Man, this is great!" His shirt was unbuttoned. Like Woody, he had a washboard stomach. His jeans were in better shape, but not by much. He slapped them. "I'm getting these off." With that he went to the pile of bags and backpacks the kids had brought with their personal gear.

Ellie said to Delta, "You thinking about going up there?" She inclined her head toward the house. "I want to change into my swimsuit, but I'm not doing it in any tent."

"I'm not swimming."

"I almost didn't bring my suit. But the weather . . ."

"The runoff'll be cold. You could freeze to death in that water," Delta said repressively.

"It's not that bad. I went down to the river."

Delta had no intention of scaling down the steps and ladder to the water below, even though there was a sandy spit jutting into the river where a bunch of the kids had set up one of the tents. The coach and Miss Billings had initially adamantly opposed any of the kids going down there, but had given in and let the assistant keep an eye on them. Not many of their classmates had gone down, though, because the weather hadn't been warm enough. But now, as the sun slipped past its zenith and was starting to head back down, the heat of the day was surprisingly intense.

"I didn't bring a suit," Delta admitted.

"Bummer," Ellie said.

Was she being sarcastic? Delta wondered as Ellie started walking briskly down the dirt track toward the Forsythes' mansion. Delta had overheard her telling do-gooder Rhonda about "fibbing"—basically lying—about where she was today to both her stepfather and her mother, as they'd been opposed to her coming at all. They apparently thought Ellie was at her job. Rhonda had received this news with a worried look and a raft of tumbling excuses about how Miss Billings and Coach Sutton were chaperones, and that even Reverend Proffitt had allowed Carmen to come, so everything was totally cool and safe, and Ellie should really just tell the truth. Ellie, who could be judgmental when it suited her— and it suited her a lot—had merely shrugged this time, leaving the do-gooder to gaze after her in consternation.

An hour later, Delta was still undecided about whether to leave the party but had stuck around because she couldn't bear to leave Tanner with Amanda. The roasting of the pig was into its final hour, and preparations were being made for the big feast. The group had swelled, and many more senior classmates had arrived, with only a few leaving. Several of the senior class teachers had shown up as well, among them Anne Reade, who taught English, and Brian Timmons, the math teacher and senior class adviser. There had been speculation all year that Ms. Reade and Mr. Timmons were an item, but Delta had wondered if they even liked each other all that much. Neither of them appeared to have any joie de vivre; they seemed more like careful allies than friends.

But . . . at least Tanner seemed to have given up his allegiance to only Amanda. He swept by to smile goofily at Delta and say, "This is great, isn't it?" and then he was talking to the guys and other girls and even the teachers. Delta began to realize that he was wasted. But where had he gotten the stuff? There was no alcohol in sight, and she doubted they could hide it in the tents. She'd seen him and others drift toward the woods a time or two, and she'd begun to realize a number of members of the senior class were stealing away to misbehave. She was hurt that she hadn't been invited. Did they think she would give the game away to the chaperones, who didn't appear to have caught on yet, or did they just not want her?

Her suspicions were confirmed when Woody appeared from the nearest copse of trees smelling of skunk. Skunkweed. Marijuana.

Shit.

She wanted to grab Tanner and yank him away. He couldn't afford to mess this up. He was on academic scholarship and hoped to walk on to the football team. Maybe the black mark of a "minor in possession," should Coach or someone else find out and feel duty-bound to turn him in, wouldn't much matter, but it sure wasn't going to help.

"Who's going swimming?" Chris McCrae called out.

"I am!" Tanner shouted, ripping off his shirt. He also had the lean muscular torso of an athlete.

"Me, too!" Woody said, yanking off his jeans right then and there, revealing a pair of Speedos that made the girls gasp and laugh; there was quite a bit filling them out, which Woody was clearly proud of.

"Me, too!" Carmen suddenly joined in. She'd changed into a pair of shorts and a tank top, and now she yanked the shirt over her head to reveal a black swim bra and ran after Tanner, McCrae, and Woody, who were all heading for the steps.

"Jesus," Zora said, who'd finally apparently left the "Amanda group" of the Five Firsts to join her. "I'm not freezing my butt off."

"I don't have a suit," Delta said.

Bailey had walked quickly after Carmen and now stood by as other kids clambered down the steps.

"Wait a minute. Wait a minute!" Coach Sutton bellowed. "Watch out for the undertow!"

Amanda said, "The rapids are down the river, Coach. The swimming hole by the beach is fine and roped off for us."

"You think these guys care?" he growled.

"They all know. And you told 'em again and again."

"Your mom and dad put me in charge, and that's what I intend to be."

Amanda rolled her eyes. Her parents had taken a trip to the beach and left the party to the coach, but she clearly thought he was taking his job too seriously.

Counselor Billings said, "Freddie's manning the rope at the edge of the swimming hole."

75

Freddie. That was the name of the aide.

Coach snorted, and Delta agreed with him. Freddie might as well save his energy for all the good that would do anyone if the guys like Woody and Penske and McCrae decided to float down the river. The rapids would be tough, though, and there was that undertow where the river dumped into Grimm's Pond, the swimming hole near the highway that was feared by parents and beloved by daredevils.

Counselor Billings started heading down the cliff side.

Delta decided she wasn't going to stay on the headland if everyone else was scaling down the cliff side, so she followed after Amanda and Counselor Billings. She'd worn black capri pants, a red short-sleeved top, and flip-flops and had some difficulty negotiating the narrow steps down; once there, she wished she'd brought her swimsuit after all. Tanner, McCrae, Carmen, and others, including Bailey and Amanda, were already in the river splashing each other, while Counselor Billings stood on the beach along with about ten other kids and watched them. The water had to be icy cold, but they obviously didn't care. The river moved slowly alongside the scrawny beach before hurrying down a narrowing canyon. There was a shelf cut into the near side, a walking trail of sorts that was almost an echo of the jogging trail above. The shelf gradually rose as the river headed around a bend and then, with increasing speed, over a series of rapids on its way to Grimm's Pond. Delta had once traveled those rapids with Amanda when they were much younger, both of them huddled in a rubber boat that was oared by Amanda's father. It had been a scary and thrilling ride . . . and she'd never wanted to do it again. Neither had Amanda, and her father had teased her mercilessly until she was fighting tears.

Now Delta gazed down the canyon, seeing the rush of white water far down as the river made its left-hand turn at the beginning of the rapids. Later in the year, it would be rated "easy" by river rafters; not so in the spring.

Miss Billings was warning them all to be careful. Freddie had stretched the "barrier," a plastic rope threaded with several red and white floats, running it from one shore to the other. He was wearing a life vest and holding another one up high, silently asking them to do the same. No one paid him any attention.

"Come on up!" Coach Sutton bellowed down, barely heard by the crowd below. "Pig's roasted! Corn on the cob's done!"

Delta stepped her flip-flops into the water, which was cold but bearable. Amanda was up to her knees, trying to gain Tanner's attention and failing miserably. He was actually splashing around with Carmen, who was good in the water, her height and strength putting her on par with the boys.

"Time for barbeque!" Counselor Billings yelled, waving them all out of the swimming hole.

Reluctantly, in twos and threes, they all staggered out of the water, shivering. Woody got near Delta and shook his head like a wild dog.

"Woody!" she sputtered. Wet drops were flung all over her red shirt.

"Sorry," he said with a huge grin, then whooped and hollered and clambered up the bank. It was like a challenge to the other guys, who damn near stepped on each other's heads as they followed him up, water dripping on the steps and rungs, making everything ten times slipperier than it had been on the way down.

Carmen followed after them like a galloping dog. Bailey, who'd descended with Delta and Amanda, looked somewhat pained as she grabbed a rung and headed back up.

Amanda looked at Delta. Delta looked at Amanda. "Go ahead," Amanda said.

"No, go on. I'm going to stick down here for a little while."

Amanda looked as if she were going to argue but stopped herself and gave a shrug. Then she followed after the others.

Chris McCrae was seated on a nearby log, eyeing Delta. His cutoff jeans were wet, and his torso was too, but it was drying in the slanting sunlight. He squinted at her. "Aren't you going up?"

"No."

He stood and ran a hand through his hair, pulling out some of the water. "Gonna stay down here for the rest of your life?"

"I just might," Delta said. She heard her belligerent tone, a far cry from the happy, enthusiastic Delta they all knew.

"He doesn't give a shit about her, you know."

"Who?" Delta asked automatically.

He gave her the "Are we really going to play this game?" look.

"If you're talking about Tanner, I'd rather not."

He snorted. "Who are you—Ellie?"

"What do you mean?"

"You gotta watch yourself. You sound about as judgmental as she is."

She turned her back on him. She didn't want to talk about Ellie, or Tanner, or anyone.

"He doesn't give a shit about anybody," McCrae went on. "Not trying to dis Tanner. Just the truth."

"Well, that's *not* true," she argued.

"He cares about one person, himself. And he likes you because you're the prettiest girl in the school."

Delta was half-infuriated, half-flattered. She

turned back around and faced him. McCrae could be so charmingly infuriating. "I'm not the prettiest—"

"Yeah, you are. Don't take it as a compliment." His blue eyes glimmered somewhere between mirth and anger. "He picked you because of your looks and popularity. He's screwing around because he can. Amanda . . . Carmen . . . Ellie . . . they'd all lie down for him and probably already have."

"Ellie?" she squeezed out, shocked, suddenly finding it hard to breathe.

"I'm just saying, don't be naïve. We're all graduating. Going our separate ways. Tanner wants to sow some wild oats, and you don't put out."

Her breath expelled in a rush.

"That's what he said," McCrae told her.

"So, if I 'put out,' I could have him back?" She was bitter.

"For a while."

"What does that mean?"

He was heading for the stairs himself, but now he turned around and walked the rest of the way backward, keeping her in his vision. "High school's over. All of this doesn't matter. You and your friends . . . the *Firsts* . . ." His tone was mocking. "It's done. Move on." He reached the steps, turned around, and started climbing as Delta absorbed his words.

"Turn on, tune in, and drop out . . ."

She followed him to the bottom of the stairs. "What?" she asked, looking up at him.

"Just something from my parents. An old saying."

"Are you smoking dope too?"

He was several feet above her, and now he glanced down, smiling. "If you truly want Tanner Stahd, you're going to have to stop sounding as self-righteous as Ellie."

Then he grabbed a rung and clambered the rest of the way up, like Woody had.

Bailey held a plate of roast pig, corn on the cob, and a deformed and burned biscuit, the kind the boys wolfed down like dollar pancakes but she couldn't stomach. Kids had been wandering in and out of the copse of trees and coming back drunk or high. They'd hid their forays pretty well; none of the chaperones seemed to notice, though Counselor Billings, Freddie, and Coach Sutton had moseyed over to the trees a time or two, apparently considering. So far, no one had gotten busted.

Carmen was hanging with the boys. She'd managed to convince the reverend—God knew how—that the barbeque was a school-sanctioned event and there would be strict rules enforced. Carmen had always tested her father, and this was just another way to do that. There was a part of her, a gleam in her eye, that said she wanted to defy convention. Did she want to become the bad girl? The preacher's daughter who goes rogue? Bailey sure as hell hoped not. It would just . . . be a big problem, and Bailey didn't want big problems.

She knew she was considered the goody two shoes of their group. More than once, she'd sensed the Firsts wanted to kick her out, and well, that would hurt, but it would be okay, too. She just didn't have it in her anymore to care. What had once seemed vitally important now felt sort of stupid.

What do you want?

She wanted to hang out with Carmen. Just Carmen . . . and okay, maybe Carmen's family, too. Strict as the Proffitts were, Bailey felt their love like a cozy, enveloping blanket. She got some of that feeling from her dad, too, but he was so busy and sometimes couldn't express himself quite the same way. He was cautious of her. Like he thought she might be secretly telling tales to Mom, though nothing could be further from the truth. Lill was with Mom. They were a twosome. And Mom was . . .

She couldn't quite come up with the right word. Selfish . . . ? Narcissistic . . . ? Those sentiments were almost too harsh. Mom just wanted a new life without her policeman husband. Bailey had overheard her complaining once that Dad was just too "law and order" for her. She was intent on leaving, and she was willing to give up the family for it, which she did. Though they all knew she was with an old high school boyfriend, Mom hadn't said a word about him.

Bailey had revealed to her father that she'd run into her mother at Carmen's, and Dad—whom she called Quin, like everyone else—had gone completely still. This was the same reaction she always got whenever she brought up Mom, but it was better to be honest about everything than have him find out some other way that could be more hurtful. She'd made sure Quin knew the meeting was no big deal. Unplanned and therefore unscripted. Just one of those things. Still, it was hard on him, though he would never admit as much to Bailey. She suspected he still wanted Mom back, might even take her back, but the trust between them was shattered, so, in Bailey's mind, it would never work.

At that moment, Carmen and a bunch of the other kids emerged from the trees and moved over toward the food. Bailey stepped toward Carmen.

"What's going on?" Bailey asked her, eyeing Tanner Stahd, who was walking like a man concentrating on making it appear he was in complete control, even though his legs and arms were stiff, his movements wooden and off their timing by a half second. He was totally wasted, which made her nervous. She didn't want Sutton, or Billings, or Freddie, or anybody else finding out.

Carmen was looking in Tanner's direction, too. Bailey could pick up on her anxiety, even though she was silent. It was there in the creases on her forehead and the opening and closing of her fists.

"You okay?" Bailey asked.

"Yeah . . ."

"Tanner looks wasted."

"Yeah." This time she was more positive.

"What were you guys doing? Smells kinda like weed."

"Uh . . . no. That's not . . . Penske had some whiskey or something . . . brown stuff."

"Carmen Proffitt, are you drunk?" Bailey asked, purposely adding a smile to her voice when she felt worried and anxious.

"No." Carmen gave her her full attention. There was something odd in her expression.

"What's wrong?" Bailey asked, her heart jumping. Her friend's demeanor sent little darts of fear through her bloodstream.

Though Carmen was looking at Bailey, it was clear she was seeing something else.

"Something happened," Bailey said, as serious as a heart attack.

Carmen didn't respond immediately. Her skin was ashen, and she looked like she'd had a good fright.

"What?" Bailey pressed.

She glanced back at Tanner and the guys, then around the campsite a little wildly. "I saw something . . . ," she whispered softly.

"What?"

"Tanner was with . . . he wasn't the only one. They were all kind of . . . with each other."

Bailey had a bad feeling growing in her gut. "You saw Tanner . . . ?"

"I saw them." Her voice was so soft, Bailey had to strain to hear. "They didn't know I was there . . ."

"Who?"

"The guys . . . some of the guys . . . and the girls . . . They were smoking dope and drinking and . . ." She glanced up wildly. "I wasn't supposed to be there. I just sort of crept up, and they saw me—"

"Carmen."

The staccato rebuke of her name made Carmen jump and Bailey's head jerk around. It was Amanda. She stood legs apart, eyes flashing, as if ready for battle.

"Amanda?" Carmen gulped.

A tense moment ensued, then Amanda's angry expression dissolved into a big smile, and she laughed and grabbed Carmen's arm. "Just joking. You looked so . . . I don't know . . . weird. Come on, let's get something to eat."

Bailey started to follow them, but she already had a plate of food, and she wasn't sure what had just happened anyway. It wasn't like Amanda to appropriate any one of the Firsts the way she had Carmen. Had Amanda purposely stopped Carmen from talking? Well, no matter. As soon as she had her friend alone, Bailey intended to find out just exactly what had spooked Carmen so much.

Chapter 5

It was twilight, and everybody was packing up and getting ready to leave. Delta was on one foot and the other, while Coach Sutton, Counselor Billings, and Freddie, along with Mr. Timmons, Ms. Reade, and do-gooders Rhonda and Trent, were collecting everything. Amanda, Bailey, and Carmen were taking down the tents and had rejected Delta's offer of help, Amanda saying curtly that they had it handled.

So now Delta was standing to one side, kind of by Ellie, who'd also made overtures of help, only to be denied. Neither of them had tried to join the do-gooders in aiding the chaperones. They knew in advance that they would be cheerfully told no. The head of the do-gooders, Rhonda, was in her own way an autocrat.

So that left Delta and Ellie, who'd never liked each other much, as the outsiders. Delta, because their leader, Amanda, had stolen her boyfriend and was somehow persona non grata now, and Ellie because of her "better than thou" attitude that drove them all to distraction. Though Delta suspected Ellie's attitude came from being passed over by the Five Firsts, it nevertheless got under her skin, and it left Delta standing near Ellie in uncomfortable silence. She suspected Ellie would drop her posturing in a nanosecond if she were invited into their group, but maybe not. Maybe Ellie's disinterest was real.

The Five Firsts . . . McCrae's barely hidden disdain might be correct and it really was over. It was a childish construct that didn't really matter to anyone anymore, and maybe even was laughed at by a few.

Delta squinted through the gathering gloom to see where Tanner was. He and a bunch of kids had spent half the afternoon going off in twos and threes into the woods on the north side of the camp. They were drinking, and since Woody was one of them, probably smoking dope, too. They were all pretty trashed, Tanner especially. He clearly wasn't going home with her, but by the thin line of Amanda's lips, it didn't look like he was going with her either.

Good.

"Okay," Coach declared. He'd gone and gotten his pickup, and they'd thrown all the gear from the cookout inside the truck bed along with the leftover food encased in plastic containers. They'd doused the coals in the pit with river water, causing them to steam for a good twenty minutes or so, but now they'd stopped, and Coach had raked through the wet ash, making sure no fire could start anew.

After McCrae's indictment of her holier-than-thou attitude, Delta had taken a turn or two in the trees herself, swallowing a few hurried sips of straight vodka. Vodka, so the party chaperones wouldn't smell it on her. The chaperones had been remarkably unaware of what was going on. Either that, or they'd chosen not to make a fuss about it.

"Okay," Coach said, climbing into his pickup cab and slamming the door. Mr. Timmons and Ms. Reade had started walking together the quarter mile to the house and were already shrunken figures in the distance as Coach leaned out the open window and added, "I'm coming right back, and we're all getting out of here, okay? We've had a fun time, and now it's time to go."

The kids all gave him a cheery thumbs-up as they watched his pickup bounce across the bumpy field. When it had crested the rise toward the Forsythe house, Tanner suddenly yelled, "One last time!" and bolted for the cliff side.

Delta inhaled sharply, and everyone else froze. Then the guys tore after him. A half beat later some of the girls did, too.

"Wait! Wait!" she called.

"Don't!" somebody else yelled. Amanda, maybe. Delta stumbled toward the cliff's edge herself, watching as the guys and girls all worked their way down the steps, jumping the last few feet, racing across the short beach, splashing into the river, and diving into the water. It was growing dark, and what was left of the sun hadn't made it down the walls of the canyon, so they were all in shadow.

Freddie and Counselor Billings had raced to the cliff's edge, too, and now gazed down at the students in dismay, as did Delta, who'd been torn about climbing back down. After a moment of hesitation, Ellie had joined the group at the bottom and was ripping off her shirt and heading for the water. Carmen and Bailey rushed up beside Delta, and Carmen immediately headed down.

"What are you doing?" Bailey demanded. "Somebody's gonna get hurt."

"Yeah, *you!*"

"I'm going down, too," Miss Billings said, sounding angry, and Freddie nodded vigorously in agreement. Amanda was on their heels.

Well, shit.

Delta descended after them once more as well. She dropped the last few feet onto the beach and felt sand in her flip-flops. Now it was hard to make out whose dark hair was bobbing above the surface. Tanner? McCrae? Woody or one of the do-gooders? Definitely stupid, whatever the case.

Counselor Billings said tightly, "We gotta get them outta there."

Carmen, a few yards away, was keeping her eyes on Tanner and saying nothing, which kind of pissed Delta off. Not as much as Amanda, though, whose laser focus was on Carmen, not the idiots in the water.

Delta wondered if she was going to have to jump in too, clothes and all, and would that even help? The partiers in the water needed to wake up and realize the potential danger.

"This isn't cool," shouted Amanda. "My parents will freak. I had to beg to get them to allow us to have this party, and now . . ."

Zora, who'd stayed away from everything, dropped down beside Delta, emitting frightened whimpers. She stared at the kids in the water dully. Delta realized Zora was wasted. She wished she'd just stayed topside.

Carmen waded into the water.

"Carmen!" Bailey barked.

"Don't worry. I know what I'm doing."

Freddie followed after her. "Don't go in. You need a vest."

"I'm not doing anything stupid." She took a few more steps, up to her waist. "Tanner, come here," she coaxed, as if to a young child.

"What the hell?" breathed Amanda.

Tanner grinned stupidly at Carmen, his gaze sliding over the others on the beach. For a moment, it seemed like he actually might be listening, but then he ducked under the plastic rope and headed downriver on his back, arms outstretched, gaze up to the darkening skies.

Delta shrieked, and she thought she heard Clarice Billings mutter, "Fuck," but realized it was Amanda. Several of the guys hesitated, then slipped under the barrier as well. Bailey, or Carmen, or someone screamed. Then Carmen was in the water, going after Tanner.

Delta scrabbled along the bank, scraping her toes, one flip-flop snapping apart. She headed toward the shelf of land along the side of the river, but she was practically trampled by Counselor Billings and Freddie in their race to catch up with the swimmers. Someone grabbed Delta's arm and yanked her back toward the beach.

Amanda.

Delta regarded her dazedly as she screamed, "Jesus Christ!" in Delta's face.

Behind her, Zora was crying, her hand pressed to her mouth, unable to stop the sobbing.

Bailey was scrambling after the chaperones, barefoot, having kicked off her shoes. Some of the guys came out of the water, dripping, staring after those who'd gone under the rope and the group running and slipping along the muddy pathway. As they watched, Freddie fell or jumped into the water.

McCrae barked at Bailey. "Go get your dad!"

"My dad?" she repeated blankly, even while turning toward the stairs.

"The police," he clarified.

"The police?" That squeak-shriek erupted from Amanda.

"Damn it, Amanda," he snarled. "People could die!"

He was already heading toward the stairs himself, nearly overtaking Bailey. Amanda whipped around to follow him, and Delta brought up the rear. Her face was wet, and she realized she was silently crying. She gazed after the swimmers who'd reached the first curve of the river, which turned and turned again, racing down the rapids and eventually dumping out into Grimm's Pond with its treacherous undertow.

Delta was good and frightened. Still . . . Tanner *couldn't* die. He *wouldn't*. He was too good a swimmer. Even weed and alcohol compromised, he was an athlete. An amazing athlete. Carmen too. They would just go with the rapids . . . and come out on the other side.

She swallowed hard. They were going to be okay. They were, she thought fiercely.

She was more worried about bringing in a rescue team, the police . . . What if Tanner's drug use was found out? He could jeopardize everything he'd worked for. And he would freak out if he couldn't play football.

Oh, God . . . What an idiot! His dad had already paid that price. Tanner wanted to be a doctor above all else. Was he trying to purposely screw things up? She wanted to scream at him, tell him to wake up and think about the future.

But more than that, she wanted him in her arms. Cradling him, kissing him, finally making love with the man she loved more than anything . . .

"My dad is going to shit," Amanda moaned at the top of the cliff.

McCrae was at the golf cart. "Does this damn thing have a key?"

Amanda stalked toward the cart and got it going.

Delta wanted to run after them but couldn't walk. Her toe was bleeding, one flip-flop ruined.

Zora was hovering next to her, teeth chattering, whispering, "Oh, God, oh, God, oh, God . . ."

"Shhh." Delta shushed her. She couldn't just stand here. She had to do something!

After several tense moments, she tried to put her flip-flop back on, but it dangled from her foot like a hanged man. Her frustration morphed into fear. What if she was wrong? What if something happened to Tanner?

She started hobbling toward the house, her tender foot scratched and jabbed by thick grasses till it was bloody and wretchedly sore. Zora kept beside her, silent now, but sniffing back her runny nose as she cried silently. It took nearly twenty minutes and was full dark by the time they got back to the Forsythe manor. Delta hobbled to the back patio and stood there in anxious horror.

"You're hurt," Zora said, seeing the blood trail coming from beneath Delta's right foot.

"Where do you think they are?" Delta looked through the pane of one of the French doors that led into the kitchen nook. The room was empty, although all the lights were on.

Zora tried the door, and it opened beneath her hand. She stepped in, but stopped when Delta didn't follow.

"I don't want to bleed all over their house. Go on in. Find out what's going on."

"I . . . smoked some dope. Do you think they'll know?" Zora quavered.

"God, Zora. Please . . . just get help."

Delta felt like crumpling down and crying. Her foot throbbed, but it was her heart that hurt the most.

Zora tiptoed into the bowels of the house, and Delta limped to an outdoor chair. Her body was buzzing, and she was aware of time passing in a visceral way. Her fear grew as a real crisis loomed. Was Tanner okay? Why had he done that? It was like he'd lifted his middle finger at all of them.

"Delta."

She gasped in surprise when the voice sounded from the darkness.

Ellie O'Brien emerged into the squares of light blasting from the house onto the patio. She was wet and shaking uncontrollably.

95

Delta immediately felt a surge of rage. "You jumped in the water, too!"

"Where is everybody?"

"What happened down there? Why did you do that?" Delta asked at the same time. "You got out? Where's Tanner? And the rest of them."

"They went down the rapids. I . . . pulled myself out before that. Miss Billings helped me. Freddie jumped in, though, and he went down the rapids. Bailey was running after Carmen, and she slipped . . ."

"*What?* It's freaking *dark,*" Delta yelled. "McCrae said to call the police."

"I don't know. I don't know. Do you think that's where Coach Sutton is? At Grimm's Pond? Waiting for them?"

Grimm's Pond. Delta thought of the deceptively calm waters after the rapids.

"Is that blood?" Ellie asked. Between words, her teeth chattered.

"Go inside and warm up."

"What happened to your foot?"

What do you care? "I cut it." Delta's responses were shorter and shorter. If she didn't get answers soon, she would start screaming and never be able to stop.

'Where's Amanda?"

"*I don't know!* Zora's inside, trying to find out. I think they're all gone. Probably at Grimm's Pond. Oh, God . . . oh, God . . ."

"Coach has a cell phone. He's bound to be calling someone."

At that moment, the phone inside the Forsythe home began ringing. "Get . . . get that," Delta stuttered, but Ellie was already running inside. Her clothes were stuck to her, and her hair was lank and wet. Like Zora, she disappeared, and then the ringing stopped. Delta's ears roared in the silence that followed. She couldn't think.

She held her breath, heart pounding. It was all a bad dream. Had to be.

Nothing really terrible was going to happen. It couldn't. Terrible things happened to other people, not the Five Firsts and not their friends.

Delta heard a desperate shriek from inside the house, and her blood chilled. Zora. *What?*

Now Zora was screaming and crying, and Delta stumbled to the door, uncaring about the blood smearing on the floor or the pain as she stepped inside, her heart nearly shattering her rib cage. She staggered forward through the house. Zora was clinging to a stunned and frozen Ellie, who was holding the Forsythes' handheld receiver to the landline at the end of her limp arm.

"What?" Delta cried. *"What?"*

The receiver slipped from Ellie's hand.

"Is it Tanner?" Delta shrieked. "It's Tanner? Oh, God! *God!"*

"It's Carmen. Amanda said . . ." Ellie broke off, gulped.

"What?"

Zora's crying intensified.

"She's dead. Drowned . . . ," said Ellie.

Zora's crying turned to a shriek.

Delta threw her hands over her ears. Discombobulated, she couldn't adjust that quickly. "Tanner?"

"The rest of them have been rescued. Freddie broke his leg in the rapids. I don't know . . . some other stuff happened."

She should feel something. Anything . . . anything but this terrible numbness. "Where's Bailey?"

Ellie shook her head. "They're all at Grimm's Pond, I think."

And that's when Delta heard the distant sirens. The police . . . rescue vehicles, approaching.

Bailey sat shivering, wrapped in a blanket on the rocky shore on the west side of Grimm's Pond. Her father was beside her. A kaleidoscope of red and blue and white lights swirled around them. Quin was soaked to the skin from jumping in and saving Tanner and Freddie, who both were being pulled under. McCrae was there, hauling out Brad Sumpter, while Justin Penske staggered to the shore on his own power. Woody Deavers had tried to help McCrae, but ended up slamming into a rocky outcropping and breaking a few ribs. He'd managed to crawl to shore and was being taken to the hospital. Tanner, whose head was bleeding, and Freddie, whose leg had been turned at an unnatural angle with a jagged white end of bone sticking through that had made Bailey feel light-headed, were being looked at. More gurneys were being readied.

On the shelf pathway, Bailey had raced past Miss Billings, who'd tried to stop her. She'd damn near jumped into the river at that point, but had gone on ahead, trying to find Carmen, as Miss Billings helped Ellie out of the water right before she'd reached the beginning of the rapids. Bailey had seen Carmen's head and had hurried to reach her. One foot slipped, and she lost her balance and was thrown into the strong current, rushed away, tumbled through the rapids, not sure what was up and what was down, unable to help Carmen, and then unable to save herself. She gulped air between downward dunks and spins in the water. Her knee hit a rock with great force, and she was glad it wasn't her head. She was spit out into Grimm's Pond, grabbed by the undertow, and then suddenly hauled out of the water by Mr. Timmons, an unlikely rescuer. He and Anne Reade had still been at the house when McCrae and Amanda showed up, and the four of them had jumped in vehicles, and all raced to Grimm's Pond.

Bailey was waiting for her friend to reappear. When it didn't happen, she prayed Miss Billings had grabbed Carmen like she'd grabbed Ellie. Neither of them had showed up at Grimm's Pond yet, though Bailey kept an eagle eye on the end of the shelf path, where she expected them both to appear. Unless they went back to Amanda's.

She watched Tanner and Freddie being strapped onto two gurneys and lifted into the back of the ambulance. She glanced down at her knee, which was swollen and purple. Brad Sumpter had a trickle of blood rolling down his temple but otherwise seemed okay. Justin Penske was unscathed, though his freckles stood out on his white face.

Coach Sutton had returned and was talking to the half-drowned classmates. Bailey could tell he was upset and worried and fighting anger. They'd done exactly what he'd ordered them not to and were lucky to be alive. Quin had splashed into the water to help her classmates out, and his uniform was soaked and sticking to his skin. McCrae, Amanda, Mr. Timmons, and Ms. Reade were double-checking with Sumpter and Penske and a couple of other guys who'd refused an ambulance, making sure they were all right.

But where was Carmen? *Where was she?*

Bailey prayed and prayed she was okay. She was a strong swimmer. She'd gone under during the rapids, but she'd popped up once; Bailey had seen her. She could just be navigating her way down.

Miss Billings reached the group gathered at the pond and was also given a blanket. "Where's Carmen? Is she all right?" she asked, stumbling into the shallow end of the pond where the shelf pathway ended. Her hair and shirt were soaked.

Bailey's heart nearly stopped, and everyone looked around at each other.

"She isn't here," Amanda said. She was standing by the ambulance, trying to catch a ride with Tanner. The EMT denied her as he slammed the doors.

McCrae demanded, "Did anyone see her?"

"I did." Counselor Billings looked stricken. "I tried to pull her out of the water, but she . . . let go. I fell in trying to get her out and hung onto a rock." Her eyes desperately searched the group, focusing on Bailey. "She said, 'Bailey' . . ."

Oh, God . . . oh, God . . . Carmen went after me!

Bailey leaned over and lost the contents of her stomach. Quin came up to her and put a supporting hand on her back as she retched.

Penske had been huddled in blankets on the rocky shore with the others, but now he stood up. "Where's Delta?" he asked sharply.

"They're at the campsite, or maybe at the house by now," Amanda said. "Maybe Carmen turned back and is with them."

"No." Counselor Billings shook her head, one

hand covering her mouth. She looked about to cry.

"I'm going to the hospital," Amanda announced. "Drive me back to my car?" she asked McCrae.

"I can take you," Mr. Timmons said. He looked to Ms. Reade. "Do you want to stay, or . . . ?"

"I'll come with you," she said, and the three of them started to leave.

"We'll find her," Quin assured Bailey.

She nodded.

And then someone shouted. One of the guys standing by the shore. He was pointing.

Something was floating down the river into the pond.

A body.

"Oh, Jesus . . ." McCrae ran splashing into the water, Quin right behind him.

Carmen.

Bailey stood up as if electrified. No! She threw off the blanket and ran forward. Her knee collapsed as she slipped on the round stones beneath her bare feet, and she fell forward, scraping her hands.

She's all right. She's all right.

I saw something . . .

No, she's all right. She's . . .

McCrae got hold of Carmen's arm and gently pulled her toward him before she could get sucked into the main body of the pond. Her skin was blue. Her eyes open.

She's okay . . . she's really all right . . .

"Bailey, get back," her dad said, his voice raspy with emotion.

"No . . . no . . . no . . ."

It was McCrae who got between Bailey and the body while Quin and Coach collected Carmen. Bailey tried to get around him, using all her force to scramble away from McCrae's grip.

"She's gone, Bailey," he said. "She's gone."

"No, no. That's not true. She's—"

"She's gone," he said solemnly.

Some rational part of her mind heard him, but she completely shut it down.

I saw something . . .

"What did you see?"

"What?" Quin asked. He was beside her now, and she was shaking, quaking, and cold, so cold.

"She saw something, Dad. Something she shouldn't have. And it killed her."

He regarded her with real alarm. "Sweetheart, this was a tragic accident."

They were all looking at her now. Miss Billings's face was drawn and ravaged. McCrae was assessing her as if she'd grown another head. Penske came her way, frowning. Coach Sutton looked like he wanted to say something, but he just ran his hand over his face.

"I'm going to take you home," Quin said.

Later, much later, when she surfaced painfully from the numb horror of seeing her best friend's lifeless form and staring eyes, Bailey pulled out her journal, a book she'd barely written two words in since she'd gotten it as a gift from her wayward mother at the beginning of the school year.

What had Carmen said?

I saw something . . . I saw them . . . they didn't know I was there . . .

She'd mentioned Tanner, too.

Tanner was with . . .

Bailey wrote his name in block letters—TANNER—and circled them. Fresh tears filled her eyes.

"What did Tanner do?" Bailey asked aloud.

Chapter 6

L ast day of school.

Ellie looked at herself in the gilded princess mirror above her dresser, part of the furniture her parents had bought for her when she was six years old, the whole set of which she now fervently hated.

But that was of little consequence now.

She unzipped the makeup container with shaking fingers. It was empty save for the toilet-paper-wrapped pregnancy wand she'd peed on. She hadn't had the courage to look at it and had nearly jumped out of her skin when the twins had rattled the bathroom door, yelling that they needed to go *right now!*

She'd yelled right back, telling them to use the bathroom upstairs, and had quickly wrapped the wand in yards of toilet paper and shoved it in the makeup container she'd brought from her bedroom just for this purpose.

Her bedroom door didn't have a lock, so she'd shoved the extra dining room chair that had migrated to her room underneath the doorknob. Hopefully it would slow down the twins, or anyone else, long enough for her to have this one, single moment of privacy.

Her hands trembled. Her period was late, and she was never late. Never.

She'd gotten her wish. Not Tanner, but McCrae. She'd followed him and some of the other guys into the woods and chugged some vodka. She'd been offered a joint, but smoking anything sent her into coughing jags that doubled her over. McCrae was feeling no pain when she took his hand and led him a ways away, deeper into the woods. She kissed him, and he said something like, "I don't think this is a good idea," though he hadn't resisted. He had, in fact, leaned into the kiss and parted her lips with his tongue. Ellie had French-kissed before, but this time it felt like a jolt to her senses. She'd made a vow to have sex with either Tanner or McCrae, but had only half-meant it. Still, she'd watched both of them with an eagle eye throughout that terrible day, kind of dreaming about having Tanner mostly. But Tanner got really wasted, and there were so many of the girls, especially the Five Firsts—God, how she hated that label!—watching him, trying to be close to him, just flat-out, fucking adoring him. She couldn't be one of those girls.

And then she'd seen McCrae's washboard stomach, and something felt like it sprang loose inside her. Like she was melting. Okay. He wasn't Tanner Stahd, but he was damn good-looking and was going places. Tanner was, too, obviously. He was going to be a doctor, maybe a surgeon, like his father. McCrae's dad was a businessman and involved in real estate deals, and McCrae . . . *Chris,* she reminded herself. She couldn't call him McCrae if they were, like, a couple. Anyway, she thought Chris was likely to follow his father into the business.

McCrae had sobered up really fast, and by the time he'd come back from Grimm's Pond, he'd been calm and in control. What they'd shared wasn't even in the glint of a sideways look to her after the shock of Carmen's death. He'd just made sure she and Delta and Zora had someone picking them up, or that they were emotionally stable enough to drive.

She shivered and carefully unwrapped the wand.

Mrs. Christopher McCrae. Oh, God, she wanted it.

Please . . .

Only one pink line. She blinked. Looked again . . .

Negative.

Ellie plopped down on her bed, staring at the single pink line in consternation. Not pregnant.

Well . . . shit.

She should be jumping for joy. Delirious with relief. Instead, she was kind of crushed.

"Ellie?"

Quickly, she shoved the wand back into the makeup case and zipped it up. "What?" she demanded angrily. "Can't I have any privacy?"

"Well, hurry up. We want to take pictures."

Her mother sounded joyous. It was a big day. Graduation was tomorrow. And then it would all be over.

Ellie shoved the makeup kit into the middle-sized suitcase of her set and locked it with its three-digit code, three zeros. She should have changed it when she got the set but never had. Now she didn't have time, but she knew no one else would dig into her closet, and it didn't matter anyway. She wasn't pregnant. It had all been for *nothing*. Later, after graduation, she would get rid of the evidence.

The picture taking took about fifteen minutes, and then Ellie was being driven to school by Oliver. She hated being with him, so she huddled in the passenger seat and stared out the window like she did on any morning he drove her in.

"Last day, huh?" he said.

She didn't respond.

"How's everybody doing now. Better?"

Again, she didn't respond, though this question appeared to be more from the heart. Since Carmen's death and the others' various injuries, the whole school had been in a state of shock. Certainly, the senior class had.

Ellie thought back to that night. Coming home to Mom and Oliver. Mom bursting into tears when she saw Ellie's damp, bedraggled form.

She'd tried to convince herself, apparently, that her brainiac daughter hadn't been one of those "dope-smoking degenerates," as Oliver put it, that Ellie had been at work like she'd said when all the terrible things went down at the party. But it was clear by how Ellie had acted that her mother's hope was unfounded. Carmen Proffitt's death was a terrible tragedy, yet Ellie had sensed that the real tragedy for her mother and stepfather was that Ellie'd been any part of the debacle at all.

But through all the grounding, and "talking to," and general disappointment from her mother and Oliver, and the overall shock and horror of losing a classmate, Ellie had carried the memory of having sex with McCrae as a kind of talisman against misery. She would think back to those moments over and over again. He might hardly remember them, but she did. And yes, though there had been some discomfort in the feel of the grass and small sticks against her back as she and McCrae—*Chris*—rolled around on the ground for a while before he undid his jeans and she took the moment to pull hers down and kick them away.

"Ellie . . . ," he'd said, sounding way too sober. Sensing he was about to change his mind, she'd yanked her bathing suit bottoms off as well and pulled him down atop her.

Unbelievable now. Especially with the events

afterward. She'd been shocked when Tanner yelled he was going back in the water. And a bit rejected when McCrae, who'd hovered kind of near her after they'd returned to the party from their secret tryst, seeming torn about how to behave, had suddenly charged after Tanner along with the other guys. She hadn't wanted to go back down to the beach, but very quickly she realized she'd be the last one left if she didn't. She'd clambered down to the spit and stood on the shore awhile, her gaze searching out McCrae, but also Tanner, who'd turned out to be the real problem.

What had possessed him to go under the rope? What the hell was the matter with him? Nihilistic behavior, for sure. Ellie had jumped in the water after them. A kind of knee-jerk response, as if she'd thought she could save them somehow.

As if he could read her thoughts, Oliver said, for about the fiftieth time, "Lucky for you that young teacher pulled you out of the river."

Ellie ground her teeth together. Miss Billings hadn't helped her all that much, though she'd certainly taken the credit for saving "one of the students." Principal Kiefer was especially proud of her, and though she pretended to be shy and humble, Miss Billings had clearly basked in the praise these last few weeks.

"She's a student counselor," Ellie corrected him.

"At least someone was using their head that night."

It was clear that Oliver found Billings memorable, and not just because she'd been such a savior. Meanly, Ellie said, "She didn't save Carmen."

"Ellie," he said in rebuke.

Ellie shrank down in her seat. She should be grief-stricken and sad and sober, like all the rest of them, mourning the loss of a friend and classmate. And it wasn't that she didn't feel sick about losing Carmen; she did. It was almost impossible to comprehend. But everything had gone to hell since that night in so many ways. She couldn't keep mourning Carmen the same way some of the others were, especially Bailey. It was nearly too hard to keep pushing forward with her own life. These last few weeks of school, with the grief counselors, and the talks with the police and the general horror and malaise . . . it was a nightmare. The Five Firsts had cracked apart like a broken egg. Amanda and Delta weren't talking because of Tanner, who'd spent a few days in the hospital but seemed to be okay now. Bailey was completely destroyed, losing her best friend and maybe lesbian crush—it was still hard to tell on that—and basically had broken with Carmen's family, who kind of blamed her as the bad influence, which was crazy too, but Reverend Proffitt was a strict disciplinarian who allowed no room for error. Bailey had split from the Proffitts and, as a by-product, her own mother, who'd left the family anyway apparently. She'd aligned with her father and had actually spoken at one of the grief meetings they'd been forced to attend and announced that she was going into law enforcement herself.

Great. Knock yourself out.

Ellie caught herself up, surprised by her callousness. Bailey had damn near killed herself trying to help Carmen.

And Zora . . . her parents were divorcing, and it was getting really ugly, apparently, although Ellie almost envied her. She would be delighted if Mom and Oliver called it quits.

They'd held a school assembly, a candlelight vigil, and then the funeral. Reverend Proffitt had talked about his little girl, so pure, so innocent, so . . . ripe to be taken advantage of, and he'd looked straight at Bailey. It had been terribly unfair of him. Ellie and most of the other kids surmised he'd heard the lesbian rumors, which really was a crime for Bailey. Made her grief twice as hard.

Now, however, most of that was behind them, and there were just hours left until graduation. Tanner had recovered and was going to walk with them. Freddie, the aide, was on crutches, but he was back at school and being hailed as a hero because he'd been responsible for keeping

Tanner's head above water after he'd knocked himself out in the rapids.

Woody Deavers, Justin Penske, and Brad Sumpter, the first guys to follow after Tanner, had been counseled and counseled by Miss Billings and professional psychiatrists as well. Ellie could have told them there was nothing wrong with them. They'd followed the most popular guy in school. Stupid. Rash. But not unexpected. It happened. It was a bad deal, but it just was. Ellie had interviewed them herself, in a kind of casual way, with her own sort of journalistic method, along with all the kids who'd been at the barbecue. She'd talked to Coach Sutton and Miss Billings and Freddie and written it all down in a report. She'd done it for herself, but she'd shown it to McCrae, and he urged her to send it into the West Knoll paper. She'd been surprised. She'd mostly done it as a means to gather her thoughts, and then she'd used it as an intro to talk to McCrae, who'd been hard to get close to since their night together. She'd feared he'd been purposely avoiding her, but when she finally buttonholed him and practically shoved the report into his hands, which he'd initially tried hard not to take, and then learned his reaction, her heart had warmed. Maybe he was a little embarrassed about what had happened. Or maybe Carmen's death had tainted everything for him. It had for her, so maybe it was like that for him a bit too.

The high school paper wouldn't print it. There were lawsuits hovering around the Forsythes and the school. With that, she'd done as McCrae—Chris—suggested and taken it to the city paper, which was printed once a week, and the *West Knoll Sentinel* had published it without a qualm. It brought Ellie a bit of notoriety and even helped thaw Mom and Oliver a bit.

Of course, Bailey was keeping a journal now too. A copycat? Ellie had been pissed, though she'd realized Bailey was using her writing as a coping tool.

Ellie slammed the door on Oliver's "Enjoy your last day," which sounded a bit ominous, like he was warning her that things were going to be different from here on out. They undoubtedly would be. She was going to make them be. But it still put a shiver sliding down her back like a cold drop of rain.

Delta felt like she was floating . . . or on drugs . . . or *something* as she walked up the steps to the stage and accepted her diploma from Principal Kiefer.

They'd made it through the ceremony. One by one, walking up the stairs to the media-room stage, accepting their diplomas, shaking hands with Principal Kiefer, a short, wiry, gray-haired man with a wide smile that somehow worried Delta. There was just something anxious about him that she couldn't put her finger on. Worse now, since the barbeque.

Or maybe she was flat-out crazy. The events of the past few weeks had sent her over the edge. Maybe her aversion to the principal was a symptom of a neurotic, paranoiac mind.

She walked back to her seat, clutching her leather-bound certificate, eyes on the myriad maroon gowns and mortarboards with their yellow tassels. They were the Cougars, and above, painted on the wall, a tawny, prowling beast came straight at the group, stealthily watching with cold, yellow eyes, although the paint was chipping slightly, which you'd think would render the image harmless but somehow didn't. Delta had never liked sitting beneath the stalking cat, and today was no exception. Again, neurotic. Susceptible. Too imaginative. Although Amanda, once upon a time, had offered up a similar view.

"I hate that cat," she'd said, jerking her head in the direction of the cougar mural.

"You do?" Delta had asked, thrilled that her friend felt the same way she did.

"I hate this school. I hate the teachers. I hate the staff." Amanda bit the words out. "My parents wanted to send me to Jesuit or Catlin Gabel," she said, naming two private schools in Portland's western suburbs, "but I didn't want to leave the Five Firsts."

"Well, that's good."

Amanda snorted. "At least I can audition without having to worry that I'll get behind in school. This place is a breeze."

Is it? Delta had thought. Sure, some classes were fairly easy. She was good at English and history and even Earth science, but math didn't come all that naturally. She'd had Bailey help her a time or two. Once, she'd even gotten up the nerve to ask Ellie for some help, and Ellie had grudgingly shown her a simpler way to come to the answer. Ellie was a whiz at everything.

Amanda was no slouch, either, but she was always busy. In those days, she had enjoyed auditioning. She'd been cast a lot as the blond, blue-eyed darling daughter. There'd been talk about moving to Los Angeles to try to get a national commercial, or maybe even a part in a film. But that had all disappeared as Amanda had become a teen, and now she was disgruntled and sort of fed up in that bohemian, "I'm too cool for this whole thing" way.

Now Delta's gaze searched out Tanner. She knew just where he was seated. She'd had a dark night of the soul after she'd learned that he'd been pulled from the river unconscious, and she'd nearly been out of her mind all the while he was in the hospital and she couldn't get to him. She, Ellie, and Zora had been at the Forsythe home when Mr. and Mrs. Forsythe had returned from the beach, both of them white with shock, though Mr. Forsythe hadn't held back, berating his wife for allowing the party in the first place. He accused her of trying too hard to be a cool mom to the high schoolers, and now she'd left them open to all kinds of lawsuits.

Delta had wrapped her foot in yards of toilet paper and called her parents. Her dad had swung by to pick her up at the same time Zora's mom and Ellie's mother and stepfather arrived. Delta had wanted to go straight to the hospital, but her dad had driven her home in a kind of quiet bewilderment. "What did you think you were doing?" he asked, as he helped her into the house, where Mom had gasped at her ravaged foot, then gone about cleaning out the cuts, slathering on some antibiotic cream and wrapping it in gauze and an Ace bandage. Delta had begged to have the car so she could go to the hospital, but her parents had said no. They did, however, call the Stahds, and Tanner's stepmother had said that she would keep them informed.

She never did.

Delta awoke the next morning in a panic. She just knew if she didn't see Tanner ASAP that something bad would happen to him. She couldn't wear a shoe, so she didn't. Just wrapped her Ace bandage around the whole of her foot and hobbled on it.

She talked her parents into borrowing the car and drove to the hospital. Directed to Tanner's room, she was stunned to find Amanda there, chatting with Tanner's dad and stepmom. His mother, who lived in Seattle and whom Delta had met only once, was just leaving the room. She made eye contact with Delta but didn't seem to recognize her. Her skin was stretched tight, and she looked older than her years. When Delta moved into the room, she saw the current Mrs. Stahd, who was at least ten years younger than her predecessor and dressed in a tight blue dress with matching heels. She ignored Delta, her attention on Tanner, who apart from a bandage slung around his forehead looked well enough for Delta to release a huge sigh of relief.

But it was Amanda, standing in the room as if she owned the place, who really dealt Delta's confidence and ego a serious blow. Everyone seemed to expect Delta to say something first, so she managed a "You look pretty good, considering," directed at Tanner.

"Doesn't he?" his stepmother said.

"Head injuries are nothing to fool with," his father, Dr. Stahd, put in repressively.

"I agree," said Amanda, regarding Tanner indulgently. "Your father knows best."

When had they all become so chummy?

Tanner said, "Hurts like a bitch," lifting a hand to his forehead.

"Let it be," his dad ordered. "I don't want them releasing you until we have further tests run."

118

His gaze settled on Amanda, and Delta tried to read his expression. He was angry, she realized, and no wonder. The accident had taken place on her parents' property.

Lawsuits, Amanda's father had spit at his wife.

Amanda, for all her smarts, seemed completely oblivious to this dynamic, but Delta saw it . . . and felt better.

And now, here they were, at the end of high school. The graduation ceremony was the period at the end of the sentence. There was no post-graduation party. The pig roast/barbecue debacle had been more than enough. Delta had heard that Coach Sutton's job had been on the line, maybe still was. But he was here today in a suit that looked a bit too small for his growing girth, the shirt pinching his collar. Coach was sober as a judge and looked as if all the energy had been knocked out of him. Counselor Billings, on the other hand, was in her element. In a soft green dress, her blond hair upswept, showing off pearl earrings on her delicate earlobes, she looked fresh and lovely, and she stood by proudly as the class filed up for their awards. Mr. Timmons was there, too, and, near him, Ms. Reade. Neither of them seemed to be able to quite grasp the moment in the same way.

Delta's gaze swept over Justin Penske, and she automatically searched for his friend, Brad Sumpter, who, like Justin, was a decent enough guy when he wasn't influenced by the other "bros." But when they were members of a pack, there wasn't much to be said for them.

Brad turned her way, maybe feeling the weight of her stare.

Delta watched Tanner step lightly up the stairs. He'd been a little unsteady on his feet right after his head injury, and she knew he'd been worried about his balance. But he was more than okay. The whole student body and faculty and everyone who knew him seemed to have heaved a huge sigh of relief that he was going to be fine.

Delta's gaze traveled to where she knew Amanda was seated. Amanda's eyes were following Tanner as if they were magnetized. Delta's simmering anger flared. She'd attempted to give Amanda a pass, thinking that maybe she was trying to make nice with the Stahds to help her family avoid a lawsuit, but Amanda was after Tanner. Delta wished Amanda would spontaneously combust and, *poof,* be off the planet. She sent her mental messages of doom.

Die, bitch, she thought, then immediately said silently to God, *I didn't mean it. I really didn't mean it. I just want her to leave Tanner alone.*

Then it was over, all of the classmates spilling outside onto the lawn. Earlier the temperature had been wonderfully warm, but now there was a chilly June breeze flitting around the soft night, suddenly surprising with a cold slap, if you weren't careful.

Mr. Timmons was standing to one side with Ms. Reade. They were both in their thirties, unmarried, and maybe having an affair. The events of the barbeque seemed to have brought them together, but it was hard to really tell. Ms. Reade was slim and rawhide tough, as if she exercised herself into a bundle of stiff muscle on a regular basis. She had a sweet expression that belied her standoffish manner. Her eyes were on Miss Billings, who was talking with Principal Kiefer. Mr. Timmons, softer than Ms. Reade, in body and tone, possessed a brilliant smile and nice blue eyes. He was also looking at Counselor Billings, but Delta thought it was in a more admiring way. When Ms. Reade suddenly glanced back at him, he pretended to look away. Seeing Delta watching him, Mr. Timmons came her way.

Shit, thought Delta. No, she didn't want to commune with the teachers. She wanted to be with Tanner. Where was he, anyway? She glanced around hurriedly, but then Mr. Timmons was there, blocking her way toward the parking lot, where everyone was heading.

"Congratulations, Delta, if I didn't say so before. So, now, what are you planning? Rock Creek Community College, I hear?"

"Something like that. I'm not really sure yet."

"Are you going to the service tonight?"

There was a special service for Carmen at the Church of Our God, Reverend Proffitt's church. In lieu of graduation parties, there had been a number of events to honor Carmen, and Delta had found each one more difficult than the last. She'd told herself it was the least she could do, but she didn't want to cry anymore, she didn't want to feel bad, she didn't want to see Amanda and Tanner sitting by each other, because that's what had happened at the other events, bowing their heads together and acting all sad, when she just wanted to tear into them, call them out as hypocrites because neither of them had cared that much for Carmen. Only Bailey had truly cared, and she was being unfairly punished by the reverend.

"Is Bailey invited?" she asked a bit belligerently.

Timmons blinked. "Well, I think anyone can certainly join in."

"Can they, though?"

Timmons looked at Delta in surprise, and no wonder. She'd always been the easygoing, good-humored one, but she'd given up her signature style since Amanda and Tanner had become . . . whatever they were. Now she felt like ripping out her hair and screaming curse words and launching herself at her one-time BFF. The Five Firsts were finishing with high school, and maybe they'd been a fake sisterhood all along.

"I just know the reverend blames Bailey for Carmen's death."

"I don't think that's true," Timmons said, looking past her and nodding to someone, or maybe no one, as he quickly moved away. Well, that was apparently one way to free herself from small talk: discuss the truth.

Zora caught up with Delta as she was walking up the concrete steps to the top section of the parking lot. "Jesus, I need a drink," she said. "I hate this. I hate school. I hate all the lies."

"Lies?" Delta asked.

"Did you know my parents sold our house? I have the choice of going with Mom or Dad. They're both moving into *apartments*. Can't afford anything else now."

"What happened?" asked Delta.

"I don't know. Bad investments? They expect me to make some kind of decision about my future. I don't want to do anything!"

"We're all going to have to do something."

"Why don't you and I get an apartment together? Go to PCC. Just get the hell away. My parents aren't completely broke yet, I guess."

Portland Community College had several campuses around the city, Rock Creek being one of them. But Delta was itching to get down to Eugene and the University of Oregon. "PCC isn't far enough away."

"Well, where else are you going?" she queried.

Nowhere.

Delta realized Zora's plan wasn't all that bad. Zora's family would undoubtedly pay for the apartment. Delta could possibly get a break on the rent . . . maybe.

But it wouldn't be U of O. And it wouldn't be with Tanner.

And then Tanner and Amanda appeared together, walking together, looking at each other, holding hands.

Delta drew in a long breath. "I guess it's really over," she said.

I wish they'd both die.

"You don't mean that," Zora said on a gasp.

Delta hadn't realized she'd spoken aloud.

"No, I don't," she murmured miserably, walking away, nearly blinded by tears.

Somehow, she found her parents and managed to get away from the crowd without being seen falling apart. Her parents assumed she was thinking of Carmen and let her be. And then she did think of Carmen, and she felt small and petty, and she decided to go to the service. Her parents offered to take her, but she turned them down. Finally, in the depths of her own personal despair, she was able to really feel the anguish of losing her friend forever. Carmen had been a member of the Five Firsts. Without her, there was no clique. Without her, the sun had dimmed a little. Delta

124

was ashamed she hadn't been able to really see that till now.

Bailey was at the church when Delta arrived, standing just inside the door, possibly working up her courage to enter the lion's den, so to speak, since she'd been treated so unfairly by the Proffitts.

"Hey," Delta said to her.

"The reverend isn't here. He's left the church. The new minister is a woman," Bailey said. She was pale, wearing a plain, midi-length black dress, her ponytail limp. But there was a determination in her set jaw that spoke of a stiff spine.

Delta peered through the doors to the pews, which were filling up with her classmates and other students from the school. There were parents there, too, but by far this was an event for the kids.

"They're moving away," Bailey went on. "Leaving West Knoll. It's too much to bear."

"They shouldn't have blamed you," Delta said.

"They didn't like what I had to say. It hurt them too much."

"What do you mean?"

"I don't think Carmen's death was an accident. I pushed for an autopsy. They thought it was blasphemous."

"Bailey, you were there. Carmen drowned."

"Did she? Something happened. She was with the guys, following Tanner around . . ." She made

125

a sharp movement with her hand, indicating they didn't need to go further down that road. Carmen's obsession with Tanner was well known. "They'd gone and had something. I didn't think Carmen imbibed, but maybe . . . She said she saw something. She didn't want to tell me, but she almost did, and then we were interrupted, and she never said what it was."

"Okay, but—"

"It was something about Tanner and some of the other kids. But she was focused on Tanner. What he did mattered to her, and he did something that really bothered her. Maybe he realized she saw and he spiked her drink and she couldn't swim as well as she could have and she drowned."

"Tanner wouldn't spike her drink!" Delta defended, affronted.

"Something happened!"

"Well, he wouldn't do that. You're way off. He never even paid attention to Carmen. Never looked at her. Why would he spike her drink? She didn't . . . she wasn't his type."

It was cruel to say and made Delta sound like she thought she was so much better than Carmen, but it was also the truth. Bailey was talking crazy, which maybe she was . . . crazy with grief.

"Somebody did something to her," she insisted stubbornly.

"You're blaming Tanner for going under the rope. They were all stupid. *Stupid!* Tanner too. It was just this terrible tragedy, and I can't believe Carmen's gone. I just want to . . . scream." Tears sprang to her eyes at this admission. She felt terrible. She looked down at her feet. The black flat on one foot, the other in a now thinner bandage and a black sneaker. She'd really messed up her foot and had finally gone to the doctor, who'd undone the bandages and added a line of stitches that she hoped would not leave marks as they marched across her sole and curved around her ankle.

"I know that you love Tanner," Bailey said. "But he's a shit, Delta."

Delta fought back an instant denial. "I guess you're entitled to your opinion."

"I guess I am."

At that, Bailey entered the church ahead of her, and Delta, after a moment, slowly followed. But now she didn't want to sit by Bailey. She wanted to be magnanimous and give Bailey a pass, but she was getting pissed and hurt and worried, which was better than the despair that had filled her for weeks.

The Five Firsts were officially dead. Carmen was gone, and Bailey was making wild accusations about Tanner.

Delta saw that Tanner had squeezed into a pew between McCrae and Justin Penske. Brad Sumpter was next to Penske, and then the do-gooders, Trent and Rhonda. There was no room for Delta next to him, but then he'd been distant since the barbeque, and she didn't know where she stood. A couple rows behind the guys were Amanda and Zora. Zora spied Delta and indicated there was just enough room for her between them and the rest of the kids, a group of underclassmen Delta recognized but didn't know well, crushed together on the bench.

Delta squeezed past the underclassmen, murmuring apologies as the service started. A middle-aged woman with graying hair and a wide girth took her place at the podium. She introduced herself as Pastor Stevens and gave them a soft smile of greeting before launching into a healing prayer. When it was over, she said that, though she hadn't known Carmen Proffitt personally, she'd heard only good things about her. As she went on in that vein, Delta glanced around, wondering, like everyone else, what had happened to the reverend. He'd given a brief eulogy for his daughter right after her death, the words clearly wrenched from his soul.

Zora leaned toward her. "I heard the reverend took his family to Colorado, which is where they're from. The mom was good friends with Bailey's, but that's over, too."

"Shhh," Amanda said loudly, shooting them a dark glance.

Pastor Stevens next invited the kids from their class to come up and talk about Carmen, tell a story, a remembrance, anything they wanted. This was a far cry from the fire and brimstone that was Reverend Proffitt's brand of delivery. Delta didn't expect anyone to go up to the dais, and she was shocked and riveted when the first person to head up the steps was Tanner.

Chapter 7

Tanner looked out at the sea of faces, knowing he had a lot of ground to make up since, in his father's words, the "head-up-your-ass stunt you pulled at that barbeque!"

"Um . . . I guess you all know what happened to me," he began. "I'm still recovering from hitting the rocks with my head. Thank you, Freddie. Sincerely. You saved my life . . ." He swept an arm toward the teacher's aide who, he'd been told, kept his head above water—otherwise, he would have drowned, like Carmen. Freddie Mouton stood up and balanced on his crutches. The church exploded in applause. There was a lot looser vibe now that Reverend Proffitt was gone.

He glanced at the pastor, who smiled at him encouragingly. Swallowing, he was determined to soldier on, though he'd been half-sick at the thought of getting up in front of the school. Grades, school, learning . . . it was all easy for him, but public speaking, not so much. Still, he knew that he needed to tell his story and change a few minds about him. He could see Brad, who'd walked to the back with his video camera. He wanted this on record.

"We've all already said good-bye to Carmen,

but I wanted to say to her family and all her friends how sorry I am personally. It shouldn't have happened the way it did."

His heart was pounding, and he made a point of not looking at the camera. He felt bad about Carmen. He hadn't known her all that well, really, but he'd been aware that she had a big crush on him. Anytime he looked up, she was staring at him, and though he would never say so, he'd found it creepy. Like she was almost a stalker.

But he never thought she'd die . . . that she would follow him under the rope. God, he'd been messed up. The letter he'd been waiting for from U of O's athletic department had come that afternoon and dashed all his last dreams of making the team. His dad didn't care. He was only interested in Tanner's scholastics. He didn't understand about football.

Now he exhaled. With his apology out of the way and the sympathetic nods of the crowd, some of them wiping away tears, he could relax a bit. His gaze searched the crowd, and he found Delta. Part D of the Five Firsts. Dark haired, dark-eyed with smooth skin, the most gorgeous girl in the whole class. His stepmother, Lori, had smiled at Tanner in that silky way of hers when she'd first seen Delta and said, "Mmm-mmm," which had made him feel weird at first, until he'd learned that was just her way.

And there was Amanda, Part A. He briefly thought of her blond head lying on his stomach, her tongue moving downward while her fingers unbuckled his belt . . .

"I remember Carmen in fifth grade," he said, quickly pushing that dangerous thought aside. "She was the best soccer player on the team. The girls went undefeated that year, and their team was on the reader board outside Palisades Market."

There was a rumble of conversation, a bit of laughter, and one of the girls raised her fist, pumping it a few times. Bailey Quintar. Tanner's lifting mood took a tumble. Bailey blamed him for Carmen's death. He'd tried to tell her it was just an accident, but she wouldn't listen.

He went on, "Carmen, though, gave up soccer for volleyball."

"And softball," a guy yelled from the back. Trent Collingsworth. At one time, he and Tanner had been good friends, but they'd split around junior high. Trent, really more religious than Carmen, had become one of the do-gooders. It was a wonder that Carmen, being the minister's daughter, had veered away a bit, but then maybe that was the way it always was.

"Yeah," Tanner agreed. This was way better. He was on familiar ground.

He saw Zora, tucked in between Delta and Amanda. She was petite and cute, and he suspected she would lie down for him anytime. They'd already indulged in a heavy make-out session once, but she'd sworn him to secrecy, saying he could never, never, *never*, tell anyone, that being in the Five Firsts was the most important thing to her, that she would be kicked out, so he could *never* tell.

His gaze swept over some of the senior faculty—Principal Kiefer, Ms. Reade, and Mr. Timmons—were they really a couple?—Counselor Billings in that pink sweater that showed off her breasts, Coach Sutton, whose hangdog face had grown even longer . . .

Then he glanced at his friends: Penske with his freckles and cowlick, Sumpter the steroid buff. McCrae and Woody Deavers were there, too, but he'd never been real bros with them.

His father had said all his friends were chaff. Not a wheat stalk among them. Tanner had argued and fought for them, but in the end, he sensed his father was right. He, Tanner, was going to med school. Sure, his old man had fucked up, had gotten his medical license suspended, but it had turned into a blessing in disguise. His father's line of energy products, vitamins, and stuff was in all the regional stores, part of the "natural" section, and he was making a small fortune.

"I just wanted to say we all miss her," he finished. "She was one of us, and it shouldn't have happened this way."

He felt something and saw Bailey's eyes burning into him. His spit dried up, and he wrenched his gaze away. She knew something, and she was blaming him. What did she know? Had Carmen said something to her? Carmen should have never followed after him into the woods . . . She sure as hell got more than she'd bargained for. He felt a flash of rage at both Carmen and Bailey. It wasn't his fault things had happened the way they had, and it sure as hell better not become a problem.

"Thanks," he said, abruptly, needing to get away. His head throbbed.

As he was walking down the steps and back to the main floor, he saw Ellie O'Brien rise from her seat and pass by him on her way to the podium. She was a redhead, and he sensed she was readily available, too. She sent out that vibe. Was she as fiery as her hair suggested? His cock stirred a bit at the thought, and he quickly forced his mind away from her.

At his own row, Tanner worked his way back into a spot that McCrae had damn near overtaken.

"Move," he muttered, shoving in.

McCrae grudgingly gave him room.

"Everyone liked Carmen," Ellie's voice was saying in a commanding way. "She had lots of friends."

Yeah, right.

He saw her gaze settle almost accusingly on

135

Amanda, Delta, and Zora. "She was a best friend to everyone, but especially Bailey Quintar. I remember horseback riding with Carmen. Neither one of us was any good—well, at first—but Carmen caught on right away and helped me stay on my horse, which really wanted to scrape me off his back. I know it's been said before, but she was a natural athlete . . ."

Tanner lost the thread of what she was saying. Ellie was too skinny for his taste and too serious, but she always had a way in front of a crowd. He could give her that. She told a couple more lame stories that the church crowd appreciated with laughter and tears. Pretty soon she finished up, but then Bailey took the microphone from her.

Tanner braced himself. *Here we go . . .*

"Only the good die young," Bailey stated flatly, her gaze laser-focused on Tanner in a way that made his heart galumph.

Jesus. He could feel her hate. He'd apologized, hadn't he?

"What the fuck," he muttered.

McCrae slid him a sideways glance but didn't say anything. Woody, on the other side of him, said, "Lesbian grief's the worst. Ow!"

McCrae had elbowed him hard. Tanner was glad. He didn't want Woody screwing things up. This was a solemn affair, and Tanner had done his part. That's what he wanted people to remember.

Crystal Gilles, Woody's girlfriend, who'd

recently traded in a Goth look for something more hippie-like—"bohemian," Delta had told him—looked past Woody to catch Tanner's eye. "Let's all act like adults," she said in a speaking voice, which kind of pissed Tanner off. She wasn't part of the popular crowd, and Tanner suspected Woody was only with her because he couldn't get any other girl. Tanner wished Woody would kick her to the curb.

The Fives thought Woody was annoying, and, yeah, he could be. But he was funny. It was Crystal who was the problem.

Tanner flicked McCrae a look. Everyone thought they were good bros, but McCrae was really kind of a pain in the ass as well. Too intense. Sure, he could cut loose sometimes, but overall he had this "do right" thing going. Tanner could admit that it had kept them out of serious trouble a time or two, and God knew he couldn't afford to get caught seriously fucking up, not with college and his whole future in front of him, but did McCrae always have to put the kibosh on the good stuff?

You shoulda listened to him at the river . . .

That was true, sure, but Carmen had made her own choice. It wasn't his fault.

But that's lucky for you . . .

He shut his mind down on that, shaken by his thoughts. *I'm a good guy,* he reminded himself. *I'm a really good guy.*

Bailey's homage to Carmen was half teary reminiscence, half call to arms. She finished with, "I made a promise to Carmen to do everything in my power to find out how this could have happened. A lot of people are saying it's God's will. If that's so, I'll accept it. But if it's not, if there was someone's hand in this, whether they meant it to be or not, I will find that out, too."

There was silence as she walked away, making the sound of her footsteps loud beneath the cathedral ceiling of the old wooden church.

Tanner made certain he didn't look her way as Bailey walked past him . . . and right out of the church.

McCrae let out a long breath.

Tanner said, "She's kinda outta control."

Woody leaned forward so he could look around McCrae at Tanner. "Ya think?"

"Give her a break," Crystal said on a sigh.

The room grew restive when, after Bailey, no one else went for the podium. Pastor Stevens stepped in and hurried up the steps, addressing the room with her somewhat sad smile.

"If no one else has something to say, I'd like to finish with a hymn and a prayer."

Tanner stared straight ahead through both, moving his lips through the hymn though he didn't know the words. His mind was back at the barbecue, in the woods, kids all laughing softly, secretly getting high . . . the feel of warm lips around his cock . . . He'd looked over, and there was Carmen. They'd locked eyes. Through his haze of weed and alcohol, he'd seen a tall, somewhat gangly, kind of plain girl staring at him with betrayal.

She'd seen. She'd seen him with her . . . and she'd seen him earlier, too . . .

He'd thought, *I could still have her right now,* and he made up his mind then and there to pop her cherry before the night was over.

Only things hadn't quite worked out that way. He'd gone under the rope, and so had Carmen, and only one of them had survived.

Bailey knows.

He swiveled around to look at her, but Bailey hadn't gone back to her seat. She'd left after her speech.

No . . . if Bailey knew, she would have said something.

The pastor made a few closing remarks, and then the crowd slowly exited the church. Penske caught up with him on the way out. He was a loser with girls. Too awkward to get anybody hot. But he was a good friend.

"Hey, man," Tanner said. "Keep an eye on Bailey, okay?"

"Yeah?" Penske asked.

"Yeah."

They looked at each other. "She gonna be a problem?"

"Nothing to be a problem about."

"Sure."

Sumpter wandered over. He'd once been a big, affable guy, but lately he'd had a flash temper. 'Roids, Tanner suspected. He'd thought about going that route himself, but his dad's mistakes, coupled with a healthy fear of what that would do to his long-term career plans, had kept him straight.

"Gotcha," Penske said.

"What's going on?" Sumpter asked.

Tanner clapped him on his broad shoulder. "Come over to my place. Play some video games. Put this damn chapter behind us."

Three weeks later, Delta was working at the store, running the cash register while Mom took a break in the back room with Dad. She could hear the murmur of their voices but couldn't make out the words. She knew that they were talking about her, about her desire to move into an apartment with Zora. If Tanner was going to Oregon, she needed to at least be able to go visit him without her parents waiting up each night for her to come home. She'd asked them for some financial help. Not a lot, as Zora was, as expected, being super great about keeping her portion of the rent something she could handle. She had some savings and would use them to pay for tuition and books and most of the rent, but maybe they would help her on other expenses?

She'd seen Tanner exactly once since the memorial service for Carmen. He'd been making plans of his own this summer. He was working for his dad, saving up his own money for college in the fall. He was also dealing with some disappointments because the football team hadn't offered him a position. He could walk on, if he wanted, though his father was against it. Dr. Les Stahd thought football was a waste of time and only went along with Tanner's obsession as long as it didn't get in the way of his own ambitions. Les felt that his son needed all his extra time for his studies, not football. If Tanner got accepted to the team, go with God and play football, but if he didn't, if Les was footing the entire bill for his son's schooling, then there was no "walking on." That was the rule.

The one night Tanner had deigned to stop by, Delta had put on her best jeans and a light blue silk blouse and a pair of black flats without bandages on her right foot. She'd felt the injured tissue, and little stabs of pain reminded her every time she took a step. But she wanted to look her best, as Tanner, who had managed to text her some when he wasn't working, had definitely become more of a stranger ever since taking up with Amanda and after the disaster of the barbecue.

Still, he'd made a point of wanting to stop by, so she'd gone straight into the frantic zone to make sure she looked as good as possible. If he was going to leave her for Amanda, she wanted to make sure he knew what he was going to be missing. With that grim thought in mind, she'd washed her hair and let it dry straight. She'd combed it down wet, then worked on smoky eyes; upon seeing she'd overdone the eye shadow, she'd wiped off all her makeup and started over, then, satisfied with the results, had added soft pink lipstick and a shiny gloss. She'd done her nails herself with a clear nail polish.

She'd stood back and examined herself critically. Tried on a smile, which fell instantly. She couldn't fake happiness, and she was anything but happy. The Five Firsts were over. School was over. Carmen was gone. And if things didn't improve, she and Tanner were over as well.

Her heart had weighed a ton. No matter how much she pretended to be looking forward to moving into an apartment with Zora—*if* her parents agreed to help, that is—the truth was that Delta didn't want to contemplate a future without Tanner.

She'd heard his car's familiar engine approaching and her pulse had sped up. It was a Thursday evening. Not Friday. Not their night. Those days were over. He'd told her he needed to work through the weekend, and she'd told him she had to do the same . . . though her schedule was pretty loose, and she would have moved heaven and earth to be with him, were he available.

Hurrying through the house to the front door, she'd purposely avoided her mother, in the kitchen. Her father had still been at the store. Pushing open the screen door, she'd stepped out into a cool June evening. The longest day of the year, she realized as Tanner, looking heart-breakingly handsome, had headed up the front sidewalk and met her in front of the porch. He'd stopped about ten steps from her, just looking at her. His sober expression made her hold her breath. Suddenly, she hadn't wanted to know why he'd come to see her. There was something wrong. Something big.

"Delta, I . . ." He swallowed.

"Do you want to come in? Have a lemonade? There's bound to be some chips around. Jalapeño. Your favorite. You know we always have something from the store."

She'd been babbling on purpose. *Don't talk. Don't talk. Don't say anything I don't want to hear.*

"You look great. Really beautiful."

The admission had melted her. Stopped her from another rush of words. But he'd looked so . . . sad? Apprehensive? "You look good too."

"I've missed you."

"Tanner . . . oh, my God! I've missed *you!* It's been terrible this last month or so. The worst time ever!"

She'd hurried down the steps, and he'd come to her, pulling her to him and holding her like he never wanted to let her go. Her heart soared. It really did. She'd heard that phrase but had never really experienced it before. Tears dampened her lashes. She'd wanted to kiss him, love him, make love to him like she'd promised herself she would but hadn't had the chance.

But instead of any of those things, he'd gently pulled himself away, his hands moving to her shoulders, where he'd kept her literally at arm's length.

"I've really messed things up," he said.

"You can't blame yourself for Carmen."

"It's not about that. Not about going under the rope. That was stupid, but . . ."

"What?"

"Something else happened."

She'd drawn a careful breath. "At the barbecue?"

He'd flinched as if she'd hit him. "All I've ever wanted was to play football, for a while at least. College football. Maybe make it to the pros, but that's kind of a pipe dream, I know."

"I thought you wanted to be a doctor."

"Well, yeah. I do. That's always been there. My dad wants it for me, and he screwed up, and we all know how that came out, and yeah, I want to be that for him."

"You don't sound convinced." She wasn't sure where he was going with this.

"It's not about that. I fucked up, okay. *I fucked up.* Would you believe me if I told you I love you?" Before she could respond, he added fervently, "I love you, Delta. I love you."

"Oh, Tanner. I love you too!"

"And I want to be with you. Marry you. There's no one like you."

This was more than she'd hoped for! "I want that too . . ." Tears stood in his eyes, and her overflowing joy was tempered by a very real, building fear.

Something else happened.

He'd stopped talking. He pulled his hands away from her and took a step backward, dashing the tears from his eyes.

"Amanda's pregnant," he said, when he finally spoke again. "I shoulda used a condom, but I didn't. It was at the barbeque. One fucking time, so to speak." He grimaced. "I wanted to be the one to tell you. Hit me, if you want. Punch me in the gut. This has been the shittiest time of my life, and it looks like it's going to get shittier. I love you. Not her. Guess it took too long to figure that out, huh?"

He'd looked at her hopefully, wanting her to absolve him. Begging for understanding.

Amanda's pregnant.

She'd tried to think of something to say, but words eluded her. For an answer she simply turned around, walked back up the steps into the house, and closed the door behind her.

Now she checked behind her at the clock that hung on the wall. Nearly 5:00 p.m. It was three days after the Fourth of July, a holiday she'd spent with her parents at a party on the Willamette River, miles and miles from the West Knoll River, where her high school friends normally gathered. But that was before Carmen's death. Before Tanner left her. Before Amanda was pregnant.

Mom and Dad came out of the back of the store and smiled at her in that shit-eating way that denoted they had some big secret. "We have a nest egg for you," Mom said. "It's not huge, but it should help you with the rent if you want to get that apartment with Zora."

Delta was overcome. She'd given up thinking about her future. Without Tanner, there wasn't one. She hadn't told her parents about Amanda's pregnancy, but they'd certainly noticed how sad and miserable she'd been.

"Thank you," she choked.

"We wish we could send you to Oregon," her father said. "Just don't have quite enough right now, and we don't want you to take on too much student debt."

"That's okay. Thank you. I mean it. It's more than enough. Thank you!"

She reached for them both, and they had a happy, awkward group hug.

After they pulled apart, her dad said, "I don't know what happened between you and Tanner, but you know how I feel."

Delta immediately wanted to argue with him about Tanner's merits. Both of her parents had been lukewarm on their relationship. They didn't understand what he meant to her.

When she kept her thoughts to herself, he went on, "High school romances often belong in high school."

"I know, Dad." She was curt.

"We want you to be happy and successful," Mom said, which her dad echoed.

Delta smiled, and luckily the bell above the door jingled, and a family came in with their four children, taking up both of her parents' attention. Delta was off at 5:00, so she said good-bye to them both and then drove home in her mom's car, as Mom was sticking around the store tonight till closing.

When she let herself into the house, she looked around at the home she'd lived in since she was born. She'd always wanted more, and still did, but her parents had done everything for her. They wanted her to succeed, and though she'd dismissed their belief in their own success, she had a new appreciation now. They'd lived a happy life together and had secretly saved money for her. They'd done everything they wanted to. They were satisfied, whereas most of her friends' families were ripping apart or facing terrible tragedy. She'd been selfish and self-interested.

But I'd leave with Tanner in a heartbeat.

An hour later, after she'd made herself a can of chicken noodle soup and a nearly out-of-date Caesar salad in a bag, she heard the familiar roar of an engine outside her front door.

Tanner?

She raced to the window. Yes! It was his Trailblazer!

She threw open the door, so glad to see him she was shaking. It was dumb. She was foolish. She knew it and didn't care.

When he came half-jogging up the walk, she stood in the doorway like she'd been frozen. "What are you doing here?" she managed.

"She miscarried. Amanda's not pregnant anymore!" He laughed. "I'm not going to make that mistake again. I'm loaded with condoms, and please God . . . don't let them break."

"Oh . . . great." She was thrilled, wasn't she? Amanda had no claim on him anymore, and he'd *come to her door.*

"Wanna use one?" he asked suggestively.

"You're sure that . . . she miscarried?"

"That's what she told me. Delta, I never was

interested in her. You know that. It's you and me all the way."

But you slept with her.

Tanner added, "I told you before, I love you. I want to marry you."

He expects you to feel the same. Do you? Of course, you do. "There's a lot of school ahead of us."

"A lot of school," he agreed, pulling her onto the porch and taking her into his arms. "But you love me. And I love you. What else matters?"

"I guess nothing."

"But . . . ?"

"Why Amanda? I mean . . . why?" *When you knew it would hurt me?*

He shrugged, said, "Why anything?"

"That's not an answer."

He suddenly grinned. "Okay, the devil made me do it."

"Tanner," she said achingly.

"Now stop," he said. "We're together, right?"

She loved the smell of him, the feel of him. "Yes," she said, "we're together," and then, "I can't believe you're back."

"Oh, you can't get rid of me now," he said on a chuckle, and then he was kissing her and she was kissing him, and they were laughing and falling back into the house, closing the door firmly behind them.

PART TWO

The Stabbing

Chapter 8

Three Days Ago . . .

Delta drove west from Portland toward the Stahd Clinic, her jaw set, her hair pulled into a ponytail at her nape, her makeup flawless. Her skin was lightly tanned, kissed by the sun, and her white dress with black piping and her black pumps were new. She'd just come from a soirée at the Bengal Room in downtown Portland, a tea that had turned into cocktails and hors d'oeuvres, so she'd called her mother and asked her to stay a little longer and look after Owen, who always begged to stay up later but fell asleep by 6:30, no matter how hard he tried. The curse of an active six-year-old boy.

She smiled at the thought. And then her mind turned back to the meeting. It had ostensibly been a meet and greet for parents of incoming kindergartners to the Englewood Academy, one of the most prestigious elementary schools in the tri-county area. Owen had been accepted, and Delta was bursting with pride. If there was one drawback, it was that all the students came from mega-wealthy families, and she'd heard there was a definite clique of brilliant, rich students, and it might be hard for someone of merely upper-middle-class means to be accepted by these little darlings.

"I'm not sure this is the right plan," she'd said over and over again, even while a part of her had wanted so *badly* for Owen to be chosen. In truth, her son couldn't care less. He was happy anywhere, and fairly oblivious to social stigma at this age.

But . . . what the hell. He'd been accepted, and so she'd attended the tea. If she had to back out, she would back out. But it was a fun ride while it was going on. The other parents had been welcoming. She hadn't had the most expensive dress, handbag, and shoes, but she'd made a good showing. Her personality had risen to the fore in all its effervescence; she'd made certain of it. She'd charmed the others, and then that handsome single dad had gently taken her by the crook of her arm and led her to a quiet corner where they couldn't be overheard and had flirted outrageously. Delta had laughed off his more scandalous suggestions and told him lightly, "You, I see, are very bad news."

"Bad news? Moi?" He'd feigned hurt.

"I'm going to leave now."

"Not before giving me a good-bye kiss."

"Not gonna happen."

"Oh, c'mon. Stay. Let's have another drink. On me, of course."

"The Me Too movement hasn't penetrated with you, has it?"

Her smile took out the sting. He didn't seem to care, in any case. "I was married for ten years, and nine of them were happy. The last year was hell. I lasted as long as I could, even when she was seeing any guy with a bigger wallet. She married one of those guys. I learned to get over her by meeting beautiful women."

"And are you over her?"

"A beautiful woman like yourself could certainly help me over the hump," he said suggestively.

She'd laughed. It was so blatant, and truth be told, she kind of enjoyed his outrageousness. It had been a while since she'd been so admired. "One drink. And I buy my own," she told him.

"You don't have—"

"I buy my own," she said again, and he lifted his hands in acquiescence.

"You're the book writer, I hear," he said.

"How'd you hear that?"

He'd nodded his head toward a group of women who were still collected at the table where Delta had been sitting. One of them had asked Delta what she did for a living, or if she worked, and Delta had told her that she used to bookkeep for her husband's business, but now she was a full-time mother who dabbled as a fiction writer. She wondered if he'd picked up that she was married.

He didn't get his kiss. He didn't really even try. But they had a lively conversation about their six-year-olds. He had a girl named Elise. And in the end, they shook hands and parted as friends.

The encounter had kept a smile on Delta's face all the way from Portland to West Knoll, but as she approached her small hometown's city limits, the smile became a frozen grimace, then fell from her face entirely when his call came through. Snapping her cell phone into its car holder, she swiped her finger across the glass and held her face close. After facial recognition gave her access, she answered with, "Hi, there."

"I need you stop by the clinic," Tanner said shortly.

"Why?"

"Just stop by."

"I'm busy. I just got back from—"

"For fuck's sake, Delta. Come to the clinic. I have something to tell you, and I'm not going to do it over the phone."

There's nothing you can tell me that I want to know. "Fine. But only for a few minutes. My mom's still at the house, and she needs to get back for my dad, so I won't—"

Click.

He hung up on her. Her husband. Her cheating, cheating husband. Tanner Stahd, the teenage god.

Well, you knew what he was when you married him, right?

They had a lot of things to work out. More, since their fateful ten-year reunion. But she'd stood by him through all these fifteen years since high school graduation, even though there had been plenty of rough patches. Ha. Rough patches? They'd been through rough landscapes, planets . . . universes.

But . . . he'd given her Owen. Her child. The love of her life. She smiled, but then her thoughts returned to Tanner, and her features set. Their last fight had been a real doozy. Screaming and yelling, and Delta had even swept their wedding photo to the hardwood bedroom floor, where it had smashed down and shattered when she'd found further proof of his dallying, this time with one of his receptionists. Hell, maybe it was with both of them. Maybe at the same time. That's what she'd coolly thrown at him, and he'd been so infuriated, he'd kicked the wedding picture into the wall, where a corner of the metal frame had punched into the sheetrock. The noise had woken Owen. Delta had rushed to soothe him back to sleep and then had stalked back to the bedroom she still shared with Tanner.

"It's the last time," she'd told him through gritted teeth.

"I'm not having an affair with Amy or Tia," he shot back in cold fury. "And I'm certainly not having a threesome. They work for me, and they're professional, just like Candy."

Candy was his nurse at the nutrition clinic he ran using his father's health products, which had actually seen their day and, after a scare of traces of lead and God knew what else found in the mix, had fallen out of favor and off the shelves. Les Stahd had lost nearly all his fortune, but he'd managed to hang on to his business, such as it was at that point, but not his wife. Lori had swanned off to greener pastures with an older gentleman still in control of his money. Les had then made a play for his first wife, Tanner's mother, again, who'd seemed interested for a while, but had then also drifted away. Luckily for Les, Lori's greener pastures had turned out to be dried-up wasteland, apparently. Her new man cut her loose, and she'd returned to Les, wiser and contrite. Delta wasn't entirely convinced of Lori's conversion, but whatever. Les and Lori were together again.

Tanner didn't see either of his parents or his stepmother any longer. And so far, he'd kept his hands away from Candy, but maybe because she was about six feet tall with an even taller, larger husband and two teenage boys, also tall and large. Amy and Tia were young and luscious, barely older than Delta had been that last year of high school. The kind of women Tanner invariably eyed lasciviously.

Prior to the high school reunion, she'd made herself believe she and Tanner were a team.

But then everything had blown apart. Amanda had been there. Cool, blond, and still beautiful, with a wealthy, far less attractive husband whom she ignored most of the night and whom she'd since divorced. Amanda had hung up her acting aspirations and become a lawyer. Her husband was one, too. Delta had caught Tanner and Amanda in a tight embrace, even though Tanner had sworn he despised her for lying about being pregnant, which was the way Tanner wanted to remember those weeks after graduation, when she'd supposedly been pregnant and miscarried. To this day, Delta wasn't sure whether Amanda had miscarried or simply lied to steal Tanner away from her. Either one could be the truth, but what did it matter? Tanner Stahd was a liar and a cheat.

Amanda hadn't explained the reunion embrace, but then Amanda never explained anything, and Tanner had said she was reading too much into two old friends catching up. Oh, was that what it was? It had been up to Delta to decide what to do, but as Owen was only a year old at the time, she just couldn't up and leave her husband. She wanted them to try to be a family, so she determined she would work things out with him.

Fast-forward to now. Tanner's infidelity had only increased since the reunion. It was almost as if he didn't care enough anymore to even put up a pretense. He was an inveterate cheater and always would be. The marriage was on a long, slow road to destruction and probably had been since the beginning.

So she was going to stop by the clinic, quickly, and see what he had to tell her. It was unlikely to be anything she cared to hear. Excuses, most likely. She still didn't want to go, but it was after hours, and the clinic would be empty, so . . . sure. Might as well see what he had to say one more time.

She pulled into the Stahd Clinic and drove her Audi into the back of the lot, out of the expanded circle of illumination from the streetlight, in a space by the back doors. She hurried up the steps and found them locked. Well, hell. If he hadn't left the front doors open, then she was out of here. She didn't have time for this. Her father was in the early stages of some kind of mental decline, and Mom didn't like to leave him alone for too long. This meeting of the Englewood Academy's kindergarten parents had been set for weeks, and she'd agreed to babysit, though Delta had promised she and Tanner wouldn't be late. Then Tanner had begged off at the last minute, claiming he had to work—par for the course—so Delta had gone by herself . . . and been entertained and flattered by that single dad, Jonah Masters . . . or Masterer . . . something like that.

She threw the strap of her purse over her

shoulder, circled the building by its brick-lined, cement walkway, and entered through the first set of double doors that led into the clinic. They were open, as were the inner doors, as it turned out, and she pushed into the clinic's waiting room. Toward the left was the reception counter, its silver metal curtain pulled down and locked as it was nearly 8:00 p.m. The waiting room's gray upholstered, steel-framed chairs were tucked against the wall; an array of dog-eared magazines had been stacked neatly on tables and filed in a rack attached to the wall in tidy rows.

Delta walked toward the door that led to the inner sanctum, grabbed the knob, twisted and pushed, but met resistance. For a moment, she wondered if she'd been locked out, which instantly annoyed her. Had he already forgotten he'd asked her to stop by? But then she realized the knob was turning in her hand.

She pushed again, and the door opened a crack. Something was up against it.

"Tanner!" she called through the crack in the door. With a sound of disgust, she pressed harder, throwing her shoulder into it to shove back whatever was holding the door closed. Her force caused it to suddenly give way, and she stumbled into the room, hanging on to the knob, but slipping, the heel of her right foot twisting. She fell forward, and her right hand hit a stain on the carpet; she felt moisture. Her left hand went down, and something sliced into her palm. A knife. She yanked her hand back and, in that same moment, saw the body. Lying on the floor. Smashed between the door she'd thrust open and the wall.

She'd fallen onto her hands and knees. Her ankle throbbed, and she'd lost her heel. Her left hand was bleeding. She stared at the body in total shock.

"Tanner," she whispered.

His chest was covered in blood, his white shirt stained with spreading red spots in a half-dozen places. Knife wounds? In a daze, she picked up the knife that had cut her. It was one from their set at home. A steak knife he'd taken to work to cut the apples and pears he took for afternoon snacks. Her brain couldn't connect.

"Tanner," she whimpered. She dropped the knife. Her pulse rocketed into high gear. "Tanner!"

His eyes were closed, but he was breathing.

She hesitated. Was this some kind of gruesome, sick prank?

But no. Blood was still seeping, soaking into the cloth. Oozing up between the tiny rips in the shirt. Knife slits. Real. It was all real. Oh, God. *Oh, God!*

"Tanner!" she shrieked. His breaths were shallow. Labored. Slowing . . .

Her phone.

She staggered back to her feet. Her right ankle throbbed. She'd done something to that foot. She was always injuring that foot.

Her purse had flown off her shoulder when she'd fallen to her knees. She stumbled forward, scooping it up. Her phone was in there . . . somewhere . . . somewhere . . .

Someone stabbed him.

Fear sliced through her. She dropped the phone. Picked it up, gazed at her husband, her breath coming fast, quaking.

His eyes opened, and he looked around wildly.

"Tanner! *Tanner!*"

The phone was slippery. It squirted from her hand, landing on his chest, bouncing to the floor, skittering against the knife. She snatched it up, and the knife flipped away, its blood-covered blade leaving a trail of red on the commercial-grade gray carpet. London Fog. She'd picked the color out herself.

"Dee," Tanner said dully, staring at nothing.

"Oh, Tanner. Right here. Right here. I'm calling nine-one-one . . . What happened? Oh, God, what happened?"

"Dee?"

"I'm right here. I'm—"

"Nine-one-one. What is the nature of your emergency?" The voice broke in on the telephone.

"My . . . my husband's been stabbed in the chest at his clinic." She had a blank moment, then rattled off the address. "Dr. Tanner Stahd. The Stahd Clinic in West Knoll."

"Dee?"

"I'm right here," she said to Tanner again, her voice shaking. She loved him. She loved him. She did. She always had.

But it was a hollow thought, one that made her feel like the fraud she was. She listened to the operator's questions and directions in a kind of rote trance.

Three minutes, and then the ambulance was there, and the EMTs were rushing in, tending to Tanner, who'd lapsed into unconsciousness again.

Delta stood back, spent. The drinks she'd had earlier didn't help the fuzzy, out-of-sync surreal quality she felt. Her legs were quivering. She staggered into the waiting room and collapsed into a chair before she could fall onto the carpet.

The police arrived.

Bob "Quin" Quintar.

Not Bailey.

Her eyes closed, and she began silently crying.

"Delta."

A new voice. One she recognized even though they hadn't spoken since high school.

She opened her eyes into the cool blue ones of Chris McCrae.

"Oh, it's you," she said.

Bailey wasn't the only one who'd gone through

164

the police academy. McCrae had chosen to become a police officer as well. Tonight, he was sans the beard she remembered him sporting at the reunion, and he was dressed in a pair of jeans and a gray shirt, open at the throat. She recalled his washboard stomach from the pig roast. He looked in as good shape now as then, fifteen years past graduation, but the bloodless pallor of his skin spoke of his reaction to finding his old classmate on the floor, stabbed a dozen times or so.

She saw the unspoken question in his eyes and realized she was holding the knife.

"I didn't do it. I loved him. I didn't do it. We . . . we loved each other. Always."

That was her first lie. He'd loved Amanda too, hadn't he?

Delta was numb. While McCrae bagged the knife, she told him about the locked back door, which Tanner normally left open for her. He ordered her to stay back with the EMTs while he and Quin searched the clinic in case the attacker was still around. By the time they returned, the ambulance had taken Tanner away, and she'd found her way to one of the waiting-room chairs. There was a smear of blood on the hem of her dress, red against the white fabric and black piping.

"It's all clear," McCrae said of the clinic.

Quin said, "I'll close the place down and get a team in here tomorrow."

"Good," said McCrae, his eyes fixed on Delta.

"I fell on the knife," Delta said, looking at her palm and the deep scratch the serrated edge had made.

"Looks like a steak knife." McCrae bent down to where Delta had dropped it. "It's not one of yours?"

She shook her head even while her mind's eye saw Tanner plucking it from their knife set in the wooden block on her counter.

That was her second lie.

The next several hours passed in a hellish blur. She drove to the ER at Laurelton General, where'd they'd taken Tanner, about twenty miles east of West Knoll. He was in a curtained cubicle in the ER when she got there. She was asked to stay in the waiting room. She half-expected to be hauled away for questioning by Quin and McCrae. The lie about the knife was eating her up. Why hadn't she said it was from their set?

Because you touched it.

Yes, but now she was going to have to compound the lie. Get rid of the rest of the set. Amy and Tia would be able to say that Tanner had brought the knife to work, wouldn't they? Or maybe they didn't know.

It was ridiculous. She needed to straighten that out right away.

It's always the spouse, though, isn't it?

But Tanner just needed to get better! He could tell them what happened! He could tell them who had done this to him. Who had stabbed him over and over again.

Who was that?

Delta shivered. Someone had viciously attacked him. Someone was out there. She could see them . . . locking the back door from the inside . . . making it look like an outside job when it was really someone inside . . . someone who knew him well and wanted him dead . . .

Delta jerked awake in her seat. She'd fallen into a daze. Her pulse ran fast and hard. Outside it had begun to rain even though it was late July, the precipitation flung against the windows by a hard, accusing wind. Delta felt under attack, singled out by the elements.

You're in trouble, girl.

She lifted her head and looked around and asked herself the question that had been at the back of her brain but now came roaring again to the front. Who had stabbed Tanner? Who would do that? Who wanted him dead?

You did.

"No . . ."

He could die.

The thought knocked the breath from her. No. Not Tanner. He was almost larger than life. The kid who'd made good on his dream of becoming a doctor. His dad had taken shortcuts and paid the price, but Tanner had put his nose to the grindstone and worked like a Trojan. His efforts had paid off, because he was an excellent physician, a gastroenterologist who worked with a combination of diet, exercise, health supplements, drugs, and surgery to help obese people, or even anyone who wanted to lose a few pounds, drop the extra weight, and gain a new, healthier lifestyle. He was beloved.

What if he doesn't make it through the night?

She couldn't think like that. She couldn't *think* at all!

With a kind of dreaded expectation, she watched McCrae walk into the ER. His eye fell on her, and he headed her way. Behind him, Quin—Officer Quintar, she reminded herself—entered through the sliding double doors. Quin took a look at Delta, and she read the accusation he didn't try to hide. But instead of joining McCrae, he peeled off to the reception desk.

"Delta," McCrae said, taking a seat next to her. "Quin's going to ask you some questions about what happened, but you might not want to answer them here."

"I don't want to leave Tanner. My mom's taking care of Owen, but she needs to go home, too. I don't know what to do."

"We need to find out what happened."

"I don't know what to do," she repeated.

She gazed at him, taking him in. He'd aged

since high school and the reunion, but hadn't they all? Some more than others. McCrae's crow's feet at the edges of his eyes spoke of a sense of humor—or squinting into the sun, she supposed—though she sensed it was the former. She remembered him saying the night of the barbeque that they needed to call the police, then taking off in the golf cart with Amanda. He'd also accused her of being as judgmental as Ellie, or something to that effect, and yet here he was, the lawman. She also remembered him at the reunion. A bit apart from the guys' group, where Tanner had held court.

He was saying something, something she'd missed: ". . . was a classmate and friend, so Officer Quintar will be the lead on the case."

"Quin's in charge?"

He heard her skepticism. They both knew Quin was no more removed from Tanner than McCrae was. He wasn't unbiased.

"We may have to draft an outside investigator," McCrae admitted, which made Delta's heart clutch.

"I need to go home to my son," she said. "I need to be with Tanner, but I have to go."

He glanced around to Quin, who was still talking to the nurse, but they were both edging toward the double doors that led to the emergency room cubicles. The receptionist pushed a large button on the wall, and the admitting doors slowly swung inward. Quin strode through them as they were still opening.

She said, "He's going in. I want to, too."

"Wait."

McCrae's voice was clipped, and Delta, who'd risen to her feet and was about to hurry toward the now closing doors, stopped short.

"You can't go in there. Tanner was attacked. He's . . . in a kind of lockdown until we know more."

"He's my husband."

He just looked at her.

"You do think I did it," she said, her heart twisting. Of course, he did. Of course, they both did. "I didn't. I would never. Could never!"

He grabbed her elbow and steered her out of the ER and into a long, windowed hallway that led toward the main doors and hospital reception. Outside, the rain was still peppering the glass windows, obscuring the parking lights beyond through a watery shield. Currently, they were the only ones within earshot of their conversation. "Give me a quick recap of your evening, and Tanner's, to the best of your knowledge."

"I thought you couldn't help me," she said.

"I can take down some information. You'll probably be telling your story to a number of us."

"So get it straight the first time?"

"That would be helpful," he said, refusing to be baited.

Delta suddenly felt extremely tired. There was a narrow bench in the hallway, and she walked over to it and sank down. "I need to call my mom again," she said on a sigh, pulling her phone from her purse, and then did so while McCrae walked a few feet away to give her some privacy.

"Hi, Mom," she said, and her throat closed. She couldn't say anything more. She was over-whelmed and felt so bereft that she couldn't speak.

"How's Tanner?" Mom asked fearfully when Delta choked up. "Oh, honey. Is he okay?"

"I don't know," she managed. "I'm . . . I'm talking to the police, and I wanted to say that . . . I might be a while."

"Okay. Don't worry. I'll stay as long as you need me."

"Thanks, Mom."

She hung up and put her head in her hands and cried. After a few minutes, she pulled it together and had the presence of mind to worry about the state of her makeup. She looked up at McCrae. "What do you want to know? Oh, yeah. Where I've been . . ."

She launched into the tale of her evening, the event at the Bengal Room. She wondered how much she should say about Jonah Masterer, or whatever his last name was, and ended up not saying anything at all. It had been nothing. A mild flirtation, and it had nothing to do with her real life.

Then she told him about finding Tanner, the stuck door, about the blood seeping through the white shirt covering his chest, his eyes rolling around.

"He called out to me several times, Dee . . . Dee . . . but even when I answered, he didn't say anything else."

"He calls you Dee?"

"It's short for Part D. The whole Five First thing, you might remember." She felt silly, suddenly, and she could feel face heat from a rising blush. Was that good, that she could still feel embarrassment even through the devastation of Tanner's situation? Or was that narcissism?

"I remember," he said.

"No one was in reception when I entered, so I pushed through into the inner offices, but his body was in the way. I didn't know what it was, so I just kept pushing and it gave way and then—" She drew a breath. "I saw him and I just . . . panicked a bit. I leaned over him. I didn't know if he was breathing. Then I called nine-one-one."

She'd already said as much, and now she was repeating herself.

Quin walked into the hallway from Emergency.

Spying McCrae and Delta, he lifted his chin. McCrae looked at Delta. "I'll talk to Quin, and maybe we can send you home for tonight."

"That would be great."

Delta wasn't sure if she should follow after him as he met up with the older man, but she stayed seated. She didn't want to engage with Quin. He was a decent guy, a fair man, and a loving family man. But he was no fan of Tanner's. Tanner may have been beloved by most, but that was not the case for the Quintars.

She thought about Bailey, who'd been certain Tanner was somehow responsible for Carmen's death.

McCrae came back her way. "Quin agreed that it's fine to let you go home. You need a ride."

"I can take an Uber. My car's fine at the clinic for tonight."

"Sure? I can drop you."

She shook her head. McCrae was being nice to her, but she suspected it was part of his job, and she really didn't want to be stuck in a car with him. What he really thought of her she couldn't tell. All she knew was that she wanted to get home to Owen.

He nodded his agreement, and when she walked out into the rain, she inhaled a deep, cleansing breath.

Half an hour later, she was relieving her mother, who tasked her with questions she couldn't answer. She felt completely wiped out, especially when Mom asked worriedly, "Did you tell them you and Tanner were splitting up?"

"Well, it's . . . nothing's been decided."

The lines of worry between her mother's eyes were deep, and Delta's answer didn't dispel them.

"Have you talked to Dad?" Delta asked.

"He's doing fine."

"Sorry I had to keep you so late."

"I just want everything to be okay."

If only it could be.

Delta rallied the last of her strength and helped usher her mother out to her car. "You okay to drive home?" she asked, head ducked against the rain outside the car parked in front of her house.

Mom waved a hand behind the driver's window. "You need a coat!"

Delta nodded. Too late for that now. Her mother rarely drove at night, and this was hours past the time she'd expected Delta to return. She held up a hand of good-bye in return and watched her mother's taillights disappear down the road.

Some July, she thought, running a hand over her rain-dampened hair.

She could hear the croaking of a bullfrog in the pond at the bottom of the waterfall on the side of the house. It all seemed so . . . normal. Meanwhile her husband was fighting for his life. Her cheating SOB of a husband—the man she'd loved more than life itself, the asshole she'd been planning to divorce—was fighting for his life in a hospital ER.

McCrae had said that they, the police, would be in touch and hinted at the fact that she might be required to come to the station for more interviews.

She went inside and locked the door, shook the rain off herself in the downstairs bath, then checked all the other doors to make sure her mother had secured them all. Then she headed upstairs to the room halfway down the hall and looked in on her son. Seeing his sweet face relaxed in sleep in the illumination from the night-light, one arm wrapped around a Lego truck, the other around his much-loved fleecy bear, Delta headed inside the room. The truck was almost out of his grasp, slipping down the edge of the comforter, so Delta gently took it from him and placed it on the shelf above his headboard, part of a "track" that ran all the way around his room. She kissed him lightly on the forehead, then walked back into the hall, allowing herself one last look. She would do anything for Owen. He was the purpose she'd missed until his birth. The career-driven plow through life that had propelled Amanda and Ellie and Bailey had totally missed her. She'd found it in being Owen's mom.

Downstairs in the kitchen, she walked through the unlit room to the butcher-block knife caddy with its array of carving knife, bread knife, paring knife, and utility knife fronted by its neat row of steak knives. Even in the semi-darkness, it was clear one slot was empty.

Delta picked up the entire block and carried it to her master closet. She pressed a button, and the automatic attic ladder in the ceiling hummed downward, unfolding slowly. Carefully, she climbed the ladder, balancing the knife block. She switched on the light as she straightened into the attic. Tomorrow she would go to Bed Bath and Beyond and buy a new set. Something similar, but not the same.

If Tanner recovered . . . She stopped herself. *When* Tanner recovered, he would know what she'd done when the knife didn't match, but it wouldn't matter because he would be able to identify his attacker. In the meantime, she wanted the police to stop looking at her and get on the right track and find whoever stabbed him.

"Who is that?" she asked the empty space.

Dust motes drifted in the light from the bare bulb.

She tucked the knife block under an eave, then shifted over a box of books to completely obscure the space. She was ducking back toward the ladder when she saw the gilt-edged volume that said *West Knoll Class of 2005: Ten-Year Reunion*. Picking it up, she smeared her hand across the dusty surface, then hauled it back downstairs.

Fifteen minutes later, she was in bed, holding the newly cleaned book in her hands. She looked at the clock. Midnight to the minute.

Heart pounding, she opened the cover, thinking of all her classmates. They'd all had varied and not necessarily joyful experiences when they'd gathered for their reunion, five years ago.

It had been a very hard time for Delta.

But now things were so much worse.

PART THREE

The Reunion

Chapter 9

West Knoll High School Class of 2005
Ten-Year Reunion

Zora teetered a bit unsteadily on her four-inch silver heels. She'd always been the shortest of the Five Firsts, even shorter than Bailey, and it made her feel a tad insecure. She hadn't seen much of any of them since high school, apart from that short time she and Delta had shared an apartment, when Zora's parents had still been footing the bill for her housing and tuition. Boy, how things changed. Luckily, she'd found Max, who'd fallen madly in love with her in that blur time of her parents' divorce when they'd sold the house, split their assets, and taken their respective bank accounts with them, neither of them all that eager to share with their daughter. Zora, unfortunately, hadn't realized the funds were going to dry up so quickly, so she'd allowed Delta reduced rent, and the two of them had navigated their first year living together while taking community college classes. Delta had chosen basic courses in business, and Zora had taken drama. Neither of them had been particularly thrilled with their choices. Zora just wanted to be famous and skip all the drudgery, and a small part of her kind of thought maybe her dad would pay her way in somehow, but, uh, no. Dad had skipped off with a new girlfriend, and Mom had moved to Bend, purchased a condo, and gleefully become a ski bunny, not that she knew how to ski, but she sure knew how to hang around a ski lodge and wear close-fitting ski gear. She'd landed a doctor who was on ski patrol, and they moved in together right away. Neither of Zora's parents seemed to quite remember they had a daughter who was barely eighteen and making it on her own.

Zora had been reeling that year and was glad that Delta had her own issues, namely Tanner Stahd. Delta was determined to save that relationship, come hell or high water. Zora could have told her it might not be worth the effort. She herself had engaged in a serious make-out session with Tanner once. She would have gone all the way, except he didn't have a condom, and one thing about Tanner Stahd, he wasn't going to let an unwanted pregnancy get in the way of his ambitions, at least that time. So they'd done a lot of kissing and rubbing and sucking, damn near everything except complete sex, and . . . it had been great *and* on the pool table where Amanda later had her own make-out session *and more* with him. Zora would have liked to really rank on Amanda and Tanner about that. It was all she could do to downplay their hot sex as just a few kisses, but she knew that if she told the truth, Tanner would rat her out as well, and she preferred that to remain a secret.

But that was all ten years ago now. *Ten years.* It didn't seem possible, and yet Zora and Max had been married six. Max had worked for his dad at Pilsber Construction at first, and things had been pretty good, but then the company had gone broke during the recession, and there were lawsuits abounding against "Piss-poor Construction," as it was dubbed, which prompted Zora to go back to her maiden name, DeMarco. So Max had taken a job as a foreman for another, bigger construction business, and they'd managed to hang on to the small house they'd bought in West Knoll. It wasn't the dream life Zora had envisioned, but it was okay. She'd wanted to move to Portland, even nearby Laurelton, a bigger city, but the house had been a good buy, even before the recession; though it hadn't been anywhere near the same league as the Forsythes' estate, it was located in a part of West Knoll that had at one time been rows of cottages, which had turned into hot, hot, hot properties before the bottom dropped out of the real estate market, so they'd done okay . . . for a while, until they were forced to sell anyway.

Now that property was undoubtedly worth a small fortune. She and Max had sold it when the market was recovering and moved into a rented condo. They were currently holding on to their cash and seeing what the market would do next. Unfortunately, prices were increasing every year. If they didn't buy soon, they might be priced out completely.

God, she hated worrying about money.

She looked in her bathroom mirror, touched the back of her upswept hair with a sparkling rhinestone comb. Her dress was black. Plain. She couldn't afford to buy something sleek and silky and colorful. Maybe red, or a rich blue, like cobalt or cerulean. Not only were she and Max saving money for another house, but there was the cost of those IVF treatments. Man, those were expensive! Zora had been sure she could have a baby without any problem, and to realize it wasn't happening had surprised and upset her. When a year went by, and then three, and four and five, she grew desperate. Max had said they could never afford the treatments, and only in the last year had she gotten him to finally open the purse strings and give it a try. But zippo. No luck. Nada. She blamed him for their problems, but the doctor couldn't say for sure what the holdup was. The woman's suggestion: for Zora to relax and try not to think about it so much. Great. What a plan. That was just sooooo easy.

And how much did that advice cost?

When she'd heard that Delta and Tanner had a

perfect little boy, that they'd named him Owen and Tanner called him "O," she'd smiled and smiled and smiled until she thought her face would break. So cute! she'd raved. So perfect! So happy for them.

So the life she should have had.

Again she recalled fooling around with Tanner on the pool table. How she wished she could rewind history and have made love to him. Maybe she would've gotten pregnant, and then she'd be the one married to the doctor now, not Delta, and she'd have a baby who was . . . ten years old now? They'd have money and a family and everything.

But . . . it was Amanda who'd hooked up with Tanner and gotten pregnant in those days, a case of a broken condom, according to her. Bullshit. Knowing Amanda, Zora believed Amanda had maybe sabotaged the prophylactic. Zora could just see Amanda sticking a wee, teensy hole in the latex tip and then carrying the condom around with her, waiting for an opportunity to pretend she was all prepared. Of course, it had happened on Zora's pool table . . . where *she* and Tanner had engaged in heavy petting just a few weeks earlier . . . which really sucked. But Amanda was relentless. She would do whatever was necessary to get what she wanted, and in those days, she'd wanted Tanner. In her single-minded purposefulness, she and Tanner were a lot alike.

But Amanda's pregnancy hadn't lasted. Miscarriage, she'd said. Unless it had been an elaborate lie that was going to be found out. Didn't matter anymore. Delta won in the end, and she and Tanner eloped. He'd just gotten into med school in Arizona, and Delta ran away with him and helped support him. She never finished her college degree, but she'd taken enough business classes to work as a bookkeeper, which helped them get by until he was in his residency. His dad had actually started the health clinic in West Knoll before Tanner was fully graduated, and Tanner joined in the business as soon as he could as the resident "Dr. Oz"—just before that whole "additive" business that scared everybody shitless. Lead? Seriously? Anyway, the upshot was that Tanner's dad's health supplement company had suffered a hard hit. Dr. Stahd Senior couldn't catch a break. But then Tanner took over the clinic from him and brought it back to glory, and everything worked out for Delta and him, and they had baby Owen.

She'd seen pictures of him on Facebook. Gorgeous little boy.

It all made Zora's stomach hurt.

Especially since Max was . . . not living up to what she needed in a partner.

She slid on some lip gloss with the tip of her little finger, wiped off the excess on a tissue, then went in search of her husband.

She found him lounging in front of the television in the same sweatshirt and jeans he'd been in all day.

"You're not going to make me go alone," she warned him, hands on her hips.

"Who would I know there?" he asked for about the fiftieth time.

"You've met Bailey Quintar."

"The cop obsessed with her friend's death? Yes."

"And you know of Amanda and Delta."

"The Fucking First Fifths."

Zora ground her teeth together rather than correcting him. He was goading her. Making fun of her friends. Maybe she did talk too much about them. They'd had a big impact on her life.

"And Delta has a son," he singsonged, "who's about one now, and she chased down her husband, the inestimable Dr. Tanner Stahd of the Stahd Clinic, handing out nutritional supplements that contain lead—"

Zora interrupted, "That was his dad. It was trace amounts. A bad batch."

"—like the quack that he is."

"And they don't do that anymore. It's a good clinic. You've been there."

"Yessirree. Which is why I know better than to go back."

Zora fought back another angry retort. Max

knew as well as anyone that Tanner was a celebrated doctor who shouldn't be blamed for his father's mistakes. Even Dr. Stahd Senior was a victim of the tainted products, which had ultimately been determined to be the manufacturer's fault, though that was too late to save his career. Max knew all that and didn't care. If Zora had to put her finger on what Max's problem with Tanner Stahd was, she would label it envy.

Which is exactly what Zora felt when she ran into Delta one day, about six months into her pregnancy. Delta had been as beautiful as ever. Her burgeoning stomach only seemed to add to her beauty. For God's sake, she'd actually *glowed,* something Zora had always thought was a myth.

Delta had put on a few pounds, though. Hopefully ones that were hard to lose. If Delta showed up at the reunion with ten or twenty extra plumping her up, it might even the scales out a little in the cosmic "who has the most" race.

"What's so funny?" Max asked.

Immediately, Zora stopped the smile that had crept over her face. She couldn't let Max know how she felt. Delta was supposed to be her friend. She *was* her friend. Zora didn't really want bad things to happen to her. She just wanted everything that Delta had.

"Okay," she snapped, gathering up her small

silver purse, a Target buy that she hoped no one would recognize. She hadn't really expected Max to accompany her anyway. She'd just been hoping.

Once in her ancient white Mazda, she turned her thoughts to the upcoming reunion. She was nervous, for sure, but eager, too. She wanted them all to see that she'd done all right. Maybe not as grand a life as she'd once had—thanks a lot, Mom and Dad—but not as bad as, say, Woody, who'd basically peaked in high school and then become a garage mechanic or something . . . although she had heard that he'd actually bought the business, but that could be just a rumor.

Zora grimaced. She was being unkind, and she didn't want to be unkind. And though it was mean and shallow—la di da di la and all that—she resented the fact that the other Fives, and Ellie, had all gotten what they wanted out of life. Delta was married to Tanner and had an adorable one-year-old, Bailey had become the cop she wanted to be, Amanda was a successful defense attorney, and Ellie, for God's sake, was a television weather girl, her journalistic aspirations taking her to TV. Why was she the only one still struggling?

You chose Max.

Okay, yes. She'd chosen Max. He'd saved her in the beginning, and he'd really seemed to be going places. Funny how things turn out. How was it that Amanda, who'd taken her shot in Hollywood and failed—there, at least, was failure—how had she come back to Oregon, enrolled in college, and then law school and been accepted by a prestigious Portland firm right away and was supposedly *brilliant?* Oh, and married to Hal Brennan, one of the firm's partners. Zora would like to believe that Amanda had been given the job by nepotism, but it was the other way around. She had apparently blown their socks off with her decisive manner and scrupulous attention to detail. This she'd learned from do-gooder Rhonda Clanton, who'd run into Zora at the only decent restaurant in West Knoll, an Italian eatery called Nona's, and who'd been only too happy to tell Zora all about her old friend.

"My husband's friends with one of the partners at Amanda's firm, and he just raved about her," Rhonda declared. She'd then leaned in and whispered, "She always was intense."

Not such a do-gooder anymore, Zora had realized, and she and Rhonda had dished a bit about Amanda.

But though Zora was mildly irked at Amanda's success, she didn't feel the anger and despair she did toward her that she did toward Delta. Amanda could have her career. *Go for it, girl.* But Delta . . . with her husband and baby . . .

Max was the problem.

And what if, though no one was saying it, Zora's inability to conceive was *his* problem, not hers? What if she'd just picked the wrong guy? What if somebody else could do the trick? She was twenty-eight years old, and her eggs weren't getting any younger. How many years was she supposed to wait?

She growled low in her throat and then, with an effort, pushed those thoughts from her head and concentrated on driving to the event, but as she negotiated the traffic, the niggling thought that she needed to rethink her marriage kept circling back to the forefront of her mind. It wasn't a new thought, but it was one that was growing in intensity. Becoming increasingly critical. A decision had to be made and soon. That goddamn biological clock.

Maybe . . . maybe it was time to look for someone new.

She considered. She needed some sperm. Preferably rich sperm . . . and smart sperm. Not Max's sperm, apparently. Someone else's.

Well, she was heading to a reunion. There oughta be plenty there.

Delta pulled up the Spanx over her legs and torso with an effort. A year, they'd said. A year to lose the baby weight. Well, it had been a year, and though she'd dropped ten of the extra twenty pounds she'd put on, the second ten were being really stubborn. Her mother had flapped a hand at her when she'd complained. "You look beautiful. You were always too skinny."

This was patently untrue, but Delta appreciated Mom saying so. But now it was reunion time, and she felt almost queasy thinking about the silent body shaming she could expect from the Five Firsts.

Four firsts, she reminded herself, as she had every time since graduation that she'd thought about the name they'd christened their group.

Resignedly, she eyed her figure. The Spanx took care of the worst of the softness around her waist, but it was hellishly uncomfortable.

"Beauty hurts," she reminded herself through her teeth.

"What?" Tanner asked as he moved into their master bath. He was half-dressed, his shirt unbuttoned, his tie loose around his neck. Were they going to be overdressed? she wondered. Though the invitation had specified formal wear for a dinner at the West Knoll Golf Club, the venue and food were generally pretty casual.

She was embarrassed to be seen in the Spanx and slid out of the room and quickly grabbed up the dress she'd purchased for this occasion. It was yellow, a lemony shade that she'd fretted over but that set off her dark hair and the tan she'd developed this summer. Her shoes were champagne-colored strappy sandals with a shorter heel than she would've liked, but the color was perfect.

She quickly dressed and then pinned up her dark hair into a loose bun. She added wide gold hoops to her ears and surveyed the results. She'd already put on makeup earlier. Not bad. The Spanx made her image bearable.

Tanner came out of the bathroom, smelling like citrus aftershave, buttoning up his shirt. Delta smiled at him, more sure of herself now that she was dressed. Their lovemaking had taken a hit since Owen's birth—well, since her pregnancy . . . and maybe even before that.

"Who's taking care of 'O'?" he asked in an offhand way.

Delta was a little surprised he'd even asked. He didn't concern himself with the baby in any way. He'd been happy when Owen had taken his first steps and toddled his way, saying, "Look at that!" and then he'd gotten on his cell phone and left the room to talk "business" with one of his people.

People . . .

Although he mostly covered up his conversations, she'd heard him snickering a time or two, joking, slyly muttering some double entendres. Those *people* were females, almost to a one, Delta believed.

Somehow, over the course of their marriage,

maybe their whole relationship, she'd become the mother to both him and Owen.

Maybe you always were.

"Mom's coming over," she answered. *Like always. If you ever paid attention.*

"You look nice. How do I look?" he asked, holding each end of his tie and thrusting out his hips, striking a pose.

"Good."

"Just good?" He smiled at her. His sexy smile. Delta smiled back faintly.

"Superb," she said.

He laughed and finished tying his tie, smoothing it down in front, looking at himself in the full-length mirror that Delta had moved out of the way of. Tanner was a peacock. She hadn't known that when they were young. How had she not known that? Was she that love-blind?

"I talked to Woody," he revealed. "He's going to be there with Crystal."

Woody had married his on-again, off-again girlfriend from high school, Crystal of the tattoos and penchant for Goth attire. Into crystals, like her name, and eschewing any kind of high school traditions, or expectations, or day-to-day experiences. She had rejected coming to the fateful pig roast barbecue, but had always had a lot of opinions about it and what they all should have done. McCrae might have accused Delta of

194

sounding judgmental like Ellie, but Crystal beat both of them by a mile.

"Maybe we should get a table together," Tanner suggested.

Delta made a noncommittal sound. She supposed that would be fine, though it might be a tad awkward as Delta had made a big deal out of marrying *Dr.* Tanner Stahd, even before he completed med school, implying that he would be so successful, bragging about how quickly he'd made it through school.

"Couldn't have done it without Delta," Tanner always said with that same sexy smile that somehow negated his words, when in reality Delta had worked day and night making sure he made it through, dragging him awake when he was near exhaustion, quizzing him over and over again, helping him with presentations. Tanner was a quick study, but he also had a wide streak of laziness, and it was only through Delta's constant organization and rigid timetable that he squeaked through without being shit-canned.

But those days were behind them. He was just finishing up his residency at Laurelton General, and he already had one foot in the door of his father's clinic. Delta had been working hard to make sure the clinic's reputation improved from the sort of new-age herbs and potions his father had peddled to a full-on facility where Tanner could take over from long-in-the-tooth Dr.

Gervais, who was regarded by most as a sweet old quack.

They left for the event in Tanner's BMW. It was ten years old, a graduation gift from his parents, and there was a ding in its right front fender. "Pretty soon," Tanner often told her. "Pretty soon we'll be living the life we were meant to have."

Delta stared out the passenger window at the streets of West Knoll, an eclectic residential area with some yards neatly trimmed, others ragged and bursting with dandelions in the summer heat. Delta helped pay the mortgage on their house with her hours at Smith & Jones and the part-time bookkeeping she did for the clinic. She'd never minded the work. She'd always been looking for the big payoff when Tanner was on his own, but maybe he needed to specialize to really raise his salary and their standard of living. That would be another three to four years. Was it worth it, or could the clinic be enough? Maybe they could find another doctor to share expenses and—

"Why are you so quiet?" Tanner broke into her thoughts.

"I'm just thinking."

"About what?"

"Oh, the business, I guess."

"Well, stop thinking about it. We've got a reunion to go to. People to impress. You're a doctor's wife, Delta Stahd. Time for you to strut your stuff."

Delta didn't respond. She remembered how she felt that day he'd come to her and announced that Amanda was pregnant. Even now, Delta wasn't sure if she'd been more upset that he'd had sex with her "friend" or that he just seemed to think it was a tragedy for him, no one else. Delta had gone to hell and back in those days and weeks before Tanner had told her Amanda had miscarried.

Was she ever really pregnant?

When he'd believed Amanda was pregnant, Tanner had told Delta how much he loved her, how sorry he was, how his life was over . . . the life they should have had together. Delta had spent hours in her room sick and crying, alternating between hating Amanda and Tanner, and anguished that she'd lost one of her best friends and the man she loved in one fell swoop. To this day, she didn't know the full truth of it, but one thing was clear: they'd both betrayed her because neither was denying that they'd made love.

Made love . . . She hated that euphemism. It made it sound like it was almost okay to cheat. You were making love, a beautiful act of sharing. Except they'd been screwing like rabbits on Zora DeMarco's pool table.

Delta could feel how tense she was as they pulled up to the golf club. She'd teamed her dress with a white loose-knit shawl tossed over

197

her shoulders. She braced herself. She didn't want to be here. She didn't want to see anyone. She didn't want to be with Tanner, but here he was, holding out his arm to her, enjoying his bit of gallantry.

The first person she ran into was Bailey Quintar, who, upon seeing Tanner and her approaching, held open the door. Bailey was dressed in a blue skirt and blouse and flat black shoes. Her hair was pulled back into a ponytail, like always, although she'd fashioned it bun-like at the back of her head. She had on discreet silver stud earrings, and she wore more makeup than she had in high school, which wasn't hard as she'd worn practically none in those days.

"Hi," Delta greeted her, suddenly filled with warm emotion upon seeing her old friend.

"Hi." Bailey's response wasn't nearly as welcoming. She gave Tanner a sideways look, then stepped back to let them enter.

"How've you been?" Delta asked.

"Better," she said.

Better? From getting over Carmen's death?

Tanner practically bolted away from both Bailey and Delta as soon as they entered, and he spied some of the old classmates hanging around the keg, which was set on the ground a few feet away from a punch bowl that graced the center of a table covered by a white tablecloth.

Bailey observed, "You're still with him."

198

Delta regarded her with a raised eyebrow. "We're married, and we have a son now."

"Ah, that's right. Congratulations."

"Thank you."

"I was just remembering the last time we talked."

"When was that?" Delta asked automatically.

"At the memorial service for Carmen. You said you wanted them both to die, Tanner and Amanda."

Chapter 10

I don't think that's exactly what I said. I was hurt, and we were all reeling and sad about Carmen. It just was a terrible time." Delta felt the spit dry in her mouth.

Bailey offered up a quick smile that fell off her face. "I guess some things just get imprinted in your mind, and you can't let them go."

"Have you seen anyone else here yet?" Delta asked, taking a few steps away from Bailey.

"Zora."

"Ah, I see her," Delta murmured, though she really didn't. She thought the person by the back windows might be Zora, though, and she headed in that direction with relief.

Bailey watched her go, completely aware that Delta was ditching her, also completely aware of why she'd done it. She, Bailey, had become rigid and unforgiving. At least that's what Delta thought, and probably everyone else at this event. Was that the real her? Maybe. These past ten years had taken their toll, for sure.

She wandered toward the punch bowl, wondering idly if any of the class miscreants had seen fit to spike the fruity, red liquid. Unlikely, when you could order whatever you wanted at the open bar.

She poured herself a cupful and then turned around and surveyed the room. Delta was with Zora, though they both looked tense. Onetime roommates. No longer friends.

The punch was not spiked. But it was full of sugar. After a couple of sips, Bailey looked for a way to get rid of the scarlet concoction. As she was holding the glass, Rhonda Clanton whisked up to her and declared, "What do you think of the punch? It's got coconut water in it, and it's yummy! I had it at a baby shower and thought it was divine."

"It's . . . punch-y," Bailey told the do-gooder.

"Yes! Exactly!" Rhonda beamed at Bailey and then moved on. She wore a pink skirt and matching twinset. She'd always seemed a little out of another era, and she looked like she hadn't aged a day since high school. Maybe it was magic punch.

Bailey surreptitiously set her glass down at the end of the table and walked toward the back wall. She'd made a life for herself at the West Knoll Police Department after several years of college, insisted upon by her father, and several more training at the police academy. It had taken a while to get hired on at West Knoll. There wasn't a ton of serious crime, and it was considered a plum position, but she finally made it. Now she worked with her father, who seemed to have had a change of heart; he was busting-his-buttons proud of her. The department was small enough that they mostly didn't have set divisions. She worked B&E and Homicide and everything else, even had a rotation as a traffic cop, and was hoping and planning to work her way up to detective. She liked the job, though she recognized it didn't feed her soul or fuel her sense of justice like she'd expected it would. After Carmen's death, she'd just wanted to go nuts on everyone. Someone was responsible for Carmen's death. She drove her father crazy, and anyone else who crossed her path, with her theories and questions and fury. She had even twisted the truth in her mind, coming up with conspiracy theory after conspiracy theory, even if said theories belied what everyone knew to be the truth. Carmen had been lured into the water. Someone had pushed her. Someone had fed her something that caused a cramp. She'd seen something—something she shouldn't, and that person had killed her over it. When Justin Penske casually asked, "Have you considered suicide over a broken heart?" she'd almost launched herself at him like a wildcat.

Her obsession nearly cost her her job, as it came up when she applied to the academy. Because she had to, she'd forced herself to tamp down her near-consuming surety that someone, or something, was responsible for Carmen's death. She had to pretend to let it go.

"I wanted answers when there were no answers," she explained in an interview. "I was grieving, and I wanted there to be a reason she was taken."

"And now?" the middle-aged woman with the skeptical look on her face had asked.

"Sometimes there is no reason."

But she'd lied. She'd believed then, as she did now, that other factors had been at play when Carmen stepped into the river after Tanner. Suicide? Never. But maybe . . . just maybe . . . needing to prove something? Like that she was strong. Better than the other girls that chased after him? The ones that were too afraid to go in the water.

Bailey hated that possible answer. Over the years, she'd kept a journal of all the memories of high school and especially those last weeks of their senior year. She'd written her theories down, all her theories and bits of information. She wrote the names down. She put the facts in order and made a time line. She pored over her own work, looking for a key. There were unanswered questions that may or may not have any bearing on the events of that day, but she felt if she just tried hard enough, she would figure it out.

In the center of her chart was Tanner Stahd.

She'd blamed him once, fully, but now she kept those thoughts to herself. Spokes radiated outward from him toward all their friends, the coach, the staff, his parents, everything and everyone connected with West Knoll High and its community.

Though Bailey had told the academy interviewer she understood that her friend's death was an accident, inside she believed something else.

Tanner and his friends had killed Carmen, and she wanted them to pay.

Greg, her ex-boyfriend, had discovered her journal one day when Bailey had been in a rush and hadn't locked it away in the wall safe she'd had installed in her apartment. He'd been silent, but she could tell he was spooked. She'd tried to brush it off as part of her therapy after Carmen's death, but he hadn't believed her. Shortly thereafter, they'd decided to take time off from each other. That time off had stretched into six months. She had her dog, a small mutt with black-and-white fur and a bad attitude toward anyone but Bailey, which was definitely one of the reasons Greg had left, but the real reason was because he'd found out about her obsession.

Now, as Bailey looked around the room, seeing her ten-years-older classmates, she tried not to look at them all as complicit in Carmen's death, but it was nigh impossible. There was Tanner, maybe no longer a teenager, but still a god, by the looks of things. And his acolytes—Woody, Penske, Brad Sumpter, even Trent Collingsworth, one of the do-gooders. She didn't count McCrae, who was on the force with her, but she'd seen him and Tanner share a few words and a hand-shake, so yeah, that "bro bond" was still a real thing.

And then there were the other Firsts—Amanda, Delta, and Zora, and, of course, Ellie. Coach Sutton, the man behind the pig roast, was absent tonight, but a number of the other teachers were in attendance: Anne Reade, Brian Timmons, and Clarice Billings. Also, Freddie Mouton, who'd been a last-minute invite to this reunion, and Amanda's parents, who, though they weren't here today, had been embroiled in a lawsuit with both Tanner's family and Carmen's afterward, both of which had since been settled.

You're the only one who isn't settled.

Well, yes, that was true, but even with the passage of time, Bailey hadn't given up her belief that someone else was responsible. She looked over at Coach Sutton, who was in his late forties now. He'd gotten himself in better shape over the years and looked fit and strong, although the hair at the sides of his temples had completely grayed out. He was talking with Clarice Billings, who had recently taken a job in administration at a junior college, and there were rumors that she might even be heading to a Pac-12 school soon. Her star had definitely risen, but Bailey still recalled how wet and scared and miserable she'd been after falling into the river trying to save Carmen. Anne Reade was standing to one side, trying to appear remote and uninterested in the goings-on of the reunion, but Bailey saw her eyes stray toward Brian Timmons a few times. She was still carrying a torch for the guy? Timmons, for his part, had put on a few pounds, but he still wore the welcoming smile she remembered all through high school, although it was maybe a little sadder. Principal Kiefer was talking to Rhonda Clanton, who'd damn near arranged the whole event by herself, to hear her tell it.

Principal Kiefer . . . Bailey had a bone to pick with him . . . she could hardly look at the man. He was the lover her mother had left her father for. It hadn't been some other nameless guy from high school; that had just been the lie her mother told. Over the years, Bailey had come to grips with that shocking reality, but she still didn't feel quite right about it. Now she forced herself to give him a once-over and was glad that the last ten years had thinned his hair and deepened the lines on his face. Though her mother's affair with him had burned bright and hot for a while—ruining Kiefer's marriage, apparently—they'd eventually ended it. When the

Proffitts had moved away after Carmen's death, her mother had lost her friend and confidante. Shortly thereafter, her relationship with Kiefer had ended as well.

Kiefer, possibly feeling the weight of her gaze, glanced her way. Bailey's eyes slid toward the guys' group. She didn't want any contact with the man and also didn't want him to misinterpret her quick look as an invitation for a confab. Hell, no.

One of her classmates separated himself from the guys' group, which had moved from the keg to stand near the door and eye the women coming through as if they planned to pick one off, just like in high school. That lone man was Justin Penske, she realized. His cowlick was tamed tonight, and he'd lost some of the starkness of his freckles, as they seemed to have melted into his skin tone some. No more alabaster skin and brown spots. He'd been unusually attentive to her after Carmen's death, but that had only lasted through the summer and then had seemed to fade away.

Now he met her gaze and started heading her way. "Bailey," he said with a slight smirk. His attitude apparently hadn't changed a whole lot.

"Penske," she responded, as no one had called him by his first name in high school and still didn't, as far as she knew.

"What are you doing, hiding out here?"

"Don't think I'm hiding out."

He glanced over at Zora and Delta. "Then why aren't you with your old friends?"

"Why are you with yours?" she countered.

" 'Cause I like 'em. Don't you like yours?"

"What do you want, Penske?" Bailey asked, through with the chitchat.

"Do I have to want something? Aren't we friends?"

We never were before.

He waved a hand, slapping that away. "This reunion got me thinking a lot about high school. Probably the same for all of us. Reminded me of the pig roast and all. Your friend Carmen and everything that happened . . ." He trailed off, his gaze on her.

Bailey nodded and then, under his harsh eye, said, "I've tried to put it behind me."

"Bullshit, Quintar. You were really upset, understandably so, but you were really mean. Really, on all of us, like it was our fault."

It was your fault. All of you. Led by Tanner.

"You still feel that way," he added. Bailey was deciding whether she would cop to that or not, when he put in, "I talked to Greg."

She felt her insides go cold. Carefully, putting on her "cop face," she said, "I didn't know you knew Greg."

"We're both in real estate. We see each other around."

209

"Greg works for Cipole Industries, Internet security, and—"

"And Cipole has commercial properties they're trying to sell. I'm their guy. Hey, it's you who introduced us."

Ah, yes. It had been one time, when Penske had wandered into a Portland restaurant and spied Bailey, who'd inwardly groaned. Yes, she worked in West Knoll, and yes, she'd rented an apartment there, but she really tried to keep her personal and business lives separated.

Greg never told you he knew Penske. Never even mentioned his name. "Is this friendship fairly new?" she asked.

"Guess it's heated up the last few months. Why? Jealous?"

Bailey knew everyone thought she'd gone a bit mad and maybe still felt that way about her. She figured it was time to end this conversation and made as if to move away.

"Okay, wait, wait . . ." Penske held out his hands when she took a few steps to go around him. "I'm not trying to yank your chain. Greg just said you'd . . . well, that he'd seen your journal."

"My journal," she repeated coldly.

"The one you were writing that summer, right after she died."

"*She* was Carmen."

"I know, Bailey. And I know how you felt about

it that summer . . . maybe how you still feel about it."

"Yes."

"It's good that you've . . . calmed down," he added lamely.

Is that what I've done? Bailey bristled inside, but she kept a stony outward demeanor.

He glanced back to the group of guys. Tanner was saying something in a low voice, and all the guys were leaning in. Whatever it was had them all reeling back and guffawing. A couple of them looked around the room at the women. Brad Sumpter's wild gaze settled on Amanda, who'd shown up in a gray dress with a plunging neckline, a silver medallion on a thin silver wire nestling between her breasts. Her husband was with her, but he seemed out of place among the classmates. As if finally unable to take it anymore, he suddenly headed for the bar.

"I know she talked to you about what she saw," said Penske.

Bailey dragged her attention to him once more. She was thrown back in time to Carmen at the barbecue. *"I saw something . . ."* But she had never had a chance to say what that was. The thought had plagued Bailey for years.

There was a long pause between them. Bailey wanted to ask what the hell Carmen had seen, but she knew Penske wouldn't tell her if she showed too much interest. She managed to hold the silence longer than he could, because finally Penske spoke as if a dam had broken. "It was just so obvious how Carmen felt about him. Tanner knew. We all knew. You knew. So when she saw him with her, his hand down her pants, you know, and them getting it on, it threw her. She shouldn't have been looking for him. I mean, what? Did she really think he and Amanda were just good friends?"

Bailey slid a look toward Amanda, who was standing to one side with her husband. It appeared she was drinking straight vodka, but Bailey sensed it was probably water. Amanda had never been a huge drinker, even when they'd all binged in high school. She'd always been a loner, however, and now she was an island.

"Tanner felt bad that she saw, but . . ." He spread his hands.

"Carmen saw Tanner and Amanda together." That was it? All those years thinking her words held deeper meaning, and *that was it?*

"Uh-huh. Always wondered if Carmen couldn't take it and just decided to end things right then and there."

"No."

"I know that's what you said at the time. I just thought maybe, with time going by and all of us moving on, sort of . . ." This time she saw him glance back at Tanner and then Delta.

"Carmen did not commit suicide."

"But Counselor Billings tried to help her, and she pushed her away. Nearly drowned them both. Wouldn't accept help."

"She didn't let Miss Billings help her because I'd fallen in and she wanted to help me. She just didn't reach me in time."

"You survived, and she didn't."

"I think she was messed up. Someone messed her up, with drugs maybe."

He let that go by with a shrug. "Amanda wasn't the only one he was with, y'know? If Carmen saw him with somebody else, too, somebody or somebodies maybe worse . . . ?"

"Somebodies?"

"Like, you know . . ."

"Spell it out for me, Penske."

"A couple girls."

"At the same time?"

"Nah. He wasn't trying to get himself killed." He barked out a laugh, throwing a glance toward Tanner, who was now standing beside his wife. Delta looked stiff and cold as a glacier. "But there were others willing to . . . well, we were all drunk, and it was the end of school. He wasn't the only one getting laid. But I know Carmen saw him with someone, maybe several people, and she wasn't the most stable. Don't get pissed. She was single-minded when it came to Tanner, and like you said, he was never going to be with

213

her. I'm just saying. It's possible she went into that water on purpose."

"She did go in on purpose. Like the rest of you followers," Bailey said coolly.

"You went in, too."

"I just said I fell in. Jesus, Penske."

He lifted his hands. "Okay . . . But we agree Carmen went in on purpose."

"To prove she was an athlete. That she could do it."

"I was around her, too, Bailey. She was *sad*. I mean, fucking slit-your-throat sad. That's what happened to her. When Greg told me about your journal, I wanted to talk to you. Let you know. Carmen saw him with Amanda, among others. She just gave up."

"What others?"

He held out his arms, encompassing the whole room. "Easier to find the ones he didn't have hookups with. And a lot of 'em took place that night."

"Carmen did not kill herself. Maybe her death was an accident, maybe it wasn't. I don't give a damn how many girls Tanner slept with that night, or any other time. Carmen knew he was with Delta, who flat-out told me she wanted to kill him, by the way, but Carmen knew Tanner wasn't hers. Maybe she lost some hero worship that night, but she wasn't suicidal."

He waggled his hand from side to side.

"You didn't know her. None of you guys knew her. And I'm done talking about her." Bailey turned to leave.

"There's just no conspiracy, Bailey. Carmen died. Maybe she meant to do it, maybe she didn't. But it just happened. And Tanner's always felt bad."

"Oh, sure."

"He never wanted anything bad to happen to anyone."

"I'm not in love with him like you and everybody else," she said coldly.

He snorted. "Oh, not everyone's in love with him anymore. I could tell you stories . . ."

"I don't want to talk about Tanner anymore, either."

"You're as bad as McCrae, y'know? Is it a cop thing? Neither of you wants to revisit high school, even though you're both here."

At the mention of her coworker, Bailey glanced over to Chris McCrae, who was hanging near the keg. He was holding a beer, and Bailey noticed, not for the first time, how he, like Penske, had gotten better-looking as they neared thirty. McCrae's hair was thick and dark brown, brushing his collar. He had a close-clipped beard that Bailey's dad had griped wasn't really regulation, which amused Bailey. Her father could be such a stodge. But sometimes, looking at McCrae directly, she sort of forgot what was being said. He was that appealing.

"McCrae has some sense," she said.

"You didn't think so when we were in high school."

"He didn't have as much then."

"Do you talk to him about your Carmen theories?"

"We talk about our jobs, Penske. That's what we talk about. The Crassleys? That's what we talk about."

He lifted his hands, and this time Bailey did move away from him. He knew, as well as anyone in West Knoll, that the Crassleys were a family of bullies, brawlers, and thieves. The Crassleys hadn't had a student in Bailey's graduating class, but it was about the only year one of the eight Crassleys had skipped. Above and below their class had been Gale and Booker, who had been in constant trouble as kids and were into ever-deepening criminal activity now. The Crassleys took up a lot of the West Knoll department's time and energy.

"What are you doing afterward?" Penske suddenly asked, before Bailey got out of earshot.

She stopped trying to edge away and looked back at him. "After this? Nothing. Going home to my dog."

"Would you like to do something else?"

"No. But . . . thanks." She was flummoxed. Not because she wanted to spend any more time with

216

Penske, but it had been a while since any guy had shown any interest in her at all.

"I was thinking of getting some real food. Not just 'light hors d'oeuvres.' You could join me?"

"I just got here."

"How about this? We do a little more reconnoitering, say hi to everyone we've missed, then vamoose?" His eyes took a trip around the room. The decibel level had increased, and Bailey had had to return a step back closer to him to hear. She saw his gaze linger on someone, his lids narrow a bit, but when she turned around to look, there was no one in his direct line of sight. Amanda and her husband were still standing together again, albeit like two frozen robots, McCrae seemed to be walking toward Ellie, Zora and Delta had turned their backs to each other and were talking to other people, Coach Sutton and Counselor Billings were gazing at Principal Kiefer and Mr. Timmons, who were both looking deadly serious in a way that seemed out of place.

"I don't—"

"Shhh." He placed a finger over her lips. "We'll circle the room, meet up again in half an hour, and you can reject me then."

She hesitated, but he'd already turned away. Bailey seriously thought about just leaving. What the hell was she doing here anyway? What had she expected to find? But, say what you will,

Penske had intrigued her a bit, so she decided to stay awhile longer, face some old friends, engage in more meaningless chitchat. What the hell. She probably would never go to another reunion.

Inhaling a deep breath, she headed in the general direction of Zora and Delta and Amanda, the remaining members of the Five Firsts.

Chapter 11

Ellie felt her heart flutter as Chris McCrae walked toward her, and she inhaled a slow, calming breath. Ten years. *Ten years.* She hadn't seriously thought about him since their one-night stand. Well, she had, but when she'd realized the encounter had meant nothing to him, she'd purposely dropped him from her mind. He was high school. The past. They hadn't had any kind of relationship, and no one had known about them doing it at the barbecue, so it was like it had never happened. In truth, she'd thought more about Tanner in the time since than McCrae. She and Tanner had at least had a whirlwind affair that first year of college when Delta had been stuck back in community college. It had been a lark. A fun time. She hadn't wanted anything further from him then or now.

McCrae had been her second choice behind Tanner the night of the barbecue. She'd used him for the experience she lacked. That was all.

Still . . . he looked damn good. No escaping that. Even though he was a cop, and she didn't know exactly how to feel about that. The twins, at sixteen, had already had a few scrapes with the law and, despite Oliver and Mom's best efforts to smooth things over, they were developing reputations with West Knoll's finest.

As McCrae neared, she also remembered how she'd thought she was pregnant, wished for it almost. The thought gave her a jolt of disbelief. It was shocking to remember the little idiot she'd been. It almost felt like someone else's memory. When Amanda's pregnancy had been revealed, Ellie had realized how much she'd dodged a bullet. If they'd both been knocked up by the hottest guys in the class at the same time, somehow Amanda would have eclipsed her on that as well. Not that she'd been looking for that particular kind of notoriety, but good God, she couldn't even lose her virginity without one of those goddamn Firsts stealing the spotlight from her.

"Hi, Ellie," said McCrae.

She was surprised by how aware she was of him. Not romantically, of course. It had never been about that, and anyway she had someone she was desperately in love with and their affair was burning hot as wildfire. Unfortunately, that relationship was taboo, not to be talked about. She hadn't been able to bring him to the reunion, and Alton would have thought it was a joke anyway. And if it were to come out somehow, and his wife found out . . . KABOOM. Nuclear explosion. Ellie would lose him, her job, and maybe even future jobs in the industry.

"Hi, McCrae," she said. "Chris." She inwardly groaned recalling how she'd tried to call him by his first name when she dreamed of marrying him, the father of her unborn child.

"I see you on the news almost every night."

"You tune in to Channel Seven?" She reported the weather, which was an okay position but not where she wanted to be. She'd been working on moving up, but so far, no dice. That's how her relationship with Alton had begun. Sleeping with the boss. But she really did love him. She did. And, yes, it was a cliché, but his wife, Coco, bitch of the highest order, did not understand him.

"It's on at the station, and I'm there usually after six."

"Yes, I heard you and Bailey were on the West Knoll force. Congratulations, I guess."

He inclined his head in acknowledgment. She almost brought up Joey and Michael and their delinquent behavior but decided against it.

"At least you didn't greet me with 'How's the weather?' That's one I've never heard before," she said.

McCrae smiled, and the transformation was magical. One moment he was intense and stern, maybe even condescending—or was that just her own guilt?—but then that *smile*. She wanted to bask in its brilliant warmth.

"How's the weather?" he asked, and they both laughed.

"Partially sunny, but there's rain in the forecast."

"Typical June," he said.

"How are things at West Knoll's finest? You still living around here?"

"My dad's place."

"Oh, right. Somebody said you bought it?"

"My dad died." He looked past her for a moment. "Didn't intend to stick around, but it was an opportunity."

Ellie wanted to turn and see what he was looking at and decided she would. If he was looking for somebody better, so be it. She didn't feel like hanging around with him all night, either.

"Mr. Timmons's dad died recently," he said as she glanced around. She realized then that he hadn't been trying to look past her. Their conversation had cued him because of his own father's death.

"Oh. Maybe he'll quit teaching." It was rumored the Timmons family had money.

"That would be too bad. I always liked his class."

Ellie had, too. Timmons's classes in analytic geometry and calculus had been difficult, but she'd always been good with numbers. Strange that she'd forged a career in journalism, while

Delta, who hadn't shown any aptitude in math, had found work as a bookkeeper.

"McCrae!" a male voice boomed, and he turned around slowly to see Tanner surging toward him. Tanner threw one arm around McCrae's shoulders. "Come on back, man. We got things to talk about."

"See ya," Ellie said, sliding away.

"Don't go away mad," Tanner singsonged after her.

Asshole.

She walked toward the bar, ignoring him, kind of angry at herself for coming at all. It was hell without a date, and yet she wouldn't have wanted to bring Alton even if she could. She glanced at Delta who, along with Bailey, was surprisingly talking to Amanda. God, to be a fly on the wall there! Despite being married, the Stahds sure weren't hanging by each other's side, so maybe bringing a date to this event wasn't the end all, be all in any case.

She moved toward Delta and Amanda but was beaten to their confab by Zora, who upon spying the two frenemies together had zeroed in on them.

". . . with Jimmy Dewars in that car accident," Amanda was saying in her precise way. "They were high."

Ellie realized they had migrated to the Memory Table, a virtual shrine to all the classmates who had fallen since high school. Jimmy Dewars and Howie Tuttle had been the friends Amanda was speaking of who'd died in the car accident during their junior year. There was a picture of Jenny Worthers, too, who'd suffered from bone cancer and had succumbed to the disease, and another of Jacob Corley, who'd died in military combat.

And of course, Carmen Proffitt.

Ellie looked long and hard at Carmen's picture, remembering the somewhat gangly girl who'd carried such a bright torch for Tanner Stahd. Well, they all had, really. Carmen's had just been so blazing. But Tanner, who spread his love around with abandon, had never shown any interest in Carmen. Ellie suspected Tanner just didn't want to get involved with her. Let's face it. Any relationship with Reverend Proffitt's daughter would have been a problem, not to mention that Carmen's blatant adoration had bordered on a cult obsession.

"You still think Carmen's death wasn't an accident?" Amanda asked Bailey. Was there censure in her tone? Ellie couldn't tell.

"No, she doesn't," said Zora.

"I can speak for myself," said Bailey.

"Of course, it was an accident," Delta broke in. "Carmen drowned. They were all reckless and stupid, and Carmen died because of it." Her eyes drifted toward her husband, and her mouth tightened a bit.

"Coming here brings it all back, doesn't it?" Bailey said. "Hi, Ellie."

They had all sort of stepped back from the Memory Table and had somewhat reluctantly allowed Ellie to join their group. *Nice of you all. Just like high school.*

Bailey answered Amanda, "Carmen saw something that night that she never got to tell me."

"Well, you've said that a few times." Amanda smiled to take some of the sting out of it.

"Something happened," Bailey said. "And I think it changed the course of everything."

"What happened was my husband went under the rope, and all the rest of them followed," said Delta. At that exact moment, another guffaw went up from the guy group, and Delta's gaze turned back to them. Ellie didn't much care for her, but she could sympathize. The guys seemed like they were having a bang-up time in that regressive "guy" way. They were boys still, and Delta was married to the ringleader.

You had your thing for Tanner, too, don't forget . . .

She slid a glance toward them as well and witnessed McCrae extricating himself from the group, heading back to the bar. She watched as he ordered another.

Amanda said to Bailey, "I saw you talking with Penske."

Bailey answered, "Yep."

225

Ellie's attention swung back to Bailey at her short comment. She didn't seem to want to discuss it.

"You were talking about Carmen," Amanda said. At Bailey's nod, she added, "And your *journal*."

There was laughter hidden in Amanda's tone. *She really can be such a bitch,* Ellie thought.

Color crawled up Bailey's neck at the snide inference. "I wrote down what happened, and I made some suppositions, some theories. Carmen didn't kill herself. I was helping her out of the water when I fell in."

"Ever think you just have survivor's guilt?" Amanda asked.

"Penske was actually interested in my journal," said Bailey.

Amanda's look said, *Or was pretending . . .*

Ellie was tired of listening to them trade shots back and forth. "It was terrible what happened to Carmen, and we all still feel bad."

Another wave of laughter erupted from the guys' group, seeming to belie her words.

Zora looked over at them. "I should've never married Max."

That snapped all of their attention back to her, even Delta's. That was probably Zora's game plan, actually, as she loved being the center of attention, and it so often wasn't hers to grab if either Amanda or Delta was anywhere around.

Amanda said blandly, "Get a divorce. That's what I did."

"You're divorced?" Ellie blurted, surprised. Everyone else murmured their own shock as Ellie looked at Amanda's husband. "But . . ."

"He just came along tonight to piss me off," Amanda said. "It's what he does. He's a leech. Always trying to get his hands on my parents' money. Luckily, they left it all in trust for me."

Ellie almost objected. Hadn't she married one of the firm's partners? Amanda's parents had moved away in the years following the barbeque debacle and a myriad of lawsuits placed against them. Upon a short and unsuccessful post-college stint in Hollywood, Amanda had enrolled at Willamette University Law School and currently was employed at Layton, Keyes, and Brennan, a downtown Portland firm where she'd met her husband, Hal Brennan, one of the partners. The firm was well known and defended some of the wealthiest clients in the state.

"Aren't you both lawyers?" Bailey asked.

"Yes, but only one of us is a success."

Amanda made it sound like her husband's credentials were dubious, at best, even though he was one of the firm's partners. There's a story there, Ellie thought. Young as she was, Amanda had been moving up the ranks in the firm. Ellie had heard her name mentioned at the station when one of the owners had employed their firm. She'd also heard some of Amanda's coworkers refer to her as "Hollywood" in a pejorative way. She might be successful, but she wasn't well-liked.

"I don't know if I could divorce Max," Zora said, a little put off by the idea.

"What about you, Delta?" Amanda challenged. "You ready to put that cheating husband of yours behind you?"

Delta's lips parted in either disbelief or shock, maybe a little of both, since Amanda could be seen as the fly in the ointment to Delta's marital happiness. Ellie almost admired her. Amanda just didn't give a shit what she said.

"Don't have any plans to leave him," Delta responded, once she'd recovered. "Marriage isn't perfect for anyone, I guess. But we chose each other. I didn't fake a pregnancy to get him to ask me."

The self-satisfied smile fell from Amanda's face. "If you're referring to me, I never faked that pregnancy. It was real."

"Okay." Delta clearly didn't believe her.

"And the only reason he went back to you was because I miscarried, thank God," Amanda declared, warming up. "So I got to have a life. What have you got? Tanner Stahd? Big fucking deal."

"I have Owen," Delta retorted, regarding

Amanda uneasily from what clearly looked like rage building inside her old rival. Ellie almost took a step back herself.

"A Tanner mini-me. Hopefully he has a little more discretion than his father. Ask Zora, or Ellie . . ." She swept an expansive arm Ellie's way. "Ask them what it's like screwing your husband. They both know. Maybe Bailey does, too."

He wasn't your husband then! Ellie immediately wanted to scream. It was all she could do to keep her mouth shut and stop from defending herself. Not so Bailey, who blurted, "I never hooked up with him!" and Zora, who cried, "That's not . . . we didn't . . . you're such a *bitch,* Amanda!"

"Agreed," snapped Delta.

Amanda merely shrugged. "I'm a truth teller. Some people have trouble with the truth." She cast a hard glance at her husband, who seemed to be having a grand time talking to whoever crossed his path. She then looked at the guys' group, her lip curling faintly. "Tanner's a piece of shit, but so are all men, if you really want to know."

"Wow," Delta said.

"When did you become such a man-hater?" Ellie asked.

"When I married one. That's not to say they don't have their place. I mean, sex isn't the same without them, at least from my point of view, and Tanner still looks good. Not as good as McCrae, these days, but I'd do him again."

Delta inhaled sharply, and Zora muttered, "Jesus, Mary, and Joseph."

Everyone's gaze shifted to Delta, who stared at Amanda with a look of mixed horror and amusement before saying, "Maybe you should just go ask him. He'd probably oblige."

"Would he?" A small smile played at Amanda's lips.

"Oh, please, don't fight," Bailey murmured as Ellie held her breath.

"Maybe I will," Amanda said blithely. She set down her drink on the Memory Table, but it caught the edge of a stack of cardboard coasters with their "2005" graduating year imprinted on them and tipped over. Dark red punch raced toward the board of pictures. The bloody fluid immediately soaked into the cardboard edge and seeped into Carmen's picture. Mesmerized, Ellie dragged her gaze away from the ruined photo and, along with the Fives, watched as Amanda headed over to Tanner and tapped him on the shoulder.

"Oh, Lordy," whispered Zora.

None of the women watching said a word, and then Delta deliberately set down her own drink, a nearly empty glass of white wine, and followed after Amanda.

• • •

Goddamnit, Delta thought. *Goddamnit.* Amanda was the ultimate bitch. Flagrant. Mocking. Careless . . . that was it. Careless. Amanda just didn't care. She'd never cared, and it was . . . *infuriating!* Amanda just cruised through bitch-dom like a conqueror. She knew Delta would flip out, and yes, she was flipping out. She wanted to strangle *both* Amanda and Tanner.

Keep cool . . . keep cool.

But how could she do that, with Amanda slipping her arm through Tanner's and laughingly dragging him away from the other guys, who were watching this happen in slow, dawning surprise and then suddenly looking around for Delta to see her reaction? She tried hard to keep a smile on her face, but it was cemented in place— and, she hoped to God, not in a Joker-esque grimace.

Is Amanda right about Tanner screwing around with Zora and Ellie and . . . everyone?

Now was not the time to think about that. She'd always known Tanner was unfaithful, but with her other high school friends? When? Long ago, or *now?*

Don't make yourself crazy.

Amanda had always wanted Tanner, and she'd always felt like Delta didn't deserve him. That was a fact. But she'd never loved him, not the way Delta had. She'd just wanted him, wanted to win him. Amanda had always craved beating everyone at everything. That was truly who she was. Except Delta had beat her in this one way. This. One. Way. She'd won his heart, and Amanda hadn't.

He did sleep with her, though. Believed he got her pregnant, whatever the case. Don't forget that. And maybe he slept with some of your other so-called friends . . .

Delta ached inside. She didn't want to. She wanted to be tough and unaffected, but it really, really hurt.

Do you still love him? Or is this just ego? Do you want this marriage to work, or is it on its last legs?

"I want it to work," she whispered.

"What?" Justin Penske heard her as she approached the group. He was a bit apart from the crowd of them.

Delta curved her smile into one of irony. "Think I'd better rescue my husband?" she asked lightly. There was no escaping the fact that Amanda had whisked Tanner away from the others. *When there's a glaring problem, don't ignore it, point an arrow at it.*

"You mean from Forsythe?"

"Brennan now, but yes."

"Keeping a leash on him's a full-time job, isn't it?" He grinned.

She'd never liked Penske much. She hadn't

liked Brad Sumpter, the workout fanatic, his shadow, either. She hadn't liked a lot of the guys in the class, come to that, but maybe that was because they'd always tried to shut her out. They'd wanted to keep Tanner in their inner circle of "bros." Bros before hos, and all of that shit. She'd been so proud of the fact that she'd managed to win him away from them and everyone else.

"I hear you have a kid now," Penske said.

"Owen. He's fourteen months."

"Still counting in months, huh. When does that stop?"

"Probably at two."

"Glad I don't have any kids. They'd be ass-holes, like I am."

"I'm surprised you know it. And can admit it."

"That I'm an asshole?" He chortled. "Aren't we all?" He swept an arm to encompass the guys' group.

"Yeah, maybe," she said. Talking to Penske wasn't half as bad as she'd thought it would be. Unlike Tanner, he seemed to possess some sort of self-deprecation. She tried to move past him and confront Amanda and Tanner.

"You still love that shithead?" Penske asked.

Amanda was smiling up into Tanner's face, and he was eating it up.

"Yes," Delta said automatically.

Her chest was constricted. Maybe there was

something still there between them, something worth saving. Some small part of her that still loved her husband. He'd been all she could think about from the first moment they were together. She'd wanted to breathe him in every moment. Be with him. *Tanner Stahd, the teenage god.* He'd been all she'd ever wanted . . . then . . . and now?

She swallowed. It still burned her to watch Amanda move in on her husband, even if she was doing it just to piss Delta off, which was what she suspected.

But what if she really does want him? Will you fight for him? Is he worth it? Is the marriage worth saving? For Owen?

Did he really sleep with Zora and Ellie and God knows who else?

She thought about the way her husband had turned on his personality for the young receptionist, barely out of high school, who'd been all legs, skinny as a colt, and naïve in that totally *adorbs* way. She'd been just too cute for words, and Delta had felt the prick of jealousy. And she wasn't the only one. There'd been a parade of them through the years. Slim, pretty, flirty . . .

Oh, hell, be honest with yourself. You wanted to scratch their eyes out.

"Hey, doll," Tanner said, easing himself away from Amanda as Delta approached.

"No, don't stop," Delta said with steel in her

voice. "We're all just one big happy family, right?"

"How progressive of you," said Amanda.

"You just said he'd screwed all my friends and that I should divorce him. I'm pretending you meant that as friendly advice."

"What?" Tanner asked. He was swaying a bit on his feet, grinning, but with pinched brows, aware he wasn't quite following.

"It was friendly advice," she agreed.

"What are you guys talking about?" asked Tanner. He lost his balance a bit, lurching, putting one hand on the edge of the bar to steady himself.

"Did you really sleep with Zora and Ellie and Bailey?" Delta asked.

"Bailey? *What?* What the fuck? No!"

"I guess at least she was telling the truth," Delta said drily.

Her pulse was running fast and hard. She was playing a part. Pretending to not care, pride making her hard and cold. And she wasn't going to let Amanda win. Tanner might be a piece of shit, but he was her piece of shit.

"Okay, this was fun, but I'm done," Amanda said on a huge sigh as she stalked away from the both of them.

"I didn't schleep with them . . . them . . ."

"I think you maybe did."

"No . . . no . . . you don't know."

"You're drunk," she observed. "Maybe it's time to leave."

"Ahm not ready."

"Well, I am."

"Too fuckin' bad, Delta."

"I'll drive myself home, and you can cadge a ride or an Uber, I don't care." She turned away from him, and he made a grab for her elbow but missed. Tried again, caught her, then hung on for dear life as she stood like a wooden statue. She sensed everyone watching them and curbed the impulse to push him away. He was a belligerent drunk when he had too much. But she didn't want to make a scene . . . at least one any worse than was already in progress.

"It's too early!" he practically shouted in her ear.

"I'd say too late."

"You were friends with Amanda!"

"Yeah, how about that? Strange things happen." She tried to ease her arm from his grip, but he was hanging on tight.

"C'mon, Delta. We jes got here. People . . . people wanna see us."

"I've seen everyone I want to."

"Everything all right here?"

Delta almost laughed. It was Principal Kiefer, older, grayer, but just as cloyingly sincere as always, worried about "his students" and propriety, which was funny as hell as she'd heard he'd had an affair with Bailey's mom, the true reason for the Quintars' divorce.

"Everything's fine," she assured him.

She took a few moments to say good-bye to Zora and Bailey, who in turn said how glad they'd been to see her, and then she headed out the main door. The night was cool, the air was slightly crisp, and she could feel the weight of impending rain in the air. Roses nodded their weighty heads at her as she walked the path toward the parking lot and remotely unlocked the doors to her Mercedes.

She stood beside her car for long minutes, thinking. Didn't want to go home just yet.

Then Amanda suddenly shot out of the double doors of the golf club and raced to a Lexus near to Delta.

"What's wrong?" Delta asked her automatically.

"My brother's been in a car wreck," she bit out, as she jumped behind the wheel and screeched out of the lot. Her husband—ex-husband—followed after her and stood at the top of the steps, along with several others who must've seen Amanda tear out as if her hair were on fire.

Chapter 12

Zora swilled down the truly awful white wine they were pouring as she watched the Tanner/Amanda/Delta debacle unfold. At least Delta hadn't pressed her on what Amanda meant. That would've been all she needed. To have to recount her own dalliance with Tanner. Great.

Her attention had been divided while it was going on, however, as she'd been buttonholed by Rhonda Clanton, er, Sharpley, and her husband, Eric, a man as earnest and gung ho as his wife, which was saying a lot. She'd wanted to be in on the drama over Tanner, but Rhonda and Eric had been so insistent and enthusiastic that Zora had been forced to pay them some attention. She'd listened with half an ear at the back-and-forth conversation the two of them were having. They were both full of affirmations. Life was just so *good,* so full of *possibilities,* didn't Zora think so?

It made her head hurt.

But the catfight she'd been expecting between Delta and Amanda hadn't come to be. Delta had walked away, and then shortly thereafter, Amanda had received a phone call and zipped out the door after her.

Zora was trying to edge away from Rhonda and Eric as, with a sad clown face, Rhonda said, "Poor Mr. Timmons. His dad just died yesterday. It's awful. They were really close, and Mr. Timmons was taking care of him."

Zora said politely, "That's too bad."

"Parkinson's," Eric told her, equally sad-clown-faced.

"But maybe now he and Ms. Reade can get together!" Rhonda said with an uplift to her voice. Her expression was elastic. Sorrow one moment, joy the next. Like a switch she could turn on and off.

Eric chided, "Oh, don't go playing matchmaker again."

Rhonda nudged him with her elbow. "I told you. They've been *almost* together for years. Maybe now it'll finally happen. Brian—I mean Mr. Timmons—is free, and she's never been married, either, so . . ."

"Well, financially, it's a good time. That's a big inheritance," said Eric.

"Oh, don't talk about that," Rhonda said with a giggle. "It's true love for them."

Zora finally heard something of interest. "What's a big inheritance?"

"Oh, you know, Mr. Timmons's dad owns that company that makes fences, or something?" Rhonda looked at Zora expectantly.

"Fences?" Zora asked blankly.

"Columbia Fence," said Eric. "Commercial fencing. You've probably seen their signs around."

She thought about it. Yes, she'd seen the small plaques embedded in the sides of chain-link fencing all over the area.

Eric put a hand up to his mouth and leaned toward her, saying in an aside, "Big, big bucks."

Rhonda playfully slapped at him. "Stop it, Sharpley. I told you. It's true love!"

Zora finally saw an opportunity to excuse herself, and she headed back to the bar to refill her glass. She nearly ran into Woody's wife, Crystal Gilles, whose tattooed arms were on full display outside a sleeveless and shapeless ecru cotton dress and sandals. She was a preschool teacher; go figure.

"Sorry," Zora murmured politely. She was surprised Crystal had even come. She'd purposely avoided the pre-graduation barbecue at the Forsythes', a good move as it turned out, but she'd managed to make it to their ten-year reunion. Maybe she'd had a change of heart over the years. At least the Goth period seemed to be over.

"Woody told me about you," Crystal said with a mysterious smile.

"Told you what?"

She turned her head, still smiling, and wandered to where Woody was regaling the guys' group with a story that elicited a wave of laughter. Zora found herself more uneasy about her comment than she would have credited. What was there to know about her? Was it the heavy make-out session with Tanner? Amanda had already spilled those beans, though maybe Crystal didn't know it.

"Bitch," Zora muttered under her breath, carefully holding a protective hand in front of her wineglass as she maneuvered back through the crowd.

Mr. Timmons was talking to Anne Reade, who had one hand on his forearm and was regarding him intently. Clarice Billings cruised up to them and, like Anne, seemed to be offering condolences. Anne pulled back, and Zora could practically read her mind. *Get away from him, you blond bitch.* Unlike Anne, who'd grown softer over time with a bit of a pudgy belly, Clarice still had a slim runner's body, and her face was smooth and unlined. Botox, or good genes? Maybe both. Seeming to sense she was unwanted, Clarice moved away from Timmons . . . and Zora took her place, causing Anne to frown.

"Mr. Timmons, hi, I just wanted to say I heard about your dad, and I'm really sorry. They said that you were really close. That you were taking care of him. I'm sure it's really hard," Zora said in her most heartfelt voice.

The math teacher looked at Zora in an

unfocused way. For a moment, she wondered if he'd imbibed a bit too heavily, but his hands were empty, and he didn't seem drunk. Emotion, she decided, as he answered, "Thank you, Zora. Um . . . call me Brian, please. High school was ten years ago."

Anne said, "Doesn't seem that long."

"I know, right?" Zora agreed. "And then sometimes it feels like nothing's changed."

"Everything's changed," he said. Then, as if realizing what a downer he sounded like, he allowed, "Some things for the better."

"This reunion just brings up all the sadness about Carmen Proffitt," said Anne. "We haven't had a student's death since, while they were in school. It's still difficult."

Though she was saying the words, there was something wooden about her delivery that made it seem like she was, well, just saying the words.

"I think it's on everyone's minds," Zora said. "Certainly Bailey's."

"They were good friends," Timmons agreed.

"BFFs." Zora gave them both a nod. Maybe it was time to leave. She'd given her condolences, and sticking around might get awkward.

Anne said, "Clarice should have been able to pull Carmen out of the water. She's all muscle, and I've never known anyone so determined. I just don't know how Carmen drowned."

There was jealousy lurking in Anne's rebuke

of Miss Billings. Zora reminded them, "Carmen was five-ten and all muscle herself. Bailey tried to get her to come out of the water, but Carmen wouldn't even listen. Then Bailey fell in, and Carmen went after her."

"Is your husband here?" Mr. Timmons asked Zora.

"No, he couldn't make it." She was a little surprised he knew she was married.

"Reunions are made for the classmates," Anne observed.

Zora felt herself grow stubborn. Anne was treating Mr. Timmons as if he were hers, and hers alone. But she'd had years to land him, and it hadn't happened yet, so . . . "Tell me about your dad, Brian," Zora said, testing out his name on her tongue. It felt a bit strange, as she'd always thought of him as her teacher, one who knew that her talent for numbers wasn't exactly up to the same level as Amanda's or Ellie's. "My parents split up right after I graduated, and my relationship with them has been, well . . ." She waggled her free hand back and forth. "It's hard to lose family."

Anne made a sound of disbelief, but the math teacher regarded Zora with damp eyes. "Thank you," he said, meaning it.

"I think I'll get something to drink," Anne said drily. "Want anything?"

Brian shook his head. He moved closer to Zora

244

as soon as Anne, with a lingering look back that could have melted steel, headed away.

Zora gazed into his eyes. Blue. She liked blue eyes. She liked the color blue. He wasn't all that bad-looking, and he wasn't all that old.

"Tell me about him," she invited again.

"You sure you want to hear?" He looked at her askance, but she could sense the eagerness beneath his words.

"Yes."

Shrugging, he smiled a bit, then launched into a tale about how his grandfather had been born poor and worked and worked until he had enough money to buy a small company that primarily manufactured fences for farmers; how his father had taken that small company and turned it into one that sold regionally and now, nationally; how that modest company had just exploded in sales over the last few years; how his father was a salesman's salesman, a great guy all around. While he talked, Zora led him over to a bank of chairs that was somewhat isolated from the rest of the group. Anne returned with her glass of punch but looked like she didn't know how to rejoin them now that they were seated. Clarice Billings glanced over at them with narrowed eyes, as well, but Zora ignored them both. They could think Zora was moving in on territory that belonged to Anne. It may or may not be true. Zora hadn't decided yet.

But blue wasn't the only color Zora liked.

She had a great preference for green, too.

"You ready?" Penske asked in Bailey's ear; he'd sneaked up behind her causing her to jump.

She'd been talking to—more like listening to—Principal Kiefer, Anne Reade, and Clarice Billings, who'd been in a confab of sorts, but who'd all looked a little tense. Most of that tension seemed to emanate from Anne, whose body language was stiff and indignant; the way her eyes kept being pulled magnetically toward Zora and Mr. Timmons sitting by themselves in some kind of tête-à-tête answered the question of why without it being asked.

Principal Kiefer was telling Miss Billings about several new teachers at the high school who'd gotten in trouble with some of the parents because they'd allowed their students to leave the school grounds to march in a protest against school shootings and therefore guns.

"It's a very hot button," Kiefer was saying, "as Bailey well knows, being a peacekeeper, right?"

Bailey was still thinking about Delta and Amanda's dustup, and how they'd left a few minutes apart from each other, so she wasn't paying particular attention. She realized Kiefer was looking at her. She was irked. He'd been trying to engage her in conversation all evening, maybe as a way to assuage his guilt. She could have told him she didn't care what he did or didn't do.

She could hear Penske breathing directly behind her. "Gun control? Yes. It's a very hot button," he answered for her.

"How do you feel about it?" Miss Billings asked Bailey. "You carry a gun."

"Regulation," Bailey responded. The last thing she wanted was to get drawn into a political discussion. And what the hell was Penske doing now? Blowing gently on her nape? She wasn't sure if she was annoyed or slightly thrilled. Justin Penske was not the kind of guy for her, but it felt good to be on a man's radar, nevertheless.

What is the kind of guy for you?

"But how do you feel about it?" Billings pressed.

Bailey met her gaze. Miss Billings had left West Knoll High years earlier, fairly soon after their graduation and Carmen's death. Some people believed she felt responsible for not saving Carmen, and sure, Bailey could believe that was part of it, but Miss Billings' career had thrived over the years, and she was now working at a small, conservative, private college on the outskirts of Laurelton, and it was rumored she was up for a job with a Pac-12 school.

"Oh, don't put Bailey on the spot," Penske drawled, smiling at the trio of school teachers and administrators. "This is fun, right? We're all here for fun."

Principal Kiefer slid a look at Miss Billings, who seemed to want to say more, but then smiled and let it go. Anne Reade's gaze kept returning to Zora and Mr. Timmons. Bailey wasn't even sure she was in the moment.

"I'm heading out," Penske said, giving Bailey a wink.

Bailey hesitated, not quite sure what that meant. Were they going to dinner?

She followed behind him after a brief hesitation in which she felt like Miss Billings and Anne Reade were regarding her with unspoken questions. She didn't know exactly what she wanted, but she was done with the reunion.

Outside, Penske was already clicking his remote to unlock his SUV, which flashed its lights at him. The last fingers of cool evening light were receding, striping the hotel parking lot as the sun set behind the hotel's upper floors.

"How about Danny O's?" Penske said as he waited for her to reach him.

Danny O's was a twenty-four-hour pancake restaurant on the outside of West Knoll, about as far from the golf club as you could get and still be inside the city limits. It had been, and still was, a popular high school hangout for teenagers on the west side of the Willamette.

"Sure," Bailey said, somewhat disappointed.

What did you expect? That this was real a date?

"I'll meet you there," Penske said and climbed into his vehicle.

Bailey followed in her blue Ford Focus, given to her by her father. She found herself reflecting on Ronald Kiefer some more. He might still be West Knoll High's principal, but luckily he'd never fully become Bailey's stepfather. She was still mad at her mom about it all, but okay . . . what was, was. She needed to get over it.

But that's what everyone had told her about Carmen, too. She needed to get over it. And maybe she was being somewhat obsessive. But it also felt important not to forget, not to let her best friend disappear into the past.

Danny O's shared a parking lot with an Irish bar called Lundeen's that was a few grades down from the twenty-four-hour diner. Lundeen's spilled its drunken bar closers into the parking lot in the wee hours of the morning, and a good number of them staggered into Danny O's to sober up before driving home. In the past, teen-agers tried to talk the barflies into buying them booze, but a few stings with officers posing as kids and catching the adult suppliers had pretty much taken care of that issue.

Bailey pulled around the back of Lundeen's as all the spots closest to Danny O's were taken. Penske had managed to squeeze his SUV between two cars, each of them a bit over the line.

"Hey, let's have a few at Lundeen's first," he said as Bailey joined him.

Her steps slowed. She would have rather stayed at the reunion than swallow anything poured at Lundeen's . . . but here she was.

Inside, she followed Penske up to the scarred bar that spanned twenty feet beneath dim hanging lights in the shape of old-time lanterns. When he ordered himself an Irish whiskey, Bailey opted for a light beer.

"Oh, get your drink on," he said, pointing to his whiskey and putting up two fingers for the bartender, who nodded his graying, ponytailed head.

"I don't drink whiskey."

"Should I have made it vodka? Give it a try."

"I don't even know why I'm standing here with you," she said.

"Because you were bored. It was boring. And now it's time for the real reunion to begin. We didn't hang out in high school. We gotta make up for that."

"You were in the cool group."

"You were one of the Five Firsts," he said right back.

"Yeah, but only Amanda, Delta, and Zora were the ones you guys hung out with. Carmen and I were—"

"Lesbians," Penske cut her off. "That's what we all thought anyway."

"Everybody knew Carmen had a serious thing for Tanner."

"Maybe she was bi," he allowed, "but you were definitely into girl on girl."

"I don't know why I'm still standing here." Bailey shook her head and set her beer down on the counter.

"Don't leave," he begged. "Okay. You want me to believe all this time you've liked guys?"

"I've had boyfriends," she told him hotly. *A boyfriend. For a short time.*

"Really, who?"

"No one you'd know."

He snorted. "But you're still obsessed with Carmen. Got that journal going."

He made her sound half-crazy. "The journal is my way of dealing with her death."

"Show it to me."

"No."

"Oh, come on, Bailey."

She shook her head. "It's mostly for me. Everyone says her death was an accident, and yes, she didn't intend to die, but I have a lot of questions. I've talked to my dad about it."

Penske had knocked back his whiskey, and now he looked hard at Bailey. There was a loud billiards game going on behind them that sounded like it could be turning into a raging fight. Bailey half-turned to check out the players, but she could feel Penske's appraisal of her.

"What does your dad think? He's a senior officer, right?"

"He thinks . . ." She wondered if she should be honest. Quin didn't actually believe in the kind of suppositions, which he tended to label "conspiracies," that Bailey had laid out over the years about Carmen's death, but he was proud of her research.

"You're a darn good investigator," he'd told his daughter upon examining her notes on not only Carmen's death but other crimes that, though she wasn't a detective per se, she'd analyzed in depth and had offered up avenues of investigation that had led to solving them.

"He thinks I'm still too involved personally to be clear-eyed about Carmen."

"Well, yeah."

"But he told me he liked the way I've been investigating and the conclusions I've drawn, and he thinks I should work to be a detective."

He pulled her beer bottle away and slid the whiskey glass along the bar, closer to her. "Is that what you're going to do, then?"

"There are no openings at West Knoll, but that's my plan. I've been stuck in a rut. Might as well move on."

"And if you're a detective, you can look further into Carmen's death."

It wasn't really a question, but Bailey smiled faintly and answered, "You're onto me."

"Drink," he said, nodding toward the glass of whiskey.

"I told you. It's not my drink."

"Drink," he insisted.

"This is worse than high school."

"You're an officer of the law now, and it's my duty to make certain you remember how to have fun. You do remember, right? Fun?"

Bailey shook her head. Not because she was answering him, because she didn't know what the hell was holding her here with him. He was too pushy. Too ready to do the wrong thing. He hadn't matured all that much from high school, and yet . . .

"I think you qualify for the 'Bad Influence' label," she told him.

He grinned at that. "Most definitely."

"You've changed since high school."

"I was always a bad influence."

"No."

"No?" he queried, one eyebrow lifted.

"You and Sumpter were just Tanner followers, not really bad."

She heard her words as soon as they were out and cringed a little inside. No man liked to be called a follower. She should have chosen what she said more carefully.

But Penske just gave her a crooked smile. "Jesus, it's hell to be dumb, isn't it? I wanted to be Tanner. I saw him there, with all those girls, women, after him, and it seemed like he had everything. I wanted it all. Right then. Right now."

She was relieved he hadn't taken offense. "We all paid him a little bit of homage," Bailey admitted.

Another roar came from the billiards table. Bailey looked over at them sharply. She half-expected one of them to bash their pool cue down on the other's head, and she tensed. She'd dealt with the Crassleys enough to know what she needed to do before things got out of control.

The pressure of a glass into her palm brought her head snapping back around.

"Take a sip or two," he said. "For fun." When he was certain she wasn't going to drop her drink, he held his nearly empty one up to his own lips.

The pool players were grudgingly racking up another game. No blood. No fight. Bailey resisted the urge to look at the time on her cell phone and instead lifted up her glass in a toast. "To fun."

"To fun!" He grinned, tossing back the last swallow of his as Bailey brought the glass of whiskey to her lips. She sipped, thought, "Yuk . . . but not horrifically terrible." She took a second sip and a third, none of them more than a small swallow.

"There ya go," he said.

"Are we going to go eat at Danny O's?"

"We could. Like we used to. Or we could stay here."

She looked into his eyes, seeing the way they narrowed slightly as he assessed her. She was assessing him right back.

"Here," Bailey opted.

Penske's grin widened, and he signaled the bartender. "Two more," he said, pointing to the bar in front of them.

"You're drinking both of them yourself," Bailey warned, to which he said in his cocksure way, "We'll see."

His cell phone rang, and he pulled it from his pocket and squinted at the screen.

"Need some help seeing?" she asked.

"Nah." He tucked it back in his pocket.

He drank another whiskey pretty fast, but Bailey was still sipping away on her first. She started to feel very warm in the chest.

A slow country-music song came on, and Penske pulled her away from the bar and into his arms. She felt a bit silly, dancing, but it was really nice.

"Let's get outta here," he whispered in her ear.

"I thought we were staying."

"Can't a guy change his mind?"

Pretty sure she was making a big mistake, Bailey nevertheless let herself be guided through the door and into the parking lot. She started toward Danny O's, but Penske twirled her around and into his arms.

"Wanna fool around?" he asked, pressing her body close to his.

She could feel his hardness, and a thrill zinged through her. She let her hands move down to his hips, pulling him closer, intensifying the feeling.

"I'll take that as a yes," he said breathlessly, moving her toward their vehicles at the back of the lot.

Chapter 13

The First Fives had all left the reunion except for Zora, and there definitely was that "party's *over*" vibe as Ellie poured the rest of her wine down the bathroom sink. She glanced around. The golf club was definitely lower tier in the decorating department. Faded flowered wallpaper, pinkish tiles on the floor, ornate and gilded fixtures, tarnished in spots. It probably hadn't been redone since the eighties, but it was about the only game in town in West Knoll for an event this size.

You shouldn't have come, she told her reflection.

She'd thought for a moment that Delta and Amanda might really get into it. Now, that would have been a story. Old rivals duke it out at the ten-year reunion. She could have a field day writing a tongue-in-cheek article that maybe, just maybe, she might be able to sell as a human-interest story. She wanted to write. Her gig at Channel Seven wasn't really giving her what she needed creatively.

She walked back out of the bathroom. There were still a number of people around, but the place was definitely starting to thin out. Almost to a one, her classmates had brought up that they'd seen her on the news . . . and almost to a one they called her the "weather girl." She wasn't the meteorologist, she was just the fill-in. She supposed she should be gratified that they'd seen her at all, but she found it more annoying than anything else. She was a journalist who'd written for a number of local newspapers and then went off on her own to interview different people for stories around Portland, sending her tapes into the Portland television stations, hoping for a bite.

Nada.

But she wouldn't give up. Alton had called her his fierce Chihuahua, which she didn't like either, but he and his wife, Coco, had a Chihuahua named Penny who was mean as dirt. That dog could only snarl and growl and glare, as far as Ellie could see, but she'd pretended to think it was just darling because Alton was an anchor on Channel Seven and he told her he had a thing for redheads when she stalked him into a bar after work one night and struck up a friendship. He'd seemed half-interested in her work, more interested in getting her into bed, but she held off on the latter until he'd read some of what she'd written. "It's good," he told her, sounding surprised, and then they ended up in a downtown Portland hotel room for a couple of hours before he had to go home to Coco.

After that, Ellie worked her way into meeting

the production staff. One of the producers took a liking to her, and she almost jettisoned Alton in favor of Rob, but luckily she stuck with Alton, who she could tell was really falling for her. Rob was a bit younger and brasher, and he was definitely a decision maker, but he was engaged to a woman whose family had money, according to Alton, and so Rob wasn't going to stray too far.

She managed to keep Rob at arm's length, but not much farther away, and she learned her hair color was a plus on television. "People notice red hair," Rob told her. "And yours is natural."

It took a little bit more time before they put her on screen. Ellie wanted to be a reporter, but Channel Seven was the domain of that bitch on wheels Pauline Kirby, who, though getting a little long in the tooth, had a big following around the Portland area. Ellie sometimes fantasized that Pauline would just keel over and die and she, Ellie, would be able to pick up the mantle as Channel Seven's number-one reporter. Not so. She was . . . the weather girl . . . part-time.

But she had Alton. He was leaving Coco, that was for certain. He was more concerned about leaving Penny, the Chihuahua, than his crazy wife. Penny was a purse dog, tucked into Coco's big bag whenever they came to the station. Ellie made faces at Penny when Coco couldn't see, and the dog went ape-shit. Rob had caught her at it once and smothered a smile. Alton loved the dog too much to ever see what a pain in the ass it was, so Ellie kept her low-grade loathing to herself as much as possible.

Now she thought about Alton as she cruised through the main room of the reunion one more time. Most of the guys were still hanging around together, and they'd traded in their beer cups for shots at the bar. Always a good idea. Justin Penske had left with Bailey; go figure.

She looked around for McCrae but didn't see him either. Damn. Even with Alton, McCrae was an itch she would like to scratch again. His body looked as hard as it ever had, maybe even more so, and she half-dreamed about having him slide in and out of her, their eyes locked, just letting their bodies do the work.

The thought brought on a wave of desire.

Whoa. That shot a thrill right through your hoohaw, didn't it?

"Have you seen McCrae?" she asked Crystal Gilles.

Crystal was nibbling on a stuffed mushroom cap. Woody was with the guys, but she didn't seem to mind. Ellie had heard they were married, but maybe it was a common-law thing. That's kind of how they rolled.

Swallowing a bite, Crystal drawled, "Trying for a replay of the barbeque?"

Ellie's heart galumphed. "What do you mean?"

"Oh, you know. You and McCrae . . ." She lifted her brows and smiled slyly.

"Did he say something?"

"God, no. The guy's a cop now. Doesn't give away anything. We all knew, Ellie."

"You weren't even there."

"Woody *saw* you. He told me about it. You thought you were the only ones out in the woods?"

Ellie was stricken. It was an odd day when she had nothing to say, but she was embarrassed and flabbergasted.

"Oh, forget it. Nobody cares. McCrae's a hottie. Happy hunting." She grimaced and put the rest of the mushroom cap on a plate with half-eaten food that had been abandoned.

Ellie wanted to scream, *It wasn't like that,* but she knew better than to make a bigger deal out of it than it was. Still . . . Woody had seen them?

She eyed the guy group with trepidation, wondering if she was a source of their "guffaws." But like Crystal had said, it was old news. Ten-year-old news, to be exact.

"Somebody said you're the weather girl on one of the local stations. What's that like?" Crystal asked.

She could tell by Crystal's tone that she was wanting to make fun of her, maybe gathering material to take back to Woody and the guys.

"About what you'd expect," she said shortly, and moved away from her.

She gave the guys a wide berth, still keeping an eye out for McCrae. Yes, she loved Alton, but he spent most evenings at home with his wife, and that left her kind of footloose and, well, horny.

She hadn't picked up any vibe from McCrae that he was interested in a "replay," as Crystal put it, and when she was talking to him earlier, she hadn't felt it either. But now she did. Her blood felt hot in her veins, and the more she thought about the two of them ripping off each other's clothes, falling onto a bed, or a couch, or the floor would even suffice, him kissing her like his life depended on it, sliding into her, thrusting, pushing, her mouth open on a silent scream—

"Ellie?"

She came back to earth with a bang. It was Brad Sumpter. He of the huge muscles and small brain. She cooled off right away. McCrae had a lean, hard sexiness, whereas Sumpter was somehow too big. Probably fake big. Enhanced.

"You wanna go somewhere after?" Brad asked.

"I can't. Got someone waiting for me." She gave him a regretful smile.

"Heard Penske say something about Danny O's. We're all kinda thinking about going."

"Like I said, I'm already booked. Tell everybody, next time." She sketched him a wave and headed for the door. Outside on the steps, she texted Alton. Maybe, just maybe, he could get away. She waited about five minutes. He kept his phone on SILENT so his wife wouldn't hear his texts, and sometimes it took him a while to ease himself free of her.

But not this time. No text back. He couldn't get away.

Damn.

She didn't have McCrae's cell number. She should have asked for it. He was reachable at the police station, but what good would that do her tonight?

Tanner was still inside the golf club, drinking with his buddies. She thought about sleeping with him, but that would be really taking a chance. What would Delta do if she found out she and Tanner had already done the dirty? Amanda had basically given the game away, but Delta was so convinced Tanner was a hero that she hadn't really listened. At least Ellie didn't think she had. In any case, she hadn't reacted when Amanda had let it be known that she'd had sex with him. And Zora, too, maybe? That was an unwelcome surprise. Tanner was far more of a man-whore than she'd known.

"I'd still do him," she said aloud; then, aware that anyone could be outside and listening, she clamped her lips together and headed for her car.

・・・

Bailey was drunk. She couldn't believe it. She'd hardly had anything to drink. But her vision was blurred. Her heart jolted. "Did you put something in my . . . drink?"

They were at her car. She'd unlocked the door, but she was swaying slightly. Penske had a hand on her arms, steadying her. He frowned. "Whad're you talkin' about?"

She realized he was swaying, too. "Did the . . . bartender?"

"I just want to be inside you," he said, pulling her close.

It melted her. She wanted that, too. It had been too long, far too long, since she'd been with Greg, even longer since they'd enjoyed sex in that wonderful way.

Penske opened the door to the back seat of her Explorer. "Let's make out inside." He practically pushed her in, and then she was lying on her back on the seat.

"We can't do this here!" she said, when he took her shoes off and her skirt and her underpants. The door was still open, and he was pulling down his own jeans.

"Yeah, we can."

"I'm a . . . cop!"

"I'm gonna fuck a cop. I love it."

"Penske . . ."

But then he was on her. The door was still open.

"Shud do door!" Her words were garbled under his marauding lips.

He twisted back and grabbed the handle, and then they were scrunched in together, fighting for space, all legs and arms. Bailey was torn between horror and a kind of maniacal amusement.

And then he was inside her, thrusting, and she was trying to keep her head from banging into the door. It felt good, so good. She grabbed his buttocks and drove him further.

"Yeah, yeah, babe, yeah," he muttered.

She lost consciousness for a heartbeat. Her eyes snapped open. Did she go out for a moment? They were still at it, and Penske was panting hard, close to climax.

Birth control.

God. Shit. *What?*

What's wrong with you?

"You can't come inside me! I'm not on the pill!"

"Oh, babe," he groaned, pumping his seed into her.

"Oh, *shit.*"

He collapsed atop her. She tried to think through the haze enveloping her. *Think.*

What just happened?

You had sex in the parking lot.

She moaned in disbelief. Had the bartender spiked her drink? Something was off.

Penske rose on his hands and pulled out of her, yanking up his boxers and pants.

"You were pretty wet," he said.

"I told you not to come."

"I couldn't help myself. You got me going so hard."

"Somethin's wrong. My head is so fuzzy."

"The booze."

"No, it's . . . I think I've been . . . roofied."

He laughed in disbelief. "Roofied? Bullshit. You'd be unconscious."

"Not necessarily . . ."

"Come on. Let's go to Danny O's."

"Don't think I can."

"You serious? You think your drink was spiked?" He moved his head back and forth. "I feel a little drunk myself. Maybe . . . huh . . ."

It was so difficult to converse, to think, to do anything. Her skirt was still in the footwell, where Penske had thrown it. She knew enough to feel embarrassed. "My clothes . . ."

"Lemme help you."

He picked up her underwear and handed it to her. With an effort, she got into a sitting position and slowly pulled the panties on.

"Sumpin's really wrong. I think . . . I need to go to Emergency . . ."

"Here." He handed her the wrinkled skirt. "I'll drive you."

"Wha? Wha? You can't drive! We need . . . Uber . . . or sumpin."

"You got a gun in this car?"

"Uh . . . um . . . what?"

Penske was out of the back seat and climbing into the driver's seat, punching the button for the glove box. "You do!" he said, pulling out her service revolver.

"Stop!" She sat up bolt upright.

"Want me to go kill him? The bartender? I think he fucked with us."

"*No!* Whad's wrong wit you?" She yanked on her skirt, struggling to get it on.

When she was dressed, she climbed out of the car, staggered a bit, knocked on the driver's door, but when Penske seemed enamored of her gun, she lurched around to the passenger side, yanked the door open. Distantly she heard people coming out of Lundeen's, and she dropped into the seat and slammed the door shut.

"Gimme that," she said, putting a hand out for her Glock.

"Is it loaded?"

"Yes."

"Wow. You really carry a gun." He handed it back to her, almost reluctantly. The glove box was open, and he glanced inside. "Is that your journal?"

Bailey took the gun back. "Yep." She put the gun in the box and snapped it closed.

"No shit. Can I see it?"

"No."

"You want to make love again?"

She tried to focus on him. It was difficult. He seemed remarkably sober all of a sudden. "I gotta figure out whad ta do already."

"You mean, like the morning-after pill? Hey, maybe we're making a baby. Would that be so bad?"

"You're nuts, Penske."

"You got any handcuffs?"

"Left 'em at the station. We're here . . . the reune . . . the reune," she tried to explain.

"You're really messed up." He laughed. "How much did you drink?"

"You know . . . you . . ."

But then he was kissing her, and she was passing out.

I need help . . . was her last thought.

Delta looked at the clock. 1:00 a.m.

She lay in the bed beside her husband, who was snoring to beat the band—the same song that always played when he drank too much. She'd left the drapes open and cracked the window, and outside a shy three-quarter moon was playing hide-and-seek behind trails of wispy clouds. When the clouds would disappear, the view of their backyard and Owen's play structure—mostly constructed for use when he was older—was thrown into sharp relief.

She threw back the covers after a few more minutes when she realized she would never fall asleep. It was still fairly early, anyway. Tanner had just gone deep with the drinks and flamed out early, while she'd come home and relieved her mother from babysitting duty, then made herself a cup of chamomile tea. She hadn't drunk enough wine to feel the effects, but she'd ended up with a blasting headache anyway. She'd then looked in on Owen, who slept on his stomach with his legs tucked in and his little butt pushed upward, one arm slung around his favorite stuffed dog, Doggie. She'd tried to keep him sleeping on his back, as recommended, but once he'd found he could flip over, that was the way he stayed, no matter how many times she tried to put him on his back again. This time, she checked his breathing and determined he was fine.

She'd been half-asleep when Tanner stumbled in, declaring loudly, "You left me," as he moved into their en suite bath, as if it had been some kind of surprise. Or maybe it was a rebuke that she'd taken the car and forced him to find another way home. When he climbed into bed and threw an arm over her and promptly fell asleep, she picked up his limp hand and flung it away from herself. Sleep had eluded her after that, so that was the first time she'd tiptoed down the hall and peeked into Owen's room. She settled him on his back that time as well, only to watch him snuggle into his favorite position, with his legs tucked under and his butt upward.

Her love for her husband might have faded away, but her love for her son was monumental. Mega-fierce. All she lived for.

Now she asked herself: Could she imagine a world without Tanner but with Owen? Would Tanner even allow it? He professed to love Owen, and did, probably, as best he could, given that all love was a diluted emotion for Tanner Stahd.

But could she do it . . . manage without him?

The thought of just her and Owen was heady indeed.

She wished Tanner was *just gone.*

Dreamily, she thought about how convenient it would be if Tanner should die. Poof, gone, leaving her with his business and, most of all, Owen, with free rein to rear him any way she chose.

There was a scratch pad on the end of the kitchen counter near the door to the garage. Her eye fell on it, and she picked it up. A moment later, she searched through the junk drawer next to the stove for a pen. She found one that advertised Woody's Auto Body.

Sitting back down, she thought for a moment, then wrote:

She wanted him dead. It was much simpler than divorce, much cleaner, and she would end up with so much more than if they had to split up what they owned together. She thought about poison, or a drug overdose, but that seemed much too risky. Too traceable. An accident of some kind would be best. He owned a gun, though he didn't keep it loaded now that they had a child, a little boy named . . . Zachary . . . but no one knew he'd taken the bullets out. He kept the gun at work, in a hiding place in his desk. If the nurses and receptionist at the clinic knew of it, they kept their mouths shut.

She planned his murder. Every day, every moment when she was awake, she planned and planned and planned. And every day that went by just convinced her more that he had to go. Her anger grew as she plotted. A gun didn't seem like the right weapon. She wanted to bash him over the head with a candlestick . . . the fireplace poker . . . the baseball bat he still revered from his long-ago days in Little League.

Delta sat up and looked at the words, scratching out the candlestick and fireplace poker. Too old-time melodramatic. She moved into Tanner's office—her office, where she did all the book-keeping, but they called it his, naturally—and opened the laptop on the desk, quickly inserting what she'd just written into the word-processing program.

But as her rage grew, so did her impatience and a sense of macabre need for pain.

And one day, while she was cutting up an apple, the knife slipped and nicked her finger. Blood oozed up in a perfect, circular drop. She sucked on her finger and looked at the knife and dreamed.

Scrolling back up to the top of the page, she wrote: *Blood Dreams* by Delta Smith-Stahd.

Bailey was being pulled along the ground, her bare heels scraping on the tarmac. She tried to lift her head, but it was more than she could accomplish. She couldn't understand what was happening.

Penske . . . Penske was dragging her around the outside of the car.

It was late. Dark. Cold. No other cars around in the lot.

"Whad're ya doin'?" she mumbled.

"Helping you."

He propped her against the car, where she sank into a heap. She blinked a few times until the parking lot, the trees beyond, the back of Lundeen's, all came back into focus.

She slowly found the strength to get to her feet, leaning hard against the car, staring down at her bare feet. "Where're my shoes?" She cleared her throat. She felt better, sharper. "What the hell, Penske?"

"Here. Put 'em on."

Her shoes were on the ground. She slid one foot into one, and then the other, moving carefully.

She still felt weird, as if her body was someone's else's. "Somebody spiked my drink," she said with more certainty.

"I did," he said. "I wanted to have sex with you."

"What?"

"I didn't think you'd go for it, so I gave you a little something."

"Jesus . . . You shit! You can't . . ." She broke off, her building fury melting away as she realized he had her Glock in his hand and was pointing it at her.

"I read your journal while you were out," he said. "Don't scream. I'll shoot you."

"What?" Bailey was in pure shock.

"We've been worried about you for years. About what Carmen might have told you. About what she saw."

"She . . . didn't . . . she . . ."

He looked past her, and she started to turn around, see what he was looking at. There were footsteps and—

Blam!

The shot hit her dead center in the chest.

Blam! Blam!

Twice more.

She smelled the cordite, felt the impact, the bursting pain, saw Penske rushing toward her as she fell forward onto the concrete, smacking her head.

"Took you long enough," she heard him say as he glared at the newcomer. "Thought I was going to have to fuck her again." Then, "Hey! Stop! Shit!"

Blam!

Penske's body folded in on itself, and he collapsed beside her.

She stared into his blue eyes, full of stunned surprise.

Although Penske was murdered by an off-stage assailant, this was later mistakenly ruled to be a murder-suicide. Penske could not have shot himself three times.

And then she knew no more.

PART FOUR

The Unraveling

Chapter 14

Tanner Stahd's been stabbed and is fighting for his life, McCrae thought in disbelief.

That fact still felt unreal, though McCrae had been called to the scene of the clinic stabbing and had spent most of last night processing the scene. After a quick few hours of sleep, he was now heading in to the station.

Twenty-four hours earlier, the day had started out fairly benignly, with a weak sun shining through McCrae's kitchen window, causing his dog, Fido, to move from one warm square of light to another before the sun slid behind some serious rain clouds. By evening, the day had been shattered by the news that there had been a stabbing at the Stahd Clinic, devolving further when the victim was learned to be Tanner himself. Not since Bailey Quintar's death had McCrae felt so uncertain and angry. Bailey's death, along with Justin Penske's, was never far from his consciousness, as it was for probably every one of their classmates who'd been at the reunion that night. It was in the forefront of his boss's, Bob Quintar's . . . Quin's . . . as well, but their hands had been tied from the get-go in any effort to investigate their homicides; Bailey's and

Penske's deaths had been ruled a murder/suicide by the special investigator, who'd swept in and taken over the case.

Now McCrae stood in today's same weak sunlight with a cup of reheated coffee. He drew a long breath and thought back to the night before. Delta had been there, her dress bloodstained, as she stood by Tanner's crumpled body. For a moment, McCrae had thought he was dead, but the ambulance had screamed in a few moments later and taken Tanner to the hospital. After taking her statement, McCrae had seen Delta to the hospital himself, then had gone back to the clinic and made sure, along with two of the four officers on staff at the West Knoll PD, that everything was secure for the night. The tech team was coming this morning to gather what evidence was on scene.

McCrae didn't know how to feel about this attack on an old classmate. What had happened? Had Delta stabbed him? That seemed impossible, but until they learned something different, she would be near the top of the suspect list, if not actually at the top.

Fido gave up his sun-worshipping snooze to trot to where McCrae was standing, his tail sweeping the battered hardwood floor of the three-bedroom ranch he'd inherited from his father. Fido was a black-and-white, long-haired, medium-sized mutt with one blue eye and one brown. He'd been whining piteously the morning McCrae had entered Bailey's apartment following her murder and had had an accident in her kitchen. McCrae had taken the dog outside for another brief potty visit, and after Fido relieved himself, he'd cleaved hard to McCrae's side. The dog knew him from the times Bailey had brought him into the station. He'd attached himself to McCrae as if they'd always been together, even though the animal was clearly confused about what had happened to his mistress. McCrae's chest had been tight as he'd recalled how he'd given Bailey a whole lot of grief about naming her dog Fido. He'd sworn that he would steal the dog away from her and change its name, but when Fido's care was transferred to him, the name stood.

Bailey.

Pouring the remains of his coffee down the sink, McCrae felt the age-old pain of losing her once more. The attack on Stahd brought it all back. Five years since her death, and it was as fresh as ever. At the time, he and Bailey had both been working their way toward detective, but her killing had made it so that he was the only one able to reach that goal. It was decided that Bailey's and Penske's deaths were the result of a murder/suicide, but Quin had never been able to accept that theory, and neither had McCrae. Supposedly, Penske had shot Bailey in the heat of passion; there was ample evidence they'd had sex in the back seat of her car. The theory was they were both drunk, an argument had ensued that had culminated in Penske shooting her outside of the car, and then, in the next moment, consumed with shock and grief, he'd turned her gun on himself. The department had brought in Timothy Hurston, an outside investigator who, despite arriving with glowing credentials, had considered it a lover's quarrel gone nuclear. Statements had been taken from bar patrons, but no one knew anything apart from the fact that Bailey and Penske had been getting pretty friendly with each other before they left together.

The problem was, it just didn't ring true for Bailey. Dead drunk? Sex in the back seat of her car? Penske with her handgun? Something was off.

Penske and Bailey weren't even an item before the night of the reunion. Bailey would have told him.

McCrae had argued that they needed a deeper dive into Bailey's death, which Quin had fervently agreed with. But the powers that be had felt Quin was too unstable to know and ordered him to go on paid administrative leave for nearly six months before bringing him back and eventually moving him up to West Knoll's chief. McCrae's arguments had been ignored for the same reason: he was Bailey's classmate, friend, and coworker and therefore was too close to the case. He'd been forced to curb his desire to correct what he perceived as justice gone wrong, but he'd never forgotten. He'd spent long hours secretly delving into Bailey's death, even if the department considered it a closed case. Two pieces of information stuck out as important to follow up on: one, the bartender on duty at Lundeen's the night of Bailey's death, who had allowed interviews with the special investigator and had offered up that Penske had been pushing Bailey to drink, quit his job three weeks after the homicide and disappeared into the ether; and two, Bailey's journal was missing. Quin had made a big fuss about the journal, had said she sometimes kept it in her car, but no amount of searching had turned it up. Quin had told anyone who would listen that his daughter had written down notes on crimes, which had, a number of times, helped catch the perpetrators, and that she'd also begun the journal after the death of her closest friend, Carmen Proffitt, a death Bailey felt had not fully been an accident. The special investigator had quizzed Quin long and hard on the journal as Quin was the only one besides Bailey who'd seen her notes, but he'd been unable to give any information that could be construed as conclusive, and therefore that line of inquiry was dropped.

McCrae, like Quin, knew how much that journal had been a part of Bailey, and how much

Bailey had believed Carmen's death was due to unnamed forces and pressures. McCrae had never really accepted Bailey's theories; she'd damn near blamed everyone at the barbeque for Carmen's death. But why had Penske killed her? Had Bailey learned something about him that had harkened back to Carmen? The special investigator had intimated that McCrae was just looking for something or someone to blame when he posed the question to him.

"You're looking for zebras when there are just horses," Timothy Hurston had said, with that superior smirk that McCrae had wanted to smack from his supercilious face. Instead, he'd begun his own underground investigation, which Quin understood and secretly encouraged. Bailey's father had never gotten over feeling that more could be done, and McCrae had worked behind the scenes, mostly on his own time, trying to trace the bartender, James Carville. By coincidence, he'd just discovered a solid lead on the man's current whereabouts when Delta's call came through about the attack on Tanner.

His first thought had been: Are the two crimes related? How could they be?

His second: *How could they not be?*

Now he'd had time to think that over. Maybe he was seeing zebras instead of horses. Maybe Bailey's death was unrelated. A romantic, alcohol-fueled interlude gone horribly wrong?

Or maybe it had something to do with her being a cop? Penske, it turned out, had once had a relationship with Nia Crassley, the youngest Crassley daughter, who may very well have been underage at the time. No one was saying for sure, especially not Nia, but Bailey, who'd tried for years to corral the Crassley miscreants, might have learned something that drove the last nail in Penske's coffin, forcing him to kill her to hide his secrets. Or maybe one of the Crassleys was involved with Penske in a setup to kill Bailey. McCrae had tried to talk to them, preferably alone, though the Crassleys preferred to face the cops as a group. They'd either laughed their asses off at his theories or acted like they were all deaf, dumb, and blind.

One of the Crassleys had trapped Bailey in an alley once, determined to show her what it meant to be with a real man, but Bailey had wriggled her way out of that one with a swift knee to his groin and a couple sharp elbows to his neck. Grudges were held. But time had taken care of that particular Crassley. Little Dan, who was six-three and about three hundred pounds, had gotten himself shot in a road-rage confrontation in eastern Oregon where the man he'd flipped off on one of those long, empty two-lane highways had chased him down in his truck, run him off the road, and put a bullet in his massive belly.

Little Dan had not survived.

But there were a helluva lot of other Crassleys who were still around who didn't much like the law and who remembered how Bailey had gotten the best of their dear, departed brother.

McCrae had posited that maybe there was more to Bailey's and Penske's deaths than met the eye, had gone at the Crassleys himself, but none of the higher-ups had been interested in listening to him, so McCrae had been forced to leave things alone. The DA had gone with Hurston's murder/suicide theory all the way, and no charges were brought against anyone else. Bailey Quintar had been murdered, one of their own, and there was sadness and a thirst for revenge, but her killer was dead, too. That was the prevailing theory and answer, and there was nothing more to be investigated. It was Justin Penske who killed her. All by himself. No Crassleys or anyone else involved.

Convenient that Penske couldn't answer any questions . . .

Fido had a dog door that McCrae had cut into his back door. It was big enough for the dog and maybe a very small person or child, which could be an issue if someone really wanted to get at him, but they would have to deal with the dog first, and Fido had grown territorial since Bailey had disappeared from his life. He guarded McCrae's house as if it were Fort Knox, and though he was polite when people were over, he wasn't willing to be won by a stranger just because they chortled and giggled over his name, like that made him cuddly or something. Fido didn't trust anyone, and getting past his defenses took years. McCrae's last girlfriend had lasted less than a year, and she and Fido had had a healthy respect for each other, but that was as far as it went.

"Hey, boy," McCrae said as he gathered up his wallet, Glock, and keys. He didn't need to wear a uniform these days. Mostly it was slacks and an open-collared shirt, though he kept a suit coat and tie in his locker at work in case he had to conduct an interview. People were usually both alarmed and respectful when an officer showed up in a suit. Anything less and they were likely to think the officer didn't mean business.

Fido looked at McCrae balefully. The dog knew he was being left behind, as ever. He was not a police dog, and while McCrae was at work, the dog stayed home. The same as when Fido lived with Bailey.

"Take care of things while I'm gone," McCrae told him as he headed into the garage and his black Explorer. Fido, apparently over being left behind, emitted an enthusiastic bark, a kind of "Yes, sir!" that brought a brief smile to McCrae's lips. The West Knoll Police Department had a couple of navy-blue Trailblazers with stylistic gold stripes stenciled with the name of the department on the sides that the officers traded around. McCrae preferred his own vehicle, but like the dressing-for-success rule, people liked to see police officers show up in police vehicles. He didn't blame them. With all the scam artists and grifters and cheaters and overall crooks trying to separate you from your money or your life, it was hard to know whom to trust, but he was glad, nevertheless, that he was in the Explorer this morning.

McCrae stopped by Smith & Jones, the local grocery store owned by Delta Smith-Stahd's parents. They had a counter in the back with a half-dozen stools and an array of doughnuts, coffee cakes, and general baked goods for their morning customers, along with some decent serve-yourself coffee from an electric urn. McCrae ordered a cruller to go from the girl behind the counter and poured himself another cup of coffee in a disposable cup, then headed for the door. He didn't see either of Delta's parents, which was just as well. Though a part of him wanted to ask about Delta, he was undoubtedly going to see her very soon. They'd barely scratched the surface on the events of last night in the ensuing chaos. Today would be the day.

The West Knoll Police Department was a one-story, U-shaped building that looked out at a whole lot of nothing. Empty fields that had once been part of a large farm, the land sold and parceled into lots, the lots used for building homes . . . well, two or three of the houses had sold before the whole project had gone bust and the land turned fallow and choked with weeds. Some enterprising student of agriculture had taken advantage of the fact that the land was just sitting there and had planted row upon row of onions. McCrae had watched him tend to his crop, assuming, like everyone else, that he'd leased the land for farming. Not so. After several years of bumper harvests, the land finally sold, and that year's onions were plowed under. Turned out the would-be farmer had never had any legal right to use the property, but that didn't stop him from suing over his lost crop. McCrae wasn't quite sure where that lawsuit currently stood, but since then, the land had turned back to weeds; maybe it was still going through the court system. You had to give the guy credit for the balls it took to run a scam right behind the police station and get away with it for years.

McCrae polished off the cruller and drank most of the coffee long before he entered the station and stopped by Quin's open office door. Bailey's father's gray hair was clipped short in a circle around his head, and his bald pate gleamed beneath the overhead lights. Ninety percent of the time, he wore a hat. Now, he swiveled in his chair and said, "We shoulda brought her in last night."

"How's Tanner doing?" McCrae asked, ignoring that. If there'd been a change, he would've been notified on his cell, but he wanted Quin's take.

"Alive. Not awake. Corolla's outside his room."

Jed Corolla was close to thirty, acted like he was fifteen, looked like a cop from the seventies with a huge mustache and a kind of swagger that made McCrae smile inside. Guard duty was one of his few specialties.

Quin was the unofficial head of West Knoll PD since they'd lost their chief to the county sheriff's department. McCrae was the unofficial second in command. They'd both been recommended for permanent titles by the mayor's office and were slated for a swearing-in ceremony neither particularly wanted. West Knoll was large enough to require an additional two officers and some administrative personnel, but small enough to be completely in the hands of the mayor, a stocky woman with a big smile and a heavy hand when necessary. She didn't like Quin much, McCrae even less. She'd worked hand in glove with the last chief, and now seemed to feel he'd been promoted away from her, lessening her power. Since the last chief's departure, Mayor Kathy had been taking this "demotion" out on Quin and McCrae. Luckily, Quin was impervious. Bailey's death had made him immune to any sensitivity to criticism he might have once felt. He had another daughter, Lill, whom he saw occasionally, but their relationship had never been the same as his with her sister. Since Bailey's death, he'd just moved doggedly and relentlessly forward, catching "bad hombres" and bringing them to justice.

McCrae wasn't much troubled by Mayor Kathy, either. He was diligent at his job and didn't let her know about any delving into outside investigations he might be doing.

A bigger problem was the relationship he'd had with one of the women in West Knoll PD's administration, the one that had lasted less than a year. Corinne had grown tired of the "no ring on my finger" nature of that relationship, and after their breakup, she'd moved on to a new guy within a month. To date, she treated McCrae with cool indifference, though he'd felt the weight of her stare more than once as soon as his back was turned. She was a little intense, and he was relieved she was with someone else. He'd made a mistake dating her. He knew better than to see someone within the department, and he'd done it anyway.

Briefly he thought back to Ellie O'Brien. They'd had that one night together at the barbeque, which might have been the kind of memory that gave you a smile afterward, but it had been forever tainted for McCrae since Carmen's death. Seeing Ellie at the reunion had ruined that memory some more. She'd become more of what she'd been in high school: serious, intense, and wearing a chip on her shoulder. He'd felt he needed to say something to her, and it had gone okay, with him teasing about her being the Channel Seven weather girl. She'd been trying to make the leap to full-fledged reporter, chasing stories around Portland and all of Oregon, for that matter, though she still didn't get much camera time. Whenever he'd caught her on screen, she looked good, though it seemed she was always forcing a smile. That intensity that drove her still showed. At the reunion, he'd thought about talking to her some more, but had ended up leaving shortly after Delta and Amanda had; he'd been uncomfortable with the guys that night, most of whom were diving deep into regression while they were there, especially Tanner.

McCrae sank heavily into his desk chair, feeling the weight of his sleep-deprived night. He'd stayed at the Stahd Clinic into the morning hours with the tech team and made sure, along with another officer, that Tanner's business was secure before he left. Tanner Stahd. He shook his head. What had happened last night? Who'd stabbed him so viciously? What, if anything, had Tanner done to incite such violence?

McCrae grimaced. He'd never been particularly close friends with Tanner or either of his toadies, Penske and Sumpter. At the reunion, Tanner had gravitated to Amanda, who, in the midst of divorcing her husband, had gravitated right back. He had left Delta to hang with her friends, the remaining Five Firsts, Ellie, and others, while her eyes traveled time and again toward her husband and Amanda. It had been noticed by everyone and had pissed off McCrae. He'd felt for her. It was hard to pretend to be having a good time when your significant other was drunk and all over your nemesis. There were still those rumors floating around the reunion from those last weeks of high school, when Amanda was supposedly pregnant and it was Tanner's child. Whatever the truth of it, Delta, as Tanner's girlfriend, had put on a brave face and dealt with them in her own way.

Amanda and Tanner . . . maybe they'd hooked up after the reunion, even though she'd left early . . . maybe not.

But Bailey was with Penske that night.

And then Bailey was killed, by Penske, and Penske turned the gun on himself?

There was a hell of a lot more to that story.

And now Tanner's been stabbed to within an inch of his life.

McCrae picked up the cell phone he'd laid on his desk and checked the time. 9:30. He got to his feet and headed back to Quin's office, but found it empty. Walking down the hall, he turned right into the break room, where Quin was looking dispiritedly through the windows of the revolving vending machine and its less-than-appealing choices.

"I'm going to stop by the hospital, then I'm going to see Delta," McCrae told him.

Quin looked up at him. "Bring her in. Let's both talk to her. Find out if she knows where his cell phone is."

That was a peculiar piece of the crime scene: no cell phone. Either the attacker had taken it, or it was somewhere other than the clinic or Tanner's car, which had been in the lot. Tanner could have left it at home, or somewhere else, but McCrae was betting the would-be killer had taken it with him, or her, and made sure it couldn't be traced.

McCrae asked, "What about the chances of another assigned special investigator, given that we both know Tanner?" *And Delta.*

"You wanna do that again? I don't wanna do that again."

"No, I don't wanna do that again," McCrae agreed wholeheartedly.

"Well, I'm in charge, at least for the moment, so we'll do it our way."

The corners of McCrae's mouth lifted. He hadn't seen Quin so strongly determined since his daughter's death had knocked the life from him. "Okay."

" 'Course, Stahd Senior's been making phone calls. He thinks a lot of things should be done that we're not doing and isn't afraid to say so. He wants to control the information."

McCrae nodded. Which was probably why Quin had taken such a proactive stance. *All to the good.*

Quin added, "Stahd suggested maybe the wife did it. I get the feeling he's never liked her much."

Or maybe he liked her too much.

Delta had always had that appeal, something earthy and real beneath her beauty. It had tugged at McCrae last night when she'd been so distraught. He could imagine that same appeal working on Dr. Stahd Senior, whose young wife who'd left him was far closer to Delta's age than his.

Quin added, "Channel Seven hasn't reported the stabbing yet."

"They will." Ellie would be on it at some level. And as soon as she found out, she would make a beeline for the West Knoll PD.

Quin grunted in agreement.

The break-room television was pretty much always on, but it was surprisingly dark this morning. No one had seen fit to turn it on, apparently, so McCrae grabbed the remote and pointed it at the screen. It was already tuned to Channel Seven, and the station was airing some kind of cooking show competition on which two women were chopping fast and furiously, screeching about the passing time. Not inter-

293

ested, McCrae switched it off and headed back to his office, a cramped space just big enough for a desk and a chair. He opened his computer and cleaned up a few e-mails, his mind still on Delta. Her hands had been bloody. She'd picked up the knife. Said she'd fallen on it.

And she'd been wearing a light, lemony scent that smelled of summer.

"Jesus," he muttered, shaking his head at himself.

He checked his desk-phone messages, and lo and behold, there was one from Ellie.

"McCrae," her voice said in that intense way she had. "Tanner Stahd was stabbed last night?" she accused, as if it were somehow his fault that she'd apparently just heard. "I've checked at the hospital, and they gave me the runaround. Call me. Let me know what's going on. I'm about to storm that place if they don't let me see him." She left her number.

McCrae ran a hand over his face. Channel Seven had always used Pauline Kirby as their reporter at large, but Ellie seemed to be trying to take over her job. Pauline was older, nosy, autocratic, and somewhat deceitful in her pursuit of a story, a real pain in the ass, but Ellie . . . he sensed she could be worse. If anyone could breach the hospital's defenses, it was her.

Well, it was time to check on the patient himself. He needed to see what Tanner's status was in person, and if Ellie would be allowed to see him. He listened to his other two messages. The first was from Corolla, who'd turned away Ellie O'Brien—a reporter, his voice warned—when she'd tried to see Tanner. Well, that answered that, at least so far. The second was from Dr. Lester Stahd, who wanted to make sure West Knoll's finest weren't allowing Delta Stahd anywhere near his son; if they did and Tanner took a turn for the worse, he would hold West Knoll PD and Christopher McCrae personally responsible.

McCrae snorted. People and families under crisis said a lot of things out of fear. He knew enough about Tanner's father to think the man was a total prick, but he put that aside for the moment and gave him the benefit of the doubt. Glancing at the clock, he passed over his desk phone in favor of his cell as he phoned the number Delta had given him the night before. The call rang five times, then was sent to voice mail, where Delta's voice said, "You've reached Delta Stahd. Leave a message." At the beep, McCrae said, "Delta, it's Chris McCrae. We'd like to get your statement about last night. Is it possible for you to come into the station today? I'll be here late morning and all afternoon. This is my cell number . . ."

Delta stared at her ringing cell phone on her kitchen counter, not recognizing the number. She was paralyzed with fear. It wasn't the hospital. That would show on the LCD screen. A reporter? A harasser? A supposed friend? The word was already out, and she had a number of e-mails or texts from the early risers, apparently, offering advice and good thoughts. "I'm so incredibly sorry, Delta. We're all here for you. If you need anything, call," from Miss Billings, signed Clarice, along with her number. "Tragedies are so difficult to comprehend. It takes time, but it gets better," from Bailey's mom and Principal Kiefer, husband and wife since Bailey's death. She'd also heard, surprisingly, from Woody Deavers's ex-wife, Crystal Gilles, who had her e-mail address from the reunion form Delta had filled out, apparently: "Don't let the police bully you. They're good at that" was her blunt advice. A number of do-gooders had also sent messages about God being on her side and "better days" coming.

Reluctantly, she pressed the PLAY button and listened to the message. McCrae's voice. *Come into the station . . . we'd like to get your statement . . .*

Tears burned her eyes, and she dashed them away angrily. Last night she'd been in a state of shock. Today the weight on her chest felt like ten tons. *Someone tried to kill Tanner!* It was impossible. Impossible! But it had happened.

The memory of him lying on the floor, the

blood seeping through his white shirt, made her whole body quiver. This morning, she'd stumbled into the shower on a still-tender ankle at the crack of dawn, before Owen was up, then had needed to lean against the wall to support herself. She was distracted by the scratch on her palm from the knife, almost forgetting to get Owen his breakfast. She gave up the idea of frying him an egg and let him eat cereal in front of the TV, something she was normally dead set against. But she was a wreck, barely hanging on. Owen had noticed something was wrong, so she'd told him she wasn't feeling all that hot—which wasn't a lie—and he'd accepted that and gone back to the cartoons. When he was finished with breakfast, she'd taken him to pre-K and had braced herself for the looks, stares, and maybe even some shunning from the staff, but they clearly hadn't heard yet. Maybe they would understand that she had nothing to do with the attack on her husband? Or maybe they would think she was to blame? They knew some about the fact that she and Tanner hadn't been getting along for quite a while. It was impossible to hide.

But all had gone normally at the school. On the drive over, Owen had asked where his father was, which had thrown Delta because Tanner was gone a lot, and usually Owen didn't seem to notice.

"Where's Daddy?" he'd popped out with.

Delta had looked at him in his car seat through the rearview mirror. His brown hair hadn't been combed all that well and stuck up in places, and though she'd managed to get him into his jeans and his favorite T-shirt, the blue one with the shark on the pocket, there was something slapdash about his clothes as well. She was torn between telling him the basic truth, that Tanner was in the hospital after a terrible accident—she wasn't about to say he'd been attacked—and covering up the whole thing until later this evening, when she could have him to herself for a few hours to spin some less-frightening tale. She chose the latter, telling Owen that her father was out of town for a while. If she told him his father was in the hospital, Owen wouldn't stand for it. He would demand that she take him to see his father, and Delta couldn't do that.

After dropping him at pre-K, she'd opted to drive to the hospital herself, only to be turned away by a policeman guarding the door. No visitors at this time, he'd said, eyeing her like he thought she might try to rush him. But he did inform her that Tanner was alive and being tended to. She'd tried to find a nurse to possibly glean more information, but apart from learning he was stable, she got the same runaround. She sensed no one wanted her near him, so she'd had to give up seeing him for the moment. Maybe she could call on McCrae later, see if he could help her get in, but for the moment it was a no go.

She'd just gotten home and was trying to think of anything she might want to eat, but everything she thought of seemed to make her stomach lurch. Then her phone started singing its default ringtone. Filled with dread, she checked the voice mail and learned it was McCrae . . . *We'd like to get your statement . . .*

"Oh, Lord."

Why did you lie about the knife?

She hurried upstairs—at least the ankle was not as injured as she'd originally thought, as it only tweaked a little—and looked at herself in her bathroom mirror. She was washed out, and there were huge circles under her eyes. She'd worked to hide those circles this morning but had been only partially successful. She'd thrown on a pair of jeans and a white shirt that looked like it hadn't even been ironed. Owen wasn't the only one who'd been ragged this morning. Now she changed into a dark blue blouse and reworked her makeup, adding a little more blush than she normally needed. Combing her hair, she clipped it into a ponytail at her nape. Better, she thought critically. If she was going into the lion's den, she needed to feel like she had some armor on.

The knife.

She should've just admitted it was from their set, that Tanner had taken it to work and there was nothing suspicious about it. Whoever had attacked Tanner wouldn't have expected to see the knife. It was just handy. Didn't that mean the crime was spur of the moment? No one would plan to viciously attack someone without a means to do it.

Who attacked Tanner . . . with intent to kill? Who? How? *Why?*

She moaned aloud.

She'd lied about the knife. She'd touched the knife. And then she'd lied about it.

Tell the truth. It always comes out anyway.

Screwing up her courage, Delta phoned back the number, and when McCrae answered, "Hi, Delta," she said quickly, "I can be there this afternoon about two."

"I'll be here."

There was a hesitation on both their parts, and then he told her, "The press knows." She nodded to herself, but before she could say anything else, he added, "Ellie called me."

Who are you? Ellie? . . . You sound about as judgmental . . . McCrae's words. From the night of the barbeque.

"If you would prefer me to pick you up and avoid—"

"No. I'll be there," she told him flatly. "I need to pick my son up at five, but I'll be at your station at two."

Chapter 15

Delta drove to the nearest ATM, took out five hundred dollars, and then went to the mall and into Macy's. She used cash to buy a medium-grade set of knives that came with a wooden-block holder. She took it home and out of the packaging and set it on her counter. It looked so shiny and new that she filled the sink with water and submerged the wooden holder, adding dish detergent. All the while she told herself she was making a huge mistake. She was getting in deeper and deeper for no good reason.

But they'll think it was me. They'll think I tried to kill my husband!

Her heart lurched. Her e-book. *Blood Dreams* . . . Her main character had killed her husband with a knife . . .

But it's an e-book . . . not in print . . . not a best seller . . . just a way to deal with Tanner's cheating . . . it's not real!

"Oh, my God . . . oh, my God . . ."

It was on Amazon and Apple and several other platforms, available for anyone to read, should they choose to. She received a little money for it each month, not much. She wanted to rip it off the platforms and ran upstairs to her computer to do so, then hesitated, afraid. Would it look worse for her if she took it down now? Undoubtedly. She left the book alone.

She walked back downstairs with heavy footsteps. Picked up the wooden knife block and dried it off. She put the knives back in it. When the holder dried, some of its glossy, oiled surface had bleached out and lost its luster, and there were spots darker than others, making it seem used, although it wasn't completely dry, so the jury was still out on whether it would pass as older.

This is a mistake, she told herself, her fingers clasping the edge of the farmhouse sink while she leaned forward, drawing several long breaths, before standing erect once more.

She realized she'd splashed water on herself, so she changed into her third blouse, this one a deep ochre that worked with her darker complexion and hair. She wore her same blue jeans as she headed downstairs, and just about the time she was ready to leave, her doorbell rang. She nearly dropped her cell at the sudden pealing through the house.

Her pulse sped up, and she scurried back upstairs to look out Owen's window, which had the best angle to the front door. Two people. A man and a woman. Her eyes scanned the streets, and down the way she saw a news van. Not Channel Seven. Not Ellie O'Brien. But a news van all the same.

The vultures were circling.

Wildly she wondered if she should have taken McCrae up on his offer for an escort. There was nowhere to hide.

The reporters gave up ringing her bell after a few minutes, but she watched them mosey down the street, talking to each other. Another man carrying a camera slid open the door of the news van and joined them.

Delta walked toward the stairway once more and sat down heavily on the top step. She had an instant image of Tanner on the floor—him bleeding, the knife, the bubbling stab wounds—and felt faint. She put her head between her knees and inhaled and exhaled several times.

A moment later, she ran to the bathroom and lost the little bit of blueberry muffin she'd managed to pick up from a Starbucks at the mall. Rinsing out her mouth, she took a look at herself through watery eyes. Her makeup was still in place, even if her skin had leached a few shades whiter. She realized abstractedly that she'd lost all that baby weight from having Owen and then some. Now she looked almost gaunt.

With shaking fingers, she called McCrae's line. He picked up on the second ring.

"I need a ride," she said.

"Be there in twenty," he answered, and was gone.

• • •

Ellie was in a silent, quivering rage. "Say that again," she said in a voice that could cut glass.

"Pauline's on this story," Ed, one of the assistant producers, told her.

"But it's in my hometown. About one of my classmates. A guy I know really well!" *A guy I slept with.* "No one's better for this one than I am."

He shrugged and looked around the studio break room. Ellie had been waiting, loaded for bear, and Ed was the first guy who'd walked through the doors since she'd gotten the phone call from Rob, who was now her producer: "Pauline Kirby's on the Tanner Stahd story. She's at Laurelton General now."

"That's *my* story, Rob. I've been to the hospital. I called the West Knoll police. I know a guy there, too. An officer who does investigations as well. I *know* these people."

"That's why Pauline's on it. You're too close. You can do an in-depth interview later."

"Later?" she'd practically shrieked.

"Later," he confirmed, and hung up.

Once upon a time, Rob had been her friend, but now he'd bonded with Coco, Alton's wife . . . *still* his wife, though Alton had sworn he was leaving her. But Rob and Alton were cut from the same cloth: both had wives from rich families, and it was sooo much easier to just go along and keep the wealthy ball-and-chains happy.

Still, this was Coco's doing. She hated Ellie for having an affair with her husband, and although Alton had wriggled his way back to his wife, tail between his legs, leaving Ellie to the stares and whispers around the station, Coco was still determined to ruin her. Coco owned Alton now. He'd sworn he was leaving her, but the man had no spine. The only good thing was that Ellie had worked her ass off over the last few years, and Coco had no authority at the station, apart from her family owning a significant block of shares, that is. The fact was that Alton was getting older and losing viewership, and Pauline Kirby was no spring chicken either. It was Ellie whose star was rising, and Rob *knew* it. He was just pandering to Coco and his own wife. The fact that Pauline was covering Tanner's stabbing instead of Ellie was just throwing an old dog a bone.

"I'm not giving up," she'd told anyone who cared to listen. "This is my story." Most of the other employees ignored her, but they were all on the same slow-moving, loser track. Ellie wasn't going to let that happen to her.

But then, to add insult to injury, the hospital spokesperson who'd ignored her earlier had actually talked on camera to Pauline, confirming that Tanner was still unconscious but stable. Pauline was probably already at the West Knoll police station, talking to McCrae, the rat fink.

Fuck him, she thought. She was so furious she could spit.

Ed scooted back out of the break room, and Ellie paced the floor.

This *was* her story.

Fuck Coco, too. And Pauline. And Rob.

Her cell phone rang, and she snatched it out of her purse, only partially surprised by the name that popped up. "Ellie O'Brien," she snapped out.

"Are you reporting on Tanner's stabbing case?" Amanda Forsythe asked. She'd gone back to her maiden name after the divorce from Hal Brennan, a divorce she'd managed to come out of much richer, though she'd sworn at the reunion she was the one with the money. Brennan, being a partner, might not have been the lawyer Amanda was, but he'd certainly had money.

She almost lied. She wanted to so badly she could taste it. But it wouldn't help her. "They put Pauline on it."

"Why?"

"What are you looking for, Amanda?" she demanded impatiently.

"I want to know who did it." There was something beneath her carefully enunciated words. Emotion? Amanda? Not likely.

"And sue the hell out of them?" Ellie half-joked.

"Our classmates keep dying, Ellie."

"Well . . . yes, but over fifteen years that's kind

306

of what happens. There's a natural attrition rate in any—"

"Two were killed. Possibly three, if you read Bailey's journal."

"Bailey's journal . . . what are you talking about? Did you read it?" Ellie was surprised into asking.

"We all know what was in it. Suppositions. Theories."

"Heartbreak over losing her best friend in the world," Ellie reminded her.

"I want to know who stabbed Tanner."

"Well, so do I. Though I don't think you're going to find that out in Bailey's journal. Her *missing* journal, as I recall. Is it still missing? Maybe we should ask Tanner when he wakes up," said Ellie.

She said "Mmm," in a way that sounded as if she was worried that wasn't going to happen. "Have you talked to McCrae?"

Ellie ground her teeth. Amanda, whom she hardly ever spoke with, was grilling her, not the other way around. "I left him a message."

"But you're not covering the stabbing?"

"I'm going to go to the hospital to see Tanner as soon as I can," she declared determinedly. She would do her own investigation. Fuck the whole damn station, too.

"I'll go with you. I'll call Zora."

"Zora?"

"She and Brian have connections."

More than you?

"If we can't get in to see him, I'll bet she can," Amanda added.

Ellie considered. They couldn't tell her she wasn't on this story. They couldn't stop her. They could fire her, but Alton would stand up for her . . . wouldn't he?

You just said Coco owns him. Will he really be there for you?

But if you just stand by, they'll probably fire you anyway.

"Let's try to get in to see him tomorrow," Ellie said.

"Okay," was the satisfied answer, and Ellie fleetingly wondered if Amanda was playing her somehow.

McCrae drove to Delta's in a controlled rush. He'd heard the fear in her voice. He could well imagine that she was beginning to be harassed, and it certainly didn't help that Tanner's father was leading the vanguard against her.

When he got to her home, he saw the news van and several people standing outside. They all looked at him as he turned into her driveway. One news van so far. There could be more.

He pulled up on the side of the house, driving on the pad alongside her garage until the nose of his Explorer was far enough past the garage's rear wall to leave him a clear view of her back door. As he climbed from the driver's seat, Delta suddenly appeared outside on the porch. She had the strap of her purse slung over her shoulder and wore a white, fuzzy jacket, more form than function, teamed with a pair of black slacks and flats. Mirrored sunglasses perched on her nose. As she hurried down the porch steps, she had the haunted look of a celebrity trying to evade the paparazzi.

He was around the car and opening the door for her. She slid into the seat as a man and a woman appeared behind them closer to the front of the garage.

McCrae was by the driver's door. "Police," he said, showing his badge.

They stopped short but didn't leave.

"I'm going to back out of here, and you need to move yourself from the property."

"Is Ms. Stahd under arrest?"

"No," he said shortly.

"Are you taking her in for questioning?"

McCrae climbed into his vehicle, put it in reverse, and slowly backed up. The reporters reluctantly walked backward into the street, but they looked as if they might just stay, regardless of his order. He wondered if he kept moving if he would actually hit one of them. Barely bump them and then they could scream foul. Sue the department for millions.

But they seemed to get it that he wasn't going to let them intimidate him, and they kept slowly moving out of the way. Their cameraman directed his lens on Delta through the passenger window, though, and she ducked her chin toward McCrae.

"Can you get me in to see my husband?" she asked quietly as they pulled away.

"Currently no visitors are allowed. I was at the hospital earlier and saw Tanner. No change."

"Is he going to live?"

"I don't know."

McCrae had learned one of the stab wounds had grazed Tanner's heart. There was talk of surgery. A punctured lung that had collapsed and been reinflated. He was being closely monitored, but Les Stahd, Tanner's father, had come into the station and demanded to see his son, and Quin had allowed it. The elder Dr. Stahd's skin was gray, his jaw slackened. McCrae hadn't seen the man in years, but it was clear his son's serious injuries had aged him.

"Those reporters . . ." Delta looked over at him as they drove away. Her eyes were hidden behind the glasses, but her mouth quivered slightly. "What have they been saying? Have you seen the news?"

"They're reporting that Tanner was stabbed at his clinic. They've been camped out at Laurelton General."

"I didn't do it," she blurted, as if she couldn't contain herself any longer.

He acknowledged with a nod. Until he knew more, there was nothing much to say.

She seemed to expect him to add something, but when he didn't, she fell silent the rest of the way to the station as well. A news van was waiting there, too. Channel Seven.

"Ellie?" Delta questioned, stricken.

But it was Pauline Kirby standing outside the front doors, facing a camera as if she were about to report. Her chin was lifted in that somewhat arrogant way of hers, and she was getting one last brush of her dark hair. She'd been an institution at the station for many years, although Ellie had made some inroads, as McCrae had seen her a time or two reporting on something more than the weather. Not often, but sometimes.

He whisked Delta in through the back and took her to what was considered an interrogation room at the West Knoll station: the only room besides the break room with a table where any kind of discussion or meeting could take place.

Quin entered, followed by Corinne Esterly, of the administrative staff, who brought them all chilled bottles of water.

Corinne was also the ex McCrae had become involved with at the station, his last relationship.

Corinne's eyes strayed to Delta, who'd taken off her sunglasses as she sagged into a chair.

311

Corinne was pretty in an elfin way, with curly, light brown hair. She was small and wiry and had a tendency to swell herself up whenever she met another woman. She was staring at Delta, who, though she clearly had had the stuffing knocked out of her and was paler than normal, had a natural beauty that couldn't be denied. McCrae watched Corinne swell up and thrust out her chest before she was thanked by Quin, her cue to leave.

When she was gone, Quin looked at Delta and asked, "How're you doing?"

Her dark eyes were bright with unshed tears. She reached for her water bottle, unscrewed the top, took a sip. "I'm okay."

"If Tanner stabilizes, we'll allow you to see him."

"Thank you."

Quin hesitated. This was emotional for him, too. Bailey and Delta had been close friends once upon a time.

McCrae said, "We want to find who stabbed your husband."

"I do, too," she responded quickly.

Quin first asked her if she knew where his cell phone might be. She thought about it, then slowly shook her head.

"He always had it with him," she said.

"Maybe it's at your house?" Quin suggested.

"No, he called me on it that night from the clinic."

"You're sure he was at the clinic?"

"Well, yeah. I was there within a few minutes after I spoke to him."

Quin absorbed that, then asked, "So, after you got to the clinic, what happened?"

Delta drew a breath, then told him about her discovery of Tanner collapsed on the floor, the knife, the myriad of wounds, the blood . . . She answered most of his questions monosyllabically, the color receding further from her face as she relived the scene.

McCrae stepped in and said, "We want to get a picture of Tanner's life before the attack, get an idea what the last few weeks have been like, how things have been going in his life, your marriage, like that."

She nodded, taking another swallow. She looked scared. McCrae didn't blame her. It was scary to be in a police interview. He just hoped it wasn't from something more serious.

"My husband and I love each other," she began, "but we've hit a rough spot in our marriage. Since Tanner took over his father's clinic, it's taken a lot of work to stay . . . happy. But let me say this clearly: I did not attack my husband. I found him lying on the floor with all that blood." She shook her head. "My hand touched the knife, and I got a cut." She lifted her palm. "But it was on the floor already. I don't know who would do this to him. I mean, why? I just don't understand."

313

McCrae glanced at Quin, who was watching Delta closely. McCrae couldn't tell if he was moved by her words, as his face hadn't changed expression in the slightest.

"That's what we aim to find out," McCrae told her.

Quin asked, "Is there anything else, say over the last year or so . . . anything you can remember that maybe stood out? Something that seemed off?"

Delta deliberated, then slowly shook her head, before remembering another party that she and Tanner had attended about six months prior. Tanner and another man had had some words about the way their cars were parked, how Tanner had pulled into a parking spot too fast and punched his car into the pickup across from him. Minor damage to the pickup, although Tanner's hood had lifted and buckled and the radiator had needed replacing. "They tossed some insults back and forth, but it didn't last long."

Quin moved on, but then circled back and seemed to ask further questions that really covered the same ground they'd already gone over. It was all McCrae could do to remain silent.

Finally, they were wrapping up, and Delta had scooted her chair back, when Quin asked, "Where were you just prior to going to the clinic to ostensibly meet your husband?"

"Ostensibly? I *was* meeting my husband. That's

why I was at the clinic." She looked slightly perturbed. "Before that I was at a fund-raiser for Englewood Academy."

"At the Bengal Room?"

"Well . . . uh . . . yes, it started out as a tea and sort of continued," Delta answered, flustered.

McCrae gave Quin a long look. Who'd been feeding him information today?

"And you saw Dean Sutton there?"

Delta regarded him in confusion. "Coach Sutton? No. I . . . was he there? At the Bengal Room?"

"You've talked to Sutton?" McCrae asked Quin, a little surprised he'd kept it from him.

"He called into the department and said he'd seen Mrs. Stahd at the Bengal Room last night with some people."

"We all just went to have a drink," Delta said a bit dazedly. "Seems longer ago than just last night."

"Agreed," McCrae said. He was running on fumes after a night of no sleep, and Tanner's stabbing felt as if it was days ago.

Meanwhile, Delta had grown paler, if that was possible, and had shrunk into her chair. *Something was up there.*

"What did Sutton have to say?" McCrae asked Quin.

"Maybe Delta could tell us," Quin suggested.

"I didn't see him. I wasn't there long. I had to

meet Tanner and relieve my mother from baby-sitting." She licked her lips. "I had a drink, maybe two, and then I left. I wish Coach would've talked to me."

"He said you were busy." Quin was sober.

What the hell? McCrae was feeling tense. He hated being left in the dark, and he really hated seeing Delta look so guilty. He was going to have to talk to Dean Sutton himself.

"I spoke with your receptionist and an assistant who worked at the clinic," Quin switched subjects when Delta didn't respond. "Tia Marvin and Amy Panterra."

"Yes," said Delta.

"You've been on the phone a lot today," McCrae observed to Quin.

"They said your marriage is over," Quin went on, ignoring McCrae, "and that your husband has made advances toward them."

Delta uttered a sound somewhere between a laugh and a moan.

McCrae wanted to burst in and help her. Held himself back, barely.

Quin said, "Dr. Stahd's nurse called the department as well, as soon as she heard. She reiterated what the other women said about the state of your marriage."

"Candy. She has a husband and two teenage boys, all of them over six feet, which kept Tanner from hitting on her. Or maybe she says he went after her, too. I don't really know." Delta gave a twisted smile. "They've all believed our marriage has been on the brink of failure for years."

"And has it?" Quin was relentless.

"I don't think so."

McCrae started, "If Delta—"

"I didn't stab him!" Delta broke in. "I didn't. Someone tried to kill my husband, but it wasn't me. I'll sit here and answer any and all of your questions, but it *wasn't me*. When Tanner wakes up, he'll tell you."

"If he wakes up," said Quin repressively.

McCrae said, "I'll call the hospital and get an update." He wanted to glare at Bob Quintar. It wasn't like the man to barrel forward so coldly, but then anything that had to do with his daughter's death, even peripherally, stirred an unresolved anger and sadness within the man, and Delta, by virtue of being one of Bailey's classmates, a member of the Five Firsts, had reminded him acutely of his loss.

But that didn't make Tanner's attack Delta's fault.

"We're going to find out who's behind the stabbing," McCrae added.

Quin nodded in agreement. "I just have a few more questions."

"More?" Delta asked wearily.

McCrae thought the same thing. It was clear Quin had purposely left him out of the day's developments. Maybe he felt McCrae was too close to Delta to be impartial. There was wisdom in that. He probably would've done the same thing if the situation were reversed. But he didn't have to like it.

"Mr. Sutton said you were flirting with a man at the bar at the Bengal Room," Quin said.

She drew a deep breath and let it out slowly. This, then, was what had made her go pale, McCrae decided.

"*He* was flirting with *me,*" she corrected. "It wasn't anything. I really wish Coach would've said hi to me. I would have liked to see him. He didn't come to the reunion. But now . . ." She swallowed, and for a moment, McCrae worried she was going to break down, but she tightened her lips and her resolve, straightening in her chair.

Quin switched tactics. "You said you and your husband love each other, but you seem to believe your husband has been . . . unfaithful?"

"Marriage is sometimes . . . challenging. But we love each other," Delta said doggedly.

Quin was doling out rope, letting her pick up the slack, before he yanked the line tight in the hopes of pulling her off her feet. He'd done the same thing with suspects more times than McCrae cared to count. But it just felt wrong, him doing it to Delta.

Delta, however, gamely went on with what she

knew about her husband. She seemed to want to set the record straight about their relationship. Mostly Tanner stayed late at work, and therefore she saw him only a few hours a day. She'd caught him once on an angry phone call, but when she'd asked him about it, he'd said that people expected instant miracles, and the only one who could do that was God, so she'd assumed it was one of his patients complaining about the results of his diet supplements. He'd also had several meetings with his father, one of them spilling out of the clinic and to their house after an apparently contentious encounter. The two Stahds hadn't spoken for nearly a month afterward. Delta didn't know what the rift was about but felt it had been over Tanner's running the clinic differently from what the older Dr. Stahd had started.

Quin asked a few more pointed questions, one being if Delta were dating anyone outside the marriage, to which he got a resounding "No."

Quin finally turned to McCrae and asked if he had any further questions.

"I think you've about covered it," he answered dryly.

A few minutes later, Delta got up to leave. McCrae rose from his chair to drive her home, but she waved him back down, telling him she'd catch an Uber or Lyft.

Clearly, she'd had enough of the West Knoll PD.

"Oh, one other thing," Quin added as Delta was at the door of the interview room, her hand already twisting the knob. "All three of your husband's employees said the knife he was stabbed with came from your house, but you said you'd never seen it before."

She stopped short, her back to them. A long pause and then a small voice, "I don't know . . ."

"Apparently he told them he'd taken it from a set from your house and that you hadn't wanted him to take it, but he did. You had a huge fight about it, but he took it anyway. It was on his desk. He used it to cut up fruit in the break room."

Another pause. She still didn't turn around as she said, a bit unsteadily, "No, I'm not sure . . . I need to go to my mom's and then pick up my son."

"Okay. No more questions for now. I hope your husband recovers and we can get some answers."

She glanced back then, her gaze touching on McCrae a moment before sliding back to meet Quin's. With a little more grit, she said, "I hope so, too," and then she headed out the door and down the hallway.

"That was quite a show," said McCrae.

Quin nodded. "You would've been too soft on her."

You can't blame her for Bailey's death, he thought, but what he said was, "You're probably right, but from now on, I want a heads-up."

Quin met his eyes, thought about that a moment, then nodded gravely. "She's gonna need a lawyer."

"A good one," he agreed.

Chapter 16

Zora watched the midday news with her mouth dropped open. It took her a few moments to actually shut it. Amanda had called her and told her about Tanner, and she'd asked for help getting in to see him. Zora had said she'd do what she could, although Brian could be such a butt about asking his friends for favors, it was doubtful; then she'd scoured the Internet for bits and pieces of information about Tanner, still in a state of disbelief. The live newsfeed had made it all seem so *real.*

It is real, she reminded herself. *It is.*

She was perched on the white leather chair in Brian's den. He'd wanted black or espresso, but she'd insisted upon white, and as ever, he'd given in to her. Brian was a sweet man, but he was kind of a wimp. His father's death had knocked him down, for sure, but she realized now he'd always sort of been that way. He'd only been happy teaching, it seemed, but when he'd inherited his father's estate, Zora had told him those days were behind him.

"Let's have a baby together," she'd exclaimed almost as soon as they'd started dating.

"What?" he'd responded, boggled.

"I think we could make beautiful children together."

She'd dragged him, bemused and laughingly protesting, to the bedroom on their third date. She would have tried on their first, but that had been the night of the reunion, and he'd spent most of the time concerned about whether he should have left Anne Reade and Clarice Billings and Principal Kiefer at the event. Coach Sutton hadn't made an appearance at the reunion, which Brian had said was because a lot of the blame for Carmen's death and other kids' injuries had been laid unfairly on him by the parents.

"Dean never got over it," Brian told her that night. "He's been teaching phys ed at Montgomery in Clackamas. I talked to him about the reunion, but he didn't feel right about coming."

Zora had wanted to talk about other things, more personal things, and she'd steered the conversation as best she could. She'd been only partially successful, but she had managed to catch a ride home with him that night and had thanked him profusely. She'd pretended she didn't think she should drive, when in reality she hadn't consumed enough to get a buzz on, but he'd complied.

He'd dropped her at her doorstep, and she'd fervently clasped his hand before climbing out of the car. "Can we do this again?" she asked. "I really could use someone to talk to. Max and I have been separated for years (a lie, but one she made good on as soon as possible); our relationship has been over a long time. Practically from the get-go. Sometimes you make a mistake, and it just takes a while before you have the courage to make it right."

She could tell Brian fell for her story hook, line, and sinker, so she picked a fight with Max the very next day and moved out by the end of that week. From there, she and Brian began seriously dating. Amanda told her she was railroading him into marrying her, which really hurt, but then Amanda always said mean things. Maybe she *had* railroaded him a little. Was that a crime? By the end of that year, she and Max were divorced, and she and Brian were married and spending hours in bed having sex like lovesick bunnies.

She'd been so sure it would work. She would be pregnant before a moon's turn, and yet . . . nada. Same old disappointments. Same old frustrations.

Her gynecologist could find nothing wrong with either her or Brian. Healthy sperm. Healthy people. Just no babies.

But . . . Brian had inherited tons of money. That was a fact. While they were dating, Brian had introduced her to important people, people with cold, hard cash, and life had been full of fun and expensive toys and . . . just everything. For a time, it was all just perfect. But then, while

Zora indulged her every whim, her husband grew content to live in his office easy chair and only gather himself to go out once a week-end, generally to a good restaurant. Sometimes they stayed in all weekend . . . and all week . . . It was a nice, predictable, fingernails scraping on a blackboard existence.

Zora was going out of her mind.

She found herself fixated on Delta and her little boy, Owen. Had dreams about kidnapping him—just for an afternoon or so—so she could have a child. In desperation, knowing her fantasies were dangerous, she'd gone to a shrink, Judy, a gray-haired granny type with terrible taste in clothing but a concerned manner, who'd suggested adoption. Zora had tried to be enthusiastic about that idea, but she wasn't, and when she approached Brian with the idea, he was even less eager than she was.

So . . . what? What was there in life?

She found herself aimlessly wandering around malls. She flirted with the thought of shoplifting. She was unhappy, uninterested, and uninvolved. It felt a little like death.

But now someone's stabbed Tanner!

Zora dialed Amanda again. Who could have done this? *Why* had they done it? It was just so . . . *terrible!*

Amanda didn't answer. Instead an annoyingly cool, female voice said, "You've reached Amanda

Forsythe. Leave a message with the front desk."
She was beeped back to the same cool voice,
the receptionist, who took Zora's name and
number and then disconnected. Zora sat tensely
for about ten minutes, then couldn't stand it any
longer, so she called Ellie. She still had her cell
number from the reunion but had never used
it. She was gratified and a little taken aback
when Ellie answered with an abrupt, "Ellie
O'Brien."

"Hi, Ellie. It's Zora. I just saw on the news
about Tanner and . . . and . . ."

And she abruptly burst into tears.

"I'm going to go see him," Ellie said, ignoring
her sniffling. "I tried today and failed, but they
won't keep me out tomorrow. Amanda said you
had connections."

"Well . . . um . . . I'm going to ask Brian,
but . . ."

"Don't count on it?" Ellie guessed. "Fine. I'll
figure it out."

She sounded so sure of herself that Zora said,
"I want to go with you. Please. Don't say no."

Ellie made a disparaging sound that might have
been a hushed swear word, but then she muttered
something kind of condescending about Amanda
beneath her breath before saying she would
talk to her, then abruptly hung up. Even though
high school and the Five Firsts were long over,
Zora couldn't help thinking about how com-

mandeering Ellie was, especially since she hadn't been part of their clique. She wondered what Amanda thought of her attitude.

Around 5:00 p.m., Brian stumbled out of his office—what the hell did he do in there all day anyway?—while the news replayed the story about Tanner. He looked from the TV to her accusingly. "You didn't tell me?" he questioned.

"I just found out," she lied.

"Sweet Jesus," he muttered, and she watched the color drain from his skin.

"I know. It's just terrible." She paused, then added, "We're going to try to get in to see him tomorrow."

"Who's we?"

"Ellie and Amanda and me."

"Leave the man be. If he's going to recover, he doesn't need an entourage hovering over him."

This was about as cold and unfeeling as Brian ever got. "*If* he's going to recover?" she repeated, aghast.

"It's what they're not saying that makes it sound dire."

"Well, he's not going to die! Tanner? No!"

He turned to gaze at her, and she thought she saw a flash of contempt in his eyes. Contempt of her? He was the one who never did anything. The one closeted in his office. The one who would barely touch her anymore. From all their early frantic lovemaking, they'd gone to being polite strangers. God, it was difficult to find a good man. Most of them were flat-out losers. "I was going to ask if you could call the Rawlings and ask if you could get us in . . ." She knew Gene Rawling was on the hospital board.

Brian shook his head and snorted, then stalked back to his office. Burned, Zora tiptoed to his closed door. She could hear murmuring and surmised he was on the phone. Edging closer, she pressed an ear to the panels.

". . . I don't know! God, it could be a drug addict, not, not . . . No! . . . No, it's no one who . . . I'm just saying, it's just bad, bad luck. I hope he's okay. I hope he gets better and he can tell us what happened . . . Of course, I mean it. And I know it's got nothing to do with anything else . . . You worry too much. I—"

Zora leaned so far forward that she half-fell into the door with a soft thud. As she collected herself, the door swung rapidly inward, and Brian stood on the other side, glaring at her. His cell phone was still in his hand, but the screen was dark.

"I thought we were going to go shopping this afternoon," she said lamely. Brian never went with her, unless it was to see old friends. He still kept up with Anne Reade, and she had a feeling maybe that's who'd been on the cell.

"No." He was abrupt. Then, maybe hearing himself, he said, "Why don't you go? I'm just going to stay here and keep an eye on the news."

"You're really worried about Tanner?" she asked in a small voice. She'd just assumed Tanner would recover, but clearly Brian didn't feel the same way.

"Aren't you? Based on the reporting?"

He was looking at her as if she'd come from another planet. "Well, of course I am. I just don't know who would do that. Maybe . . . maybe someone after drugs? From the clinic?"

"Did you hear me talking on the phone? That's what I said."

"Who were you talking to?"

"Ron."

Ronald Kiefer. The ex-principal of West Knoll High. For some reason, she'd been certain it was a woman on the other end of the line. Anne Reade, maybe. Or Clarice Billings, possibly. Or maybe even one of Zora's classmates . . . ?

"I hope Tanner recovers," he said.

"Yeah . . ."

He lifted his brows in that "Anything else?" look, and Zora shook her head and walked toward the garage, hearing his office door close behind her. She wanted to double back and listen in some more, but he was onto her now, and if he caught her a second time, she doubted he would shrug off her interest.

Tomorrow, she told herself. She would see Tanner for herself.

• • •

Ellie's cell phone buzzed while she was on her laptop, tucked into a small anteroom at the station that was used by personnel who didn't have actual desks. Space was at a premium, and twice while she was writing, someone looked in to see if the room was available. She would lock the door, if she could, but, alas, it was considered a common-area room.

Glancing at the number, she saw it was Joey. "God," she muttered, looking over her words. It was a chronicle of Tanner's life. She wanted to be the first to write a personal background story and therefore make a case for being the one to present it on air. She didn't have time for Joey right now.

But, Jesus. Both Joey and Michael were always in trouble, and Mom and Oliver had just given up on them. Ever since they'd both fallen deep in lust with Nia Crassley and damn near killed each other over her. Luckily, in true Crassley style, Nia, after having sex with both of them, though not at the same time—God, she hoped not at the same time—had moved on to a local West Knoll businessman who'd since gone belly up after Nia and her sticky-fingered family had sucked him dry of all his material possessions. That was the truth of the Crassleys. They were all awful. Ellie had told both her brothers to get rid of her and get out of West Knoll, and she was pretty sure they'd done neither.

Bzzzz. Bzzzz. Bzzzz.

It was an irksome alarm-sound ringtone she'd designated for both of her brothers.

"Hey, there," she finally answered, gathering her annoyance under control. Her eyes were still on her narrative. Too folksy? She hadn't had a folksy relationship with Tanner, but she wanted to infuse the story with warmth. She thought of Delta, and her expression fell into a scowl. This was her fault. If she hadn't actually stabbed him, she was involved somehow, Ellie just knew it.

Joey greeted her, "Fuck, Ell, that doctor friend of yours was stabbed in his clinic!"

"I know. Was there something else? I'm trying to put the last finishing touches on—"

"Nia's pregnant. Doesn't know if it's me or Michael."

She sat back into her chair. "What about that other guy you said she was seeing?"

"She ditched him three months ago."

"And you and Michael took up with her again?" She was practically shrieking. Her brothers were morons. *Morons!* She loved them fiercely, but they were absolute idiots.

"She's hot" was the somewhat sullen answer. "What are we supposed to do? Turn her down when she comes crying to our door?"

"Well, no. Of course not. I wouldn't want you to do that," she said sarcastically.

The twins lived in an apartment together. They'd both dropped out of college and gotten jobs with a local moving company. The idea of a ménage à trois with Nia was starting to sound far more likely than she'd hoped.

"We're going to tell Mom and Dad. Just wanted to let you know if Dad kills us, that's why."

"Get a paternity test. That girl . . . that whole family are grifters, cheats, and thieves. Make sure the results are yours. Just, for once in your life, be careful."

She clicked off. She didn't have time for this shit right now. Tanner was in the hospital, and Delta had put him there. She was going to prove it.

She worked for hours. Went home. Worked on it some more.

By the following morning, she had a well-written report on Dr. Tanner Stahd, if she did say so herself, and she was determined to read it on camera. That meant getting the okay from Rob, and she wasn't quite sure what that was going to take. Sleeping with him? He was tight with the wealthy wife, but maybe given the right incentive? Coco had accused her of trying to sleep her way to the top, and though Ellie had been outraged, it had mostly been for show. If she wanted to use sex to get ahead, so be it. Didn't mean she didn't like the guys she slept with; she did. Sure, it would be terrific if Rob would put her on screen on merit alone, but that was a pipe dream.

Nevertheless, she went into the station and waited in Rob's office with her story. "Read this," she told him when he entered a few moments later, thrusting the pages at him.

Rob took them, glanced through the first few paragraphs, and his brows lifted. "Okay," he said.

"Okay?" she asked cautiously. Was this the green light?

"Looks good, so far. Go over to the hospital. Get an update. Maybe Stahd'll wake up and give you an interview."

She thought about Zora's lackluster response to trying to get the three of them inside Tanner's room. "I'll be lucky to get a toe inside his room."

"You sell your talents short, Ellie. If anyone can get inside that hospital room, it's you." He snapped the paper with his fingers. "And these friends you all grew up with? Take some with you. A whole class reunion. That's a good story."

Chapter 17

Now . . .

*B*BBBEEEEEPPPPP!
The ominous sound of the flatline jolted Zora's pulse as she stood just outside the door of Tanner's room with Ellie and Amanda. Everyone had started running, and they'd been shooed from the room.

Zora moved back out of the way with Ellie and Amanda, huddling near them.

Ellie was spitting mad. "She tried to kill him!" she declared.

The alarm and the frantic activity surrounding Tanner were driving Zora crazy. She wanted to clap her hands over her ears. Ellie wanted to blame Delta for the attack on Tanner. "We don't know that," Zora reminded her, then, "Are you going to be reporting on this?"

"No."

"I just thought—"

"Let's wait till we find out what happens," Amanda broke in.

She stood to one side in a gray suit teamed with a white blouse with a long, loopy bow that was out of date and yet looked fantastic on her. Zora wondered if she should have worn something similar; she felt a bit overdressed compared to her friends . . . though maybe *friends* wasn't quite the right term. Ellie was in slacks and a conservative dark blue blouse, while Zora was in her Louboutins and her black Saint Laurent dress with the ruched neckline. But, hell . . . no one was paying any attention. It was all about rushing people and lights and that horrible *BBBBEEEEEEEEEPPPPP.*

Tanner . . . *not* Tanner . . .

"I'm going to find out who did this to him," Ellie declared.

"You just said it was Delta," Amanda reminded.

"Then I'm going to prove it was her," she corrected.

The policeman who'd been on guard, but who'd clearly been a bit in awe of Ellie—he'd recognized from the news—and had let them in because of it, had practically pushed them away from Tanner and into the hall when the beeping started. Now he stood by, as if unsure what they were going to do next. Zora wondered herself. She was glad to be out of the closeness of the room; she'd felt like she might pass out. But now they were just waiting . . . for what? She didn't like the beeping. It was too *urgent.*

Amanda looked at the door they'd just exited as if there were a whole scenario going on inside her head—thoughts and ideas about what she'd just seen that she apparently didn't want to share.

"Is he going to live?" Zora quavered.

"Grow a pair," Ellie snapped at her.

"That's so mean. I just wanted to know what you thought."

"If he dies, he won't be able to tell what happened," said Amanda.

"I'll find out from Delta," Ellie said tightly.

"Try to avoid torture during your third degree," Amanda suggested.

Ellie snorted.

"Do you think . . . she'll be arrested?" asked Zora.

"If there's a God," Ellie said shortly. She was digging in her purse for her cell phone.

"Do you think we're like . . . cursed?" Zora whispered.

"Oh, for God's sake." Ellie shook her head and walked away, holding her phone to her ear, waiting for a call to go through.

Zora gazed after her. Ellie really was tense, whereas Amanda seemed to never lose her cool. Zora felt bad and weird about everything, and it didn't help that Brian had retreated to his office again like a turtle. She really needed somebody to talk to. Someone like Bailey, but Bailey was gone.

"We lost Carmen, and then Bailey, and now Tanner is fighting for his life," Amanda said soberly. "We're pretty unlucky."

Ellie turned back around, apparently still waiting for her call to connect.

"Is she leaving?" Zora asked.

"I don't know." Amanda's eyes narrowed as she looked at Ellie, who clicked off her phone in disgust.

"Do you think Delta did it?"

Amanda answered, "I'm not as convinced as Ellie."

"He said 'Dee,'" Zora reminded. "You heard that, right?"

"Yes."

Ellie stalked back over to them as Zora asked Amanda, "Are you . . . staying around?"

"I want to know if he lives or dies," she responded.

"He's not going to die," Zora whispered.

"Did you hear the monitor?"

"Yes . . ."

"What do you hear now?"

Zora could have answered, "My own heartbeat," her pulse was thundering so hard through her veins. "The beep. It's loud."

"They're working on him," Ellie snapped.

"I don't hear anything but the beep," Zora said.

And just like that, the beeping stopped.

Zora's hand flew to her mouth in horror.

"They've stopped trying," Amanda said shortly, her head cocked, listening.

"He's not dead," Zora beseeched her.

"That's a pretty good clue he is," Ellie said. Both she and Amanda stood stock-still, their expressions tense.

"Bu . . . but . . . that *can't be!*" Zora blubbered.

"Jesus," Ellie said. She looked shocked.

For the first time, Amanda really focused on Zora. "Are you okay? You look like you're going to fall over."

"I'm okay," she said, but her head was spinning.

"I'll give you a ride home."

"I'm—"

And then the door to Tanner's room opened, and the nurse who'd given them such hard looks came out, her expression resigned. She didn't even react to Zora, Ellie, and Amanda hovering outside.

"Is he . . . okay?" Zora asked in a tremulous voice.

The nurse regarded them soberly and said, "The doctor will be talking to the family."

"He's gone," Ellie said bluntly.

"Come on," Amanda stated grimly, and she steered Zora toward the outside door.

After dropping Owen with her mother—Delta was afraid to take him to pre-K, afraid of what he might learn as she hadn't yet found the words to say Tanner had been attacked—Delta arrived at the hospital in time to see Amanda walking out of the building hand in hand with Zora.

339

She watched them head toward a black Lexus SUV—Amanda's car, apparently, as Amanda unlocked the doors and made sure Zora was in the passenger side, then walked around the front of the vehicle to the driver's side.

What did that mean? Nothing good.

Her hands were clasped on the wheel. Her fingers frozen. Her whole body clenched. Yesterday she'd left the police station and headed to Smith & Jones, where her dad had put his arms around her and called her Delli, and she'd broken down and completely lost it. Her father's on-and-off slips into the beginnings of dementia hadn't been on display since Tanner's attack, which was a blessing. Her mother had comforted her, too, and offered to take Owen for the night, but Delta had needed to have her son with her, though it had shaken her when, later that evening, after she'd explained that even she couldn't see daddy at the hospital just yet, Owen had looked up from his meal of macaroni and cheese and asked, "What happened to the knives?"

"What do you mean?" she'd asked, stunned.

"Those aren't the same ones."

He was six. How much could he know? *A lot,* she realized and felt the noose tightening. "Those are new ones" was her lame answer. She hoped to God he wouldn't remember exactly when the knives were exchanged. It was so ridiculous. She should have never been so stupid. Her main

340

character in *Blood Dreams*, Lynda, would never have panicked in such a ridiculous way.

And the police knew she was lying about the knife. Tia and Amy had made certain of it. She was going to have to come clean. She could put the original knife block back. It was still in the attic, and she could just blame her inaccuracy on stress, or something, but now Owen had seen the change.

"How could you be so stupid?" she asked herself now as she watched Amanda's black SUV pull out of the lot. Had she and Zora come to see Tanner? Undoubtedly. Had they gotten in? Past the police officer?

Her cell phone started ringing. LAURELTON GENERAL read across her screen.

She gazed at it in bewilderment for a moment, but a part of her knew what was coming, and her heart started a hard, erratic beat. "Hello?" she answered

"Mrs. Tanner Stahd?" a female voice asked.

"Yes." Her voice was strangled.

"I'm calling for Dr. Evanston. This is Nurse Alice Song. Is it possible for you to come into the hospital?"

"He's dead, isn't he?"

"I really think you should come in and talk to Dr. Evanston."

"I will. Tell me he's alive."

"It would be best, if you came in. . . ."

Delta checked out. Just checked out. One moment, she was listening; the next, her gaze, through the windshield, was watching a plastic bag dip and weave against a frisky little breeze. Up and down. Whipped around. Flung to the ground. Caught up again.

Nurse Song didn't have to tell her. She already knew.

"I'll go straight to the morgue," she said, her voice robotic.

Nurse Song didn't argue with her.

She hung up and sat in her car and watched the plastic bag some more.

McCrae woke up late to Fido's wet, rough tongue licking his face. He scrambled awake, looking for the time. "What took you so long?" he declared to the dog, jumping out of bed and into the shower. When he got out, Fido was waiting for him by the bathroom door. His breakfast was late.

McCrae fed him and grimaced at the time: 9:50 am. No one would get on him about being late after the all-nighter he'd pulled the night before. It was just that he had a lot of things to do.

He heard a message come in on his way to the station at the same time his cell started ringing. Seeing that Quin was calling, he answered the line first. "McCrae."

"Tanner Stahd just passed away," Quin said.

"Oh . . . shit . . ."

"You're coming in?"

"On my way."

"Corolla just called. Check your messages."

McCrae was struggling to accept the news that Tanner was gone. He read his text and saw it was from Corolla, saying he'd allowed Ellie O'Brien, Zora DeMarco, and Amanda Forsythe into Tanner's room just before he died, but he'd been there too, and he could swear they'd never gotten near him. The doctor had decreed that Tanner's injuries were just too severe for him to recover, and the body was in the hospital morgue. Delta Stahd was already there.

If he hadn't been so close to the station, he would've turned around and gone to Laurelton General right then. As it was, he wheeled into the lot and jumped up the back stairs two at a time. For some reason, he'd believed Tanner would be all right, even with the seriousness of his injuries. Impossible to imagine that he was gone forever.

And now it was a homicide.

Who killed him? Why had they done it?

He needed to find out the motive. He didn't believe Delta had murdered him, even if Quin acted like she was the prime suspect. It just didn't ring true to him that Tanner had been killed over a crumbling marriage or a workplace affair. Yes, it was a crime of passion. The multiple chest

343

wounds told that story. But Delta stabbing her husband over and over again? He couldn't see it. The motive had to lie elsewhere, but where and with whom?

He ducked his head into Quin's office and said, "I'm going to the hospital."

"Sit down a minute."

McCrae was already a half step away and had to reverse himself.

"Just for a minute," Quin reiterated, gesturing to the one other chair in the room.

McCrae did as his superior had suggested, though it was way outside of Bob Quintar's playbook. The man didn't have talks with coworkers at his desk, or anywhere else. He was quiet and methodical and occasionally had to take a meeting, but his way of working was with minimal conversation. Not that he couldn't carry on a meaningful conversation when called upon, but his day-to-day modus operandi was to speak as few words as possible.

"I know how you feel about Delta," Quin said. "I don't feel the same way. She's beautiful and possibly deadly. She's not the girl you went to school with."

"I don't remember saying she was."

"All those girls . . . Bailey's friends . . ." He looked grim.

The attack on Tanner was making Quin relive his daughter's death. McCrae hadn't told him he'd found the bartender, James Carville, not wanting to get his hopes up, but now he did.

"Where is he?" Quin demanded, half-rising from his chair.

"He recently landed in Eugene, apparently. He's staying with a sister and working at a local bar, the Duck-Duck Inn. I'll go see him as soon as we get a grip on the attack on Stahd."

"I should be interviewing him," he said tautly.

"You should *not* be interviewing him. You're Bailey's father. If the guy knows something about Bailey and Penske and that night, I'll find out."

Quin looked about to argue but kept himself in check. McCrae got up to leave again, and the older man added, "Corinne called Hurston."

McCrae stopped short and gazed hard at Quin. *"What?"*

"You didn't say anything to her about Carville, did you?"

"Hell, no."

The idea of the special investigator in contact with Corinne left McCrae feeling unsettled. He didn't want the man anywhere near him or West Knoll, especially now, when he was about to follow up on a lead that could prove that Hurston's theory on Penske's and Bailey's death was incorrect. The man was a political animal, and if he felt Quin and McCrae were trying to prove him wrong, he wouldn't take it sitting down. He cared less about right and wrong and more about how it would make him look, and an error this big would make him look bad.

McCrae drove to the hospital, his thoughts turning from Hurston to Corinne. Toward the end of their relationship, during one of their frequent fights, she'd yelled at him, "You don't give a shit about anything, Chris! There's nothing inside you. Nothing!"

This was her complaint whenever she deemed he wasn't attentive enough, which had become more and more often over time. "I care about a lot of things," he'd denied, sick of the accusation.

"People, Chris. You don't care about people. Oh, no. I'm wrong," she'd said, seeing he was about to fight her on that, too. "You care about people *you don't know.* Anyone who has a problem, you're right there for them. Any stranger in need . . . Officer Chris McCrae to the rescue!"

"It's my job, Corinne. I—"

"But you don't give one goddamn *shit* about the people you *love* . . . ," she'd snarled. "You're a hero to everyone. You suck it up like life-giving elixir. No, no." She held out her finger when he was about to argue again. "Don't say another word. I already know what you're going to say anyway, and it's just more bullshit."

"It's not bullshit."

"It's *bullshit,*" she'd shouted back.

And then she'd picked up her sweater where

she'd laid it over a kitchen chair and walked out the door. Two days later, she entered his house when he wasn't there and gathered up the rest of her belongings and smashed a picture of them together that she'd had framed and placed on the end table beside his couch. He'd swept up the pieces and thrown them into the trash.

That was the end of their relationship, except for the fact that they worked together. Worked together, but seldom spoke to each other any longer.

But now she was talking with Hurston?

McCrae searched his feelings as he pulled to a stop in the hospital parking lot. Was he jealous over the thought of Corinne and Hurston together, whatever that relationship might be? No. What he felt was betrayal. She'd gone behind his back to the enemy and joined forces, and no matter what, it wasn't going to be good.

He strode into the hospital reception area and toward the elevator bank. No one bothered him as he pushed the DOWN button for the morgue.

The elevator car opened with a *ding,* and he strode down the hallway. Outside the morgue door, he ran into Delta, who was talking to a man in a white coat, Dr. Evanston according to his name tag. She turned toward McCrae, and the look on her face told him everything he needed to know.

"He's gone," she said.

Automatically he reached for her, drawing her into the shelter of his arms.

Jesus Christ, Ellie thought, screeching to a halt as, barreling down the hallway from the elevator in search of the morgue, she came across Delta in Chris McCrae's embrace. She'd left the hospital earlier to get a signal and reach Rob, who wasn't picking up, but she'd stayed in the parking lot, determined not to leave until she talked to the doctors and staff about Tanner's death. She wanted this story. It was hers, and she meant to have it.

The doctor with them saw Ellie, but not Delta and McCrae, who had their backs to her. She pretended to examine her watch, then shook her head and reversed direction, heading back to the elevator as if suddenly remembering she had somewhere else to be. She was determining whether she was going to push the button and call the car, or just wait till Delta and McCrae came back this way, so she could interview that doctor or anyone at the morgue without them listening in.

As she stood there, the elevator bell rang, and the doors slid open. She stepped forward, then was nearly run over by Tanner's father, whose face was bright red with fury as he barreled into the hallway. An interesting emotion for a man who'd just lost his son, she thought, stepping out of the way.

He didn't even notice her, but his wife did, as she followed him into the hallway.

"Dr. Stahd," Ellie greeted him.

He shot her a quick look but didn't stop walking until he recognized her. Only then did his footsteps slow. "You're that reporter."

"Yes."

"You tell 'em. You tell 'em that she did it. She killed my son. Stabbed him to death!"

Ellie said cautiously, "You're talking about Delta?"

"He should've never married her," Lester Stahd railed. "Pretending she was pregnant. Fooled him, she did. Sucked him dry, and then wanted a divorce! My grandson'll be with me, mark my words."

"I'm not sure that was Delta," Ellie said slowly. She didn't really want to correct him, as she mostly agreed with what he was spewing, and it looked like it might continue, but Amanda had been the one who may or may not have been pregnant with Tanner's child.

"Put him under a spell, that's what she did. Used her looks and her wiles to get him!"

His wife grabbed onto his arm and held on tight, sending Ellie one of those proprietary looks that said, "Stay away from my man."

"Don't run off," she told her husband. "It's

all just too terrible, and we need to stay together."

"She with him?" Stahd asked Ellie, hooking a thumb in the direction of the morgue.

"I—um—Delta's here," she said, wondering if she should warn him that Delta was snuggled into McCrae's embrace. But it might be over by now anyway. "Could I get a statement from you? I'm with Channel Seven."

"My daughter-in-law killed my son," he said. "That's your fucking statement."

"Oh, babe," his wife cooed, pressing his head against her ample bosom, still eyeing Ellie. "Oh, babe."

Lori, Ellie remembered. Who'd left him once, but it didn't appear, by the way she was hovering over him, that she was going to make that mistake twice.

Tanner's father paused for a moment, and Ellie watched a stunned look sweep over his features as if it had finally hit him that his son was really dead, gone from this world. But then he clamped down on those emotions and headed for the morgue once more.

"Would you like to give an interview?" Ellie called after him, injecting just the right amount of empathy into the question to allay the fears of his insecure wife.

Stahd stopped and thought a moment. "Yes," he said. "Stay right here. I'll be back."

Ellie watched him and his wife head down the hallway to the morgue together, Stahd moving at a half run, while wifey mewed platitudes and dogged after him in a pair of Manolo Blahniks that Ellie had lusted after herself but couldn't afford. When they were out of sight, she tried Rob again, getting through this time with no problem—small miracle—and said she was getting a story to add to her piece from Dr. Stahd, who'd just learned his son had died from his injuries.

Rob said, "Get it."

As Ellie clicked off, she felt a pang of something akin to remorse. Immediately she squelched it. Yes, she was very sorry that Tanner had been killed, and she sure as hell wanted Delta or whoever had done it brought to justice, but there was no reason to sit back and grieve when there was work to be done, work that could inform the public and, yes, help her career.

Probably Delta did kill him. Maybe she'd just had enough of his cheating, his narcissism, his lack of character . . . all the pieces of Tanner that everyone had ignored in high school but that had become self-evident over time. He'd still looked pretty good, Ellie could admit, and she sure as hell would've done him back in the day . . . maybe even more recently . . . but, well, it was too late now.

She spared a thought for the young man who'd

been such a star in high school . . . but then her thoughts turned to Bailey and Carmen.

Amanda was right. They sure as hell were one unlucky class.

Chapter 18

Dead. Tanner was dead. Not injured and recovering. Dead.

Delta wanted to burrow deeper into the comfort of McCrae's arms, but it was a false safe harbor. Almost from the moment he reached out to comfort her, she could feel him pull back. It helped wake her from the alien world she'd been sleepwalking through.

"I saw him," she said.

McCrae looked toward the door marked MORGUE. He'd seen enough dead bodies to know the wealth of feeling behind those three words.

"Are you related?" the doctor asked McCrae as he checked his watch.

"No," Delta and McCrae answered at the same time, slowly pulling apart.

"Well . . ." He seemed momentarily stymied by their answer, then nodded to them as he returned to his duties, clearly ready to hand the matter of Delta over to McCrae, regardless of their relationship.

He'd barely gotten out of sight when Tanner's father and Lori suddenly appeared in the hallway.

"Lester," Delta managed through a tight throat.

The elder Dr. Stahd gave McCrae a hard look. Though he wasn't physically comforting Delta any longer, the vibe must have been in the air, because Stahd's mouth tightened and he glared at her.

"Already at it, girl?" he asked.

"Lester," Lori protested faintly.

"I'm so sorry," Delta said.

It wasn't a confession, but Stahd seemed to take it that way. He drew himself up and looked about to launch himself at Delta. McCrae moved between them, on alert.

"You." Stahd pointed a shaking finger at McCrae. "I'll sue the police for protecting a killer! You'll lose your job. Maybe you were even in on it."

Lori groaned.

McCrae turned to her. "You all right?"

"You leave my wife alone," Stahd growled.

"I'm fine," said Lori, though she looked ready to collapse. Delta knew she probably appeared the same way.

"I'm going to my mother's," Delta said for McCrae's benefit. "The press . . ." She lifted a hand and then wearily dropped it again. "This'll bring them back."

"You're only concerned about yourself," Stahd shot out. His jaw was thrust forward pugnaciously. Apparently, his only way to deal with grief was through anger.

"I can't believe he's gone." Delta's words were little more than a whisper.

Lester practically spit on the floor. McCrae stood by, watchful, a wall of protection, which only seemed to infuriate Lester more, though Delta was grateful for the support.

Lester ground out, "I'm taking my grandson. You're going to jail. Owen needs a stable home."

"Owen's my son. He's staying with me." Delta was sure about that.

"You killed his father."

"You don't get to say that. You know I didn't. I couldn't. And Owen's mine. I know you're grieving, but stop it. This isn't helping any of us."

"I'm suing you," he said, then, as if gaining strength from the very words, repeated them. "I'm suing you."

"Let's everybody take a breather," said McCrae.

"Lester, let's go home," said Lori.

"I want to see my son," the older man snapped. "And then justice will be served."

Delta's eyes were starting to sting. She wanted to protest her innocence some more, but Tanner's father wasn't listening.

"You took him from me," he said, his voice wavering a bit.

"No . . ."

"Somebody has to pay!"

"Lester!" Lori was more insistent this time.

"I'm going see my son," he declared belligerently, as an attendant, maybe hearing the raised voices, came to see what was wrong.

Delta turned away from them and headed blindly back toward the elevators. She was repeatedly smashing her uninjured palm against the button when McCrae came up next to her.

"I didn't do it," Delta said again. She'd lost count of how many times she'd said those words.

"Do you need a ride home?"

"No, I'm fine."

"You sure?"

"Can't keep depending on West Knoll's finest," she said, though the idea of having him take her was tempting. "I need to go to my mom's. My son's there and . . . and . . . I don't know what to do. Get groceries?" She choked out a hysterical laugh.

"Let me take you," he offered again, and this time she just shrugged and nodded. What the hell. He was right. She would probably crash if she had to drive now.

He drove her to Smith & Jones, and her mother—both of her parents, actually—swept her into their arms and hugged her tightly. The emotional response brought full-on tears to Delta's eyes, and it was a relief to cry, to get it all out. She hadn't been able to before, too shocked by Tanner's dying. It still seemed unreal and probably would for a long time to come.

Owen appeared from the back room, holding a plastic T. rex. He regarded McCrae with silent suspicion, so McCrae took his leave.

Delta felt almost bereft when he was gone. She sensed she could rely on him. Was there something wrong with her that she wanted him around? Maybe she was evil, like Tanner's dad seemed to think. Tanner had only been gone a few hours, and she was seeking comfort from another man? Was that normal? It hurt her head to even think about it, so she pushed those wearying thoughts aside and grabbed up Owen, squeezing him hard, closing her eyes, and drinking in the scent of him.

McCrae got back to the station in time to find there was a call on his voice mail from Dean Sutton. Before phoning him back, he checked on any new developments from the crime-scene team on the Stahd case, but no further clues had been found at the scene, and the only fingerprints and/or DNA picked up were from the current employees and Delta.

The killer wore gloves, McCrae figured, although he determined to look deeper into the backgrounds of Tia Marvin, Amy Panterra, and Nurse Candy to see if there was more there than met the eye. Quin might be leaning toward Delta as the killer, but McCrae's belief that she was innocent had been bolstered even more by

Lester Stahd's enraged insistence of her guilt.

"Hello, Coach," McCrae greeted the older man when Sutton picked up on the other end. "McCrae here."

"Chris McCrae," Coach responded in the "Can you believe it?" tone of someone greeting a long-lost friend.

They talked for a few minutes, with Coach Sutton fondly reminiscing and McCrae only listening with half an ear. Time was fleeting, and he had lots on his plate. Finally, McCrae said, "Quin said you saw Delta just before Tanner was stabbed at his clinic."

"I did. At the Bengal Room. You been there? It used to have a real tiger pelt on the floor, but that was years ago. Now it's all fake stuff, but it's nice. The whole place is better now, gentrified, as they say. It's not far from Montgomery, where I coach, so I go there sometimes."

"You didn't talk to Delta."

"Nooo . . . ," he said. "She was involved with another man. Name's Jonah Masterer. Comes in there a lot trying to pick up women."

"Involved," McCrae repeated. He'd already heard that Delta had been talking with a man at the bar of the Bengal Room, but Sutton made it sound more like a tryst.

"They were just flirting. Delta's always been a pretty gal, but she was glowing under the attention. Made me wonder how things were going in that marriage, y'know? If Tanner recovers, I hope he's nicer to her."

McCrae didn't tell him it was too late for that as he didn't know when and how the family was going to make his death public.

"Anyway, after she left, Masterer bragged that he was meeting her later. I guess that didn't happen, since she discovered Tanner."

"No."

"Thought you should know. I don't believe she had anything to do with the attack on Tanner, but I guess she was there in the window of time of his murder, right?" He didn't require an answer as he then waxed rhapsodic about Tanner's prowess as an athlete and what an all-around talented guy he was—a doctor, no less. "Sure hope he recovers," he wound up, and McCrae felt like a heel for not telling the truth, but he knew the older man would find out soon enough.

McCrae wrote Masterer's name down. Just because he didn't feel Delta was a killer didn't mean he shouldn't follow up.

They talked for a bit more, but as McCrae was winding up the conversation, Sutton said, "Meet me at the Bengal Room, and let's talk about a few more things."

"When I can. I'm a bit busy now."

"You gotta talk to Masterer, right? Come on by tonight around . . . uh . . . seven-thirty or so?

There's a chance you'll see him, and there're a few other things I wanna talk over."

"You want to give me a preview on that?" McCrae asked, uncertain when he would be able to make time for a tête-à-tête with West Knoll High's old coach.

"Okay, well, I always meant to talk to you about the senior barbecue. I got blamed a lot for it, and I guess I blamed myself."

McCrae glanced at the time, hoping this wasn't going to be a long jawboning session. Reminiscing was fine, but he remembered how Coach used to go on and on about things.

"I didn't go out in the woods like so many of ya, so I don't know what happened out there, exactly. Just heard rumors. Like . . . um . . . well, you were out there, with Ellie O'Brien."

McCrae felt a fresh jolt of embarrassment. Well, hell. "Yeah . . . ," he allowed cautiously.

"Okay, okay, I'll save the rest for later. See you tonight," the coach said, apparently waking up to the fact he was moving into uncomfortable territory for McCrae.

McCrae clicked off. He hoped his face-to-face with Coach Sutton was going to be more than a walk down memory lane from a time he would rather bury in the back of his mind.

Zora couldn't think. Tanner was dead. Carmen, Bailey, and now Tanner were all dead. Her friends and her classmates. Two of the Five Firsts and the boy they'd all circled around.

Once again, she recalled making out with Tanner. Fast and hurried and hidden. He'd held his hand over her mouth because she'd had an attack of the giggles that wouldn't quit, and there had been other people in her house.

Oh, if they'd only truly gotten together, made a baby. Zora had cried at Delta and Tanner's wedding, and though she'd sworn it was tears of happiness, it felt like something important had gotten away from her.

He was supposed to be the father of your children. Owen should be yours.

Well, hell.

Brushing back her tears, she grabbed a tissue in the master bath and blew her nose, shuddered at her reflection. She looked like a hag.

Painstakingly, she applied new makeup, adding a lot of blush because she was just so pale, almost *gray*. Satisfied with the results, she dug through her closet and found her light gray coatdress with the tailored pockets. She slid her feet into black flats, Manolos, then grabbed up a soft, black leather bag with a thin chain strap that she slipped over her shoulder.

Her house felt empty, even though Brian was in his office. It felt cold, too. She wished she had her car, but it was still at the hospital. She shouldn't have allowed Amanda to drive her home, but she couldn't remember one minute of that trip, so she probably would've been driving blind anyway and was lucky to be alive.

But now. Now she needed to *get out.*

She called for an Uber and fifteen minutes later was on the road to the hospital. At the Laurelton General parking lot, she thanked the driver and then found her car, a white Mercedes sedan that matched her husband's in everything but color. His was black.

She drove to the mall and wandered aimlessly around, buying a new thousand-dollar handbag. The purses were with the hats and scarves and near the shoes. Jewelry was on one side, and she stopped to finger a silver bracelet. She then went to the shoe department and spent ten minutes deciding between a pair of fiery red heels by an up-and-coming Italian designer or another pair of Manolos in silver.

She decided to buy them both and was waiting at the register when a woman with a boy of around five came in. The kid was bouncing in his shoes, walking behind her. She stopped and looked at the same bracelets Zora had just examined, and the little boy bounced into the shoe department. Zora paid for her shoes and then turned toward him. He was about five feet away.

"Hey, there," she said, squatting down, putting her packages on the floor around her.

He stared at her. "You bought stuff."

"Lots of stuff. You wanna see?"

He nodded and trotted toward her. Remembered. Started bouncing again.

She opened the bag that held the purse. It was a dark green. "I think it's the same color as dinosaurs."

"No." He shook his head.

"No? There's a toy store down the mall. I bet we could find one there the same color."

Zora's heart was pounding. She wasn't sure what she was doing. He reminded her of Owen. She'd seen the Facebook posts from Delta, although she'd really fallen off posting recently.

"I know that store!" he said, delighted.

Zora slid her eyes around. No one was paying her any attention, least of all the boy's mom. What was wrong with her?

"You wanna go?" Zora whispered.

"Yeah! *Rrraaaarrr!*" he yelled, clawing the air in an imitation of a T. rex.

"What's your name?"

"Tyler."

"Well, Tyler. Let's go see what's at the store."

"I'll tell Mom!" And he raced off to tell his mother before Zora could stop him. She quickly headed for the open doorway into the center of the mall, then made her pace drop to a stroll, heart pounding. She was just going to the toy store and he'd wanted to come along, that's all. Nothing wrong with that.

She heard his loud voice urging his mom to let him go. She didn't look back.

"She said she'd take me!" he cried.

Oh, shit.

"Who did?" the mom asked suspiciously.

"*She* did!"

And then Zora heard running footsteps behind her. The boy's. He caught up to her with a determined look on his face. "You didn't wait!"

"Excuse me," his mother said. Zora glanced back at her, heart pounding. "Don't talk to my son anymore. If I want him to go to the toy store, I'll take him."

"I don't know what you're talking about," Zora said staunchly.

They were standing in the center of the mall by now. Tyler was gazing at her with an angry expression. "You said you'd take me," he insisted.

"I don't know what's going on. Just stay away from me." The woman grabbed her son by the shoulders.

Zora was so shaken she nearly peed herself.

"Ma'am . . ." They both turned to see a woman in a navy-blue suit approach from the store. She had a tiny badge on her breast.

"Oh, fuck!" Tyler's mother exploded, then said, "Sorry. I didn't mean to take it."

She handed over the silver bracelet she apparently still had clutched in her hand as she'd chased Zora out of the store.

Zora turned away from the whole scene and walked stiffly down the mall and out a side door. She found her way back to her car and sank behind the wheel. Tears filled her eyes.

After a few moments, she turned the ignition and drove herself home. Brian was still in his office, and she almost banged on his door but didn't.

Instead, she went into their master bedroom and changed her clothes, putting on some comfy Lululemon pants and a top. She wandered into the kitchen and found some chips and a dish of *pico de gallo* and took them both into the TV room, where she'd seen the news about Tanner yesterday.

She watched HGTV blankly and ate her chips. It was 5:00, and the news would be on again soon. The whole world would learn of Tanner Stahd's death.

Feeling really low, she took her empty bowls back to the kitchen and went to her bedroom, where she'd thrown her coatdress across her silk duvet. Digging in one of the pockets, she drew out the silver bracelet, identical to the one the woman had accidentally run out of the store with.

Opening the bottom drawer of the bank of drawers designated as hers in the walk-in closet, she added to the small pile of keepsakes she'd been "given" by the major retailers in the mall.

She'd been very careful about not being caught, but today had been a close one.

She heard the door to the office squeak open, and she hurriedly tucked everything away and walked back into the bedroom. She was hanging up her dress when Brian stood in the open doorway.

"I need to talk to you," he said, and only then did she realize how shaken she was.

"I was at the hospital when it happened," she said tearily.

"What?"

"When he died. I was there."

Brian's face slackened. "Tanner?"

"Yes. Isn't that what you were going to say?"

He was gobsmacked. "No."

"What is it?"

"God, this is bad timing, but when is it ever good timing?" He ran his hands through his hair and said, "I want a divorce."

Delta's parents had decided to close the grocery store early for a family emergency, so they were at her parents' house, where Mom fixed spaghetti and meatballs, Owen's favorite. They were all still trying to figure out how to tell him about his father when the local news came on . . . and Tanner's death was one of the lead stories.

". . . prominent West Knoll physician Dr.

Tanner Stahd died as a result of his injuries from a vicious attack earlier this week . . ."

Owen, who'd been playing with Legos, looked up at the screen, frowning. "What did they say?"

Mom swept in, "Come in the kitchen, Owen. I need help serving up."

"But . . ."

Delta was already searching for the remote, which seemed nowhere in sight. She gave up and headed for the television, but couldn't immediately find the OFF button. Her father said a shade too heartily, "I want the biggest meatball. You're going to have to fight me for it."

"Were they talking about Dad?" Owen asked.

"They were saying some things." Delta nodded. "I told you there was an accident. A terrible accident."

"Is he dead?" Owen asked, his voice rising in horror.

"I'm afraid . . . so." She reached for him, but he ran into the kitchen and grabbed his grandmother, who held him close.

Delta was turning to follow after them both, when Lester Stahd's voice boomed across the airwaves. She swiveled back to the television to see him in an interview with Ellie on the patch of ground just outside the hospital that separated the parking lot from the main building.

". . . killed my son. I have proof," he was saying.

"What kind of proof?" Ellie asked him.

"She was always after the money. Everybody knew it, even my boy . . . my boy knew it, too." His voice cracked. "But I don't count on the police helping to put her away. I have to sue her myself and hope the D.A. brings charges."

"Lord," Dad said, wiping his hands over his face.

Delta stared, glassy-eyed. Tanner's father was shredding her reputation. He truly believed she was guilty. That she'd married his son for the financial support and prestige.

"Do you know a good lawyer?" her father asked, his voice quavering a bit.

Delta stared at the television, unable to completely turn it off. It was fascinating, like watching a deadly snake devour a live animal. It was horrible, and impossible to unsee.

"Amanda," she said, heading for Owen, who had lifted his tear-streaked face from the comfort of her mother to reach an arm out to her.

"Is she . . . will she do a good job for you?" her father asked.

She swept up her boy and held him close, his little arms wrapped tightly around her neck. Burying her face into him, she said, her voice muffled, "She's one of the best criminal defense attorneys around."

And once upon a time we were friends.

Chapter 19

Amanda finally listened to Delta's message. The call had come in at about 6:30, but Amanda had let it go to voice mail and then purposely hadn't checked it till nearly 9:00. She'd known it was from Delta; she'd had her number in her call list since high school. She'd purposely ignored today's call. Years had passed, but Amanda still felt raw and competitive about her onetime BFF. If Delta was reaching out to her, it had to be about Tanner, and Amanda just didn't feel like going over it with the wife.

But . . . she was also eaten up with curiosity. That fact alone made her force herself not to listen to the call before it was time. Discipline. Amanda lived by it, an aspect of her character she'd sorely lacked when she was younger. Purposely, she'd switched her phone to SILENT, then gone to visit her brother at Woodview Village, the retirement community where he'd lived for the past five years. Her parents had abdicated responsibility for him almost from the moment they all learned that the automobile accident that had nearly taken his life had stolen his ability to mature into an adult. His brain had suffered irreparable harm and left him at about a fifth-grade level of understanding. Amanda's parents had left her the house and grounds with the understanding that she was to take care of Thom. She'd done so with resentment for five years.

Her parents had magically disappeared from her life and Thom's. After Mom realized Amanda wasn't going to be the darling of stage and screen, she'd lost interest in her. She'd had even less interest in Thom, so she'd talked their father into moving to Palm Desert, where he worked as an estate lawyer for all the retirees in the community and she got to be the queen of the desert, apparently. They'd basically severed their relationship with their children, and so Amanda and Thom were on their own, and Amanda was the parent.

Fine. She didn't like them any more than they liked her.

At Woodview Village tonight, Thom had been exactly the same, remarking about the dinner that they shared, refusing all vegetables, and talking about the characters in video games as if they were his friends. As ever, Amanda told him he should watch his diet, while she barely listened to his chatter. She'd made all the arrangements for his care long ago and now just needed to show up every once in a while and pretend to be attentive. She didn't know how she felt about Thom these days. His regression to his current state had alarmed her and sent her parents flying out of their lives completely. But he'd stabilized, and this is what was left, so Amanda made sure he was safe and comfortable and left it at that. Though her parents had given her their estate to sell, she'd chosen to keep the asset and pay for Thom's care out of her own earnings. She hadn't made partner yet, thanks to her loathsome ex, whose jealousy of her success compared to his own weaker abilities—he'd made partner only because he'd had family money that he'd invested in the firm—had kept her from that coveted position. Every time she threatened to leave, however, the other partners scrambled around and found her more money. Hal's thin-lipped acceptance was worth staying for, too. Cheater. Bastard. All-around fuckhead. But in a sense, she'd married him for his money and connections also, so *c'est la vie*.

Now Amanda plucked her phone from her purse as she headed down the concrete outdoor steps of the retirement community. She'd stayed late with Thom tonight, a test to see how long she could keep from checking on Delta's phone message, and she'd made it till the sun was going down. It was amazing how late that could still be at the end of July. When Delta's name had popped onto Amanda's cell screen, she'd been extremely curious. She knew Delta hated her, whereas she didn't really feel the same way about her. She just wanted to always beat her at her game.

Delta had always been the pretty one, although she'd put on a few extra pounds around the time of the reunion, which had tickled Amanda pink. But then Hal had been determined to antagonize Amanda that night, making friends with all her classmates as if he were the best buddy of all, putting on that oh-so-agreeable personality that he dropped at the door to their house, never bringing it inside. Amanda had figured that out early in the relationship and recognized she had to get what she could from the marriage before it was over. She'd told Delta at the reunion to divorce Tanner like she was divorcing Hal, but Delta had been taken aback and somewhat horrified—it was soooo her.

And extra pounds or no, Delta had looked good that night. It was just a shitty fact. She'd been attractive in high school, but at the reunion she'd been . . . *delicious*. That was the word Hal had used to describe her that night, knowing it would piss Amanda off, which it did, even though it was true. Hal had smiled evilly at Amanda over his drink, sliding long, lingering glances over Delta's voluptuous figure whenever he caught Amanda looking. In answer, Amanda had used Tanner to bait both Delta and Hal, and Tanner was so easily attained. Once upon a time, she'd thought she was pregnant with his child and had been thrilled about the sensation she'd made, but she'd never wanted Tanner. Not really. He was too . . . available, in every way. She could read him like a children's book. And he could be lured into bed with barely a "Hello." Sure, he was good-looking, and his family was fairly well-off, and Tanner had managed somehow to get through med school—who knew? All Amanda could think was that money must've changed hands somewhere along the way—and make a decent success of his father's questionable business.

It was just a matter of competition. Amanda wanted to win, and somehow it felt like Delta was ahead of her. Like, all the fucking time. Even though Delta didn't even know she was in the game.

Ellie, actually, was the one who wanted to battle with Amanda. She had that same fire in the belly to succeed . . . and crush everyone else beneath the heel of her boot. Amanda understood because she felt the exact same way.

Finally, alone in her car, Amanda pressed the button on her cell phone to hear Delta's message.

"Hi, Amanda, it's Delta." Her voice shook some, but there was steel beneath it. *Steel magnolia.* Delta was the epitome of the term. "Tanner died earlier today, and I just ran into his father, who's blaming me. I've talked to the police and told them what I know, but now I think I need a lawyer. A good lawyer. From what I hear, you're one of the best. Is it possible for us to meet and talk about my case? If you're interested, this is my cell number. Thank you. Please call . . ." A pause, and then she hung up.

She thought that over. Delta asking *her* for help? Things must be pretty desperate.

Her cell phone rang in her hand. She gazed at the screen and felt a moment of annoyance when she saw Zora's name. She shouldn't have been so nice to her earlier. She hadn't meant to give Zora carte blanche to call her any old time.

"Hi, Zora," Amanda answered, her voice purposely flinty.

"Did you see the news? Oh, my God. Ellie was on TV giving an interview to Tanner's dad, the doctor, and he was vicious. Just *vicious* about Delta! Says she killed Tanner! Made all kinds of accusations. It was really hard to watch. Even Ellie looked kind of upset."

"Ellie thinks Delta's guilty."

"I know, but Dr. Stahd was so *mean*." She paused. "Do you think she's guilty?"

Amanda watched the passing landscape as she headed west out of Portland into the lowering sun. "Jury's out."

"Remember . . . remember what I told you she said at Carmen's memorial service?"

Amanda hated guessing games. "Refresh my memory."

"She said . . . well, she said . . . you really don't remember?"

"Zora." Amanda was losing patience.

"Delta said that she wished you and Tanner would just die," she said in a rush.

Oh, right. Amanda remembered hearing that from someone, but she'd forgotten it was Zora. She'd half-believed Delta might have been the one to say it to her face. That's how heated and wild their emotions had all been following Carmen's death.

"Maybe she meant it . . . ?" Zora said on a squeak of disbelief.

"I'm not worried about Delta."

"You're not? You don't . . . you don't think she did it?"

"I don't know."

"What'll happen to her little boy if she did? He's so adorable. I'd die for a child like that."

Amanda was mildly surprised. "You know Delta's son?"

"I've seen pictures. I just . . . I'm worried, and I'd like to help. Maybe I should call Delta and talk to her. I could be a babysitter. I'm sure she needs help."

Something desperate there, Amanda thought, but then Zora was always kind of that way. "Then call her," she said, adding, "You said were watching Channel Seven?"

"Yeah, Ellie's station. You missed it? It'll probably be on again tonight at eleven, right?"

"Probably."

Amanda meant to hang up, but Zora said, "I kinda want to talk about something."

"Zora, I am busy."

"It won't take long. I was talking to Brian about everything, you know? Even about the senior barbeque. We just started talking and . . . you know what he said?"

Amanda crushed her teeth together, trying to keep from being unspeakably rude and just hanging up.

"He wants a divorce! I think he's serious! I don't even think he ever wanted a baby! His feelings all just came pouring out. I wasn't going to tell anybody, but I just need to talk. I'm devastated."

"Zora . . ." Amanda really didn't want to go there with her. "I gotta go."

"What am I supposed to do now, huh? I think there's someone else, too; he's just not saying."

"This sounds like something you need to work out with him."

"God, Amanda. You were nice to me today. Now you're not."

"I'm just turning into my house, and I've still got work to do tonight."

"Okay, sure."

"And I want to catch the late news, so I'm going to work until it's on." Then, because she could tell she'd really hurt Zora's feelings, she added, "If it makes any difference, I don't think

Brian was ever in love with Anne Reade. He married you."

"I don't think it's Anne. I think it's Clarice Billings."

"Oh, come on." Amanda half-laughed.

"I'm serious. Miss Billings is still really cute, at least she was at the reunion."

"Clarice Billings is only interested in her career. Take it from one who knows. Don't you remember the way she played up to Principal Kiefer? How she leaned on him after he and Bailey's mom broke up after Carmen's death? I saw them on a date once that summer, and it did not look like it was going well on her part. I think he bored her to tears. Then she got that better job, probably at his recommendation, and she was outta West Knoll like a shot. Brian's lucky to have you. You're younger, sweeter, and better-looking."

"You really think so?" Zora asked in a small voice.

"Yes."

"Or maybe it's someone else in our class. You think that could be it? At the reunion he kept looking at Delta . . ."

Amanda pulled around to the back of her house. The two-bay detached garage, which was far enough away from the house to be more of an outbuilding, was filled to the gills with her parents' stuff that she'd moved out of the house.

She preferred to park on the tarmac apron in the back.

"But I heard him on the phone . . . I'm pretty sure he was talking to a woman."

"Then ask your husband. There're a million reasons people say they want a divorce. Make him give you one. And while you're at it, tell him to grow the fuck up."

She clicked off. *Swear to God, dealing with needy people is the worst.*

She thought about how the most gung ho of the do-gooders, Rhonda and Trent, had wanted to help her after Thom's accident, how she'd agreed during the worst of the crisis, and how somehow they'd both tried to worm their way into a close friendship with her, which she'd neither wanted nor needed. She'd had to cut them out. Pathetically, they'd still considered her the head of the Five Firsts, and that had apparently meant something.

She'd lied to Zora about taking work home. She'd specifically finished up everything that was pressing while she was at the office. She thought now about going for a run on the cliff path above the river, something she usually did at lunchtime, but it was too late and too dark. Switching on the TV, she set up the DVR to record the late-evening news, then she sat down and watched mindless television until it came on. So Ellie had finally gotten some prime-time air. The powers that be at her station had never put her on hard news before. She'd been trying to sleep her way to the top, in Amanda's biased estimation, and, hey, whatever works for you, Amanda always felt. She'd done much the same thing, though she'd believed she'd loved the asshole at one time. Since then, she'd learned there was no such thing as love, at least for her. She didn't feel it, and she had the sneaking suspicion that so-called love was really just desire and lust, and that was basically a chemical reaction in the brain anyway.

When the news finally came on, Ellie's segment with Dr. Lester Stahd, who continued with his rantings and accusations, was the lead story. Zora had said Stahd was vicious, which was the right word. Stahd just looked like a madman, wildly grieving for his son. His wife had gotten dolled up for the camera, but she was in the background.

Amanda watched the segment, reversed the DVR, and watched it again. She ended up watching it five times, taking the measure of the elder Dr. Stahd. No wonder Tanner had been so screwed up. His father was as much of a bullying loser as her own mother. *It's a wonder we make it to adulthood as sane as we are. Parents are destroyers.*

Except Delta's. They'd been normal and nice. Lovely people, really. Amanda had always been jealous of them.

It was almost midnight when she decided to

text Delta: *I'm in. Let's meet tomorrow around five at my house.*

She didn't really want Delta seen at the office yet, where the partners and her ex and everyone were around, until she knew exactly what she planned to do for her ex-BFF.

Message sent, Amanda climbed the spiral stairway to the bedroom she'd used ever since she was a kid. For a few minutes, she hung halfway out the window, breathing in the smells of freshly mown hay and the danker scents from the river beyond. In her mind, she could see the place where Carmen had refused to come out of the water and accept Clarice Billings's help. She had it mentally marked, the same spot where Bailey had slipped in, running the rapids by herself without a raft of any kind.

Foolish children with death wishes. That's what they'd all been.

Back inside, she stripped off her clothes, washed her face, and climbed naked beneath her sheets. The cell on her nightstand's screen lit up, and she heard the *ding* of an incoming text. Delta.

Delta: *OK.*

"Okay," Amanda whispered, staring toward her ceiling in the inky darkness, but her inner vision was on Delta Smith-Stahd.

Delta took Owen to school the next morning and returned to her own house with trepidation. There were still no reporters camped out on her door today, which was a surprise and a relief, but since Ellie had given that in-depth report on Tanner, capping it with his father screaming for her head, maybe the reporters felt her story was played out and had moved on to a new one, or at least a new angle. Either way, the lack of press was likely only a momentary reprieve.

She took a long shower and came out of it feeling marginally better. Tanner was gone. He wasn't coming back. Life felt almost spookily normal, and she had to keep reminding herself that someone had killed him.

Wiping away the fog on the bathroom mirror, she gave herself a long look. Her dark hair lay lank and wet against her neck. Tiny lines had formed at the edges of her eyes and along her mouth, seemingly overnight. Worry had also furrowed creases in her forehead.

She checked her phone and saw there was a message from Candy: *When will the clinic reopen?*

It was with a dull shock that she realized she was the owner of the clinic now lock, stock, and barrel. It had been Tanner's baby, but unless Tanner had altered his will in the last couple of weeks, it now belonged to her, and she needed to do something about it.

This'll drive Lester Stahd even further out of his mind.

She wrote back to Candy: *I will check with the police.*

After that, she made herself some toast and tea. The raspberries she'd purchased days earlier were starting to shrivel. She was going to have to get back to some semblance of a routine for Owen and her. Just the two of them now, no longer three.

She felt a rush of emotion.

Who did this to you, Tanner? Did you know them? Was it personal, or for drugs, maybe, thinking they could score at the clinic?

All those stab wounds . . . with their knife . . .

She glanced at the new block of knives sitting on the counter. Grabbing up the wooden holder, she trudged upstairs, pulled down the attic ladder, climbed up, and exchanged it with her original set with its missing knife. She had no explanation for why she "couldn't remember" that she hadn't recognized their own knife. Owen would know she'd tried to replace them, but maybe she could keep him away from the police interrogators.

God, it was all so stupid!

Maybe she should confess to McCrae? Or maybe to Amanda when she saw her later.

What if she doesn't take your case?

She put herself together and then dressed in nice jeans and a white blouse. Peering through the living room shades, she groaned at the sight of a gathering news crew. Damn. They were back sooner than she'd thought. Not Ellie, at least.

She thought back to her interview at the police station and what she'd told Quin and McCrae. The arguments and tiffs she and Tanner had gotten into. The one with his father had been over the business, and the fender bender . . . It was amazing how fast that fight had escalated between Tanner and the guy in the other car. She couldn't remember his name, but he, like Tanner, had taken his dented vehicle to Woody's Auto Body. Delta wasn't there when Tanner took it in, but he'd told her later that Woody had slapped him on the back and told him to keep clear if the other guy was there. "He's mad as hell. Let me call you," Woody had told him. "Grinning like the idiot he is," Tanner had related. "Like the accident was my fault. That jackass ran into me!" He hadn't found his old friend's jocularity as fun as it used to be, apparently.

But could a minor traffic accident end in murder? She knew it happened sometimes, but it had been half a year ago. Could this guy really carry a grudge that long?

You should talk to Woody.

Her cell buzzed, breaking into her thoughts. She pulled the phone out of her purse and regarded it carefully. Zora. Huh.

"Hi, Zora," Delta answered, still looking out at the van across the street.

"Oh, Delta," she said in a rush. "I'm so, so

sorry about Tanner. I saw it on the news. Do you need anything? Anything at all?"

"No, but thanks, really. I'm just . . . I don't know . . . numb."

"Do you need food? I could bring over something. Or . . . babysitting? I know your boy is about six."

"Owen's at pre-K. Thanks. I think I'm okay."

"Would you just like some company? I've had a kind of rough time myself and could use a friend."

"Umm . . ." Delta drew a blank. She wasn't going to meet Amanda till 5:00. No meeting at the law firm, which was fine with Delta. "There's a news crew here, so I'm planning to leave and just get away for a while."

"Come to my house," Zora invited.

"Thanks, but I think I'm going to go hit a double feature. I just want time to pass till tonight."

"I'll go with you, if you want me to. I'd love to."

Zora had never been so eager to be Delta's friend since the end of high school and the Five Firsts. "Sure," she said, and they agreed to meet at the mall cinemas.

Inside her Audi, Delta pressed the button to lift the garage door and backed out a little more quickly than she'd intended. Luckily, this crew was smart enough not to block the drive this time. Still, the young, balding male reporter from Channel Four came right up to her window as she backed into the street.

"Your book *Blood Dreams* starts with a woman stabbing her husband to death," he called through the closed window. "That's either a macabre coincidence or a blueprint for murder. Care to comment?"

"Oh, no," Delta whispered beneath her breath. They'd found her e-book.

She put the car in DRIVE and started forward, the man trotting alongside her window.

"Any other scenes we should expect to see come to life?"

Asshole. She pressed her toe to the accelerator, and the Audi jumped forward as if in a race.

Chapter 20

Quin was already at work when McCrae came through the back door of the station at 6:00 a.m. and headed for the break room, his mind full of thoughts about Delta Stahd. Before he could get settled, Quin found him and beckoned him back to his office. Corinne walked slowly by the door and stopped, looking in on them.

"You see the news?" Quin asked McCrae.

"Yep," he clipped out. Ellie O'Brien's report on Tanner's life had been fine, but the follow-up with Lester Stahd had devolved into accusations, condemnations, and recriminations against Delta that held only enmity and rage, no facts.

He looked back at Corinne, who said, "Social media's exploded, too, about half for and half against her."

"You're still in her camp?" Quin asked him.

"I'm not going to make any judgments about her on hearsay and emotion. I'm going to go through the clinic records. Talk some more to the employees. See if there are any grudges. Any previous break-ins, that kind of thing. Find some possible motives."

"Mr. Hurston is coming in to talk to you," Corinne said.

"Why?" McCrae asked.

She shrugged lightly and left.

McCrae looked at Quin, who said, "Might be a good time to go to Eugene."

"In the heat of the Stahd homicide? No. And why's Hurston coming today?"

"You sure you didn't say something to Corinne about Carville?"

"Positive."

Quin shook his head. "Hell hath no fury . . ."

"I don't have time for this," he muttered.

"Go before Hurston shuts you down and takes over the Stahd case."

"The Stahd case is ours." McCrae was positive. "I'll go when things cool down a bit."

"Then I'll go," Quin said determinedly. "Before Hurston gets in the way."

McCrae knew the mettle of Timothy Hurston better than anyone. He liked convenience, tidiness, cases that were neatly tied up and made him look good. The man was running for the state senate, a true politician. He'd decided Bailey's and Penske's deaths were a murder/suicide and, by sheer force of will, had slashed down any argument McCrae and others in the West Knoll PD had to offer. Hurston was much loved by the upper brass, so he'd gotten his way. Case closed. A feather in his cap. He'd obviously also since convinced Corinne that he was correct in his assessment of the crime, as she was apparently helping him.

And maybe it was a little bit about her twisting the knife on McCrae, as she knew how he felt about the man's findings.

"I'll go," McCrae said. "And I've got a meeting with Coach Sutton later tonight."

"Good. I'll keep checking with the lab, see if they've pulled any other DNA from the crime scene, and I'll talk to the employees again."

"I'd like to be in on any other interviews," said McCrae.

Quin nodded. "Let's connect later. Trade stories. I'll make sure your trip to"—he looked to the open doorway and lowered his voice, changing course—"Hurston won't know where you are."

"Good." If Hurston should so much as catch a whiff of someone challenging one of his settled cases, he'd move heaven and earth to keep them from overturning it.

Quin added, "There was a bar fight with the Crassleys last night. I've put Corolla on it."

McCrae snorted. There was always a bar fight with the Crassleys.

He re-gathered up his belongings and headed out, calling Delta on the way. When she didn't pick up, he left her a voice message, telling her he would be busy for most of the day, but she could call him and leave messages and texts, and he would get back to her. He also added that, if she needed anything immediately, she should call Quin. Maybe Quin wasn't Delta's biggest fan, but he was a fair man, and the way Stahd Senior had eviscerated her on television wouldn't sit well with Quin's innate chivalry.

On the drive south, he thought over the information he'd learned about Tanner Stahd's attack and subsequent death, letting his mind free-associate. He thought of Delta, the elder Dr. Stahd, the personal nature of stabbing someone, the possibility of divorce with an undoubtedly looming custody battle, and the victim himself, Tanner Stahd and his purported womanizing, from high school right on to the present. From there, he thought about Bailey and Penske and Carmen . . .

McCrae looked through the windshield at the passing landscape, fields on either side of the freeway that cut down to the Willamette Valley.

He thought about Jed Corolla, who'd allowed Ellie, Amanda, and Zora into Tanner's room.

"They didn't do anything, I swear," the earnest younger officer had said, catching up with him just before he left for Eugene. "The three of them . . . I was right there. They were just standing back, four feet or so, when Stahd had the heart attack that killed him. They never even got close. He just sat up and yelled, 'Dee,' and then dropped back down, unconscious. The staff tried to revive him, but he never came back."

When McCrae had absorbed that, Corolla added, "That redhead looked like she knew what that meant."

The redhead. Ellie O'Brien.

"What about the others?" McCrae had asked.

He shook his head. "They all were herded out of the room, and I followed them out. They left."

McCrae followed his GPS into Eugene and a street a few blocks outside of campus but close enough to get some foot traffic to the Duck-Duck Inn. He'd been given the information on Carville from a series of current and previous coworkers at Lundeen's who kept sending him from one person to another until he finally learned of Carville's whereabouts.

The Duck-Duck Inn was undoubtedly named for U of O's mascot, a Donald Duck replica that had apparently been grandfathered in by Disney to allow for the university's use. There were Donald Duck caricatures involved in various stages of comic high jinks decorating the otherwise rough board walls. McCrae doubted the image was sanctioned by businesses outside the university grounds, like the Duck-Duck, but no one appeared to be complaining.

He sat down at the end of the bar and ordered a beer. It was about 1:00 p.m. No sign of Carville. Maybe the information was wrong, or maybe he was slated to work later. McCrae turned to his phone, checking e-mails and texts. Nothing new. He'd hoped Delta would contact him, but she'd been radio silent since he left her off with her parents.

Dee, he mused, thinking of Tanner's last word. Sure, "Dee" could be for Delta, but there were other possibilities as well. Coach was Dean Sutton, he could be the "D." Or . . . Zora *De*Marco. And it certainly didn't have to be somebody's name.

After he'd been at the bar about twenty minutes, he called the bartender over, a young woman in a sleeveless shirt with arm tattoos covering nearly every square inch of skin and a series of tiny red stones pierced into an arc around one nostril. "I'm looking for somebody," he said.

"You a cop?" she asked.

McCrae was in jeans and a blue shirt with the sleeves rolled up. He was almost offended that she'd made him so quickly. "This is outside my job, and the higher-ups would not appreciate my being here."

She looked interested. "Could you get fired over it?"

"Entirely possible."

"Who is it, then?"

"James Carville."

"The old man. Huh."

"The old man?" McCrae repeated.

"Gray hair, ponytail?"

McCrae nodded. That was exactly how he would've described the man he'd met five years earlier, though he'd thought the man had just grayed early.

"He'll be in around two. Punctuality isn't his strong suit. Mine neither, but then nothing really gets going till later."

McCrae forced himself not to look at the time. "Maybe I'll have something to eat." The early-morning stale muffin he'd shared with Fido wasn't cutting it. "What's the favorite around here?"

"Duck burger. Made with beef," she added, clearly a point that had needed to be mentioned more than once. "The usual suspects—tomato, onion, lettuce, and avocado, and pepperjack cheese, too."

"Sold."

She went through a swinging door presumably into the kitchen to place the order. When she returned, she refilled his beer, though he protested he didn't need a second.

"It's on me. Gotta keep in good with the cops," she said.

"I'm not from around here."

"Doesn't matter. Karma works everywhere."

A few other customers started trickling in. McCrae nursed his second beer and worked on the piled-high hamburger and fries Marla, as she told him her name was, put in front of him. He was impatiently checking his phone every five minutes when Carville walked through the door, his ponytail a good deal longer than it had been five years earlier.

He noticed McCrae right away and looked like he wanted to bolt.

"Remember me?" McCrae asked, though he'd only seen the man once before the investigation was co-opted by Hurston.

"You were with that cop's father."

Ah, yes. He'd been with Quin, and Quin had been sick with grief, alternatively silent and seething or loud and explosive.

"Didn't get to talk to you much before the investigation moved to another investigator."

He made a sound of disgust, low in his throat. "That bullshit asshole who directed my answers."

"How do you mean, 'directed'?"

"I mean, like, he said, 'You saw no evidence that he'd roofied her, correct?' and then when I said, 'I'm pretty sure I did see him dump something into her drink,' he said, 'Well, it was dark and you couldn't see,' and I said, 'It wasn't that dark' and 'Yes, I could see,' which he didn't like, and so we went around a few times. Spooked me."

"That why you left?"

"That, and I was losing my apartment. Landlord was jacking up the price, but that cop was the last straw."

"So you did see Penske put something in the woman's drink that night."

"Yeah . . . if that's his name, Penske . . . pretty sure. She didn't know about it. I was going to tell her, but then they went outside, and they seemed all right. I don't know . . . I kinda shrugged it off. You see a lot of stuff at a bar." He made a face. "We all left when the placed closed. Didn't think about the car at the far back of the lot. People leave 'em in the lot all the time. I didn't learn till the next day they'd been shot."

"Anyone else notice them that night?"

He shrugged. "I was the one serving them. That cop talked to everybody."

"The investigator."

"Yeah, him." Carville's lips tightened. "Nobody wanted to talk to him."

McCrae could well imagine. Hurston had his narrative set before he started and was trying to make the facts fit it, not the other way around. "Anything else? Anything you can remember? Something small . . . an anomaly? Anything."

"I've thought about it a lot. Tracy said she thought there was a guy who came in and looked at them but then left."

"Tracy's another employee?"

"She was only there a few weeks before I left. She kinda made up stories, so I wouldn't put too much faith in what she said, y'know?"

McCrae recalled the staff very clearly, had

395

committed their faces to memory as a means of preserving what he knew personally of the case. He'd been too much of a junior officer to be put in charge, and Quin was Bailey's father, so Hurston had been plopped into the case. McCrae had planned to revisit it when he could, had expected it to be earlier than the five years that had passed, but at least he had some traction now. The problem was Corinne had sicced Hurston on him and Quin.

"Was Tracy the blonde or the one with the long brown braid?" McCrae asked.

"Long brown braid. Tracy Gillup. We used to call her Giddyup."

After that, Carville didn't have much more to say. McCrae thanked him and slid off his stool, checking his texts and voice mail again. Nothing from Delta. He called Quin, who wanted to know every detail about what he'd learned, then informed McCrae that Hurston was at the station.

Jolted, McCrae asked, "How's that going?"

"He wants to know about you. I said you were working on the Stahd case, which you are. I think he's too busy campaigning to try to hijack it from us, but . . ."

"Yeah?" McCrae said when Quin trailed off.

In a low voice, he added, "He might be worrying that you and I haven't given up finding Bailey's killer."

"I'm going to look for this Tracy Gillup next."

"Good."

There was a moment of silence between them, then Quin said, "And Delta called and asked when the clinic could be opened again."

"I'll look into it," he said again as he hung up.

It bothered him that Delta hadn't called him directly, but then Quin would be more likely to know the answer to that question, given that McCrae wasn't around.

Are you being played?

The thought stuck with him all the way back to West Knoll. He'd been Delta's champion, believing in her all the way. And yet what did he know about her really? He'd always liked her, but in truth he barely knew her.

He was pulling into the station around 4:00 when his cell rang. He braced himself, but once again it wasn't Delta, it was Ellie.

"Are you going to arrest her?" Ellie demanded.

"I assume you mean Delta."

"Is there enough evidence?"

"You should talk to the DA about it."

"I'm onto something here, McCrae. I've got momentum going. I don't need a whole 'on camera' interview with you; just answer yes or no. Are you going to arrest her?"

"You trying to make your move to anchor using Tanner's homicide?"

"Yes or no," she snapped.

"That's pretty low, even for you."

"You are a piece of shit, McCrae."

"That may be," he said amiably. "Just don't get in the way of my investigation."

"Your investigation?" She snorted. "I've got leads on this, and I'm not going to squander them."

"What leads?"

"Delta killed Tanner, and I'm going to prove it."

"Leave it to the police, Ellie," he warned.

"The police . . . meaning you and Bailey's dad? You haven't even been able to solve *that* mystery. Murder/suicide? Total bullshit, and you know it."

McCrae's eye narrowed. Beneath her gibes, something was going on here. "What have you got, Ellie?"

She snorted. "Thanks for nothing, McCrae," she declared, and hung up.

"I could just pick him up at the pre-K for you," Zora said. They were walking out of a lame romantic comedy that nevertheless had brought tears to Delta's eyes.

"No. My mom's picking him up today, and only people on the list at the pre-K can pick him up, which is me, my mom, my dad, and . . . Tanner . . ."

"I'm so sorry." Zora's hand shot out and touched Delta's arm as they headed to their cars.

"Thanks." Delta drew a long breath. Worry had settled in, bone deep. She needed to do something. Act. Find out why her husband had been killed. Her mind was screaming along even while she was watching the hours pass in idleness. Maybe she should check with Woody, do a little investigating of her own.

"You want to catch dinner?" Zora asked.

"No . . . thanks. I really can't."

"Oh, okay." She sounded crestfallen.

Zora was being awfully nice to her, which was weird in itself. Before the film, she'd confessed that her husband had said he was leaving her. "There's somebody else," she said, sounding lost. "He's apparently loved her since the barbecue, and I think he's talking to her all the time. He always says he's talking to someone else, but I just have a feeling he's lying."

"Who is it?"

"I don't know." She shot Delta a sheepish look. "For a while I thought it was you?"

"Is that a question?"

"No, no." She shook her head.

"I've been faithful to Tanner all along. The whole time we've been together, even during college and med school."

Delta cut herself off then. There'd been rumors about Tanner with Amanda and Ellie and even Zora. She'd chosen to ignore all the noise and concentrate on loving her husband and making a

399

home with him. When Owen came along, it was easier to shove that noise aside and concentrate on being a mom. When she thought about how much she'd hated Amanda, how it had consumed her for a while, it almost embarrassed her. Even so, she marveled that she was going to meet with her soon.

But I'm over it. All of it.

As if there'd been no break since their conversation before the film, Zora said miserably, "I thought Brian was saying he was in love with Clarice Billings at first, but now I don't know. He really hung out with Anne Reade back then, and Amanda said Clarice was too ambitious for him anyway."

"You talked to Amanda about it?"

"On the phone last night. But maybe he thought Clarice was out of reach, and so that's why he was with Anne, because she was gettable. Maybe he loved Clarice from afar back then, and now with his inheritance, he has more to work with, y'know? Like he could get her now."

"He didn't say who it was?" Delta asked.

"No. Except that it was someone at the barbecue . . . I think." Her face clouded. "Maybe it is Anne Reade. I don't know . . ."

"He married you, Zora," said Delta. She was starting to weary of the conversation. She had so many other, bigger problems.

"I know, but . . . maybe I just got in there at the

right time. Caught him just as he was becoming well . . . rich."

"Don't be so hard on yourself."

"Amanda told me I was younger and prettier than Miss Billings," Zora said, looking at Delta sideways.

Delta could see was angling for a compliment, so she gave it to her. "Amanda's right."

Zora smiled. "Amanda also told me to tell Brian to grow the fuck up."

"Sounds just like her."

"I know you guys aren't friends anymore, but I kind of want us to all get back together, the Five Firsts, you know? Is that dumb? A pipe dream? Completely out of the question?"

There are no Five Firsts any longer.

"Actually, I'm going to see Amanda today," Delta said. "I want her to be my defense attorney."

Zora's lips parted in surprise. "You're kidding."

"No. My husband's dead, and I'm a prime suspect. I need a lawyer, and I asked Amanda to be that lawyer."

"Is she . . . has she agreed to?"

"I'll find out." They were at their cars, and Delta turned to her to say good-bye. "Thanks for coming to the movie with me."

"Oh, anytime. You know, I could I help you out tomorrow, too. With Owen? *After* pre-K," she said. "You can go somewhere, or just take a

401

nap, whatever you need, and I'll get him dinner and play with him, give him a bath, put him to bed . . ."

"I'm really okay, Zora. I—"

"Please," she beseeched. "I want to. I need to get away from my life for a while. What better way than with children? Brian and I were trying, you probably know already, but now that's over."

"I don't pick him up till around five."

"Great. I'll be at your house at five-fifteen, okay?"

Delta lifted her palms and dropped them in surrender. If Zora really wanted to come over, why should she fight it?

McCrae got a total rundown from Quin on Tim Hurston's trip to the station, which had appeared to be a sniffing-around expedition and nothing more. McCrae had almost asked Corinne about him but didn't want her to know he'd even given the man's visit a thought.

With that in mind, he'd gone to his desk and immediately started a search for Tracy Gillup and got a hit for her address right away, only to learn that she was no longer there. He tried to find a cell number—or any phone number, for that matter—but struck out. He then looked up employment records and realized the girl was a roamer, out of one job at a bar or restaurant, then onto another, moving around after only a few months at any one place. He also realized she didn't stray far from a certain nexus on Portland's west side, so if she'd moved from her last place of employment, he could check with various bars in the area and see if he could find her. Since he had some time before he was supposed to meet Dean Sutton, he headed out of the station at about 4:30.

"Where are you going?" Corinne asked.

He hadn't seen her as she was walking from the break room when he was pushing through the back door. It was odd for her to ask. Especially since they didn't talk anymore.

"Working a case," he said.

"The Stahd case."

He nodded. He didn't have to tell her he was doing some digging into Bailey's homicide before he met with Sutton. "Is there a reason you want to know?"

"I'm sure you heard Tim was here today. He wanted to talk to you."

"Tim Hurston?"

"You know who I mean."

"I don't think we have anything to talk about."

"You don't have to be so pissy about him, you know. You and I have been over a long time."

McCrae smiled faintly. "As long as he stays out of my business, he's all yours."

"That's the pissy attitude I'm talking about!" she called as he headed for his Explorer.

403

McCrae actually laughed for the first time in a long time.

Delta pulled into the long drive toward Amanda's house, which she'd inherited from her parents after the accident that had permanently injured her brother. Delta had occasionally wondered about how her parents could just up and leave Amanda and Thom, but hadn't wanted to feel anything like pity for the woman who'd caused such trouble and misery for her and Tanner.

But now she needed her. Maybe there was someone else she could call, but she didn't know who that person was, and the one thing everyone said about Amanda was how good she was at her job.

The driveway circled around to the back, but Amanda's black Lexus SUV was parked outside the double-bay garage that sat back from the house and had once housed the golf cart they used to transport supplies to the barbeque. Delta pulled her Audi up beside it. Her car was nearly paid off. A blessing, as she had no idea what her future finances were going to bring. She'd asked about reopening the clinic at Candy's request, although who the doctor in charge might be was a question. Elderly Dr. Gervais wasn't anyone's idea of someone who could run the business.

She thought briefly of McCrae, whom she'd deliberately not contacted since the day before.

She'd made a point of blocking him from her mind and keeping her phone off. It was just better to keep him at arm's length right now.

She rang the back bell off the patio; it wasn't a house where anyone used the front entrance. A few minutes later, she watched Amanda approach through the back door's glass panes. She wore a light gray blouse and a pair of black slacks, and looked cool and comfortable even though the July evening was hanging onto the day's heat. She greeted Delta with, "Hello, there," as she opened the door and gestured for Delta to enter.

Delta's pulse was running light and fast as she stepped inside. The last time she'd been here was the night of the barbecue.

Amanda led her to the dining room. She sat down in an end chair, and Delta took the seat to her right. The rest of the table seemed to stretch away from them toward the interior of the house, an interior that felt empty and disused, which it probably was most of the time.

"Can I get you something to drink? Water or a soda? Coffee or tea?" Amanda asked.

"I'm fine, thanks."

"You sounded kind of urgent last night."

Delta squeaked out a half laugh. "Well . . . yeah."

Amanda's expression grew serious. "I'm going to ask you a question, and I want an honest answer. Many defense lawyers don't want to know if their client has committed the crime. That's not me. I want to know the truth, exactly what I'll be dealing with if I take your case."

"Okay."

"Did you kill your husband?"

"No."

Amanda's blue eyes stared into Delta's. "I'm not sure I believe you."

Delta could feel the heat rush to her face. "I loved him. Someone stabbed him over and over again. I want to know who that someone is. I can't believe you could think it was me. I'm just . . . holding on by a thread."

"Did you see Ellie's news report last night?"

"If you mean Lester Stahd's decimation of my character, yes."

"Before that. Ellie's . . . eulogy. I believe she was trying for intimate and warm, but that's a little out of her reach."

"I saw some of it."

"She made Tanner sound like a great guy, a wonderful human being. But we both know that's not true, don't we?"

Delta eyed Amanda cautiously. She hardly knew how to respond to that, so she didn't. "Are you going to help me?"

"We need to work out a few things. Financial and otherwise. You've hated me for years. I'm just wondering if you can put that aside."

"I haven't hated you," Delta responded automatically.

"I'm going to tell you something, and then we can move on."

"All right," Delta said carefully.

"I'm competitive."

"Really." Delta was dry.

"No, I mean deep-down competitive. On the edge of psychotic . . . competitive."

"You act like this is news."

Amanda gave a surprised laugh. "Fair enough. From the beginning, I wanted to beat you. Everybody, of course, but especially you. I wanted Tanner because you wanted him. I had to have him because he was yours. I didn't think about it that way at the time. I've come to that realization a bit late."

"Why?" she asked, dumbfounded.

"Because you were, and are, the best of us," she said. "It's just something I always knew. Ellie feels it, too, I'd wager. Watch out for her . . . and for Zora."

"Zora? What do you mean?"

"Don't trust any of us. We lie. You don't lie . . . much."

"All I know is I need a defense attorney. I'm here because that's what you are, and you're a good one. I know things are going to get worse for me, and I've got a little boy to take care of who's just learned his dad isn't coming back."

407

Her voice quavered a bit, and she pulled herself together. "He's doing okay. Wanted to go to pre-K today. I took him. I don't really know what else to do, but another shoe's going to drop."

Amanda gave a deep nod. "My job would be to do my best to keep you out of jail, but if I should fail, have you made arrangements for your son?"

"Yes. I mean, no. But my mother and father, his grandparents . . . they would take care of him." Amanda had put her finger on Delta's deepest fear. She couldn't believe she could actually go to jail. She was horror-stricken at the thought.

Several long moments elapsed during which Delta could tell Amanda was doing some serious thinking. "All right," she finally said.

"All right?" Delta repeated.

"I'll represent you."

Delta let out a pent-up breath. "Oh . . . good. Thank you. Do you need a . . . retainer? I can write you a check . . ." *As long as it's not too much.*

Amanda named a fairly reasonable figure, which caused Delta's brows to lift.

"I'm doing this as a friend," she told Delta.

Delta's throat closed, and she was glad to have to look down and search through her purse for her checkbook, a chance to gather herself. Once she'd written out the payment, she set it on the table between them.

Amanda didn't reach for it. She merely crossed

her arms atop the table and settled in. "Now that we've got that taken care of, let's go back over the last few months, maybe a year. Don't leave anything out about your relationship with Tanner and your son and anyone else you deem important in your life. Your parents? Friends? Tell me about any fights you've had and what they've been over, money, the dynamics of your household—"

"Other women," Delta cut in.

"Other women," Amanda repeated, cutting off whatever else she'd been about to say, then picking up again, "What you told the police. Anything about his business, and yours. Financial issues."

"I don't have a business."

"You wrote a book."

"Well, yes, but it's barely made a blip on anyone's radar."

"What's the book about?"

Delta drew a breath. "It's a . . . thriller."

"And in one of the first scenes, the wife stabs her husband."

"You've read it?" Delta asked, her heart clutching.

"Just know about it. Give me a recap."

"Well, my main character's been abused by her husband, so she takes matters into her own hands. She . . . stabs him to death, and then basically gets away with murder. It's not autobiographical."

Her eyes narrowed. "Okay. Other people have read your book. The police are going to know about it. I'm going to read it."

She nodded. Her throat was hot.

"Let's leave it for now. Just start talking to me. If there's anything I should know that makes you look bad, bring it out into the daylight."

The knife . . .

"What?" Amanda asked, reading her expression.

Delta tried to tell her. She closed her eyes, gathering courage. But what came out was a blurt. "Were you even ever pregnant?"

Amanda sat back in her chair. Delta held her breath, wondering if she'd blown it; she really, really hoped she hadn't. Finally, Amanda leaned forward again. "I thought I was, but probably not."

Silence fell between them, then Delta drew a breath and started in.

Chapter 21

McCrae looked at his phone, checking the time as he entered the third bar on Portland's west side where Tracy Gillup had once worked. He asked to see the manager—Jimmy, he was told—who was in his twenties and sported a shaved head and the kind of hard body achieved from weight-lifting that looks like it barely fits in a shirt. McCrae started talking the talk, discussing working out as if it were his life. Jimmy immediately sought to one-up him, bragging about how many pounds he could press.

"You sure you don't have any information on Tracy Gillup?" McCrae put in.

"Sorry, man. This place sold three months ago. I don't have any records before that." His gaze slid away, and McCrae determined he was lying about something.

"Maybe you could get me a beer?" McCrae didn't really feel like drinking, but he had some time before he was meeting Sutton. He pointed to one of the taps, and Jimmy directed one of the guys behind the bar to help him before he scooted into the back room.

There were several waitresses, but two had dark, almost black hair, and one was a bleached blond. No medium brown and no braids, but then it had been five years since Bailey's death, and Tracy could have certainly changed her hairstyle.

He nursed his beer and thought about Tanner Stahd. Someone had stabbed him using a knife that was handy. No premeditation. After hours, though, so their meeting had been clandestine, but maybe not on purpose? Delta was coming to the clinic . . . did whoever was there know that? Was she meant to take the fall? Or was it just the heat of passion? A spurned lover . . . ? Which didn't look good for Delta.

There was no theft, as far as anyone could tell, so it didn't seem like drugs.

Jimmy came out once more and looked around, his eyes sliding back and forth. He didn't like having McCrae there. It was in his body language. He disappeared into the back once again.

McCrae was finishing his beer, deciding he didn't have time to find out what was making Jimmy so anxious, when a guy at the end of the bar yelled at the short-haired blonde, "Giddyup, bring me another Cadillac margarita, no salt."

McCrae stared at the blonde, who signaled to the guy that she'd gotten his order. He'd only met Tracy Gillup once, and he wasn't sure, so he said, "Tracy?"

She turned and looked at him. "Yeah?"

Jimmy came out of the back like a shot, as if

he'd been listening, which he probably had. "You don't have to talk to him," he told her. "He's a cop."

Tracy gave him a bored look. "You ain't my dad, Jimmy," she said, then turned to McCrae. "What do you want then?"

"I want to know what you remember about the night of the murder at Lundeen's five years ago."

"Jesus Christ," Jimmy said.

"Thought that was all decided," said Tracy.

"The cop that was killed was my friend," said McCrae.

"Giddyup!" Another guy called from the same group as the first hollerer. "Get me the same!"

"Jimmy, you wanna get those Cadillacs?" Tracy said, hooking a thumb toward the loud group milling around at the end of the bar. Then she leaned forward on the bar in front of McCrae and said, "I wondered if anybody was ever going to get past that cop, investigator, whatever. He didn't give a damn about the truth."

"Tim Hurston."

"Maybe. I don't know what his name was." She paused. "You look familiar."

"I talked to you first at Lundeen's. I was the first investigator. You had longer brown hair in a braid."

"Huh." She straightened and eyed him across the bar. "I told that other asshole what I knew, but he just blew me off."

"Tracy," Jimmy said, hovering around behind her. She ignored him, and it was clear she didn't like his proprietary attitude toward her.

"He was talking to somebody. Making all kinds of plans. And she was barely hanging on to her stool. I don't think she even knew he was on the phone."

McCrae said, "There were no calls on his cell that night." Carville had called her a liar. Maybe this was what he meant.

She gave him a "Really?" look. "It was a burner. Just a plain old phone. Nothing fancy about it. I know those kind when I see 'em. I noticed, 'cause most of the guys who have 'em around here use 'em to score drugs and stuff. Keep changing 'em out. Untraceable."

"Justin Penske, the man with Officer Bailey Quintar, was using a temporary phone, not his cell?"

"Uh huh. And there was that other guy, too."

"What guy?"

"The bigger guy who came in, looked around, saw the two of them and quickly turned around and bolted. Except he was hanging around outside, trying not to be noticed. Kept waiting for something, I guess."

"That was never in any report."

"I didn't really think about it till later, after that asshole who wouldn't listen to me anyway was gone."

"You're sure this guy was watching Penske and Bailey?"

"No. That's the point, isn't it? 'The only sure thing is man is unsure.' I don't know. Fuck it. Don't believe me. Nobody ever does."

She stepped back, nearly into Jimmy. "Jesus, Jimmy," she said scornfully.

She was helping so many people, McCrae had to wait for her to come back into his space. "I believe you," he said, when he could get her attention again.

"Bully for you," she said over her shoulder, pulling a Stella for the customer seated next to McCrae, an older man.

"Do you remember what he looked like? The big man who was watching?"

"Yeah. He wore a trench coat and sunglasses and had a big birthmark on his forehead, six fingers on each hand, and wore red lipstick."

The older man beside McCrae snickered.

"Anything?" McCrae asked, ignoring the gibe.

Tracy didn't answer for a while. Kept filling glasses of beer. Checking the time, McCrae was about to slide off his stool and head toward the Bengal Room, when she came back.

"He was pretty anxious. On one foot and the other. And I thought I saw him talking to someone in a car for a while. An older car. Faded red. Like a truck of some kind, actually, maybe.

Whole front of it was like dusty pink instead of red. Maybe one of those car trucks."

"El Camino?" the older man beside McCrae said.

"Fuck if I know," Tracy said. "That's all I know. There ain't no more. You want anything else?"

"Chevy stopped making El Caminos in eighty-seven," the guy said.

"It was old, okay?" Tracy snapped at him as she walked away. "That's all I'm saying."

McCrae dropped money on the bar with a sizable tip. The old guy looked at the bills hard, and before he left, McCrae gently reminded him it was stealing if he should slip a dollar or two into his own pocket.

The Bengal Room was just as Coach Dean Sutton had described it, with real-enough-looking fake tiger skins adorning one wall to make McCrae take a second look, a sleek mahogany bar sporting under-counter lighting, and blood-red leather club chairs nestled around a scattering of tables. The lighting was low, and there was an understated elegance that drew in a crowd of fortysomethings.

"My condo's over thataway," the coach said, pointing west, after he and McCrae shook hands. Fifteen years later, Coach had short-clipped gray hair and had grown lean enough to hollow out his cheeks. His body was still fit, though the

416

faint pudginess that had defined him was long gone. This man was sober and stingier with his smiles as he gestured for McCrae to take one of the club chairs at a table crowded close to the bar.

"Oh, man, that's tough about Tanner," he said, his long face growing even more hangdog. "Saw on the news that he didn't make it. Hard to believe. So much potential . . ."

"I know what you mean."

Sutton was lost for a moment, sorrowfully shaking his head. Then he drew a breath and looked around. "Hope it doesn't turn out to be Delta."

"Yeah." McCrae tried to sound somewhat non-committal, even though he agreed completely.

"Masterer isn't here yet, but I bet he comes."

"You want me to see him."

"She was flirting pretty heavy with him, that's all."

"How are you doing?" McCrae asked him, which sent him on a long story about how good the boys' track team was at Montgomery and how it was a shame the fastest runner was more interested in soccer than football.

McCrae had trouble concentrating. His thoughts were chasing each other around and around. He felt the need to be doing something more than legwork. He wanted something to grab on to.

He let the coach go on for a while before he decided to bring the conversation back to the here and now. He wanted to call Delta again. It felt like a long, long day without any communication, which was probably another thing to think hard about, but that one he pushed away.

"You wanted to talk some more," McCrae reminded.

"Ah, yeah. I didn't know he was gone then."

"Does it make a difference?"

"Feels kinda bad to say things about a guy who just died, yeah. But it wasn't all about him. It's about all of 'em, I guess. Been thinking a lot about Carmen Proffitt. She was a good girl. A really good girl. Did you know her?"

"She was in my class," McCrae reminded.

"I mean really know her. Like a good friend."

McCrae shook his head. Carmen was the reverend's daughter, and most of the guys had steered clear of her. She was tall, gangly, connected at the hip with Bailey, and not interested in any guy but Tanner.

Sutton said, "She had a big crush on Tanner, but a lot of 'em did back then."

Tanner Stahd, the teenage god.

"Yep," McCrae agreed.

"Some of the mothers, too. The way they looked at Tanner? You could just see it. They were as giddy as kids." He paused, as if waiting for McCrae to fill the void, but when that didn't happen, added, "Bailey's mom couldn't take her eyes off him."

McCrae said uncomfortably, "Mrs. Quintar was dating Principal Kiefer." *And now they're married.*

"But she hadn't settled on Ron at that time. That was later. You know they broke up and got back together after Bailey died?"

"Yes."

"Well, before all that, she was playing the field. So was Ron, come to that. Dated both Clarice Billings and Anne Reade for a time."

"I hadn't heard that."

"Well, he was awkward as hell. Basically just called them up and asked them on dates, and if they said no, he pinned them down on when they were free and kept at it till he basically wore them down and they said okay. Didn't get the signals or didn't care. I've talked to both Billings and Reade. They both said he was hard to say no to. Never thought he'd get back with Bailey's mom, but after Bailey's death . . ." He shrugged. "You just never know, do ya?"

"You're not suggesting that Joyce Quintar was ever with Tanner . . . ?"

"Nah . . . I don't think so." But he didn't sound so sure. "It was just, Carmen was a good girl, and if she was with him at the barbecue, but she'd thought that he'd been with Bailey's mom and she felt guilty enough . . . she might take her own life."

McCrae grimaced. He didn't want to debate what had happened to Carmen again.

"I was going to tell you that, when you talk to Tanner again, you might want to ask him about Mrs. Quintar—er, Kiefer now—but that's what I mean about feeling bad about talking about him. The reverend suspected something, I think. The moms were friends, but after the barbecue where Carmen died . . . there was a falling out between them. Maybe over Tanner? I just . . . when I'd heard he'd been attacked, I wanted to say my piece."

McCrae could hear Bailey's voice in his head: *Carmen said she saw something . . . I think it had to do with Tanner . . . she didn't have a chance to tell me what . . . but she didn't kill herself . . . she would never do that . . .* She'd repeated variations on that theme all the time he'd known her since Carmen's death.

"I'm just saying, Carmen followed Tanner around like an imprinted duckling and coulda heard and seen a lot of stuff. Tanner wasn't . . . discreet. I heard afterward he was with some of the girls the night of the barbecue. He was a great kid, great athlete, but he . . . was red-blooded, y'know? He was Carmen's hero but he . . . mighta showed her a side she couldn't accept."

"I don't think she committed suicide."

He inclined his head. "You're the cop."

"You think this has some bearing on what happened to Tanner two nights ago?"

"I've just been thinking a lot. Bailey, rest her soul, thought there was something more. I ran into her a couple of times after I left West Knoll, and both times Carmen's death was the first thing she talked about. She didn't feel justice had been done."

McCrae thought about how Tim Hurston had hijacked Bailey's case and used it to increase his own profile in his long-term bid for political gain. *I feel the same,* he thought.

"There he is," Coach muttered. "Jonah Masterer."

A tall man strode into the bar and ordered a martini. He then turned to survey the crowd, leaning against the bar, elbows on it, like he owned the place. When one dark-haired woman from a group of ladies drew near him to try to catch the bartender's attention, Masterer moved in to talk to her. Whatever he was saying brought a smile to her lips, even while she shook her head.

"He's a type. Dark hair, good-looking . . . seems to have money. Tells 'em about his little girl as a warm-up." Coach was dry. "When I saw him hitting on Delta, I wanted to smack him, so I left the bar before bad things happened."

"Good thinking."

"You gonna talk to him?" Coach asked hopefully.

McCrae was dealing with a coil of jealousy winding through him. Its inappropriateness was slightly worrisome. "Maybe later."

"You didn't even order a drink," Coach said, when McCrae got to his feet.

"Can't tonight. Thanks. Good to see you."

He left Sutton staring after him, a little deflated. McCrae suspected the older man really wanted to see the slick and apparently charismatic Masterer get his comeuppance. McCrae would've liked to see that, too, but he would be better served to talk to Delta about the man in more depth.

If she would ever answer . . . he thought as he dialed her one more time.

There were several messages on Delta's phone that she'd let go to voice mail while she was interviewing with Amanda. She listened to them now while standing in her kitchen, her eyes on Owen, who was already in pajamas and munching on apple slices with cinnamon, his after-dinner snack. The first was a hang-up, the second from the funeral home where she'd sent Tanner's body after the autopsy. She'd asked that he be cremated, but they'd informed her that a Doctor Lester Stahd had gone to the place and threatened a lawsuit against them if they moved forward with Delta's request, so that hadn't happened.

422

Sighing, she'd just finished listening when her cell started ringing. She looked at the screen and saw it was McCrae. She wanted to answer so badly her arm shot out to grab the cell before she could stop it, as if it had a mind of its own. She hesitated, battling herself, then clicked on.

"Hey, there," she greeted him.

"Where are you?" he asked.

"My house."

A pause. "I just wanted to make sure you're still doing all right."

"I'm okay." Another long pause, and then she heard herself say, "You want to come over?"

She thought he was going to say no. She could almost *feel* that he wanted to say no, but his voice responded, "I'll be there in about forty-five."

She clicked off, set the cell on the kitchen counter, then slid it away from herself and ran upstairs to take a quick shower. As soon as she was finished and redressed, she joined Owen in the family room. He'd been quiet since learning of Tanner's death, asking few questions, and she'd hovered over him so much whenever they were together that he'd snapped his hand at her as if swatting at a fly. She'd tried to give him some space, but now felt guilty for inviting McCrae.

"You want anything else?" she asked him.

"No."

"The . . . detective . . . um, policeman, who's been looking into your dad's—"

"I know what a detective is."

She sat down next to him on the couch. "Okay, well, he's coming by to make sure we're okay."

"He's trying to find who killed Daddy."

The matter-of-fact way he spoke brought Delta up short. He'd seen the news. He knew the facts. She just didn't have any idea what he was thinking.

"Is it okay that he's coming over?"

Owen shrugged. "Will he kill the man who did it?"

"Well, no . . . that's not . . . he'd arrest him and put him in jail . . . or her . . ." Delta fumbled.

Owen froze for a moment, thinking that over, then he nodded gravely, put aside his unfinished plate, and snuggled closer. Delta hugged him hard.

Chapter 22

Zora got home, looked in the refrigerator, grabbed a yogurt, and then drank some wine. And then drank some more. And then the bottle was three quarters empty. She tried to imagine herself at Delta's with Owen, and the image made her feel better, for a time . . . But it was also a lie. Owen was Tanner's child. And Delta's. Not hers.

He was never going to be hers. And she couldn't steal him away. She'd never get away with it. She was crazy to even think it. Crazy! And even if Delta killed Tanner, which she could've, Zora was thinking more and more, the boy's grandparents were in the way.

She sobbed softly into one of the den pillows. She was never going to have a child. Never. It was so unfair. She'd spent the day with Delta, and all she could think about was how unfair it was that Delta had Owen. Maybe Delta did kill Tanner. She did not deserve that little boy.

After a few minutes, Zora lifted her face and brushed back the tears, worried that her cheeks were probably blotchy. Brian, of course, was locked in his office, probably talking to Miss Billings or Anne Reade or *Amanda* . . . whoever the hell he was in love with.

She lurched to her feet, then sank back down. Maybe before she confronted him, she'd have one more glass . . .

Ten minutes later, she was still sitting on the den couch, staring at a blank TV. What time was it? Too late for the news? Brian usually taped it.

It took her an inordinately long time to find the remote, turn on the television, and work her way through the menu until she found the recordings. She pressed the PLAY button and started watching the local news. Ellie's channel . . . ? No, a different one. Brian didn't watch Channel Seven as a rule.

A reporter came on, and he was yammering away about Delta. Zora blinked, ran the recording back, listened again. They were talking about Delta's book . . . about the plot . . . and . . . ? What was that?

She ran it back one more time, replayed.

"Oh, my God," she whispered, blinking hard, trying to sober up. Did they say her book had gone viral, basically, racking up thousands of purchases? Thousands and *thousands?*

"Brian," she called, forgetting for a moment how upset and hurt she was with him. "Brian! *Brian!*"

"What?" he demanded, slamming out of the office and stalking to where she leaned against the aperture to the den. She needed the support, but she didn't want him to know that.

"Did you see this . . . this news?" She pointed to the screen with the remote, but she'd stopped the recording. Now she tried to start it and fumbled around, dropping the remote to the wood floor, where its plastic back flew off.

"How much did you drink?" he demanded, bending to rescue the remote.

"But . . . Delta's book . . . she's making money . . . lots of money . . ."

Brian snapped the remote's plastic cover back in place and reversed the picture. The whirling images made Zora's head hurt. She really had drunk too much.

And then Brian played it again.

"Thousands and thousands," Zora murmured.

"People think it's a road map to killing Tanner."

"Uh huh. She killed him, and now she's making a killing."

She hadn't meant to be funny, but that was kind of funny. She giggled and then remembered how sad she was. "You don't love me anymore."

"I don't think Delta killed him."

She narrowed her gaze at him, realizing he was looking kind of . . . weird. "What?" she asked.

"When you sober up, we'll talk."

"Talk to me now."

"You won't remember it."

"Yes, I will." She sat down on the couch and folded her hands in her lap, looked at him and concentrated.

Well, she did have some trouble concentrating; that was true.

But what she heard was that he'd been secretly seeing Judy, *her* therapist, who was "helping him understand the issues in their relationship"! Was that even okay? Them sharing the same therapist? Zora thought she could probably sue the old hag. It was *Judy* who'd helped him realize he never really wanted children. *Judy* who had helped Brian go over his youth and all the years in between. *Judy* who had reminded him that he'd had a crush on Miss Billings and had suggested he get in touch with both Clarice and Anne Reade and "explore what might have been."

"You're having an affair!?" Zora really, really wished she were sober.

"No." His face darkened.

"Does she want you to sleep with them? Maybe a ménage à trois? Did she say that was okay?" Her nose felt hot. She was close to tears.

"I knew you'd do this. You're taking this the wrong way, like always." He tightened his lips. This was Brian's seriously angry face. "This is about my journey on the path to happiness."

"Oh, for God's sake." Zora leaned her head back against the cushions.

As he was wont to do, Brian's anger, such as it was, dissipated as if it had never been. He sat down beside her on the couch.

"Listen to me," he said. "We only get one

428

chance to go around in this life. I've been fooling myself, and so have you. And I want to go back to teaching, and I don't need children, but you do."

Her heart clutched. "What are you saying?"

"I'm saying we need a break, Zora."

"I don't want a divorce!"

"We'll take it one step at a time. I've been thinking a lot about Tanner, since this whole thing started. And Delta. I don't think they were ever happy, and maybe if they'd recognized that, it all wouldn't have ended so tragically."

"You think Delta killed him."

"No. I think someone else had it in for him." He gave a bark of sardonic laughter and said, "If Delta wanted to kill him, she would've done it years ago, when he really embarrassed her."

"What do you mean?"

He grew serious, and Zora worked hard to concentrate. "I saw Tanner in the woods the night of the barbeque with Amanda. So did Carmen. Carmen was looking right at him while Amanda . . . pleasured him."

"Pleasured him?"

"Amanda's blond head was bobbing up and down in the dark, y'know?"

Zora hadn't gone into the woods that day. Something she still regretted. She could picture Amanda going down on Tanner, though. She'd done the same thing.

"Carmen was staring at them, watching them. She was . . . transfixed."

"Oh, God. That's what she saw," Zora realized. "Bailey said she saw something."

"Maybe that's why she went in the water. Following after Tanner. She wanted to prove she was just as daring, somehow."

Zora shook her head, seeking to clear the fog. "Did you tell anyone?"

"We were all dealing with the shock of Carmen's death," he excused himself.

"You were a teacher," she rebuked. "And Woody and a bunch of us were smoking dope, too."

"Damn it, Zora. Should Clarice and I have turned you all in? Anne didn't even know what the smell was."

"Your girlfriends?"

He glared at her. "And you just married me for my inheritance."

"That wasn't . . . that isn't . . ."

"Sure, it is. And, yes, I should have said something about what was going on in the woods. Maybe everyone's lives would've turned out differently. Mine, too. All I know is I don't want to be unhappy anymore. I don't want you to be unhappy, either. We need to end this marriage."

"No."

His face darkened, and he threw up his hands and stalked to his office. She heard the door slam with finality.

He was looking for excuses, just like always. She felt a huge ache in her heart. Well, he was right about one thing: she *was* unhappy. But she couldn't lose him. She couldn't.

She sank back in the cushions, furious and overwhelmed and . . .

She must've fallen asleep, because she woke up suddenly. Thinking something had jogged her awake, she went to Brian's office, but the door was open, and he wasn't there. She heard his voice in the kitchen and tiptoed down the hall as far as she dared. It was quiet, except for him on his cell.

". . . told her about . . . divorce . . . no, she's drunk . . . No names. Shhh. Come on . . . It's time to start the next chapter of our lives . . . Sure. I'll be there soon."

Zora shrank back into the shadows, her anger bubbling upward. She wondered if she could slip back into the den or if she should brazenly face him? She felt pretty damn sober now. She heard him open the door to the garage, all quiet like . . . trying not to have her hear.

He was going to *her.*

She ran back to the den and found the black flats she'd worn to the movies, squinching her toes into them, then hung by the curtains in the dining room and watched through the window till she saw his taillights start to pull away before she broke for the garage door herself, yanking it

431

open. Her heart was racing as she leaped into her own car and pressed the button for the ignition, throwing her Mercedes into reverse, damn near slamming into the garage door, which he'd apparently pushed to go down while she'd hit the button to have it rise at the same time, confusing the mechanism.

"Shit!" she shrieked, standing on the brakes. She managed to just avoid disaster, taking a moment to push the button and reverse the door so it rolled upward once more.

She then backed down the drive and into the road, throwing the vehicle into DRIVE and speeding to catch up to him.

She'd been afraid she'd given him too much time, but she caught him faster than expected. He was staying within the speed limit to wherever he was going, and she had to hang back once she had him in her sights. She didn't want to tip him off.

He could talk all he wanted, but the bottom line was he was in love with someone else. He didn't care about her. He never had.

Why had he brought up Amanda? Just to tell her about Carmen? To ease away from the fact that he was leaving her?

Or . . . was it something more? Was she wrong about his lover? Could it be Amanda? Maybe she was the one he'd wanted from afar . . .

No. Impossible.

Still, she stretched out her right hand and searched blindly through her purse for her cell. As soon as she grasped it, she placed it on top of her purse, then, darting glances at the glowing screen as she drove, she punched in Amanda's number. When Amanda didn't answer, Zora stayed on the line, letting it go to voice mail. Maybe Brian was right about one thing. Maybe it was time to bring it all out in the open. Tanner was gone, and Carmen, too, and if her death was Amanda's fault, well hell. Zora didn't feel like playing nice anymore.

You cheated with him, too.

She closed her mind to that. It had only been one night, and they hadn't even gone all the way. Amanda was the one who'd done all the damage. And what did it matter now anyway? Brian was wrong. Delta maybe did kill Tanner. Okay, maybe not, but somebody did. Somebody took his life and Bailey's and Penske's . . . and maybe it wasn't Amanda, but she sure as hell was responsible for something.

Amanda's voice mail clicked on. "You've reached Amanda Forsythe. Leave a message . . ."

Beep.

"Hi. It's Zora." Instantly her anger started to collapse, like a balloon losing air. She had to work to hold on to it. "I just talked to Brian . . . Did you know he saw you with Tanner, what you were doing in the woods the night of the

433

barbeque? He said Carmen saw, too. He said he doesn't want to be unhappy anymore, like it could lead to something terrible, like what happened to her." She paused, aware that Brian's Mercedes had taken a turn and was heading a familiar route through West Knoll. "I'm not going to let him leave me. And nothing bad is going to happen to us. I just wanted you to know that." She had so much more to say, but doubt was creeping in. Amanda had been the leader of the Five Firsts, one of her best friends.

Whatever. She couldn't think about that now. She clicked off and concentrated on her driving.

McCrae told himself not to go to Delta's and then all the way back to his own house. *Don't go see her. It's a bad idea. Stay home.*

But after he checked Fido's water bowl, scratched the dog behind the ears, and grabbed an energy bar, he headed out, ignoring his conscience. It was going on 8:00, and he hadn't had much besides a couple of beers since morning.

He arrived at Delta's and pulled in the drive. When he walked to the front door, she was waiting for him. He wanted to sweep her into his arms and press her flesh to his. Less sexual, more just companionship. Okay. Maybe not less sexual, but he didn't expect anything from her. Just wanted to touch her.

She, however, gave him none of the warm

signals he thought he'd gotten on the phone, and when he entered and saw her son, Owen, in pajamas, sitting on a couch in front of the TV, he saw why.

"Hi," he said to the boy.

"This is McCrae," Delta said as she moved into the adjoining kitchen. Then, "Chris McCrae. This is my son, Owen."

"Hi," said Owen, cautiously.

Delta was at the refrigerator. "Would you like a drink?"

"Water would be great."

"Okay . . ."

"It's been a long day," he said.

The boy moved from the couch to one of the counter bar stools, strategically placing himself between McCrae and his mom.

Delta handed him the glass of water, and he saw that she was drinking a glass of rosé. There was an awkward moment. "It's about time for bed, isn't it?" she said to Owen.

Owen ignored her. "Mommy didn't kill Daddy," he related soberly.

"Owen!" said Delta. She'd lifted the glass to her lips but set it back down without drinking.

McCrae answered the boy, "We are working to find out what happened."

"Why did you say that?" Delta questioned her son.

Owen shrugged, then he focused on something.

"The knives are back!" he said on a note of discovery.

McCrae's gaze followed his. He was looking at a knife block near the sink. Delta was gazing at it, too. She'd picked up her wineglass again, and this time she took a sip with a shaking hand.

McCrae stared harder at the knife block. There was a line of seven steak knives slipped into the spots, but one was missing.

"What happened to the new ones?" Owen asked.

McCrae looked at Delta, who was avoiding his gaze.

Oh, shit, he thought, realizing with a sense of betrayal that she'd lied to him.

Brian drove toward Anne Reade's house. Or at least she thought it was. It kind of deflated her. Anne, then, was the woman he was throwing her over for?

But there wasn't a lot of traffic out this way, not all that far from Amanda's property, actually, so Zora had to cruise past the turnoff Brian had taken above Grimm's Pond, which set her on a course to Amanda's. She supposed she could turn around in Amanda's long drive, which was a good mile farther on, but she didn't want to wait that long, so she did a U-turn and headed cautiously back to the road where Brian had turned off and almost immediately pulled over and parked, mentally chewing her nails. Should she walk? She had a black windbreaker with a hood that she kept in the car.

She waited a tense thirty seconds, then grabbed the windbreaker, got out of the car, slipped into the coat, and covered her head with the hood. It was coolish, but the windbreaker still was a little on the warm side. She wanted to take it off, but she wanted the cloaked protection more.

Her white Mercedes practically glowed in the tiny sliver of moonlight. She hesitated, wondered if she should drive it farther away. But Brian had already been out of her sight for too long.

She walked rapidly down the road, praying she wouldn't be seen.

This is stupid. What are you going to do when you find him?

Tear the bitch's eyes out.

She was a little surprised at how violent she felt, but Brian was hers, and she wasn't going to give him up without a fight.

The houses were spaced far apart, with long drives that snaked into the inky night. She could see a rooftop on one, and she hurried down the drive. No black Mercedes. She backtracked, jogged down another drive. Again, no car. In fact, neither house showed any kind of light.

Was this Anne's neighborhood? Maybe she was wrong.

She ran farther down the main road, and by the

time she'd found the right drive, with Brian's car parked, still idling, down a long asphalt drive that then ended in gravel, she was in a full-blown sweat. She shouldn't have worn the Ann Taylor silk blouse, and the black flats weren't made for running, either.

In fact, she should've just stayed home with her wine. She wasn't going to give up on Brian, but this kind of nonsense, in the dead of night, ruining her clothes? She could find a hundred better ways to save their marriage. She could—

The hard poke in her back had her whipping around, and she gave an aborted scream. "What the fu—"

The handgun was now aimed right at her face. She lifted her hands in surrender automatically, her mouth an O of surprise.

"Who . . . who are you?" she stuttered, staring at the man dressed all in black, holding her at gunpoint, even as he looked kind of familiar. "Where's Brian?"

"Inside."

His voice was gravelly and cold.

"Well, what are you doing? What, *what?*"

He suddenly leapt forward, and she screamed, the sound reverberating through the quiet night a half second before the gun smashed down on her head, knocking her flat to the ground.

Zora knew no more.

Whistling, her attacker grabbed her by her

heels, making sure the black shoes stayed on her feet, and dragged her toward the house.

McCrae entered his home about 11:00 and heard the distinctive *click-click-click* of Fido's nails as he greeted him in the dark. McCrae squatted down and rubbed the dog's ears, just like he had a few hours before. Only then he'd been primed and eager to see Delta and let whatever happened happen. He'd wanted her. He still wanted her. But now . . .

He swore violently, and Fido whined slightly and began washing his face with his tongue. "I'm okay," he told the dog.

After she'd gotten Owen in bed, Delta had fallen all over herself to tell him what she'd done. Yes, she knew the knife was from their own set. Yes, she'd purchased a different set of knives, meaning to swap them out, so no one would know, but then Owen had noticed, and she'd put them back. She'd felt like an idiot. No, she hadn't used the knife. Like Tia and Amy had said, Tanner had taken it to the clinic himself. But after she'd touched it, after she'd realized it was the weapon, she'd wanted to distance herself. And once she'd started, she didn't how to stop the deception.

"I told Amanda," she said.

"Amanda," he'd repeated, surprised.

"As of today, she's my lawyer."

McCrae was playing catchup, and he didn't like the feeling at all. "Tell me how that happened," he said, and she laid out how she'd asked for Amanda based on her reputation. "It was kind of awkward, but she knows it wasn't me who killed him."

"How does she know that?"

"Because I told her. She told me not to lie. I know how lame that sounds," she added quickly. "I'm just saying what transpired."

He'd grilled her further, feeling betrayed, and she'd answered his questions fully, with no recriminations. She'd sworn she wanted everything out in the open.

Still, McCrae hadn't known what to believe. He stayed and asked questions and tried to get his own feelings under control until they were both wrung out.

"What are you going to do?" she'd asked him as he'd prepared to leave.

He'd had no answer for her.

Now he took a shower and climbed into bed. Did he believe her? Yes . . . mostly.

He swept his cell up from his night stand. The name of her book was *Blood Dreams*. He was no techie, but he figured he could download an app and purchase it to read on his phone.

It rang in his hand. He glanced at the time. 12:50.

And then he saw it was Quin calling.

"What?" he answered.

"Car went off the cliff at Grimm's Pond. Opposite side of the river from where we rescued . . . where we pulled out Carmen . . ." His voice was unsteady. "It's Brian Timmons and Zora. I need you over there, McCrae. They're both dead."

Chapter 23

It was 5:30 Friday morning, and the day was dawning overcast and dull. More July gloom. Ellie was already dressed and out the door. There was much to be done. An interview with Delta, if she could swing it. Everybody wanted her, but so far no one had gotten her. McCrae was running interference at some level. A real pisser. Had he always had a thing for Delta? Probably.

He only had sex with you at the barbeque because he was drunk.

She pushed that out of her head. That was a long, long time ago, and she didn't need any negative thoughts screwing up her day.

Her cell phone buzzed against the passenger seat of her Ford Escort where she'd thrown it. She glanced over. Amanda. Huh.

She answered, putting the phone on SPEAKER, leaving it on the seat. "What's up, Amanda?"

"I want you to do an interview with me. I'm representing Delta, and I want it out there, as soon as possible. The next news cycle. Can we do it this morning?"

"You're representing . . . ?" Ellie's brows shot up in surprise. "Delta killed him, Amanda."

"I don't think she did."

"Really?"

"Can we do this, or should I check with Channel Four?"

"Well, yeah . . . come to the studio. Anything to do with the Stahd murder is hot news." Did she mean that asshole Phil, on Channel Four? He'd been dogging Delta, from the reporting she'd seen, but hadn't gotten anywhere. Before Amanda's call, Ellie had decided she would get the interview. They were friends . . . at least classmates, but Amanda? As her lawyer?

"What makes you so sure she didn't do it?" Ellie asked.

"She told me she didn't."

"Oh. Good one."

"I've got a stop to make, but I'll be there in half an hour to forty-five," she said, and clicked off.

Ellie shook her head. Did she really want to do this? Ed's assistant, Peter, might be in already. The morning news would be going on, but they could tape an interview in another room, and she was riding high at work after her interview with Tanner's father. Big ratings. Everybody loved watching someone just on the edge of crazy.

Amanda rode the elevator to the building's sixteenth floor—the offices of Layton, Keyes, and Brennan. Her law firm took up a floor of the concrete and glass high-rise, which stood tall on Portland's west side and faced the Willamette

River and the colloquially called City of Bridges' eastern shore. Amanda dropped her briefcase off in her office, which had a peek-a-boo view as its southeast corner, jutting out just a smidge to allow some light. She smoothed her skirt, then marched down the hall to her ex's office, with its bank of windows and spacious appointments. The benefits of being a partner.

She checked her e-mails on her phone. No texts. But there was that phone message last night from Zora that she hadn't listened to. Her finger hovered over the button, but she decided not yet. She was on a mission.

She headed over to her ex-husband's office, knocking lightly on Hal's door, even though she could see he was inside talking with Merl Keyes, another partner; all the walls were glass, which came to be after the other partner, Layton, was sued for sexual harassment. Now there were no more secrets, supposedly, though Amanda knew for a fact that her ex had been a cheater and a scoundrel, and she had no reason to think he'd changed.

Hal looked over at her, and she could see his expression harden. He was embarrassed that his ex-wife was the one bringing in the business. She hoped he died of embarrassment. He signaled her to enter.

"What brings you to darken my door?" he asked with a humorless smile.

Merl Keyes lifted his palms and sidled toward the door, but Amanda was blocking it.

"You might want to hear this," Amanda said.

"I don't need more ex-marital strife than I've already got," Merl said with a fake smile.

"I've taken on Delta Stahd as a client who's more than likely going to be accused of murdering her husband, Dr. Tanner Stahd."

"That West Knoll murder?" asked Merl.

"Your ex-BFF," Hal said, surprised.

"Yep," said Amanda.

"Isn't the victim's father already threatening a lawsuit?" Merl asked.

"I believe so."

"I don't think this is a case for you," said Hal.

She'd expected as much. He couldn't stand whenever she became the center of attention, and this case was certainly going to do that for her.

Merl scooted out the door at that, but Amanda held her ground. Her ex's dismissiveness was one of his least-attractive characteristics. That and his cheating. And patronage of titty bars. She'd hired a private investigator and had him followed during the worst of their divorce, and Hal couldn't keep it in his pants, his choice being "professionals."

"I signed a contract, and she paid me a retainer," Amanda said. "Just thought I'd let you know."

Hal had never been an especially attractive guy,

but he'd been smart and clever. When Amanda first started at the firm, she'd gravitated to him for those latter reasons, though her mother had said he looked like a ghoul. The slicked-back hair hadn't helped his looks, but now, with the added hair loss and a thickness to his lips that made his smile almost grotesque, he was a ghoul and then some, although the younger women who buzzed around, trying to get the partners' attention, were able to look past that, just as she had.

"How much was the retainer?"

"Enough."

He snorted. "You always pick the hard-luck cases."

"Guess that's why I have the most billable hours around here."

"You have other cases to work on," Hal snapped. He hated it when she kept blithely knocking him down.

"Nope. You took me off them all."

"Well, I don't think it's a good idea. It's a trial that's going to be sensationalized and that we'll likely lose."

"I think I'm going to win."

He laughed harshly and shook his head, his default when he couldn't think of another way to try to keep her in her place.

She headed back out to her car. She was going to put herself on the air and tell the world she was Delta Smith-Stahd's lawyer and Delta was innocent.

Notoriety always helped in her profession, Amanda felt. And if she could suck up enough valuable airtime, she might be able to quit this shitty, misogynistic firm and start her own.

When Ellie arrived at the station, the first thing she did was check for phone messages that may have come in through the reception desk. Most people called her on her cell phone or texted her, but there were still those messages that came through the switchboard from people who didn't know her as well.

No messages.

She added Amanda's name to the visitors log and then went looking for Peter, who was in the break room, pouring a cup of coffee. They had no problem setting up, and Amanda arrived soon after Ellie got out of the makeup chair with Char, who was kind of a bitch but was a tireless worker.

As Ellie sat down for the interview with her, she asked herself what it was about Amanda that made people give in to her. It was an unorthodox interview in that Amanda ran with the ball, not giving Ellie much time to ask any questions as she touted Delta's innocence, drawing on their years of friendship—ha, ha—and then crowing some about her own accomplishments as a defense attorney. She finished up with an unexpected comment on Dr. Lester Stahd's troubled health clinic and how Tanner, not his father, had turned everything around. It was a subtle warning, Ellie realized, to Stahd Senior about going off on Delta. Ellie was miffed, as Stahd would undoubtedly blame her for this, too.

"I'll see if they'll air it," Ellie muttered, when they were finished. "The earliest would be noon."

"Okay. Wish it would be sooner."

"Who are you doing this for?"

"Delta."

"Uh-uh. You're doing this for you."

"Publicity's good. My ex might not think so, but I don't listen to him."

"You work with him."

"For the moment." There was something in her tone, some deep satisfaction that she wasn't even trying to keep secret. She wanted Ellie to notice.

"You're leaving the firm," Ellie realized. "And you want your husband's clients."

Her answer was a thin smile.

Ellie was seeing her out when Ed nearly barreled into her. "Ellie!" he said. "I think that car accident's your friend!" To her blank look, he added, "On the news? Didn't you watch ours?"

"No . . . I was interview— . . . What friend?"

"The Z one. I don't know. Zona?"

Amanda took in a sharp breath as Ellie grabbed up her phone. Amanda yanked hers from her purse as well.

"I'll talk to you later," Amanda stated crisply and stalked out.

Ellie found the news feed. She saw the mangled black Mercedes. Brian's car. Both dead. She felt numb all over.

"Where's Rob? I want to talk to him."

"Uh . . . I don't know. I don't think he's here yet. Check with Alton," Ed suggested.

"Alton's never here this early." Her years-long relationship with the man had made her aware of that.

"Yeah, well, he is."

"What?" She couldn't think. The world had tipped off its axis. "Where is he?"

Ed waved a hand down the hall toward the business offices. She went to Rob's door, and a man she didn't recognize was behind his desk. No sign of Alton.

"What's going on?" she asked.

"Ellie O'Brien," the man said with a careful smile. "I'm Russ Niedermeyer, head of production."

"Where's Rob?"

"Rob's no longer with us. And I'm sorry to have to tell you this, but we're going to be letting you go as well."

Ellie stared at him. She'd had too much devastating information in too short a time. "What? I—I just did that piece . . ."

"It was good, but Pauline is our number-one

gal, and we're going with her," he said in that fake-bonhomie way that made Ellie want to gouge his eyes out. "I'm sure you know that the station has been sold, and that—"

"Months ago. It was sold months ago!"

"—we're still making changes. Finding the proper fit, as it were, for all our employees."

Ellie focused on him, disbelieving. Niedermeyer was a good-looking guy, and he knew it, with a pressed white shirt and a trimmed beard and a smile that didn't reach his eyes. She tuned back into something about severance pay, but then she couldn't think of anything to say; she wanted to beg to have her job back, and that wouldn't do.

And Zora was gone . . . she and Brian were *gone* . . .

She walked blindly out of the office, breathing hard. She was in shock. She knew it. Couldn't seem to do anything about it.

Goddamnit. Goddamnit. They'd fired her . . . *Fired her!*

This was Coco's doing somehow. She was tight with Pauline, and she had Alton—*that worm!*—under her blood-red-nailed thumb.

How did I ever sleep with him? How did I ever think we could be a power couple when he's a dead battery?

Another station would welcome her with open arms. She'd go to Channel Four herself, push

451

Phil out. It couldn't be that hard. She'd get that interview with Delta. Didn't mean she had to believe in her innocence; *Dee* was still her number-one suspect. Maybe she could get Dr. Stahd to do another interview. Do both together, a juxtaposition. Delta innocent, or Delta guilty? Choose your own adventure.

But Zora was dead . . .

"Jesus," she muttered on a half gasp.

She was heading out, down the hall, and there in front of her were Alton and Coco, little Chihuahua Penny perched in Coco's purse. Alton looked away from Ellie, but Coco smiled deliberately.

"Hi, Ellie," Coco said, while Penny bared her little teeth and growled softly behind quivering black lips.

Ellie looked from one to the other of them.

"Fuck you all, and your little dog too," she told them and then pushed past them before she could break down and make a fool out of herself.

Delta reluctantly took Owen to preschool. She was dropping him off later than usual, the result of a sleepless night and a slow morning. "Are you sure you want to go?" she asked for about the tenth time as they neared the turn into the school. "Next year, if you go to Englewood Academy, it's real school, and I won't be able to take you out at every whim."

"I want to go." His face was set in stubborn lines.

"I just want to make sure . . . we're both okay."

"I'm okay."

"All right." She wanted him with her. Especially after the debacle of the evening before.

"Did that man stay all night?" Owen asked carefully.

"No. He left a couple hours after you went to bed."

"I don't like him."

Delta looked in the rearview mirror at her son. "You hardly talked to him. He's going to help us."

"He thinks you killed Daddy with the knife."

"That's not what he thinks. He's a policeman, and it's going to be all right."

Owen's eyes suddenly flooded with tears. "I'm sorry, Mama. I told him . . ."

"It's not your fault, Owen! It's not your fault."

Delta's throat was hot as her son blinked back tears. She tried to talk him out of pre-K some more as they pulled into a spot and parked. She felt like she'd almost convinced him when one of his friends showed up at the spot where they were stopped on the sidewalk, skipping his way ahead of his mom to the front door. Seeing him, Owen swiped the remaining tears from his face and pulled himself together. The effort broke Delta's heart.

453

He started to run on ahead of her as well, then he stopped and came back and held her hand. "I won't talk to that man anymore."

"Okay . . ."

"I won't tell him you killed Daddy."

"Owen." She sucked in a shocked breath. "I did not . . . do anything to harm your father."

He looked up at her.

"Is that really what you think?"

He shrugged his little shoulders, and this time he raced after his friend and didn't look back. She checked him in, staring after him as he joined the other kids, wanting to scoop him up and run away somewhere, anywhere safe. But he was with his friends and seemed purposely to be avoiding looking at her.

She left the pre-K on leaden feet. She felt both zapped of energy and yet charged with the pressure to do something. She needed her son to believe in her, even if no one else did. She'd handled Tanner's attack and death all wrong.

She got back in her car and fought the urge to cry. Fingers wrapped around the steering wheel, she held back the tears by sheer will. Nope. She wasn't going to cry. She'd had enough of that. She needed to be proactive. Do something. Find out something that would take her out of this terrible limbo.

Maybe she would go see Woody today. Ask about the fender bender and the guy who'd argued with Tanner. That would at least be something.

She looked back at the closed door to the pre-K, aching. First, though, she was going to Smith & Jones to see her parents.

Every nerve in Ellie's body was buzzing as she drove toward West Knoll. She kept bouncing from Zora and Brian to the fact that she'd been fired and back again.

What happened to them? An accident . . . had to be a terrible accident . . . couldn't be anything more sinister, like what happened to Tanner . . .

No, that was an act of passion. That was Delta . . . or maybe someone else, she grudgingly allowed. But Zora and Brian were an accident.

"McCrae'll be on it." she said aloud.

It occurred to her that the Five Firsts were down to just two. She was sorry they were gone individually, but as far as their special group? She was glad it was in shreds.

She picked up her phone. *Come and get me and give me a ticket.* Swiping through her favorite numbers, of which McCrae was one, she touched the screen to make a call.

McCrae was at work, at his desk after a short, damn-near sleepless night following hours at the crash site. He'd already fended off a number of reporters when Ellie's call came through. He ignored it, and she called right back. "Call the station," he answered in a growl.

"What the hell happened?" she practically screamed at him.

"You can get a statement if you call the station."

"I want *you* to tell me! C'mon, McCrae. These were *our friends!*"

He closed his eyes, her words piercing him. He'd driven like a madman to get to the crash site. Not the wisest course of action, but he'd made it, striding through the barrage of flashing red and blue lights from the West Knoll patrol cars, to arrive at the same time as the coroner's van. The ambulance had already left, empty. The coroner's van was picking up both bodies.

McCrae tightened down his emotions to look at Zora's body. There was blood, but she almost appeared to be sleeping, and Brian's . . . he was more mangled, with broken legs at odd angles, a gash across his forehead, and dull, staring eyes. Corolla had come up to him and said there was a witness, of sorts.

McCabe turned to the guy, who wore shorts, a short-sleeved shirt, and hiking boots, and was apparently camping along the West Knoll River. He hadn't seen anything, but he'd heard the car crash over the cliff from about a quarter mile away; the vehicle had tumbled down the hillside to lodge upside down on the river's shore. "No braking," the guy said. "They just went over."

McCrae had spent another three hours at the scene, grimly watching as the car was winched up the hill from the rocky shore far below. Across Grimm's Pond were the fields that separated this section of the river from the Forsythe estate.

Déjà vu. Below was where they'd all gathered after the ill-fated run down the rapids that had resulted in Carmen's death. He remembered how helpless he'd felt that day, and how angry, and experienced the same emotions anew.

He'd stuck around for a while, watching the crime-scene techs gather evidence, then had gone home and expected to go right to sleep, but mostly he had just thrashed around, consumed with the fatal car accident and also bothered by the realization that Delta had lied about the knife . . . which begged the question: What else had she lied about?

"McCrae?" Ellie's sharp voice demanded.

He grimaced. Zora's parents had been informed of her death, as had Timmons's sister, who lived in British Columbia and was making plans to come to West Knoll.

"We don't know yet," he finally answered Ellie. "There was no braking. They didn't make the corner and sailed through the guardrail."

"Were they drunk?"

"Like I said, we don't know anything yet."

"Passed out? Drugs?"

This time he didn't bother responding.

"I can't believe it. I just can't believe it," she muttered. "Tanner and now Zora and *Mr. Timmons?*"

"I don't know."

"Goddamnit, McCrae. What do you know?"

"Nothing," he said, meaning it. He had no answers and nothing to tell her.

She was breathing hard, as if she'd been running. "God, what an awful day. I'm going to the crash site."

"I think the crime techs are finished, but—"

"I'll stay out of their way," she interrupted. "McCrae . . . ?"

The expectant pause after his name somehow reminded him of the unfinished business of their last conversation, so he answered her with, "Last time we talked, you said you had leads you were working on."

"A lifetime ago. Too much has happened, and I'm not . . . following them anymore. God-damnit," she said, sounding consumed by fury and close to tears. "I've gotta go. Oh . . . did you know Amanda's decided to be Delta's lawyer?"

"Yes."

"Of course," she sneered, then added, "We did an interview, should be on the noon news, if they run it," and hung up.

Almost from the moment Delta pulled away from the pre-K, her cell phone started ringing. Eyes on the road, she pulled it from her purse, then dropped it onto the console. McCrae.

She moaned aloud.

She could still hear her panicked explanations about the knife from the night before. The memory was a spike to the heart. He hadn't believed her. He'd wanted to, she could tell. But he hadn't believed her. From that moment on, the entire rest of the evening had been awful. She'd put Owen to bed and returned downstairs. That's when she'd tried to explain, and even to her own ears it sounded lame. The thrill she'd felt on inviting him over had died a quick but painful death.

"How could you be so stupid?" she railed at herself again.

The phone was still ringing, waiting for her to pick up. She seriously thought about letting it go to voice mail, but that would only put off the inevitable. A teensy part of herself wanted to know why he was calling. A bigger part worried it had something to do with another trip to the station.

But . . . what the hell. She answered and clicked on the speaker. "Hello . . . Chris."

"Delta, I don't know if you've heard, but there's been an accident."

She slammed on the brakes at a stop sign she almost blew through. Her brain was not functioning well. "No . . . I just dropped off Owen at pre-K. What accident?"

"It's Zora and Brian Timmons."

"What?"

And then he told her. She drove blindly for a few blocks and then pulled over. McCrae described the accident—at Grimm's Pond, no less. While she listened, she stared through the windshield at the traffic passing her by, but what she was seeing was Zora, her one-time roommate, flighty, sometimes silly, maybe a bit too seduced by the finer things, but a friend, a long-time friend, one of the Five Firsts . . .

McCrae was still talking. She couldn't think. Couldn't hear.

"Was it murder?" she cut in.

That stopped him, and he took a moment before saying, "It looks like an accident." But there was a dubious tone to his voice.

"Is it connected?" she asked, almost in a whisper.

"To . . . ?"

"The other deaths. Our classmates?"

"Well . . . as soon as we get some forensic evidence, we'll know more. Maybe later today."

"I just spent the day with Zora," she said, a lump forming in her throat. "She was coming over to take care of Owen today."

"You were with her . . . yesterday?"

"Yes, we went to the movies." She could feel a headache building. She wanted to cry but couldn't seem to find the tears. "I didn't kill Tanner, but

460

somebody did . . . and now this. Maybe there's a conspiracy. Maybe whoever killed Tanner killed Zora and Brian, too."

"Where are you?" he asked.

"Parked on the side of the road. I don't believe in coincidences. It hasn't been a week since Tanner was attacked. Somebody . . . *not me* . . . killed him and maybe Zora and Brian and Bailey and Carmen . . . and Penske." Her voice was starting to quaver.

"Tell me where you are, and I'll come get you."

"I'm fine, McCrae." She got control of her voice. "I'm fine. Just fine. Thank you for telling me."

"Don't hang up."

"It's not right. Something is going on. Don't you feel it? And who's going to be next? Me? *You?*"

"I'm going to find out what this is all about," he promised.

"Good."

She clicked off and stuck her phone in the side pocket of her purse. She dropped her head into her hands. She was too raw where McCrae was concerned. She needed to *think*. To figure things out.

Maybe Zora's and Brian's deaths were an accident. *Maybe.* But it sure didn't feel that way.

Who killed Tanner? And Brian and Zora . . .

"Why?" she asked aloud.

After several minutes, she pulled herself together and headed carefully the rest of the way to her parents' grocery store.

Chapter 24

Amanda was back at her house, in her bedroom, staring across the fields toward the chasm where the West Knoll River ran—a barely visible, jagged, dark gap, from her point of view, that cut off her land from the property beyond.

Zora.

She hadn't gone back to the office. The momentum of the day had faded as soon as she'd heard the news, a punch to the gut. The interview she expected to play on the Channel Seven noon news had lost the power to make her smile. Her game with Hal hardly seemed worth it.

She'd left her phone downstairs, but she still had Zora's message, a puzzler. She'd blamed Amanda for Carmen's death, if she could read between the lines. From something that had taken place at the barbeque. Was she the only one who truly remembered what had happened that night? It was all so steeped in mystery and suspicion, when in truth they were just a bunch of drunk, stoned idiots doing exactly what drunk, stoned idiots did.

Still . . . Zora's message had been fairly specific.

Did it even matter anymore?

She shifted her gaze to the general direction of Grimm's Pond—the site of the crash, she'd learned from a news feed on her phone. What had happened that sent Zora and Brian plunging over the cliff to their deaths?

She shivered and rubbed her arms. Hearing Zora's slightly accusatory voice on the phone over and over again had spooked her. Normally, she was immune to atmosphere and innuendo, but not today.

She heard her cell phone ringing downstairs, but it was too difficult to work her way down the spiral staircase and catch it in time, so she let it go.

She didn't want to talk to anyone anyway.

. . . saw you with Tanner, what you were doing in the woods the night of the barbeque. He said Carmen saw, too . . .

Why had Brian been talking about the barbeque? Did it have anything to do with what happened to them?

What she remembered of the barbeque was how good Delta had looked, how cute and gorgeous her figure was. Ellie had looked good in her swimsuit, too, and Amanda had felt ugly and forgettable. Her talent agency had just dropped her. Nobody wanted her, except Tanner, but then he was indiscriminate. So she'd flirted outrageously with him in front of Delta, had really thought she wanted him. Funny how things turned out.

She sighed. It was unfathomable that Zora was gone.

Stripping off her clothes, Amanda put on her running gear and headed out to the path that ran along the river. She could go all the way to Grimm's Pond if she felt like it, the last half mile across an unfenced field and then down to the river and swimming hole.

The crash site offered up little and less, and the information that was available was being broadcast by every channel. Ellie felt a bit heartsick that she wasn't part of the news team, and she turned a cold shoulder to Pauline and her favorite cameraman, Darrell, when they appeared. Pauline stared her down. She could tell Pauline wanted to ask her what the hell she was doing, but Ellie wasn't going to give her the chance. She was pissed, too. She'd been let go through no fault of her own. It just wasn't fair.

Grimly, she drove toward the West Knoll police station. She'd hung up on McCrae but now realized she needed him. She was going to get this story whether she was employed or not.

But . . . with Zora and Brian's death, Tanner's murder had slipped from the very top of the news rotation. Delta might not be under such a fine microscope, so it was a good time for her to pitch for an interview. She'd been harsh about Delta, true. Maybe Delta didn't know it, though. Ellie could suck up a little, maybe get a personal one-on-one.

And where are you going to air it?

She would work that out later. The interview was the thing. That would be a coup, and if it played right, all the focus would shift back to Delta.

She heard her own thoughts and grimaced. Zora was dead. Tanner was dead. And all she could think about was getting her job back.

Her cell buzzed. She eyed it almost angrily, not trusting it wasn't more bad news.

It was her half brother, Joey.

Ellie ignored him. Not today. Her brothers were endless problems. The cell stopped ringing, then started in again. She ignored the second call, too. They had no idea she had problems herself.

The third time he called, she snatched up the phone and growled, *"What?"*

"Nia and Michael are eloping," he said through a clogged throat.

She ground her teeth together, then almost laughed. It was so ludicrous. "Tell me you're kidding."

"I'm not."

"So you and Michael are sharing . . . again?"

"Nnnooo . . ."

"You're not convincing me." She sighed. "Do you know where they are now?"

"At our apartment."

"Are you there?"

"I'm outside. We had a fight."

"Hold on. I'm coming." She clicked off and threw her phone into the passenger seat. It felt almost good to have a mission. She hoped to God she could stop Michael before he did something irrevocably stupid, and marrying a Crassley fell directly into that category.

When she got to the apartment, a two-bedroom in a fifty-unit, gray complex in desperate need of paint, Joey was pacing outside. Ellie swept up the wooden stairs to the front door, but when he tried to follow, she ordered, "Stay here." Both of her brothers had been involved with Nia Crassley, and it was bad news all around. Nia was the youngest Crassley and the only girl, with three elder brothers and a passel of half brothers, stepsiblings, and who knew what. Ellie knew, from the twins, that Nia was living with her three true brothers on the family property. She was a few years older than the twins, but looked twice their age. They were just her latest conquests. She, like her brothers, had been the bane of West Knoll for years. Her parents, both gone now, had started the dynasty of crime and bad behavior, and Nia, Gale, Booker, and Harry Crassley had gleefully continued in their wake.

The door was locked. Ellie yelled, "Michael, let me in, or I will break this down, I swear. Bad things have happened to me, and I'm off leash.

467

I will smash this lock. I will smash a window. I will—"

The door flew inward, and Nia stood there with a look of disbelief on her elfin face. "What's your problem?" she demanded. Michael hovered behind her, giving Ellie his somewhat belligerent "I know I'm in trouble" look.

Ellie gave her attention to the girl in front of her. Nia was pretty enough, small and dark and sultry, but she'd had a hard life, and it showed in the fine lines around her eyes and mouth. She regarded Ellie insolently through bangs that needed to be trimmed.

"Let's get you a pregnancy test before you guys make a run for the preacher," Ellie said calmly.

Michael said, "Butt out, Ellie."

Nia smirked.

"I'm not going to bother being nice," Ellie said. "Nia, if you are pregnant—and that's a big *if*—well, we all know that if you are, it could be anybody's."

"Ellie . . . ," Michael murmured.

"If Justin Penske were still alive, he'd be top of the list for baby-daddy, but he's about the only man I would rule out at this point," Ellie said. "I just don't think it's Michael."

An electric silence fell among them. Nia opened her eyes wide and glared at Ellie in a way that was meant to be intimidating. Ellie just waited.

"Joey should've never called you," Michael whined.

"Shut up," Nia told him.

"You shut the fuck up," Michael retorted, looking wounded.

"You can't elope!" Joey yelled from the porch.

Ellie turned to frown hard at him, and he backed down the stairs again. "Nobody's eloping," she told them.

"You think your shit don't stink," Nia snarled. "But I know something you don't . . ."

"You've never shown that you know anything."

"Oh, burn!" Michael choked out, half-inclined to laugh.

Nia turned on him, and Ellie thought she was going to rake his face with her nails.

"Stop," she ordered, her voice cold and hard. Nia froze, possibly hearing something in Ellie's tone. She hadn't been kidding when she said she was off leash. Right now, at this moment, she felt capable of anything. To Michael, Ellie said, "Am I going to have to follow you around? I could call your father. Let Oliver deal with you."

"You don't want that!" Joey called from outside.

"Joey, if you say one more word, I'm heading straight to your father," Ellie shouted at him.

Both Michael and Joey stayed silent.

Nia, having recovered a bit, defiantly lifted her chin. "You wanna know what I know? Too bad."

"I want you out of my brothers' lives. That's all I want from you."

"I know that Penske didn't kill that cop, Bailey Quintar," Nia said quickly.

Ellie could feel her anger harden. She wanted to grab Nia Crassley by her hair and drag her outside. She knew she was close to losing it completely. And if she wasn't careful, this adrenaline-pumping anger could change to grief, and she would collapse and sob her heart out.

"She deserved to die. Bitch killed my brother. I was glad when she died! We all were. I—" She gasped in shock when Ellie suddenly did grab a fistful of her hair. "*Ow!* You fucking bitch! . . . Whore! . . . *cu–*"

"*Shut up!*" Ellie screamed in her face, shocking her silent. "Bailey didn't kill your brother. That was road rage. Get it straight. I'm taking you back to your house. On the way, we're going to stop for a pregnancy test, and you're gonna pee on that stick in front of me!"

"I'll sue you. I'll say you attacked me!" Nia shrieked.

"Hey," Michael said.

Ellie rounded on him. "Pay attention to what you and your brother have been fighting over. This girl? Really?"

Nia twisted around to try to slap Ellie, and she would've gotten in a pretty good hit if Ellie hadn't held her back with a hard yank.

"Owwww!" Nia howled. "I'm gonna sue! Tell everybody about you! You'll lose your job!"

Ellie laughed without humor. *Too late.* "And I will write a story about you and your miserable family that'll put half of them in jail, where they oughtta be."

"Nia, stop it. You don't want more trouble. A couple of 'em landed there already," Michael admitted.

That caught Ellie up. "A couple Crassleys in jail? Well, that's a good start. Which ones?"

"Booker and Harry. They were in a bar fight last night," Michael said glumly.

Nia wriggled, trying to loosen Ellie's grip. "Like the kind that bitch cop always broke up!"

"Watch yourself when you say anything more about Bailey," Ellie warned.

"I'll say what I want. He never wanted to be with her. It was just a *job,*" Nia spat.

"Penske? He'd be lucky to have her," Ellie responded, but her antennae shot up nonetheless.

Nia spat like a wildcat. "He never wanted her! She was just in the way and had to be removed. We all hated her! She just wouldn't leave us alone!"

Ellie snarled sarcastically, "Oh, sure, so he killed himself too."

"He didn't kill himself! That wasn't supposed to happen! He was mmmiiiiinnnee!"

The last word came out on a long moan. The

fight went out of her, and Ellie slowly released her grip on Nia's hair.

Michael from behind her, and Joey, outside, were both utterly silent.

Ellie processed what Nia had revealed. She asked, jaw set, "Which one of your brothers killed him?"

Nia's mouth quivered. For a moment, Ellie thought she was actually going to give them up, but instead she cried, "You're trying to make me say things, you *bitch!* I'm not talking to you." She whirled around. "Goddamnit, Michael. I'm sick of this!"

"Whad I do?" he asked.

"Nothing!" With that, Nia ran out the door.

Joey looked like he was going to try to stop her, but she kicked at him as she pounded down the wooden porch steps and beat feet to an ages-old green Chevy parked on the street outside.

"Fuck, Ellie, what have you done?" Michael demanded, joining her on the porch, where they watched Nia fire up her car and burn around the corner.

"Saved your ass, like always."

"Damn you, Michael." Joey suddenly leapt up the steps toward his brother.

"Stop it. Both of you. You need to both get over her."

"But she's—" Michael began.

Ellie glared at him, and he cut himself off. After a beat of silence, she said, "She's a Crassley, and they're grifters, con artists, and all-around miserable human beings. You know it as well as I do."

"That's really harsh," Joey said.

"You heard what she said about Bailey."

"But Bailey harassed her," Michael said.

"Be careful," she warned. "Gale Crassley attacked her in an alley."

They both clammed up. Joey shuffled after Michael back inside and asked him, "You going to work today?"

"Nah, I quit."

They both worked at fast-food restaurants.

"Wanna play video games?" Joey asked him.

"Mother of God," Ellie muttered, leaving them and heading back to her car. Crisis averted for the moment, unless the girl was really pregnant. Maybe she was. If so, they would all end up back in another scene.

But it had made her forget her own problems for a moment.

Now Nia's words circled her brain as she drove back toward town: *He didn't want to be with her. It was a job.*

And: *He didn't kill himself. That wasn't supposed to happen. He was mine.*

Had one of her brothers killed Penske? Maybe Bailey, too, although the current theory was that he'd shot her and then shot himself. Same gun, but maybe . . .

She thought furiously for several moments. She could call Delta, ask for an interview, maybe then push that interview with Channel Four. Or . . .

Two Crassleys were in jail, leaving only one— Gale, maybe the worst one, but only one. Well, and Nia. But if she were ever going to interview, face off, with the Crassleys, this was the time.

But was that safe? What if . . . what if they had killed Penske? And Bailey?

Bailey for being a cop who'd constantly thwarted them, and Penske . . . because he was with Nia, before she was old enough for legal consent?

"You're asking for trouble," she murmured aloud. But hell . . . what a story, if it were true. And maybe even some closure for Bailey's family.

She knew where the Crassley compound was, a ramshackle, sprawling single-story house in dire need of repairs, with a weedy drive and a barbed-wire fence that corralled a car graveyard. She was driving in the opposite direction, so she turned around and drove past the western boundaries of West Knoll and onto the county roads.

She bumped up a long, pothole-riddled drive and parked on a grassy mound to one side, aiming her Escort for a straight shot out, if she needed it, which she might. Six or seven large dogs barked madly at her behind the barbed-wire fence in a pen of sorts as she got out of her car and stepped into a pile of dog shit. Fuming, she tried to scrape the smelly stuff onto the clots of gravel that showed through the weeds as she walk-hopped toward the sagging front porch.

Loud voices sounded from within. Angry voices. A man and a woman. Gale, most likely, and Nia. When Nia came flying out of the house, that answered that. She acted like she didn't see Ellie as she stomped down the porch steps and over to the area where about twenty vehicles in various states of disrepair were parked. Ellie realized Nia's car had been one of the paint-faded hoods—rusted cars, trucks, and what have you; there was even a tractor out there—as the girl jumped inside her green Chevy and burned away from the others. Smoke flew out of her tailpipe as she took off again.

She'd better not be going back to Michael and/or Joey.

She almost turned around, but now there was only one Crassley at home. She moved forward and rapped her knuckles against the side of the tattered screen door. She put on an expression of friendly interest, though suddenly she didn't know exactly what she planned on saying to him. She didn't really want to complain about Nia; she thought she'd heard "Penske" in the argument she'd overheard between them, and that didn't bode well.

She heard him trudge her way, and then he pushed through the screen, causing her to back up. Standing in front of her on the porch, the man had a rifle tucked under his arm.

"You're that reporter," he said.

She stopped short. *Oh, holy God,* she thought, and only after a long moment did she nod her head.

"Well, come on in," he said, opening the screen to have her walk through ahead of him.

Gale Crassley . . . possibly Penske's killer . . . possibly Bailey's . . . a man who knew the inside of a jail cell better than the walls of his own home.

With the greatest reluctance, she ordered her legs to walk inside.

McCrae knocked his knee as he was swinging away from his desk, and he bit off a string of invectives. He was mad at himself. For his feelings for Delta.

Just because she lied doesn't mean she's a killer.

Quin came looking for him. "We got a lot to discuss."

McCrae nodded. He'd avoided him on purpose. A lot had happened in the last few days that they hadn't gone over.

"Come outside."

They walked out the back door together and stood on the edge of the field. A hawk slowly cruised overhead, looking for small prey, while the sun reached out warming fingers of light through the cloud bank.

"Tech came back. They found a block of concrete in Timmons's car. Markings and dust on the accelerator."

McCrae frowned. "Someone lodged it in place on the accelerator and turned them loose?"

"Looks that way. They were likely unconscious as they went over."

"What the hell for?" McCrae exploded.

"They're looking for prints, fibers, whatever, to see if someone drove the car to Grimm's Pond. So far nothing."

"In that case, Brian and Zora likely drove themselves. Why?"

"There's a house about half a mile back on the road on that side of the cliff. Number of houses on five-acre lots, far enough apart for privacy, close enough to run into your neighbors now and again. One of 'em's just closed up and empty. Got dusty tire tracks on the tarmac that match Brian Timmons's."

"So he went there? Or someone drove him there?"

"It's Anne Reade's family's old house."

McCrae regarded him incredulously. "Anne Reade."

"She's out of town and hasn't lived there for years. She was taking care of her father, but he moved to a nursing home earlier this year. It's been uninhabited since February. I talked to her on the phone. She's in South Carolina. She's got a boyfriend there and is moving at the end of the summer to join him and start teaching there. She said Brian knew the house was empty."

"So he was meeting someone else there? Who else knew?"

"She says nobody, although it wasn't a big secret. Crime techs are going over it now, but I understand it's dusty and undisturbed like no one's actually entered in a while."

"So they met outside? I'd say maybe Brian was living a secret life, but he had Zora with him last night."

"We checked out their house this morning. Everything looks in place, except Zora's car isn't there."

McCrae frowned. "Maybe with a friend? Or in the shop or getting detailed?"

They discussed it further but came up with no new conclusions.

They headed back inside as they were wrapping up. Quin switched subjects and asked him about his interviews with Tracy Gillup and Dean Sutton. McCrae told him about Tracy seeing someone she thought was watching Bailey and Penske, but he added that Carville had warned about Tracy not always being truthful. He then said he hadn't learned anything more than what they'd already known from Sutton, purposely leaving out what the coach had said about Quin's ex-wife. Until he interviewed Bailey's mother himself, he wasn't going to stir that pot.

Which was what he thought he might do right then, along with checking in with Delta and getting some in-depth information about Zora and Brian from their friends and family. He went to his office and took his gun out of the drawer, then headed out.

"Mr. McCrae!" he heard as he was opening the back door again.

He turned slowly around and saw Tim Hurston coming his way from reception. Thinning gray hair, neatly trimmed, suit pressed to a knife's edge, pugnacious chin: the man had his hand out and a smile that looked predatory.

What was this?

McCrae shook his hand reluctantly. "Something you need?"

"I wanted to talk about the widow Stahd. Delta, her name is."

McCrae didn't respond. Just waited.

"Isn't it time she was arrested?"

"Not enough evidence," McCrae said evenly.

"Is that really the reason?" he said in a tone that suggested they both knew it wasn't.

"Yes."

"Well, I've heard differently, and I'm going to suggest you pick her up and bring her in. If she's a black widow, we need her off the street."

"That's for Quin to decide," McCrae said. His spit had dried up. His mouth felt like dust.

"Well, no, as an appointed special investigator—"

"That was before Quin was made chief."

"Your mayor has put me in charge of this case. If you don't want to be a part of it, you can step down."

McCrae wanted to argue further, but Mayor Kathy was someone who tended to be dazzled by big personalities like Hurston. She was a wild card, and it was entirely possible she may have given him some kind of special dispensation to override Quin. In any case, McCrae wasn't the one to fight him.

Out of his peripheral vision, he saw Corinne step into the hallway behind Hurston and pretend she wasn't interested in what was going on.

"I have things to do," McCrae told the man.

"None as important as this."

McCrae looked over at Corinne. *You made a bad choice,* he thought.

As if she'd heard him, she tossed back her head and marched away.

"Bring her in, or I will," Hurston threatened.

McCrae left without responding. The man sure

had a hard-on for getting inside the West Knoll police department and asserting his will. Whatever his reasons, McCrae was done placating him.

Chapter 25

Gale Crassley followed Ellie into his house as she was trying to make a call.

"Gimme that," he told her, yanking the phone from her hand.

"I was just texting my boss to let him know where I am," Ellie said. A lie. But he didn't have to know it.

For an answer, he moved the rifle up and pointed it at her. Her whole body was quivering, even while she desperately wanted to not show fear.

"I think you'd better take your clothes off and sit on that couch."

"What?" She almost laughed until she looked into his cold, staring eyes. He was only a year older than she was, maybe two, but there were light years of different experiences between them.

"You have green eyes," he said, smiling. In fact, he never stopped smiling. It was thoroughly creeping her out. A part of his reptilian self, she decided.

He very gently pushed the rifle at her, making her stumble onto the couch. A spring popped up to meet her, a hard slap to her derrière.

"I don't think—"

"Shut up. Take off your clothes," he said mildly. "Ain't nobody here but you and me. Ain't nobody gonna be here. You can tell me what you want after you take off your clothes."

She held up her hands in front of her, mind whirling, seeking to be free of him. "If I could just say something."

"Don't talk till I tell you to. You got that?"

She was staring at him, her gaze above the muzzle of the gun, hoping to make eye contact, anything.

He tucked the gun under one arm again and rubbed his jaw, looking down at her.

"Take off your goddamn clothes before I rip them off."

"And then . . . we can talk?"

"Not if you keep yappin' away."

Ellie considered her position. *C'mon, McCrae,* she whispered in her head.

Very carefully, she began to unbutton her blouse.

McCrae got the text from Ellie that was sent without being finished. *At Crassleys. Come and get—*

He was on his way to the Kiefers, determined to put Coach Sutton's theories about Bailey's mother to bed. He hadn't talked to Masterer, not because he believed anything besides flirting

484

had transpired between the man and Delta, just because he should knock it off the list. Now it could appear that McCrae was protecting Delta, and Hurston, with Corinne's help, was out for blood.

Why? How did he benefit from Delta being charged with Tanner's murder? Hurston always had his own agenda, but he couldn't see how charging Delta would help him. She was a sympathetic figure with a little boy to take care of.

But Tanner called her Dee, the name or letter he'd called out from the hospital bed . . . and she'd lied about the knife, though Hurston didn't have that bit of information yet. God knew what he'd do when he did . . . and she wrote a book with the same plot. He'd managed to read two chapters, and the similarities were eerie . . . and the marriage was in trouble because Tanner regularly slept with other women . . .

All circumstantial evidence, but damning, nonetheless.

But Ellie's text. *Come and get . . .* what?

But anything to do with the Crassleys was bad news.

"Goddamnit."

He was driving one of the West Knoll PD Trailblazers rather than his own SUV, and now he turned it around and sped through the city streets toward the hills on the east side of town, where the river made a lazy turn and headed west toward the ocean. The road to the Crassleys was well known. There was always a Crassley in trouble. That was the way of it, mostly penny-ante stuff. He wondered what Ellie's connection to them was.

When he pulled into the driveway, he saw a blue Ford Escort. A pack of dogs set up howling and barking as he tagged the license number and learned that it was indeed Ellie's car. It was the one vehicle parked in the front of the house, though sunlight was breaking through the clouds and refracting off the chrome and side mirrors of a couple dozen older vehicles. The hounds threw themselves at the fence where they were penned as he walked by, and McCrae, for all of his love of dogs, was glad he had his Glock.

He walked carefully toward the front door. He'd barely gotten to the bottom step when one of the Crassleys—Gale, he thought, though they all had a similar look: tall, hulking, and jowly with mean eyes—stepped outside. It was Gale, he decided. He was the one closest in age to their class, two grades above. McCrae's gaze slipped to the rifle under his arm, and Gale, apparently appreciating the finer points of greeting visitors while armed, carefully set the butt on the porch floorboards.

"Where is Ellie O'Brien?" McCrae asked.

"Who?" He put a hand to the back of his ear.

"Owner of that vehicle." McCrae gestured behind himself, never taking his eyes off the man.

"Don't know."

From inside the house, he heard a pounding and muffled shrieking.

"I'd venture to say you do know," McCrae said. His blood was heating up. If this piece of shit had done anything to her . . .

"Help! Help!" the faint female voice called.

"Shut up, Nia," he threw over his shoulder.

"Help!" she cried.

"That's Ellie," McCrae said grimly. He spread his feet a bit farther apart.

"You can't come in," Crassley stated. "Gotta have a search warrant."

"Not if someone's calling for help . . ." He pulled his Glock and held it in front of him, highly aware that Crassley could try to flip his rifle up and take a shot. He'd been in a number of tense spots over the years' incidents, but he'd never had to shoot at anyone. There was always a first time.

Crassley must've picked up on his intentions, because he dropped his belligerent stance, carefully propped the rifle against the wall under McCrae's watchful eye, spread his hands, then held open the screen. "You just caught us in a little fun time," he said. "Chasin' each other around. Pretendin' we need the cops."

"Help!" Ellie's voice was louder.

487

"Where are you?" McCrae asked, his Glock still trained on Crassley, whose hands were up by his ears. The rattle of a locked door tucked beneath the steps to the second floor answered the question even as he was asking it. To Crassley, he said, "Open it."

"I was just gettin' there. She was a little quicker to get 'er clothes off than me. Beggin' for it, y'know? That's how women are."

They walked toward the door together. Crassley pulled a key down from above the jamb and unlocked the door. Ellie tumbled out in bra and panties. Before McCrae could react, she launched herself at Crassley and raked his face with her nails, drawing blood. Crassley ripped her and hit her in the face, and McCrae pushed into him, slamming his gun against the man's head, dropping him to the ground. Crassley writhed in pain and howled and screamed about police brutality.

McCrae kept his gun sighted on him. "Get up and I'll shoot you," he ground out.

"Jesus, man . . . ," Gale sputtered.

"Bastard!" Ellie shrieked. She hauled off and kicked him in the side.

"Did he hurt you?" McCrae demanded.

"No," she snarled.

Gale started laughing. "Tell 'im, sweetheart. Tell 'im how you went down on me and sucked my cock."

"Don't," McCrae said as Ellie launched herself at him again, kicking for his face.

Crassley grabbed her bare foot, and she went down hard on her butt, and then scrambled to her hands and knees and then her feet, hauling back to kick him again.

Crassley was trying to rise too, but she managed a good one to the groin, though he swiveled to protect himself, and she mostly got him in the hip.

"Don't!" McCrae yelled louder as Ellie looked about to body-slam him.

She stopped herself, turned her glare on McCrae, then turned to grab up her clothes, which were strewn along the couch.

Crassley, holding a hand to his head, said, "I'm calling my lawyer. You came into my house and harassed me, hit me."

"You were going to rape me!" Ellie spit at him as she pulled on her pants.

"It ain't rape when it's consensual."

"Wait, wait." McCrae put a hand out to Ellie, who'd put on her shoes, heels, and was ready to come at him again. "Don't give him what he wants."

"I see the curtains match the drapes." Crassley grinned as his eyes fastened on the sheer scrap of panty material.

"Ellie. He'll sue you. He wants you to attack him."

Tears stood in her eyes, and her chest heaved. "It might be worth it," she said, but she backed up a few steps away from the battle and finished getting dressed.

McCrae marched Crassley outside, got cuffs from the police vehicle, and put his hands behind his back.

About that time, the other Crassleys showed up, Booker and Harry. Nia was right behind them. They all glared at McCrae, who was opening the back door of his police vehicle. Ellie stalked outside to her Escort and glared over at Gale, a red-haired virago ready to go at him again.

The other Crassleys started protesting and griping, glaring at McCrae and Ellie. "Don't say anything to her," Nia warned Gale.

For an answer, Gale made kissy noises with his pursed lips at Ellie, then thrust his crotch at her before McCrae could get him locked into the back seat.

"It's me who's going to go after you," Ellie told him, stepping forward. "Attempted rape."

"Suck my dick," he told her, grinning.

"If I ever got that thing in my mouth, I'd bite it off," she assured him.

McCrae slammed the back door.

"Hey," Booker suddenly yelled in discovery. "You two were the ones fucking the night of the barbecue! Woody told me."

"That's right!" Harry concurred, and they slapped palms.

McCrae said to Ellie, "I can call for some help and drive you."

"Nope. You take this piece of shit and dump him wherever he needs to go. I'll drive myself." She peered through the window of the Trailblazer at Gale and said, "Nia said it was 'a job.'"

"Don't listen to her!" Nia shrieked as her brothers' heads turned to look her way.

"I'm coming after you," Ellie added as she walked away. Then she slammed into her own car and backed up, creating a spray of gravel.

McCrae circled his vehicle around the three other Crassleys and followed after her. They bumped down the drive and onto the road.

"So you had her too, huh," Gale said. "That makes us brothers, in a way."

"Shut up, Crassley."

"At the barbecue. Heard all about that one. Everybody was at it, huh. Even that lesbo girl with Tanner. Funny, they're both dead now."

McCrae kept silent by sheer will.

"I heard Tanner was with every one of 'em that he could get, and that preacher's daughter was throwin' herself at him. Killed herself 'cause she wasn't a virgin, and she had that preacher daddy. Bet he wanted to kill Stahd. I would."

McCrae closed his ears. No one had ever said

Carmen had sex with Tanner that night. He went back to something Ellie had said.

"What was the 'job' Ellie brought up?" he asked Crassley.

"Don't know what you mean."

"Nia said it was a 'job'," he quoted.

"Bitch doesn't know what she's talking about," he muttered, and then subsided into silence.

Delta saw Amanda's interview with Ellie on the noon news. It felt weird to be the subject of their conversation. She'd called Amanda but hadn't heard from her, which was the way of it, she was learning. Amanda was fairly demanding when she needed something from you, hard to reach when she didn't.

And then she switched to Channel Four, thinking of the young, balding reporter who'd dogged her so much. And there he was . . . talking about *her!*

". . . in recent days *Blood Dreams* sales have skyrocketed. It's topping the e-book charts. I asked Delta Stahd about her book, but she declined to answer. The story is remarkably similar to the fate that her newly deceased husband, Doctor Tanner Stahd, suffered. The wife of a notoriously cheating doctor concocts a plan to stab her husband to death and inherit his estate. In the book, she gets away with murder, but in real life, Tanner Stahd's father, Doctor Lester

Stahd, is making a claim that Delta should not profit from killing his son, which is what he believes she did. Does the sudden 'rise to fortune' of *Blood Dreams* constitute monies Delta should not profit from as well? Tanner and Delta Stahd also have a young son, Owen Stahd, and Lester Stahd is suing for custody of him. It's a family tragedy that grows more complicated daily. If—"

Delta switched off the set. Her mother was standing at the edge of the family room. She'd heard too. "Mom, I didn't do it," she said.

"I know." Her mother came over and put her arms around her. Delta leaned her head on her shoulder. She closed her eyes, thinking about her meeting with Amanda, who'd asked as they were wrapping up, "Is there anything else? Anything you can think of that might be something we have to spin?"

She'd shaken her head. She hadn't thought about the uptick in sales of *Blood Dreams*.

Now she pulled back from her mother and tried on a smile. Her father was at the store, and her mother would be too, if Delta hadn't needed support.

"Dad's okay by himself?"

"For a little while," her mother agreed.

"Okay. I'd better get going then."

"You sure?" Mom frowned. "I don't like thinking of you alone."

"I'm sure." As much as she loved and relied on

both of them, today she was antsy and uncomfortable. Amanda's television interview hadn't really helped all that much. Just hearing about herself made her feel like a criminal.

She left around 1:00, feeling somewhat lost. Zora was gone. Another one of their group. Owen was at school. It did feel lonely.

She thought about calling McCrae, but she didn't know what he thought of her after she'd confessed about the knives. Everything just felt . . . fraught.

Back at her house—no press outside, thank God—she remembered about checking in with Woody about the guy who'd fought with Tanner over the fender bender. She imagined the police had already talked to him, and there wasn't anything for her to really do, but . . .

She had a glass of sparkling water, thought about some rosé, then decided it was still too early in the afternoon and stuck with the water. After listening to the quiet of the house, she headed out. She hadn't really seen Woody since the reunion, apart from across the street in downtown West Knoll once and at Danny O's another time, when she'd taken Owen when he was about three. Both times, he'd given her a sardonic smile and a salute, which she'd taken to be a comment on her escalating social status as Dr. Tanner Stahd's wife.

Candy had opened the clinic on a limited basis.

She'd called Delta and given her condolences, and then had said they really weren't having much business. Tanner's father's screaming decimation of Delta had apparently cooled the community's interest in the clinic.

If I'm in charge, it's not safe to go.

That was a further depressing thought.

She went to Woody's Auto Body, but there was no one there. A clock-face sign on the door had an arrow pointed to a return of 3:00 p.m.

"One helluva lunch hour, Woody," she murmured. But maybe he was on the job somewhere.

She phoned Amanda again, but the call went to voice mail once more. This time she left a message. "Hi, Amanda, it's Delta. Just checking in. I saw your interview with Ellie. It was nice to be defended. Um . . . I told McCrae the truth about the knife. It just . . . happened. Anyway, thanks. Call when you can."

She clicked off and decided to go to lunch herself at Danny O's. Might as well kill some time.

Amanda came back from her run and drank a full glass of water. She thought she heard something and cocked her head. Something outside, by the garage? She walked out to the back patio and looked to her garage. Nothing. She heard a mower, far away, and scoured the distant fields from west to east. The clouds had burned off completely, and the sky was high and blue. She closed her eyes and drank in the sense of purity that open spaces gave her, fighting the depression that hovered in the corners of her mind ever since she'd heard about Zora.

After a few moments, she went back inside and up the stairs to take a shower and clean up. She wasn't going back to the office today, or maybe any day. Hal didn't want her there. She didn't want to be there.

And she had his client list on a sheaf of papers that she'd managed to print out when he wasn't around. She would have preferred the file, but she could input them into her own contact list when she had time, which she did right now, as a matter of fact.

She took her laptop to the dining room table, along with the file containing Hal's clients. She sat down and, with her Pilot pen, started making notes to herself, first on paper, then to be inputted in the computer. She made herself an itinerary. She needed to meet with McCrae or Quin and get a feel for what the police had on Delta. She knew a lot of the county prosecutors; one of them would be assigned to Tanner's homicide case. Whether they would go after Delta or not was anyone's guess at this point. Delta felt that McCrae was sympathetic, but that only meant so much.

And there was the issue of the knife . . .

Curiously, she believed Delta on that one. She'd panicked. But it looked bad, and could to a jury, if the case went to trial. More problematic was the book she'd written, which apparently was making a small fortune and showed no signs of stopping as the story of Tanner's murder spread across the Internet. Delta hadn't mentioned her increase in book sales, but maybe she felt like the information was already readily available.

Amanda snorted. Hal had accused her of taking hard-luck cases. Maybe not so with Delta.

Ellie took a good, long shower. He hadn't really touched her. Just made her strip, which she'd done, excruciatingly slowly. He'd wanted it that way, and well, she'd been counting the minutes till McCrae got the message, her mind whirling as she'd worried he might not act in time or maybe at all.

But like the hero he was, he'd shown up, and Crassley had shoved her into the closet and locked the door. Had he really thought she'd keep quiet? Maybe he'd believed he could keep McCrae out of hearing range.

Whatever. She still felt dirty. Kind of scared and kind of exhilarated. And mad. She truly wanted to kill him. Would, if she could without facing the consequences. She could have kicked him to death.

Her cell was ringing as she toweled her hair

dry. She swept it up from her dresser and saw it was McCrae. "Hi," she answered shortly.

"Crassley's in county. Already got a lawyer. Seems to have one at the ready, and not a public defender. I'm heading back to the station now."

Ellie said, "Thieving must be profitable."

"You doing all right?"

"You keep asking. I'm fine. I have murder in my heart, but otherwise I'm fine."

"Don't do anything rash."

"Oh, like go out to the Crassleys and torch their property and all those fucking cars? And the dogs?"

"The dogs aren't part of it."

"I know, McCrae," she said wearily. "But excuse me if I want some payback. It's been a helluva day."

"What did you mean about 'a job'?"

"What?" she asked, deliberately misinterpreting.

"You said 'Nia said it was a job.' What was a job?"

Should she tell him? A part of her wanted to keep that nugget to herself, in case it was true.

But you're not even a reporter, right now . . . and he saved you . . .

"We had a fight, Nia and I. Long story, but it's why I went to the Crassleys. I thought I could . . . interview Gale. That was erroneous, as you know. There's no interviewing a Crassley. Nia was talking about Penske. She said he was on 'a job.' She was dating him off and on around that time. You know they'd hooked up while she was still in high school."

"I heard that rumor," he agreed.

"She said, 'He didn't want to be with her. It was a job.' I took it to mean that Penske didn't want to be with Bailey, that it was a job."

"Okay."

"Okay? That's it?"

"You think Nia implicated her family. That somehow Penske was with Bailey that night, on their orders. Maybe they had something on him. Maybe they could prove he'd been seeing Nia when she was underage. Something like that. The Crassleys blamed Bailey for Little Dan's death, among other things. You think Penske was used to set her up, maybe even kill her."

"Impressive, McCrae." She was a little surprised he'd followed her thinking so closely. "So what do we do now?"

"You, stay away from the Crassleys."

"What about you?"

But he had already clicked off.

Danny O's was busy, with the waitstaff holding trays of food, a lot of breakfast items from their twenty-four-hour menu, and a large population of construction workers who probably liked the size of the portions, large, and the size of the price, small to medium.

Delta hadn't been here in years. Tanner called it "slumming it," and Delta tended toward salads and lean meat and expensive wine. *I'm a snob,* she thought, the label like a kick to the gut. She'd always thought of herself as that girl whose parents owned the mom-and-pop grocery store, not Dr. Tanner Stahd's wife.

She was sitting at one of the smaller booths, perusing a menu for anything she might like to pass the time—iced tea was about all that appealed to her—when a shadow fell over her shoulder, and she glanced around quickly, apprehensively.

"Brad?" she said, seeing the hulk that was Brad Sumpter looming over her.

"Hi, Delta," he said.

He was nervous, she realized. Well, so was she. Brad had already been a bodybuilder when they were in high school, and that had continued through the reunion and apparently for the years after. He'd never said much, being more Justin Penske's sidekick.

"Can I sit down?" he asked, and then plopped down across from her, pushing the table a little closer to her side of the booth to make room for a swelling gut. Maybe his obsessive workouts had stopped, or at least petered out. He looked like he was going to seed.

"What . . . are you doing these days?" she asked him.

"I saw what Amanda said about you. I wanted you to know, I know you didn't kill him. I was glad she said something. I thought you guys still hated each other. It's good you don't."

"Yeah . . . thanks."

The waitress came and asked if they were ready. Delta almost wanted to leave, but she ordered the iced tea. After a long moment, while he apparently waited for her to order more, Brad shook his head, and the waitress moved on.

"If you ever need anything . . ." He trailed off.

"Thanks, Brad. I'm doing okay. It's hard . . . for all of us."

He looked off across the restaurant, and she could see he was wrestling with some deep emotion. His lips moved, and his eyes were sad. "You know, when it all gets straightened out and it's better, that'll be a good thing."

"Yes," Delta said slowly.

Her iced tea was delivered, and she pulled the glass close.

"Aren't you gonna put sugar in it?" he asked.

"No."

"You look good, Delta."

"Thank you."

He waited another moment, then pushed himself up from the table. "Well, I'd better be going." He hesitated, then added, "I didn't want any of this bad stuff to happen to you or Tanner."

He left before she could question him further.

A hard breeze was kicking up. As Amanda walked from the kitchen and cut across the dining room, she saw a paper bag fly up outside the front-room windows. She crossed the living room and unlocked the rarely used front door. She couldn't remember the last time she'd opened it.

There, held down with a handful of pebbles, was a manila envelope. She picked it up and brought it inside. "For you" was scratched across the front in pen.

She opened it up and shook out the contents. A notebook.

Bailey's notebook.

Chapter 26

McCrae changed his mind about returning to the station and went looking for Tracy again, but she wasn't on the schedule to work at the bar that day. Jimmy, her boss and possibly boyfriend, regarded McCrae with serious suspicion this time and wouldn't say anything apart from the fact that Tracy wasn't there.

McCrae started to leave, then looked at the stool where he'd sat the last time he was here, remembering Tracy leaning over the bar, pulling back, telling him about Penske's burner phone and the guy who was watching. The old car with the faded hood pulling up outside Lundeen's, the watcher talking to the driver.

He had a sudden mental picture of the Crassleys' car graveyard.

He left in a hurry.

Delta's cell phone rang as she was leaving Danny O's. She pulled it out of her purse, regarding it with trepidation as she crossed the parking lot to her car.

Ellie.

"Did McCrae tell you what happened?" Ellie responded to Delta's hello.

"Um . . . no, I don't know . . . what do you mean?"

"You haven't talked to him?"

"Not for a while. What happened?"

There was a pause, and then she said, "Can I do an interview with you? I'm not with the station any longer. It would be for the paper, maybe. Something written. No camera, unless you wanted that and we could figure it out."

"No."

"It would be your chance to proclaim your innocence."

Delta unlocked the driver's door. "I'm not interested, Ellie."

"With the sales of your book skyrocketing, this could be a big interview. Built-in online audience. Do you have a website?"

Delta clicked off. The hungry tone in Ellie's voice pissed her off. Not with the station any longer . . . was that even true? Didn't matter anyway. She wasn't giving interviews. Amanda had told her not to, and she hadn't planned on it anyway.

She called Amanda, who picked up on the second ring, surprising her. "I just got a call from Ellie, who wants to do an interview."

"No," Amanda responded.

"That's what I said." She sighed. "I'm sure you heard about Zora and Brian. I'm having trouble thinking of anything else. Zora was supposed to be taking care of Owen tonight, so I could have some time to myself."

"She asked you if she could babysit?" Amanda asked quickly.

"She offered, yeah."

"Delta . . . you're too trusting. Zora was . . . she had some problems. She'd been trying to get pregnant for years."

"I know. I think that's why—"

"She talked about if you were convicted of murdering Tanner, that maybe she could have your son. I'm sorry. I don't want to talk ill of the dead, but that's a fact."

Delta was struck silent.

"Don't trust anyone but me," Amanda said tautly. "And . . . stop by the house later. I have something to show you."

"What?"

"Come by after dinner . . . around eight? I've got some things to do, but I think I might have some answers to some old questions then."

"I'll have to get a sitter."

"Do it," Amanda said and hung up.

Well, great. Just after telling her that Zora had been angling for Owen . . . seriously? What had she planned to do if Delta had left Owen in her care?

She shivered. The idea of finding a sitter tonight . . . if her mother couldn't do it. She wasn't going to go.

"Mom," she said, greeting her mother a few moments later as she pulled out of Danny O's lot. "Could you babysit tonight? I need to meet with Amanda."

"Well, sure."

"Thank you," she said gratefully. "Gotta go. I'm driving, and I don't want a ticket."

"Okay, honey."

She clicked off and headed back toward Woody's Auto Body. After several miles, she noticed a big, black SUV changing lanes along with her. She changed lanes again, and the black SUV followed.

Her heart lurched.

She drove on to Woody's, one eye on the black SUV. The auto body shop was on the outskirts of Laurelton, about a half-hour drive from West Knoll. As she turned at a light, she expected the SUV to follow, but it cruised through the light and went on. She thought there was a man at the wheel. Brad Sumpter, maybe?

Unnerved, she drove back to the auto body parking lot. The note was still on the door, but through its window panel, she could see someone inside. She walked up to the door and tried the knob. The door opened, and she was inside a small room with a counter and two metal chairs. There were pictures of cars along the walls and a number of items for sale to improve the appearance of a car—chrome cleaner, chamois cloths, leather upholstery wipes, bottles and sprays of all colors and scents, scented trees in cellophane that nevertheless permeated the room with flavors that nearly obliterated the sharp scent of oil and paint.

Woody was behind the counter. His hair was still long, pulled up into a man bun and streaked with gray. He wore a wife-beater T-shirt, and she could see a portion of the landing eagle tattoo that spread across his left shoulder. Her dislike of tattoos had faded over the years, and Woody's made her feel warm, almost happy, like meeting an old friend and recognizing they hadn't really changed. His face was, as ever, more comical than handsome and was covered with a short, but raggedy beard. But it was a familiar face, and when he smiled at her, Delta's resistance fled. "Woody," she greeted him, a catch in her voice.

"Mrs. Stahd," he drawled.

She was horrified to feel tears building. She touched her finger to the corners of her eyes, seeking to hold them back. "Sorry. Tanner and then now Zora . . ."

"Hard to believe there's not some evil purpose behind it all, right?"

She nodded.

He shrugged, as if purposely setting that aside. "Whatever are you doing in a place like mine?"

"I don't know," she admitted. "Looking for some answers, maybe."

"Here?" His brows drew together.

She shook her head. Didn't know quite how to proceed, now that she was facing Woody, so she backtracked. "Crystal sent me an e-mail. I hadn't seen her since the reunion."

"She sent you an e-mail?"

"She warned me to not let the police bully me. She still a preschool teacher?"

"Nah . . . She's, uh . . . you know we're divorced."

"I guess I heard that." Delta nodded.

"She's in the marijuana business," he said.

"Really?" She couldn't hide her surprise.

"I know what you're thinking, like everyone else. Shoulda been me, right? Well, I was in it first, while she was teaching, and we had rip-roarin' fights over it. Makin' good money, but it's finally what broke us up. She ended up with the business in the divorce. How do you like that?"

"Wow."

"Yep. So if you wanna see her, you gotta head toward the beach. She lives out thataway." He hooked a thumb toward the west.

"Actually, I wanted to talk to you about the guy who ran into Tanner's car. I think you fixed both vehicles."

"You mean the guy Tanner ran into."

"I guess I heard it the other way around," said Delta.

"Look, Tanner's dead, and I liked him, but he

was a liar. No gettin' around that. Who d'ya think stabbed him?"

Delta found his way of hitting the issue straight on refreshing, and a little scary. "A lot of people think it was me."

"I know who did it."

She smiled faintly, before realizing he was dead serious. "Okay, who?"

"One of his girlfriends. Tanner always had a few extras around. One for show . . ." He swept a hand in Delta's direction. "And the others for . . . other things."

"Maybe. Who are those girlfriends?"

"One of 'em's your lawyer," he said meaningfully. "Saw that today. Couldn't believe you actually hired Amanda Forsythe."

"I needed someone good."

"I get that. Still, it's a surprise. I saw them at the barbeque, y'know, Amanda and Tanner."

"I remember you being pretty stoned."

He chuckled. "Oh, yeah, but I still saw them. In fact, I saw a lot of things. Some I really shouldn't have. Have kept 'em to myself." He put a finger to his lips. "But you wanted to know about Mr. Josh McGill. Tanner sideswiped his car and acted like it was the guy's fault, even though it was pretty easy to tell it wasn't. McGill's a hothead. He challenged Tanner in the parking lot, from what they both said, and there was a lot of shouting. Maybe some shoving, but

Tanner was smart. He backed down when he was losing. Had to, but it was hard for him. He was a guy who couldn't be wrong. You know the type."

Woody was describing Tanner in terms that were spot-on, but no one had ever had the courage to say so before.

"The police already asked me this. Bailey's dad," Woody added.

"Oh." She should've expected that. But as long as she was here . . . "Who else was he with?"

"Zora. Always liked her. Tanner said they got pretty hot and heavy on her pool table before Amanda. Ellie was a score in college. Amanda was high school."

"How do you know all this?"

"Ahhh, let's just say we had a mutual confidante, back in those days." He rubbed his nose, faintly smiling. "She's the one told me about Ellie and Chris at the barbeque too. A lot of that going around that night."

Ellie and Chris . . . McCrae. She'd ignored the rumor about them at the barbeque, had put it down to wild gossip, but maybe it was true. She wished it didn't affect her so much at this late date, but it did, to some extent.

"What about you?" Delta asked lightly.

"At the barbeque? Oh, I stayed true to Crystal."

"What about afterward?"

"You want me to kiss and tell?" He wagged his finger at her. "That could get me in serious trouble."

"You just said you're divorced."

"Why do you want to know? Could it be you're interested in little old me?"

She almost smiled. He was as outrageous as always.

"I don't kiss and tell, but yes, I know what you're thinking. I can see it. That jealous female thing mixed with a kind of intuition. You think Tanner and I might've shared a few women. Not together. Just . . . working out of the same black book."

Delta hadn't really gotten that far in her thinking, but she didn't want him to know that. "Did you?"

His grin widened. "We mighta . . . hit a few gentleman's clubs, y'know."

Delta recalled catching Tanner in a lie and learning he'd gone to an adult club with someone. Probably Woody, she saw now. She recalled her husband grinning at her and saying, "The devil made me do it." A favorite line.

"Who's this confidante you shared with Tanner? Maybe she knows something about my husband's murder," Delta said.

"Tell McCrae to come and talk to me. I have a few things to say he might be interested in."

"About Tanner?"

511

"About West Knoll High School. It's not just about the students, you know."

"What do you mean?"

He hesitated a moment, then shrugged. "Timmons had his tongue hanging on the ground for all the girls."

"Oh, come on."

"I know a horndog when I see one. Maybe he hid it from you, but it was there. I know Zora married him for the bucks, but he married her because he couldn't get the one he really wanted. And that's all I'm going to say about that."

The phone on the counter started ringing, and Woody gave it a sidelong look. He reached for it, and over his shoulder, he said, "Nice seeing you, Delta. Stay safe."

McCrae bumped along the Crassleys' weed-choked drive a second time. He had no warrant, but he didn't plan on going inside the house again. Instead he pulled to a stop outside of the yard with the parked jalopies and, ignoring the baying dogs, opened the gate and walked in.

He'd just passed by the first row of dust-shrouded vehicles when Booker and Harry poured out of the house and started yelling.

"What the fuck you doin'? Get the hell off our property!" Booker screamed.

"I'm getting the shotgun," Harry snapped, but he didn't move.

McCrae kept a careful eye on them as he wandered among the rust buckets. He'd be surprised if any of them worked. The sun was beating on them, refracting heat off the metal in waves.

Booker and Harry were poised, waiting for McCrae to do something.

Then he saw the faded red hood of the car with the truck back. "El Camino," he marveled, reading its name in the metal script that was still in place. If the guy at the bar was right—and he had no reason to doubt him—the vehicle was a 1987 model or earlier.

"What the fuck you doin'?" Booker repeated in a low growl as McCrae brushed past them and back to the Trailblazer.

McCrae turned around and left. He didn't think the two morons realized what he was looking for, but he wasn't about to take any chances. He pulled his cell from his pocket and placed a call.

"Quin," he said into the man's voice mail, wishing he were there to pick up. "There's a car at the Crassleys that I need to bring in as evidence. El Camino. Faded red hood." He debated about saying more, but if this was the car outside Lundeen's the night Bailey and Penske were shot, the one where the driver stopped to talk to the guy Tracy thought was keeping tabs on them . . . then he couldn't afford for it to disappear. Tracy might not be the liar people had accused her of being. So far, she was batting a

513

thousand. And the burner phone . . . the "job" Penske was doing . . . it didn't add up to murder/suicide any way you cut it.

He was almost to the station when Delta called. Surprised, he answered, "Chris McCrae."

"Hi," she said diffidently. "I just thought I should let you know that I . . . uh . . . went to see Woody, and he said I should have you call him. I guess he thought I had a direct line to the cops."

"You went to see Woody?"

"I wanted to ask about Tanner's fender bender, but he'd already talked to Mr. Quintar—Chief Quintar," she corrected herself.

"He wants me to call him?" McCrae was having trouble with the thought of Delta going to see Woody.

"We talked about the past . . . the barbeque . . . a lot of things."

"What things?" He was keying in, now.

"He said that . . . a lot of things about Tanner that I already knew. His cheating. With my *friends*. Sounded like Woody went with him to men's clubs, maybe. And he mentioned that Brian Timmons . . ." She heaved a sigh. "You should talk to him. I don't want to say anything about Brian. I don't even think it's true."

"What did he say?" McCrae asked patiently, even though he wanted to yell at her to stay the hell away from the investigation. It was bad enough already. He didn't want her doing anything that anyone could misconstrue.

"He said he was a horndog. That his 'tongue was on the ground' looking at the teens."

"I don't remember that," McCrae murmured, wondering what Woody's angle was. "I'll call him. But, Delta, stay away from him and anyone who has anything to do with Tanner's homicide. Leave the investigating to us."

"I can't just sit around," she said with a note of belligerence. "I feel set up, and I can't just sit around. And I think someone was following me, and I don't want to go home yet."

"Following you?" he snapped.

"Maybe . . . I don't know . . ." She backed down quickly.

McCrae slowed before he was about to turn into the station, then sped up and drove past. "You know where I live? My dad's house."

"Yes, I think so."

"Meet me there. I'm on my way now."

"You think that's a good idea?" she asked after a weighty pause.

Hell, no. "Just be there, okay?"

"Okay," she said.

What are you doing, buddy? What are you doing?

His phone rang. Quin. "Hey," he greeted his boss. "You get my message about the car?"

"Yeah, what's it about?"

McCrae tersely gave him a rundown of the vehicle and what it meant to Bailey's case. "The Crassleys are involved. I don't know how yet, but I will."

"Goddamn," Quin said soberly.

"I know. We're getting traction on Bailey's case, finally, but there's something else." He then told him about Ellie's encounter with the Crassleys and taking Gale Crassley to the county jail.

Quin sounded flabbergasted. "I'm sorry I haven't been available. I've been putting out fires on your behalf. Hurston had a whole list of reasons why he wants Delta charged with her husband's murder, and he wants you off the case."

"He doesn't have any jurisdiction! This isn't his investigation!" McCrae exploded.

"I told him that. Reminded him I was the chief. He's got Mayor Kathy twisted around his finger, but until I'm removed from office, he can flap his arms and fly around like a headless goose, which is what he's doing. Don't come in. Keep doing whatever you're doing. He's been ready to pounce on you all day."

"Okay." McCrae felt a little better about meeting Delta instead of going into work.

"This is good work, McCrae," Quin added. "And I'm sorry about Ellie. Is she okay?"

"I think so. I've checked in. I'll keep making sure."

"Those Crassleys . . . ," he muttered coldly.

"I'm going to pin them down," said McCrae. "Find out what really happened that night."

"It never was a murder/suicide," he said.

"No."

"McCrae," he said suddenly, when they were about to end their call.

"Uh huh?"

"Be careful of Delta Stahd. I don't agree with Hurston on much, but he makes some good points. She's a prime suspect and may have very well killed her husband. I know you like her. But don't forget to keep your eyes and ears open. If anything further should come to light about her, we're at that tipping point. I'm not saying for sure that she did it. I'm just saying be careful."

McCrae hung up, his mouth dry. Quin didn't know about the knife. He didn't know McCrae was meeting Delta at his house.

Ellie thought about it and thought about it and thought some more. The Crassleys were somehow involved in Bailey's death. Penske had made her his "job." She didn't have enough for a full story, but she had some of it.

She was driving to the Channel Four station to track down Andy, a producer who'd always had a thing for her. You could just tell these things.

Last year, she'd run into him at a hotel function, and his eyes had been all over her. She'd been with Alton then, but she'd taken note.

She put a call in as she pulled into the lot. She was told he wasn't in, but she left her name and number, and he called right back. The chicken-shit. Screening his calls.

"Hey, Andy, I'm right outside," Ellie said, putting a smile into her voice. "I want to come work for you, and I'm bringing a couple really good stories with me."

"I heard heads were rolling at Seven. Sorry."

He didn't sound sorry at all.

"I can get an interview with Delta Stahd," she lied. "One on one. Her side of the marriage."

"That would be good."

"And I also have a story to tell about myself. Today, and I mean *today*, I was held at gunpoint by Gale Crassley, who's currently in the county jail over the incident. He had me strip naked."

"*You* were held at gunpoint."

"Yes. *I* was held at gunpoint."

He whistled, surprised. "Wow. That is a story."

"But I need a job. And I want to come to Channel Four."

"Well, Ellie, I'm not in charge of that, you know. You'd have to talk to the big boss, and he hates being talked to, which you probably also know. And you gotta check with HR, of course."

"I also think I've got new information on that

cop killing five years ago, the current chief's daughter," said Ellie, undaunted.

He chuckled, sounding a bit embarrassed. "That would be something, for sure."

"You don't believe me," she realized, aghast.

"We've got some good reporters already, and there's not a lot of room. You know how it is. Staff gets overblown and you gotta cut. Maybe you could talk to one of 'em, in fact—"

"This is all bullshit about the *'big boss.'* You're giving me the runaround and don't have the balls to admit it." Andy was supposed to be her friend!

He said, pained, "Ellie . . . I'm going to be straight with you. You have a reputation as hard to work with."

"Who said that? *Alton?*"

"And, well, that's another thing. The, er, bonds of matrimony don't seem to matter a lot to you."

"You piece of shit."

"You're a darn good reporter, Ellie, but it's that kind of attitude that gets you in trouble. And at Channel Four, we do real news. Not biased innuendo. Not stunts, and—"

"Stunts?" She couldn't breathe.

"—not incomplete stories with half-baked theories masquerading as fact."

"My life was in real danger, you asshole."

He clucked his tongue. "Name calling is counterprod—"

She clicked off. Tossed her phone into the passenger seat but overthrew, and it smacked into the window, bounced down to the seat and then the footwell. Real news? *Real news?*

She fumed for long moments. Her life had been in danger. In real danger! And Andy was talking about *stunts?*

She let out a primal scream that made her ears ring and pounded the steering wheel. How much was she expected to do? Save the twins from the vile Crassleys? Save her own self—with McCrae's help, okay, but hello? Fucking Gale Crassley could have raped her! Crassley was a prick, but McCrae was an asshole. All men were assholes. It was just a fact.

And she'd *given* him what Nia had said about Penske's interest in Bailey being a job. Just given it to him. Bestowed it on him with barely an acknowledgment. Now he was out playing cops and robbers with the Crassleys, and she was persona non grata at Channel Seven *and* Channel Four.

Well, Andy was going to be sorry. She was going to delve some more, get all the facts, all the pieces, everything and write the story of the century, maybe film it on her camera, put in on YouTube.

She drummed her fingers on the steering wheel until she came up with a plan. She would get that interview from Delta . . . *Dee* . . . chase her down if she had to, force a confession out of her, and tape it on her phone.

What time was it? 4:30. The longest day of her life. Delta would most likely be picking up her kid from pre-K soon.

Time to go wait outside her house.

Chapter 27

Delta had never been inside McCrae's family's house and had expected a somewhat neglected home with years of deferred maintenance. But the kitchen was warm and bright, with honey-colored cabinets in good repair and refurbished oak floors that gleamed. He'd kept what was good and teamed it with a farmhouse sink and quartz countertops.

"Someone did some nice work here," she said.

The dog stayed stiff and unmoving. Not growling. Just not accepting.

McCrae snapped his fingers, and the animal came to sit at his side.

He'd been just turning off his vehicle, one of the West Knoll blue-and-gold Trailblazers, when she'd pulled in the drive behind him. The first awkward moments were eased by him opening the door and greeting the frisky little dog, who'd changed his position upon seeing Delta. His obvious joy had instantly developed into threatening silence.

"Don't mind Fido," McCrae said. "He'll get over it."

"Fido?"

"Was Bailey's dog. I took him in."

"Oh."

Now he looked around the kitchen as if seeing it for the first time. "Had to fix it up after Dad died. Hired an interior designer who had a lot of ideas. Took some talking to, but we eventually saw eye to eye."

"It's really good."

"I called Woody after I got off the phone with you."

"What did he say?" Delta asked curiously.

"He couldn't give a straight answer if it was his ticket out of hell."

"Do you think he knows something?"

McCrae shook his head. "I felt like he was . . ."

"What?"

He glanced at her, and she remembered thinking how blue his eyes were all those years ago when they were at the river and he was stripping down to his faded cutoffs. They looked exactly the same now. Deep, deep blue.

". . . throwing shade at everyone else. Brian Timmons. His ex-wife. Tanner."

"Tanner, for certain. I knew he was a cheater; I mean, I turned my back on it, but I knew. But I didn't know how much."

"He brought up going to adult clubs, like you said."

Delta looked away. "Whenever he was in trouble, he would lie and try to squirm out of it.

He'd say, 'The devil made me do it.' Like that's all it took to be absolved."

McCrae frowned. Fido, looking up at him, started whining, and McCrae absently reached down and petted his head. Fido pushed into McCrae's hand. His eyes closed, his tongue slipped out, and he started panting happily.

"You want something to drink? I've got water . . . and coffee, tea . . . beer . . . ?"

"Thanks, no." Delta smiled. "It's just kind of nice to make it stop for a minute. Oh, I saw Brad Sumpter today. He came up to me at Danny O's and sat down in my booth. He told me he knew I didn't kill Tanner. That was nice to hear." She gave a short, humorless laugh. "He said he never wanted any of the bad stuff to happen to me and Tanner."

Fido took a few steps forward, and Delta leaned down, holding her palm open for him to sniff. He looked up at her with those doggy eyes and pushed his head into her hand, hoping for a pet or a scratch apparently, and she obliged.

"That's pretty good," McCrae said. "He's fairly picky about who he thinks should be allowed in the house."

"I'm going to have to go get my son soon. I'm . . . I think I'm taking him to my mom's. I'm meeting Amanda tonight. She has some things to go over."

"You trust her to do right by you?"

"I do. Why? Don't you?"

"Yes, she should."

"I've heard so much stuff lately, about the barbeque, and how she was in the woods with Tanner and *everyone* saw, apparently." She paused, wondering if she should take this further, then decided, why not? "You were with Ellie."

"Um, yes."

"And there I was, waiting for Tanner, being this good, good girl, I thought, while the rest of you were having fun."

"Ellie and I . . . that was . . ."

"Not fun?" She lifted her brows, calling him a liar.

"Not a good idea. We've been at odds ever since."

"Maybe it's true love."

He shook his head. "No."

That confession warmed Delta's heart. It was way too soon to be having the feelings she was having. Transference, yes. But it felt great, and she needed to feel great, just for a little while at least.

"I thought I was being followed, but now I don't know. They kept switching lanes like I was, but they shot on by when I turned off to go to Woody's Auto Body."

"What kind of vehicle?"

"Oh, I don't think it was anything. I'm just getting paranoid. It feels like everybody's out to get me." Seeing he was waiting, she said, "Big. Black. Big sidewalls, and I think it was like a Suburban? Something like that."

"If you see it again, call me."

She nodded. "I'd better go. It's nice to talk in person, though. And not at the police station . . . or the hospital."

"Agreed."

They started to walk to the kitchen door at the same time and bumped into each other. He reached out a hand to her arm to steady her. The contact felt electric against her bare skin. She remembered him holding her at the hospital and wanted to be held again. She looked up, and those blue eyes were steady and full of something primal that he probably didn't know she could see.

"You can kiss me," she whispered, heart thudding.

His mouth opened to spout objections, she thought. She placed a finger over his lips, not wanting to hear them.

Slowly, almost reluctantly, she thought, he cupped the back of her neck and brought her lips to his. She felt the hard warmth of his mouth and responded to the kiss, wrapping her arms around his waist. The kiss became more urgent. Full of desire. She would have lain down right there on the kitchen table if Fido hadn't squeezed between them, yipping and trying to jump.

They broke apart, each breathing hard.

McCrae said, "I . . . I didn't . . ."

"Mean for that to happen?" Delta finished, hearing the breathless sound of her own voice.

His mouth quirked. "Want that to stop."

They looked at each other.

"You have to go," he said.

"I have to go," she agreed.

He nodded, finally breaking eye contact. This time, Delta walked ahead of him out the door, and he followed her to her car, seeing the way the breeze teased her blouse, pressing it against her back, messing with the long, lustrous tresses of her dark hair. He watched as she backed out of his drive, lifting a hand in good-bye.

"Holy shit," she whispered.

"Holy shit," he muttered as he walked back in the house, running his hands through his hair. Not what was supposed to happen. Way off what was supposed to happen.

Fido cocked his head to and fro. McCrae realized it was time to feed him and poured kibbles into his bowl. Fido scarfed them down as if he was starving. Typical behavior.

But kissing Delta was not typical behavior for McCrae.

He purposely worked on shutting down his mind on her. Tried to remember all Quin's warnings.

To hell with it. That wasn't going to work. Instead, he concentrated on what she'd said that had sparked a negative feeling in him. Nothing to do with her. Something in what she'd said.

The black SUV. Suburban-like, she'd said. Zora and Brian had been run off the road . . . although preliminary reports suggested that maybe they'd already been dead, or unconscious, and that a block of concrete had been wedged against the accelerator, propelling them off the cliff.

Was someone following her? The more she'd dismissed it, the more concerned he'd become, even though he'd sought to hide his feelings.

He thought about Woody. He hadn't seen his old classmate since the reunion. They'd never been fast friends. Woody was just naturally too much of an anarchist, while McCrae leaned toward law and order . . . Delta notwithstanding.

Stay away from the station, Quin had said. Hurston was hovering like a dark cloud. Why? Why was he going after Delta so hard?

There was a new lead into proving Bailey's and Penske's deaths were not a murder/suicide. Hurston would fight to prove they were. Not for justice's sake. Just not to be wrong. But Delta . . . what the hell was with Hurston's interest in the Stahd case?

He called Quin, who answered formally, "Robert Quin," even though he had to know it was McCrae. Someone must be around. Hurston?

Was he still at the station? Or maybe it was Corinne, listening with big ears.

"Meet me at the county jail. Let's talk to Gale Crassley about that car," McCrae said. "He's the ringleader of that clan."

"Uh huh. Sure, I'll look into it."

"Can you make it in half an hour?"

"Likely."

"Okay. See you there . . ."

"I don't want to go to Grandma and Grandpa's. I want to go home and be with you," Owen said.

Now he wanted to be with her?

"I have one appointment. I'll pick you up as soon as I'm done," Delta told him.

"I want my blanket," he said stubbornly.

She understood the reversion. She should have seen this coming. And Owen was adroit at picking up feelings. When she wanted to be with him, he pulled away. When she had something to do, he sometimes clung to her. Not as often now that he was older, but they were in uncharted emotional territory. It was gratifying in a way, that he was turning to her.

She said, "Okay, we'll go home and get it, but then over to Grandma and Grandpa's."

"Promise?"

"Yes."

It took her forty minutes, twenty minutes to the house from the school, another twenty over to her parents' house, to make the full trip. By the time she was back, it was nearly 7:00.

Ellie was exhausted. Sitting in her car, not moving, watching Delta's house . . . a terrible job. Her whole body felt shut down. Luckily, she'd peed before she came here; otherwise, she'd have to leave and take care of business. Where was Delta? What the hell was taking her so long?

She was half-afraid she'd fall asleep and this whole endeavor would be a bust. But luckily enough, her brain just wouldn't relax, and while her body cried for sleep, her mind wouldn't abide.

She thought of all the people who'd wronged her. Oliver, her stepfather. Mom, who'd married the fucker. Joey and Michael for just being the miscreants they were, though she would still do anything for them. Morons. If Nia were actually pregnant . . . no. She wouldn't go there. She'd figure it out later. Alton and Coco . . . and Niedermeyer, the bastard, and Andy, that squirmy little rat fink.

And McCrae.

She wasn't as clear on his transgressions as the others, but she always felt angry with him. He withheld from her, and he loved Delta. Maybe love was too strong a word. He *cared* about Delta in a way he would never care about her.

And she wanted him to care about her. Love

531

her. Come in on a white steed and carry her away to a castle.

She snorted. Okay, he'd saved her today, although she was pretty sure she could have saved herself, if she could have gotten the gun away from Crassley, so she wasn't going to give him too much credit.

Still . . .

She wanted Delta to be Tanner's killer. That would get her out of the picture.

But is she? Really? Do you really think so, Ellie?

She wrestled with her conscience. She wanted it to be Delta so badly it was almost like she could will it to be true.

But it wasn't.

"Damn it," she whispered, feeling tears of frustration gather in her eyes.

She had hated them all, the Five Firsts, but especially Delta. Amanda was the meanest, but Delta was the best. Carmen didn't count. She'd been gone so long and was so gaga over Tanner, she just never felt like a rival. And Bailey, she'd been small and wiry and tough in her way, but there hadn't been the least bit of sexual energy coming off her that Ellie had felt competitive about. Zora, the same. She never challenged Ellie in the same way Amanda and Delta did. Still, she'd hated them for being in the clique and purposely keeping her out.

But now it was just down to Amanda and Delta, and truthfully, she didn't actively hate Amanda anymore. Not at the same level as she had, anyway. Amanda was such a cold bitch and always had been, and everyone knew it.

Ellie thought about what Andy had said about her and pressed her lips together. Well, you had to be a bitch sometimes in her profession and Amanda's. You had to prove you were "man enough" for the job.

But Delta . . . Mrs. Delta Stahd, married to Dr. Tanner Stahd, the teenage god. Wow. Tanner'd sure proved that moniker wrong. A cheater. A liar. An over-and-under bad guy. And Delta had married him. Ellie had been so jealous of her at the time.

You still are. She's got McCrae . . .

Her brain shied away from thoughts of him. She could get herself so riled up when it came to him. Sometimes she hated him most of all. A lot of sometimes. Was that love masquerading as hate?

She refused to think about him anymore. Think of something else. Like what's your next job going to be? How're you going to pay the rent? Buy food? And gas? What if this dearth of employment goes on a while?

She was calculating the number of months she had before her meager savings gave out when she saw Delta's car come along and pull into the garage. Finally. She checked her watch and was surprised to see that her excruciating wait had been an hour and ten minutes.

She was just getting herself psyched to charge up to Delta's front door and rap loudly—it was past time Delta gave her that interview—when Delta's car whipped back out of the garage, and she took off.

Where are you going in such a hurry? Is your kid in the car?

Questions, questions, questions.

Ellie reached for the key to turn on her ignition but stopped in the process as a large black Tahoe pulled away from the curb, turned on its blinker, then slipped around the curb after Delta's car.

"Who're you?" she asked aloud, then started her car and slid onto the road after them.

Amanda put down Bailey's journal, having read it cover to cover. She was hungry. She'd made a trip to see Thom, but she hadn't stayed through dinner. He'd been more interested in being with others at the care facility, which had been the slow trend, a good one, since the accident. The less he needed her, the better, for both of them.

And she had another appointment to keep.

Rising from her seat at the table, she stretched her back. She had an idea who'd killed Tanner Stahd. Not from Bailey's notes, which mostly were a series of scenarios explaining Carmen's death as either accidental or stemming from a lack of caring on the part of the classmates . . . all the way to flat-out murder. No, it was thinking about Zora that had put it in play, so she had some questions. She would show her hand if she was right, but if so, she would head straight to the police. Maybe she was playing with fire. Or maybe she could be completely wrong.

Delta would be coming over, and Amanda hadn't had anything to eat since some carrot sticks and hummus after her run.

Should you tell Delta?

No, not yet.

She heard something outside again. In the direction of the garage. She'd thought the noises she'd heard earlier were from whoever had left Bailey's notebook—her front-door camera picked up a man in a gray hoodie, hunched over, hiding his face—but here they were again.

It was 7:00. Light and hot and still breezy. In fact, the wind was picking up.

She heard a banging sound and saw that an upper window of the garage had come open and was swinging back and forth against the building, slamming into the wall, rattling the panes.

The garage was locked. She kept a key in a drawer just inside the back door. If she was going to fix the window, she was going to have to get the key and go up the stairs that bisected the two bays of the garage. The golf cart was kept in one side. The other side was empty; Amanda preferred to park right outside the back door.

Grabbing up the key, she headed to the garage. She unlocked the door and stopped in sudden surprise.

"What the hell?" she asked aloud.

A black-shrouded figure suddenly rushed from behind the golf cart. Amanda screamed and turned to run. The attacker grabbed her from behind. Swung her around. Crashed her head into the newel post at the bottom of the stairway. She saw stars. A swimming circle of them, just like in the cartoons. She tried to say something, but her tongue was too thick.

She'd lost a shoe in the fight, and her assailant picked it up and jammed it back on her foot. Then he dragged her out of the door of the garage and bumped her along the tarmac toward the back door of her house.

"Are you okay?" Mom asked, concerned, as Delta dropped Owen and his blanket off at their house.

"I won't be long. It's just a meeting with my lawyer."

"But are you okay?"

"Why? Do I not look okay?"

"No, it's just, has something happened? You seem . . . lighter?" she asked hopefully.

"Really? No. Do you have something for dinner for Owen? I'm sorry. I'm running so late."

Her mother flapped a hand at her. "Dad's still at the store. Owen and I will get something when we pick him up."

Owen wouldn't let go of her hand. Delta waited patiently, even though a part of her wanted to get to Amanda's right away.

"Mommy, don't leave."

"Okay. Let me make a phone call."

Amanda's phone rang. She heard it through a watery blur. She was on the floor. A wooden floor with a rug. Her dining room.

She'd left the phone on the table when she'd gone in search of the noise.

Noise . . . garage . . . *attack!*

Her whole body jerked at the memory. She almost opened her eyes but remained still, afraid, aware that she needed to keep feigning unconsciousness or . . . She quivered all over, couldn't stop herself.

Faint voices. On the back patio?

". . . lure them here," an unidentified male voice said.

A female voice answered. Quietly. Too quietly.

"What do you want me to do with her?" the man asked.

Again, the female voice was ultra soft. Did she know Amanda was listening?

The phone. If she could get the phone.

She tried to lift her head. It felt like it was

splitting apart. Her hand reached up. She raised her body as much as she could. Fumbled around atop the table. A page fluttered down, and her pen rolled off and thumped softly on the carpet.

Amanda's hand closed around the pen. The paper was nearby. She wrote without looking, painfully writing down a name. Her hand drooped. She wanted to say something more. A message to Delta. An apology . . . in case . . . in case . . .

She scribbled below the name, but as she reached for the paper, intending to hide it— where? On her person? Under the edge of the carpet?—the paper *rrrriiiippped.*

She slid the piece she still grasped under the carpet, searched around and grabbed the other.

"What sound?" the guy asked.

Footsteps approaching.

Amanda closed her fist over the scrap of paper she possessed, crumpling it.

"The bitch is trying to write a warning note," the female voice said now, not bothering to hide her voice.

Amanda kept her eyes closed, silently praying.

"Thank your husband for the keys," the voice whispered in Amanda's ear as her fist was pried open, the crumpled slip of paper removed. Then, "My name, huh. Who're you trying to tell?"

"We good here?" the man asked.

"Finish it," was the cold answer.

Bam!

Amanda had a last moment of sentience and pain as something crashed onto her head, and then she was gone.

Chapter 28

Crassley tried to refuse to see them, but Quin prevailed, and he was brought handcuffed into an interview room. "Man, my lawyer's gonna hear about this. I got nothin' to say to you."

"Who is your lawyer?" asked McCrae.

"Brennan." He smiled, showing teeth that really needed the attentions of a dental hygienist.

"Hal Brennan?" McCrae was surprised. Amanda's ex?

"I got friends in high places." The smile widened.

"We've got you for my daughter's homicide," Quin said coldly.

The grin faltered a teensy bit. "Your . . . what now? Have you lost your idiot mind?"

Quin was pushing it. They were far from having enough evidence to convict Crassley, but he didn't have to know that. McCrae played along, adding, "You, or one of your brothers, pulled that trigger."

"You got that wrong."

Quin went on, "And then you took out Penske. You used him, and then you killed him. You had a grudge against my daughter, and you killed her; then you killed Penske."

Gale Crassley lifted his palms. "You are way, way off. I heard that thing was a murder/suicide."

"You were seen," Quin said.

"No way I was seen, because I wasn't there."

"Your car was," McCrae said. "With one of you Crassleys in it."

He froze. A telltale moment of tension, before he relaxed. "We got a lot of cars."

"Was it you? Or Booker? Or Harry?" McCrae pushed.

"None of us. You don't have videotape. Lundeen's didn't have no cameras then."

"Didn't have any cameras," McCrae corrected. "Interesting you know that."

"Everybody knows that."

"So it was a good place to hide a homicide." Quin stared him down.

"You were seen by a witness," McCrae told him. "And we know about the burner phone Penske was using. You guys were trying to keep it off the grid, but you've been found out."

"No witness," he said, but he couldn't quite hide his apprehension.

"You got Penske to kill Bailey because you had him for sex with a minor," McCrae said. "He was a pawn in your game."

Crassley's smile returned. "You think you're so smart. You don't know fucking anything."

"Why, then?" McCrae pushed.

Crassley twisted in his seat. "Guard!" he called,

then to Quin and McCrae. "I'm not talking to you guys anymore."

"Next time, you'll be talking to a prosecutor. And Hal Brennan, when he hears what we've got on you, is gonna have to beg for you not to get life." Quin rose from the table.

McCrae added, "Your troubles are just starting. You shouldn't have messed with Ellie O'Brien today, either."

"Couldn't help myself . . . that red hair," he said, wiggling his tongue suggestively.

"You knew she'd turn you in. You're too smart to let that happen without a reason, and from what I know of you, you'd throw your whole family under the bus to save your own skin, so why?"

"I think you have a real sorry opinion of me, and it is inaccurate."

"Why?" he pressed.

He spread his hands. "The devil made me do it," he said with a cold chuckle as the guard came to the door to escort Crassley back to his cell.

Once outside the county courthouse, Quin asked, "What do you think?"

"One of the Crassleys did it," he said with certainty.

"But?" Quin asked, hearing something more unspoken than said.

"Holding sex with a minor over Penske isn't what they had on him. They don't consider that all that bad, nor do they pay a lot of attention to Nia. It's something else."

Quin looked at him. "What?" he asked.

" 'The devil made me do it'? Delta just mentioned that's what Tanner said as an excuse for bad behavior."

"A lot of people do."

McCrae nodded. He didn't know quite why the phrase nudged at him so much. He felt like it was just outside his grasp, lingering in some forgotten whorl of his brain. Something to do with high school? The Crassleys? Tanner?

"I'm talking to the union about Hurston," Quin said suddenly. "Sick of him in my face."

"Does that mean I can come in to work tomorrow?"

"Already told Mayor Kathy to butt out, nicely. She's under the mistaken impression that Hurston solved my daughter's case and should be allowed to look at Tanner's. She wants Stahd Senior to stop threatening to sue everyone and anyone. She thinks the stall on the case makes her look bad."

"Stall? It hasn't been a week yet," McCrae declared.

"She watches too much television," he snapped as they headed to their vehicles.

When Delta finally sneaked away from her parents' house and beeped her remote to open her car doors, it was close to 8:00. She drove away, glancing in her rearview. She'd thought she'd seen the black SUV again but wasn't sure. Now she headed west toward the Forsythe property. It was still light. Wouldn't get dark till nearly 9:00 at this time of year.

She was going to drive over the bridge that spanned the tapering end of Grimm's Pond, right past where Zora and Brian's car had gone over. As she approached that area, she slowed, looking to her left to see the crime-scene tape, the sheared bark of trees, trampled grasses, and disturbed gravel. To her shock, the black vehicle was suddenly in her rearview. The driver stomped on the brakes as Delta hit the gas, her Audi jumping forward as if eager to race. She tore down the road, zooming past the drive to Amanda's and heading farther west twenty miles into the Coast Range before she caught the turnoff that would take her back to Highway 26 to circle back to West Knoll. Hands shaking, she dug through her purse for her phone. Of course, it wasn't at hand. Of course, it wasn't.

Finally, her hand closed over it. She pulled it out and called McCrae but got his voice mail. "I saw the black SUV! It was following me. I just drove—"

Beep-beep-beep. And the phone went dead. Dropped signal.

"Aargh!" she yelled. And then she laughed

a bit hysterically. She was safe, at least for the moment. No black SUV in sight.

Ellie stood on her brakes at the same time the menacing SUV did. She nearly ran into the back of it, while it nearly ran into the back of Delta's Audi. But then Delta sped away from it so fast Ellie wondered if she knew who was driving it. Was this some game of cat and mouse?

The Tahoe didn't follow. Ahead of her, it made a three-point turn and started heading back the way it had come. Ellie stayed frozen in her car. Should she dash off too? Save her skin? Call the police or, more accurately, McCrae?

She stayed where she was, her eyes following the big vehicle as it came her way. The driver looked over as they came even.

He stopped.

Ellie pushed the button to roll down her window as the Tahoe's driver did the same.

"Brad," she said.

"Ellie," he responded.

"What the fuck are you doing, man? You scared Delta. You see the way she ripped outta here?"

"What are you doing here?"

"Following you! I was waiting for Delta, and I saw you move in after her. You've been hanging back, hoping she wouldn't see you. What are you doing?" Then, as it came to her, "Who're you working for?" For some reason, she wasn't scared. She should be, she supposed. What did she know about Brad Sumpter, really? Nothing. He was always in the background. Just hanging with the guys. No one of serious importance.

"I'm trying to save her."

"Yeah? From whom?"

"My cousins."

"Your cousins? Who're—" But she suddenly knew. "*The Crassleys? You're a Crassley?*"

"My mom was."

"Okay, Jesus, Brad. Drive into town. Stop at . . . the police station. I'm calling McCrae."

"I don't want to get in trouble." He started to look scared.

"No, no. You're not going to get in trouble. You're saving Delta, right? From your cousins? What are they planning to do with her?"

"You're going to turn me in. You're going to blame me for everything. I didn't do it. I swear I didn't do it."

"I believe you, Brad. I do."

"No, you don't." He threw his behemoth into gear and tore toward West Knoll.

"Shit." Ellie shoved her Escort into DRIVE and turned it around with more ease than Brad had demonstrated as he herded his Tahoe. Still, he was way ahead. Not that she couldn't find him, but did she really want to race after him? Yes! No . . .

Should she tell McCrae? Yes . . . but the story

would get away from her then. She'd already given him a tip that he'd taken as his due, not giving her another thought. If she didn't push to fit herself into the investigation, she would be forgotten. But this was her story. Hers. And Brad was harmless, right? He was trying to save Delta from his cousins. Jesus. The Crassleys were his cousins!

Did she have Brad's number? No. She knew she didn't. Where did he live? Did she know? But he wasn't going there. He was going back to Delta's, to pick up her trail there. That made sense. But would Delta go back home?

No. She would go to her parents'. That's where the kid had to be.

Immediately, Ellie aimed for Smith & Jones.

Delta didn't trust going through town, so she wound around the outskirts, avoiding the city center. She tried to call Amanda. No answer. "Pick up!" she cried. Maybe she should go back to her parents'. Be with them and Owen. Wait for McCrae to get back to her. He hadn't yet. She had cell service again, but she'd been driving and expected him to call any second.

At this end of town, she was closer to Amanda's than her parents'. What if the black SUV found her *or knew where she was going?*

Her phone rang, and she stared at the screen for a moment before answering carefully, "Hello?"

"Delta, it's Ellie. I saw the guy who was following you. Brad Sumpter. In the black Tahoe? He says he's trying to keep you safe."

"What?" She was stopped at a crossroads, and there was no traffic, which was just as well because it felt like her bones were melting.

"Are you going to your parents'? I've been trying to get through to you. Together we've got a real story. Brad Sumpter's mom is a Crassley! One of those pieces of shit attacked me today."

"What?"

"Where are you going? I'll tell you about it in person. Or meet me somewhere? Your house."

"I'm going to Amanda's. I'm meeting my lawyer."

"Oh. Then meet me afterward."

"Ellie, are you sure about Brad?"

"Yes. So, your house. What time?"

"No. I've gotta go."

"Delta, don't put me off. I think the Crassleys are behind Bailey's death, too."

"I'll—I'll call you and let you know." Then, "Thanks," and she clicked off.

Good Lord. Her pulse was racing. Too much information in too short a time. Had Brad started following her after they ran into each other at Danny O's? He was related to the *Crassleys?* Why were the Crassleys after her? She'd never done anything to them. She'd avoided them as much as anyone else. It didn't seem right.

She drove on toward Amanda's, glancing once more toward the spot where Zora and Brian died, though she warned herself not to. She'd told McCrae there was a conspiracy. There had to be. Her friends just couldn't die like this.

"Dee," McCrae said aloud, on his way back to the station. Something or someone had brought Tanner's nickname for Delta to the front of his mind. *Dee.* He'd thought it could stand for Dean Sutton or Zora DeMarco . . . But Zora was gone now, and it didn't feel like it could be Coach Sutton. It didn't even have to be a name . . . although Woody's last name was Deavers . . .

He grimaced, knowing he was searching for anything other than "Dee," as in Delta's initial.

But what had cued that? What was his brain trying to remember? Something from high school?

He'd powered down his phone while he was in the jail. His battery was low, and he'd left the charger in his own car, which he was on his way to retrieve. Now he switched the phone back on and was gratified to have a whole seven percent of battery life left. It was enough to get him to the station, where he could switch back to his car.

Two messages. The first one from Ellie. "I want to talk to you. I've got information that I want to share, but I need to be in on the story. Here's some: Brad Sumpter's been following Delta in a black Tahoe. He says he's watching out for her because his cousins, *the Crassleys,* have it in for her. Call me for more details."

McCrae thought that over. Almost called her, but listened to the second message.

Delta's voice, on the edge of hysteria, "I saw the black SUV! It was following me. I drove—" and it cut off.

He quickly phoned her back.

Delta drove around to the back of the Forsythe property and parked next to Amanda's Lexus. There were lights on in the kitchen, and she stepped outside onto the patio, the breeze tugging at her hair. Memories stirred, and she looked down at her foot, faint scars still visible around her tender ankle from the injuries sustained at the barbeque.

She knocked on the door, and when nothing happened, pushed it in. "Amanda?"

No answer.

She stepped into the kitchen and listened. Nothing.

In the dining room, she found Amanda's laptop and a notepad and papers . . . and a journal. Bailey's journal?! She'd seen it enough times before it disappeared that she knew it instantly. Amanda had Bailey's journal? How?

"Amanda?" she called again, the creeps coming over her. Something was wrong here.

She reached for the journal but pulled her hand back and waited, counting her heartbeats. Carefully, she reversed her steps and then saw what looked like drops of blood on the carpet. Mouth dry, she leaned down to look. The wood floor looked as if someone had hurriedly wiped up some liquid. Was that blood in the tiny cracks? Blood drops on the carpet? *Amanda's* blood?

A teensy corner of blue paper was caught beneath the edge of the carpet. She was torn between finding out what it was and running for the back door. She got her fingernail around the ragged piece of paper and carefully slipped it out.

Not me & T at bbq

Amanda's writing? A message for *her?*

An icy feeling settled between her shoulder blades.

The journal. Something in the journal had prompted the message?

Is that blood?

Where was Amanda?

Is this some kind of trap?

Delta bolted for the back door, racing for her car. She'd locked it automatically and now couldn't seem to get her hands around the keys, digging wildly through her purse.

Was that a noise? A footfall? *Was Amanda playing games with her?*

It was dusk. Shadows lengthening. The wind

beginning to moan. She could smell the river. The grasses.

Get a grip. Get in your car. Call McCrae.

She saw something on the patio. A black puddle?

One of the garage doors suddenly started to rise. Delta froze, her eyes darting to the garage. A woman stepped from the shadows. Amanda, finally.

Behind her Delta glimpsed the rear end of a white car. A Mercedes.

"Amanda?" she asked, suddenly not so sure about this blond woman.

"Amanda's in her bedroom," the woman told her.

Delta automatically looked upward.

Amanda was hanging out her bedroom window. Limp. Arms thrown forward in abandon. Eyes open.

Dead.

Delta stumbled forward, a shriek of horror bursting from her throat.

Hard hands grabbed her from behind, wrenching her shoulders back.

Clarice Billings stood in front of her, but not the Miss Billings with the blond hair clipped at her nape and the trim suits and warm smile and kind words of counsel. This Clarice was cool and hard and capable.

"Put her in the garage," she told Delta's captor.

Chapter 29

McCrae tried to reach Delta three times before he gave up, his calls going to her voice mail. He next tried Ellie, who also didn't answer.

Brad Sumpter was a Crassley.

He called in and ordered an APB on Brad Sumpter, then stopped trying to make it to the station and drove directly to the Crassley compound just as it was getting dark. The dogs burst into frenzied song as soon as he stepped out. He stalked to the front door and banged on it with his fist. It was wide open, only shut by the screen, which wasn't latched. "Booker? Harry?"

He stepped inside. Pulled his gun. Eased himself through the rooms, clearing them one by one. Headed upstairs. Messy. Dirty. But empty. Downstairs. To the basement. No one. Nothing but car parts—and a small arsenal of guns.

Back to the main floor and outside, looking over the cars. A slanting sun sent its last rays over them, touching them with gold. Nothing.

Back in the Trailblazer, he searched for Delta's parents' number. Found it. Called them.

"Hello?" It was Delta's mother.

"Hi, this is Chris McCrae. Is Delta there?"

"No." Alarm in her tone. "She was meeting her lawyer, and she said she would be right back."

"Is that Mommy?" he heard in the background.

"No, honey. It's a friend of Mommy's," Mrs. Smith told him. "Is everything okay?"

"As far as I know." He injected surety into his voice. "Did she say where she was meeting Amanda?"

"At her office? Maybe?"

"You hear from her, would you have her call me?"

"Okay."

He hung up before he gave anything away. Amanda's office was in downtown Portland. Would she really meet there this late? Maybe. Especially if the meeting started earlier and had already broken up.

Delta. Dee.

Dee.

He had a sudden memory from high school. Tanner and Woody.

Tanner: "Let's go to a titty bar."

Woody: "They closed the best one down."

Tanner: "Years ago, but there are others. Good ones."

Woody: "McCrae should meet Diabla."

Tanner, suddenly angry: "Diabla's not in the game."

Woody: "Well, maybe not now . . ."

Tanner: "C'mon, McCrae. Don't be a pussy. Let's go find you a real woman."

He'd declined, and Tanner had called him a pussy for weeks afterward. McCrae had wondered if he should tell Delta, who believed, at that point, that Tanner was being true to her. A misguided sense of brotherhood and the uncomfortable feeling he would be a rat kept him from speaking. But maybe he should've.

Diabla. Female devil.

The devil made me do it.

Crassley had said those words with amusement mere hours ago, a hidden joke. Woody had reminded Delta of Tanner going to adult men's clubs, and Delta had remembered Tanner using "the devil made me do it" as an all-encompassing excuse.

Was Diabla a myth?

He called Woody for the second time that day.

"Hey, McCrae, my man," Woody greeted him, recognizing the number. "Are we BFFs all of a sudden?"

"The devil made me do it."

McCrae guffawed. "So, you know?"

"About Diabla? I'm learning."

"You know who she is?"

McCrae searched his mind. Someone older than they were. Someone who'd been "in the game." One of the parents or the teachers? He ran through the list and, like a dial, click, click, clicked down to a few choices.

Bailey said Carmen saw something in the woods.

Carmen died when Clarice Billings couldn't pull her from the water.

"Miss Billings."

"Bingo, brother. I tried to get you with her that one time, remember?"

"Clarice Billings worked at an adult men's club?"

"That's how she paid for college. Gave it all up to be a teacher—well, mostly."

"What do you mean?"

"I mean, she ran through the male faculty at West Knoll. Brian Timmons never got over her, but Tanner kind of thought she'd screwed around with Kiefer, and that's why he recommended her for that job she's got now. Let's face it, he married the chief's ex-wife, so neither Kiefer nor Diabla probably wanted her to be hanging around West Knoll anymore."

"And she was with Tanner?"

"He was of age," Woody defended. "I woulda done her, wouldn't you? If you had the chance?"

"Tanner died on Monday," McCrae said coldly. "You've had all week to bring this up."

"Well, she didn't kill him," Woody denied. "She's not a killer. And she and Tanner were long over."

"You know that for a fact?"

"Well . . . yeah . . . but I don't see much of Tanner anymore . . ."

McCrae said tautly, "Carmen saw Clarice with Tanner at the barbeque. In the woods together."

"Might be," Woody allowed cautiously. Then, "Y'think that's what sent Carmen over the edge?"

I think that's why she wasn't rescued, McCrae thought.

He got off the phone with hardly a good-bye. Then he called Quin.

Delta was seated on a hard metal chair. She'd tried to escape when her captor first grabbed her, but he'd wrenched her arms back so hard she was practically immobilized. He'd brought her into the garage, sat her in the chair, and was standing somewhere behind her. The golf cart was to her left, and in front of the door was Miss Billings, Clarice.

"You've had your fun, Harry," Clarice told him. "Now push the body out the window."

Harry snickered. "What about her?"

Clarice looked at Delta. "I've got her."

Delta poised her muscles, ready to jump, but Clarice pulled a pistol from the small of her back and aimed it straight at her. "I will shoot you," she said conversationally. "I would prefer not to, but I will."

Harry walked around her and through the other garage door, which was still open.

"That's Zora's car," Delta said through a dry throat.

Clarice glanced at the white Mercedes. "Yes, it is. We weren't sure what to do with it. She followed Brian to Anne's house. Her empty house, I should say. Anne's good about telling me what she's doing. We're good friends. Everyone thought we were rivals, but . . . well, Brian's no prize. He looked better when he inherited, but dear little Zora snapped him right up. Oh, Anne doesn't know about me. She only knows about Clarice, the educator and counselor."

Delta wasn't following. Her mind was still filled by the image of Amanda's dead body hanging from her window. She had to get away. Now. While Harry was off doing his deed.

"Then . . . inspiration. We would take Zora's car to Amanda's. I had the keys . . . a little gift from her husband, who I've known for years. He's a cheater too. Just like Tanner."

Keep her talking. Buy time.

"You killed Zora and Brian," Delta said, tensing. Could she jump forward? Could she survive a shot?

No! You have Owen to think of.

But I can't stay here!

"Brian was becoming a problem. He was stupid in love, starting to tell Zora about me. We were waiting for him at Anne's. Just him. But then Zora showed up too, and we had to improvise. Put 'em in the car and over the cliff." She smiled thinly. "You Five Firsts . . . Clarice thought you were ridiculous."

"You're not Clarice?" asked Delta carefully.

"I just told you. Clarice is a construct. I'm not crazy. No multiple personalities or any of that shit," she added. "Clarice is my given name, but I'm not her. She's just the angel I play."

"Why are you doing this?" The question was ripped from her soul.

"Men are easy to control, but women are relentless." She shook her head. "I've had to do things I really didn't want to. It started a long time ago. Your class . . . I made mistakes. I can admit that. I was far more reckless in those days. Didn't think enough about self-preservation. I've been having to do a lot of cleanup."

"You killed Tanner."

"He was going to out me. After all these years. I was shocked. Really shocked. That chapter at West Knoll High was long over. This guy, this cheating, arrogant bastard was having a crisis of conscience? He had a son. He needed to be 'a better man.' That was what he said. I could've laughed, but he was going to tell you about all the women he'd cheated with and beg your forgiveness. I doubt he would've gone through with it. He couldn't ever keep his dick in his

561

pants. I'm sure you know that, too. But I couldn't take the chance. I watched the clinic, and the night came when he stayed after everyone else had left. I confronted him, warned him that it would ruin him too, but he wouldn't listen. And the knife was there, on his desk. Just like it was supposed to be. I picked it up when he wasn't looking, followed him out, and . . ." She sighed. "I gave him one last chance, but he was stubborn. He sealed his own fate. I didn't know how perfect it would be with you showing up right afterward and picking up the knife!"

Delta heard a hard *thunk* outside and felt ill. Amanda's body hitting the ground.

"Don't move," Clarice ordered, sensing Delta's panic, sighting down the pistol.

Crash!

The noise from outside caused both Delta and Clarice to jump. Then Clarice cocked an ear, moved closer to Delta, and doubled down on her terrorism as she leveled the barrel of the pistol at her forehead.

Have to keep her talking. Lower the tension. Keep yourself alive . . .

"How . . . did you know that I picked up the knife? That wasn't public information," Delta asked, licking dry lips.

"Hal Brennan isn't my only powerful friend."

Someone in the police department? Not McCrae, never McCrae, she prayed, knowing he was too honorable, but scared anyway. And not Quin. He was a justice seeker. More so after Bailey's death.

"The special investigator," Delta realized.

"You're very good. Surprising really, given what you were in high school. Beauty, no brains. Clarice always had both, and it's served her well."

Footsteps. Harry was returning. Delta tensed, testing her bonds.

Now or never!

BANG.

Clarice's shot zinged past Delta's ear. She screamed and froze.

"Stay put," Clarice warned her coldly.

"What the fuck?" Harry demanded, running into the garage.

Only it wasn't Harry. It was another man who bore a resemblance to him. Hulking and scraggly.

Crassleys. She'd never really known them, though she'd heard about them for years.

"What happened? Where's Harry?" Clarice demanded.

"We had some trouble. He's here."

"*Where,* Booker?" she snapped.

He half-turned, and Clarice followed his gaze outside the open garage door.

They could hear someone coming, though it sounded like they were dragging something across the tarmac. A body? Amanda's body?

God, please, no. Delta steeled herself, but it wasn't Amanda Harry flung onto the garage floor.

It was Ellie.

Ellie hadn't felt like waiting for Delta any longer and knew she'd just gotten the brush-off. Well, no more.

She'd been driving home, thinking, and decided to turn around and break in on their lawyer/client meeting. But she was famished, so she ran up the steps to her apartment, hit the refrigerator, and groaned when there was no food. She needed sustenance to continue, and she was bound and determined to continue.

There was only one drive-thru in West Knoll, and it was a coffee shop that closed at 9:30. She raced into the drive-thru lane and had to get out and rap on the window. The girl shook her head and pointed at the clock.

"There are three minutes left!" Ellie screamed.

Reluctantly, the girl opened the window, and Ellie ordered a maple scone, the only item left from the day's sales. She munched it as she drove to Amanda's, dropping crumbs, not caring. As she turned in the Forsythe drive, she thought she saw a figure move in the shadows of an oak tree, and she dropped the remainder of her muffin into the footwell.

"Shit." She looked down, her foot on the brake.

Crash!

The driver's window burst in. Ellie moved her foot from the brake to the accelerator, and the Escort jumped forward, but the assailant had thrown his upper body inside and grabbed Ellie by the neck. She fought him, scratching and clawing as the car slowed to a stop. Ellie's toe sought to find the accelerator again, intending to rush forward and throw him out, but then everything went black.

"You killed her?" Delta whispered in horror.

"Nah, she's alive," Harry said.

"Was that crash her car?" Clarice snapped.

"Had to smash the window in."

"Damn you, Harry. Another vehicle . . ." She looked ready to explode.

"Bitch's lawyer's down from the window," he informed her with an uncaring shrug.

Clarice thought hard for a moment. "Good. Suicide." Then, referring to Delta, said, "Tie her to the chair."

Delta instantly stood up, but Booker strode forward, knocked her back onto her seat and held her down with viselike fingers. There was a discussion about what to tie her up with. Harry rummaged around and found, of all things, a jump rope from a box of toys. Delta stared at the rope and remembered playing with Amanda when they were young. Amanda's initials were stamped in pink onto the ends of the rope's handles. Delta had begged her parents to do the same for her. It hadn't happened.

Harry handed the rope to Booker, who strapped Delta in. She exclaimed when he pulled it tight and, satisfied, knotted it in the back. Ellie was lying on the floor a few feet away, and Delta could just make out her breathing.

"Gale should be here," Clarice snarked at the two men.

"He shouldn't a' done what he did. Then he woulda been here," Harry said, somewhat resentfully.

"He's the brains of your family. You all know it."

"He's the one who gets *paid*," Booker said suggestively, his eyes roaming over her body.

"He knew you needed him tonight, but he went and made her strip anyway." Harry jerked his head in Ellie's direction.

"It's good she dies. She would sue him, otherwise," said Booker.

"If he got himself arrested on purpose . . . ," Clarice shook her head, her mouth tight.

"We're here for ya, Dee," Harry said.

Dee?

"Get the gasoline," she ordered.

What? Delta jerked her head around.

"Douse the grounds around the house. We'll make it a hellfire."

566

Harry and Booker both left the garage.

"What are you doing?" Delta demanded in a squeaking voice.

"Amanda was your enemy. And she didn't like Ellie much either, come to that, so it's okay that she's here. Wasn't in my plan, but Ellie's become a bigger and bigger problem as well. Not a Five First, but might as well have been." She lowered the gun now that Delta was strapped to the chair. "This is how it'll play: You killed Tanner, and Amanda snapped. Took you out and Ellie, and maybe they'll even find a link to Zora and Brian's 'accident.' Luckily, Bailey and Penske were put down to murder/suicide, although Chris McCrae and Bob Quintar can't quite give it up. I heard that they're still working on it, off the books. I don't like messing with police, but if they become too big a problem . . ."

Delta tested her bonds, which were tight, but not as tight as she'd pretended when she'd cried out. She needed to alert McCrae, but her phone was in her purse, and her purse was on the ground beside her car, dropped when she'd been seized. And Dee would never let her make the call anyway before she pulled the trigger.

She cocked her head, smiling a little sadly at Delta. "And then there's Carmen."

Delta shuddered at her tone and thought of the note from Amanda. *Not me & T at bbq.* She suddenly got why she'd left it.

"Amanda realized it was you Carmen saw with Tanner," Delta said on an intake of breath.

"Everyone else thought I was Amanda. The blond hair. But not Carmen. She saw me with him in a . . . compromising position. The preacher's daughter? I knew she was going to tell. It was pure chance that I had my moment, and I took it."

"You killed her. You never tried to help her!"

"Bailey wanted to save her, but she got swept away. I reached a hand for Carmen, but then I held her down. I had to."

She said it so matter-of-factly Delta's insides chilled.

Delta had a distant memory of sitting in Clarice Billings's office talking about her career after high school . . . and how she planned on getting married to Tanner Stahd.

She heard the clomp of approaching footsteps. The Crassleys returning.

Delta worked her bonds as best she could, but though they were looser than Booker had undoubtedly meant them to be, they held her fast.

The men were arguing. Pissed-off and angry. At each other and at Gale.

"He shoulda been here. You're a piece of shit." That sounded like Harry.

"Fuck you, man." Booker came in and slammed down several large cans of gasoline. He said to Dee, "The house'll blow like a volcano!"

"I gotta do everything!" Harry shouted at him from outside Delta's vision. "If Gale was here—"

"Shut up, asshole."

Clonk. Harry apparently dropped his load of gasoline cans onto the tarmac. There was a scrambling noise, and Booker yelled, "No!"

BANG.

Booker grabbed his chest, staggered, and went down.

"You stupid shits!" Clarice shrieked, running outside, her pistol back in hand.

Delta frantically worked her bonds. Ellie stirred, rolling an eye at Delta. "We gotta get outta here," she whispered, and Delta realized she'd been playing possum.

"Booker!" Harry called in distress, as if he hadn't just shot him.

Ellie tried to get up, groaned softly, hung her head for a moment.

"Help," Delta said softly.

Ellie edged her way closer. Booker was groaning, Harry was crying, and Clarice was shouting.

Ellie's fingers found the knot.

"Can you get it?" Delta asked.

"Almost."

BANG. BANG.

Delta jerked and gasped. That sounded like the same gun Harry had fired.

A moment later, Ellie collapsed on the floor in much the same position as before as Clarice appeared in the garage doorway. She was carrying a much larger gun than the pistol. Booker was still moaning and writhing on the ground, but there was no sound from Harry.

"They killed each other," she said, trying out the idea to see how it sounded. "They were helping Amanda kill the people she hated."

Then she picked up one of the cans and starting pouring gasoline.

Delta feverishly worked at the knot Ellie had loosened.

As if suddenly aware, Clarice looked up from pouring out a second can. She came over to Ellie and Delta, holding the half-empty can. Delta regarded her warily as she nudged Ellie with a toe.

In the next second, she smashed the can down on Ellie's head.

"Where are we going?" Quin demanded into the phone.

"The Forsythe house. I don't believe Delta is meeting Amanda at her office. I think they're there. I'm on my way." McCrae had driven to the Portland outskirts talking to Woody, but had turned around directly afterward. Quin had sent officers to Brad Sumpter's house, and Brad had apparently admitted that he was the guy who'd been sent to spy on Bailey and Penske, that he'd made sure Penske was doctoring Bailey's drink, and that the purpose of drugging Bailey was to get the notebook. But then Penske had been a loose end, apparently, and Gale killed him. Brad swore no one was supposed to get hurt—no one!—and he'd been sick at heart and horrified ever since. He also swore he'd never partici- pated in any further Crassley scheme and had filched the notebook from where Gale Crassley had hidden it to give to Delta or Amanda. He'd left it on Amanda's front porch.

"I'll meet you there," Quin growled.

"Get Portland PD to check on Amanda's office in case I'm wrong. Layton, Keyes, and Brennan." They already had a team heading to Clarice Billings's home.

Quin grunted an "Okay" and clicked off.

McCrae hit the accelerator but not the siren. Maybe he was overreacting, but he didn't think so. Neither Ellie nor Delta was answering. Something was wrong.

Clarice dragged Booker and Harry by their heels into the garage and left them by Zora's Mercedes. Booker was no longer making any noise. She then returned to pouring the gasoline. The fumes were filling both garages, choking Delta.

Ellie's head was bleeding profusely. She was out cold.

"Gotta bring that other car in," Clarice was muttering. "Gotta bring it in."

When four cans of gasoline were spread all over, Clarice opened the garage door in front of Delta, who gulped in air by the lungful. Clarice then looked at the golf cart. From where she sat, Delta was in line with it and could see the key was in place as Clarice stepped over Ellie, climbed onto the cart, turned the switch. The electric vehicle came to life, and Clarice put it in gear and ran over Ellie's prone body.

The plug for the vehicle was yanked from the wall. Something sparked.

Whoosh! The wall behind Delta erupted in flames. She felt the heat on her back and yanked with all her might. One hand came free, and she frantically sought to untie herself.

She and Ellie were in a ring of fire. Outside, Clarice stopped the golf cart and looked back, her mouth an O of surprise.

Then she saw Delta was free.

She ran back inside as Delta was trying to grasp Ellie's arm.

Clarice grabbed Delta's hair. Delta elbowed her with all her might, but the older woman hung on, screaming.

"You bitch! All you bitches! Fucking bitches!"

Clarice slapped Delta hard with her free hand, making her ears ring. Infuriated, Delta head-butted Clarice, which finally got her to release her hair. Clarice jumped at her, and they tumbled to the ground. Heat and roaring flames and this *rabid witch* were all around! Delta hit her as hard as she could, and Clarice howled, finally released her arm, then staggered to her feet.

"I'll kill you!" she screamed, but Delta too was getting a knee under herself, attempting to rise.

And then there was someone else there, grabbing Clarice from behind, pinning her arms back like Harry had pinned Delta's, dragging her from the fire while she struggled like a madwoman. Quin. Gripped on hard. His face set and dangerous.

And McCrae. In front of Delta, helping her up, holding her.

"Ellie," she cried.

"Get out!" He pushed her to the open doorway. Flames surrounded it, spitting and crackling, catching fire to the structure, racing along the garage doorjambs. Delta hesitated, then saw McCrae picking up Ellie.

She ran through the doorway as something from above crashed down hard behind her.

"McCrae!" she screamed, as he came through the smoke with Ellie in his arms.

Only later did she realize that a piece of jagged wood from the debris falling from the ceiling had speared his shoulder.

Clarice was sobbing, choking, and pleading with Quin to understand that she was an innocent victim in a grand scheme, even while she struggled for freedom. The chief was unmoved.

An ambulance screamed to a halt outside the conflagration of the garage. "Ellie," Delta moaned as the attendants jumped out. They quickly brought out the gurney and loaded Ellie atop it. That's when one of the EMTs noticed McCrae's shoulder just as a police car swung into the drive, lights flashing. Officer Corolla had been called to pick up Clarice, whose screaming intensified, only switching from Quin to Corolla as she was muscled into the police vehicle and locked into the back seat.

"Take her to county. I'll be right behind you," Quin directed tautly. "And watch her."

"You'd better come with us," the EMT said to McCrae.

"McCrae . . . Chris . . . ," Delta choked, horrified, seeing the thick spike in his shoulder.

"Can you drive me to the hospital?" he asked her calmly.

"Yes."

It was the longest, and the shortest, ride to Laurelton General. Delta watched McCrae being pulled into Emergency as Ellie, white and unconscious, was taken to the fourth floor. She'd called her mother, who was desperate to come to the hospital, but Delta asked her to stay with Owen. "I'm fine," she assured her, "but I'm about the only one."

"You might want to wash up," one of the aides, who'd been hovering around, finally had the courage to say.

Delta found a women's restroom and looked at her smoke- and tear-streaked face. Her normally dark hair was gray with ash. Her clothes . . . forget about them. She looked like she'd been through a war.

She rinsed off her face and managed to smear soot into her hair, but at least it was off her skin. She returned to the emergency room and asked if she could see either McCrae or Ellie. They allowed her see McCrae, who was scheduled for an out-patient procedure to remove the jagged stick that had speared him, which was nevertheless going to require some major cleaning out and stitching. Ellie was going in for surgery to repair a broken tibia and fibula; both bones in her right leg had been snapped by the weight of the cart, but it was her head injury that was causing the most concern.

Though they said she could see McCrae, they asked her to wait . . . and wait . . . and wait. By the time she got into his room, he was bandaged from neck to waist along his right shoulder.

She didn't stand on ceremony. Just ran right in and clasped his left hand. "You saved Ellie," she said, her throat raw. "And me."

"You were doing okay, as far as I could tell. You darn near took Diabla down."

"Diabla? That's what she called herself?"

"Her professional name, apparently. You beat the devil, Delta, and you're still standing."

His hand squeezed hers tightly.

She supposed it was too soon to tell him she loved him . . . but she did it anyway.

Epilogue

Three weeks later, Ellie sat on the chair in Russ Niedermeyer's office, her right leg in a cast over her knee so it stuck out almost straight. The breaks on her shinbones had been close to the knee, so it was difficult to maneuver. Her head was tender. A concussion and a brain contusion that they'd caught before she was seriously affected. She didn't really remember what happened, but Delta had related the events, creating a deep and abiding hatred for Clarice Billings, aka Diabla, burning within Ellie's soul.

". . . might have been a little hasty about letting you go," Niedermeyer was saying. "There's room for more than one reporter. Pauline is considering cutting back her time."

Oh, sure. That was just like Pauline to cede airtime to Ellie.

"I want to anchor the evening news," Ellie told him. The Diabla case had rocked the area, and the names of high-profile clients the one-time adult entertainment star—currently an academic at a well-respected private college, although that was bound to be over—was giving up, had reached into every level of Northwest society and beyond. Good old Diabla had wormed her way into so many executives' beds, once her years at West Knoll High were behind her, that it was, as they say, a veritable list of who's whos.

"You know Alton is the anchor and—"

"I'll cohost. I have no problem sharing, for now."

"Well, let's talk some more when you're ready to come back."

"I'll be here next week," Ellie told him with a smile as she struggled to her crutches.

Her star had suddenly risen with her takedown of Diabla, who was currently being charged with the murders of Tanner Stahd, Amanda Forsythe, Zora DeMarco, Brian Timmons, Booker and Harry Crassley, Justin Penske, Bailey Quintar, and Carmen Proffitt. Gale Crassley was charged, right along with her, on many of the counts as well. Though it had been Delta who'd physically fought with the woman, she'd demurred on all the notoriety, and, in fact, she was the one who'd told the media that Ellie had been injured while trying to save her, which was true. In any case, Ellie was happy to be regarded as a hero. Delta had ended up with McCrae, which was kind of a pisser, but she was getting over it.

And . . . it looked like she was going to be an aunt. Nia was truly pregnant and swore it was Michael's, or maybe Joey's, she wasn't really sure, but it was one of theirs. Maybe. A paternity test would at least say whether it was the child of one of the twins. Currently, the three of them were living together, and nobody wanted advice from Ellie. Gale Crassley was being held in jail, and regardless of the numerous charges already against him, Ellie was going to go after him tooth and nail herself. He'd played with her that day; though there was suspicion that he'd known what was going down with Diabla and hadn't wanted to be a part of the scene at the Forsythe estate, he had used Ellie as a convenient means of going to jail, no matter what his reasons. She wanted his ass convicted of sexual assault, too.

She stepped outside and rested on her crutches, surveying the parking lot of the station. A Range Rover pulled in, and Alton stepped out, smoothing his hair. Seeing Ellie, he stopped short. "Hi, partner," she said with a smile. "Looking forward to Monday."

Fido circled and circled Owen's legs, and the little boy giggled and chortled, trying to grab the dog as it weaved in and out. Delta, sitting on McCrae's couch, cradling a cup of coffee from the pot she'd made, couldn't help grinning at them.

McCrae sat beside her, his uninjured left arm draped casually over her shoulders.

"You said the special investigator is no more?" asked Delta.

"Tim Hurston has been found to be in Diabla's

black book. Along with Hal Brennan, who has been trying to wriggle his way into Amanda's parents' estate, so he may actually be disbarred."

"And Amanda's brother, Thom?"

"Her parents are running true to form. They've ceded his care to a cousin, given him power of attorney."

"A better cousin than Brad Sumpter, I hope," Delta murmured.

Brad had stated that he'd been trying to atone from the moment Bailey and Penske died. He felt responsible for reporting on them to the Crassleys. He was an abettor, for sure, but he'd also worked against them, whenever he could.

"Sumpter'll probably get some leniency," McCrae said.

Delta nodded. "So how was today?" she asked after a moment.

McCrae had put in his first full day of work since his injury. He'd been surprised to find Joyce Quintar Kiefer visiting Quin, but had realized they were sharing a moment of remembrance about the daughter they'd lost. Lill, their surviving daughter, was an elementary school teacher and was moving back from Arizona; they were planning a welcome home party. McCrae had briefly thought of Coach Sutton's comments about Joyce being unable to take her eyes off Tanner, but had kept it to himself. Was it true, or a fiction from Coach's possibly jealous mind? Didn't matter anymore.

"It was good. Mayor Kathy's going to swear in Quin as chief."

"Good." She smiled over at him, and they locked eyes.

"So, what's going to happen now?" he asked into the silence that followed.

She looked at him. "You mean . . ." She waved her hand back and forth to include him and her.

"You're gonna get married!" Owen suddenly declared. "Or just live together in sin."

"Where did you hear that?" Delta asked, startled, as McCrae half-laughed in surprise.

"That's what Cara's mom and D.J.'s dad are doing," he said wisely.

"I don't think 'living in sin' is the way I would put it," Delta told him.

"Is that even a thing anymore?" McCrae asked.

Owen flipped up his palms. "I just know what I heard. And I want to live with Fido, so . . . C'mon, boy." He opened the door and took Fido into the backyard.

Delta gazed after him in consternation. "He was devastated about his father. It's all so soon. I don't know if I can trust this new Owen. I wonder if a crash is coming."

"Maybe." He paused. "So what do you think?"

Delta slid another look at him. "About?"

"Living together, in sin or otherwise."

"Seriously?"

"Owen is planning to move in with Fido. Seems like he knows what he wants."

"He wants the dog, but it might not last about you and me."

"He's come a long way with me."

"I wouldn't mind a trial," she admitted slowly. "Maybe a few nights here, then some at my house? See how Owen does?" She smiled faintly. "He knows you saved me."

"You were doing a pretty good job of saving yourself," he said. "You and Owen could start out here. I'm closer to West Knoll Elementary, unless you're planning on Englewood Academy."

"No, I'm over that. And well, financially, I could really use a roommate. Tanner's father wants to buy the clinic, get back in the business, but I don't know. He seems to accept that I didn't kill his son, but he's still an arrogant son of a bitch."

"Your book's doing well."

"That's . . . not for me." She shook her head. "College fund for Owen."

Owen came bursting back in, with Fido leaping against him, knocking the back of his knees so that Owen fell over and rolled on the ground, laughing in a way Delta had never heard as the dog barked and jumped and fake-growled.

"You never answered my question," McCrae reminded. "What you said at the hospital?"

"I don't remember."

"You're seriously going to make me wait to hear it again?"

"It's too soon . . . isn't it?"

He looked into her worried face and shook his head.

She glanced back at her son, leaning her head against his shoulder. "What did I say? I believe it was—"

"I love you," he whispered.

"Yeah . . . right . . ." Her mouth curved into a smile. "That was it."

Books are produced in the United States using U.S.-based materials

Books are printed using a revolutionary new process called THINKtech™ that lowers energy usage by 70% and increases overall quality

Books are durable and flexible because of Smyth-sewing

Paper is sourced using environmentally responsible foresting methods and the paper is acid-free

Center Point Large Print
600 Brooks Road / PO Box 1
Thorndike, ME 04986-0001 USA

(207) 568-3717

US & Canada:
1 800 929-9108
www.centerpointlargeprint.com